CONALL IV

A BRACE OF EAGLES

SNAIDHM IOLAR

DAVID H. MILLAR

TITLES BY DAVID H. MILLAR

Conall IV
A Brace of Eagles
Snaidhm Iolar
DAVID H. MILLAR

A Wee Publishing Company
Houston, TX, USA
http://www.aweepublishingco.com/
Paperback ISBN 978-0-9916640-6-1
eBook ISBN 978-0-9916640-7-8
ISBN-10: 0-9916640-6-1
ISBN-13: 978-0-9916640-6-1
Library of Congress Control Number: 2019900010
A Wee Publishing Company, LLC, Houston, TX

To Unexpected Arrivals. Welcome, Jake.

ACKNOWLEDGEMENTS

I doubt whether there is a perfect way to acknowledge everyone who made Conall IV possible without being repetitive or tiresome. Yet no author is an island.

Thanks go to Ida at Amygdala Design for the excellent cover artwork and interior formatting. Also, thanks to my friend and artist, Michael McEvoy, for the map illustration. A new member of the team is Andrew Noakes, who provided welcome comment and suggestions in his structural report, and arranged for the copy editing of the manuscript. He also broke me from my attraction to the use of 'pendulous' to describe Mòrag's breasts!

Last but certainly not the least, a big round of appreciation to my beta readers—Brendan, Jolie, Judith, and Pam.

CONTENTS

PRONUNCIATIONS

Conall IV: A Brace of Eagles—Snaidhm Iolar is a yarn set in ancient times. It revolves around the Celts and primarily Irish and Scottish Celts. As far as possible, I have attempted to use old Irish and Scots Gaelic words and phrases for personal and place names, and the odd curse or two.

Gaelic in all its forms (Irish, Scottish, Welsh, Manx, Breton and Cornish) is a difficult language to comprehend. It is made more challenging by the many regional dialects. I have often considered the language to be the result of a warped Celtic sense of humour. Rather than give a complete listing of the Gaelic words and phrases used in the story, I have opted for compromise. In the not-too-distant future, I will upload a Conall Pronunciation Guide to A Wee Publishing Company's website (http://aweepublishingco.com/). In the meantime, the following pages lists the personal names of the main characters. When all is said and done, it is the tale that counts. Feel free to pronounce the Gaelic in the way that gives you the most enjoyment.

Finally, *Conall IV: A Brace of Eagles—Snaidhm Iolar* is written in British English, if only because it makes little sense to use American English for a novel series set in Europe.

IRISH GAELIC

Áine Ni Dedad	AWN-ya nee DAY-da
Aodán Mac Conall	AY-awn MAK KON-ul
Aoibheann Ni Fionnséach	AY-veen nee FINN-shay-ah
Barra Mac Conall	BA-ra MAK KON-ul
Beacán Ó Cathasaigh	B'YAG-awn o KAS-akh
Bláithín Ni Néill	BLAW-heen o NEE-ul
Bricriu Ó Cathasaigh	BRICK-roo o KAS-akh
Brighid Ni Conall	BREED nee KON-ul
Brion Ó Cathasaigh	BREE-un o KAS-akh
Brocc Ó Cathasaigh	BRUK o KAS-akh
Conall Mac Gabhann	KON-ul MAK GAWN
Craiftine Ó Cuileannáin	KRAFT-in o QUILL-an-awn
Cuán Ó Néill	KOO-awn o NEE-ul
Cúscraid Mac Conchobar	KOO-skri MAK KRUH-who'r
Danu Ni Conall	DAH-noo nee KON-ul
Deaglán Ó Néill	DEG-lawn o NEE-ul
Deda Mac Sin	DAY-da MAK SHEEN
Eirnín Mac Gabhann	ER-neen MAK GAWN
Eochaidh Ruad	OHY ROO-uh
Fearghal Ruad	FER-ul ROO-uh
Fionnbharr Ó Cuileannáin	FYUN-var o QUILL-an-awn
Íar Mac Dedad	EER MAK DAY-da
Labhraidh Ó Cuileannáin	LA-ra o QUILL-an-awn
Lonán Ó Néill	LUH-nawn o NEE-ul
Macha Mong-Ruad	Maha MUNN ROO-uh
Manannán Mac Lir	MAN-na-nawn MAK LEER
Medb	MAY-ve
Mongfhionn	MUNN-yung
Mórrígan Ni Cathasaigh	Moe-rig-gAHn nee KAS-akh
Neamhain Ni Fearghal	NYAV-in nee FER-ul

Onchú Ó an Cháintigh	UN-choo Awn HAWN-tyg
Ròs Ni Torcán	ROS nee TURK-awn
Sárán Mac Craobhach	SAWR-awn MAK CRAY-v-akh
Sorchae Ni Íar	SUR-a-ka nee EER
Tadhg Ó Cuileannáin	TYG o QUILL-an-awn
Toirneach	TOR-nah
Torcán Ó Dubhghaill	TURK-awn o DOO-l
Uallachán Ó Dubhghaill	OOL-akh-awn o DOO-l
Urard	UR-urd

SCOTS GAELIC

Brandubh Mac Artair	BRAN-doow MAK ASH-ter
Brianag Ni Brion	BREE-uh-nak nee BREE-un
Carmag Mac an t-Sionnaich	KAR-ah-mak MAK an-CHUN-ich
Crum Dubh	CROM Doow
Diadhaidh	JE-ah-ee
Drostan Ruadh	DROST-an Roo-ag
Gràinne Ni Fearghal	GRAN-yuh nee FER-ul
Iasg	EE-ask
Mòrag Ni Artair	MOR-ak nee ASH-ter

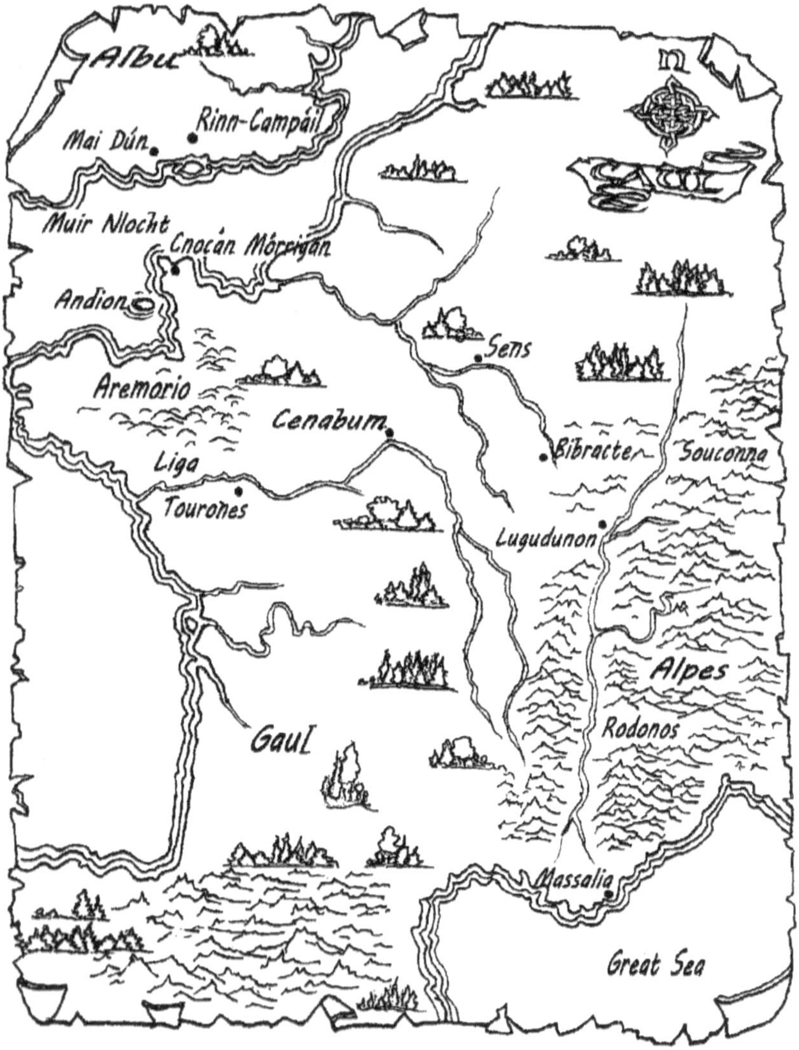
Albu
n
Rinn-Campáil
Mai Dún
Muir Nlocht
Cnocán Mórrigan
Andion
Aremorio
Cenabum
Sens
Bibracte
Souconna
Liga
Tourones
Lugudunon
Alpes
Rodonos
Gaul
Massalia
Great Sea

CHAPTER 1

405 B.C.—Lugnasad—Southern Albu

Butter-gold and cruelly hooked, the beak ripped a ragged gash across the newborn's throat. Bright, arterial blood splashed the grey, stone slab. Denied a final voice, the innocent's lips trembled. A second, mortal slash delivered by a pitiless talon laid open the sacrifice's belly. Released from the bonds of skin and muscle, entrails burst forth to lie steaming on the rock's cool, pitted surface.

"Did you receive a message you approve of?" Fate attempted to maintain a haughty distance from the violence, but in this guise, the smell of blood and warm flesh challenged his fortitude.

With a nod of her heavy, golden-brown head the Goddess replied, "The Ancients have given their consent. I will cross the Muir nIocht and enter the land of the Gauls."

"Gods and goddesses do not usually cross territories."

"Extenuating circumstances. Rome must be stopped. My servants—the druids—must be protected. My Hand must fulfil his destiny. The people need to worship."

"Surely, it is *you* who needs the people's worship?"

"Bah! Semantics."

Fate changed the topic. "The Roman gods did not protest?"

Such was her distaste for her fellow gods, if the Goddess could have spat, she would have. "The Romans got their gods from the Greeks. Likely the Greeks got theirs from the Egyptians. All the Roman gods desire is to pose for yet more marble statues. Affecting an air of ennui, they abstained."

The scent of the warm flesh and blood tormented Fate. Conversation and debate faded. He screeched at the Goddess, and she returned his cry. Soon there was little left of the carcass, but cracked bones and skin. Satisfied, the eagles bent powerful legs and swept upwards. The stones of Choir-Gaur quickly became a grey mirage in the distance.

***

Stripped to the waist, Conall Mac Gabhann, Rí Ruirech—king over kings—of Clann Ui Flaithimh sat on the cliff's edge. His perch overlooked the harbour, which was located at the apex of a roughly equal-sided triangle. The other points were the great hillforts of Southern Albu—Mai Dún and Rinn-Campáil. He enjoyed the warmth of the summer sun as he surveyed the array of ships in the harbour. The sound of waves breaking on the shore and the rhythmic clunking of wooden hulls against jetties soothed away his morning headache.

To Conall, it seemed that the longer he sojourned in the pleasant kingdom of Mai Dún, the more frequent were his headaches. Nightmares, in graphic detail, recalled his mother pinned to the solid wooden table with iron spikes through her hands, her dress torn and her arse bloodied from multiple penetrations. His blacksmith father shackled to the stanchions of the forge, his back charred and eyes sightless, burst by hot irons. Tearless, his last moments were filled with the dying screams of his hand-fast partner. His little sisters, too young to rape, were tossed aside. Deep gashes across their throats smiled ghoulishly at Conall. Bathed in sweat, he awoke, screaming at the Goddess. "Your Hand needs no visions to remind him of his duty. I will avenge my family and destroy the Romans who paid for the murders." Only the soothing embrace and tears of Mórrígan that splattered his chest restored his sanity.

With an effort of will, Conall pushed the memory aside. Enjoying the juices released, he chewed and sucked on a stalk of coastal grass. He mused that it had probably been pissed on by multiple sheep and goats. A smile ghosted his lips before he stretched well-toned arms and rolled his muscled neck and shoulders. Sighing, he pulled soft, calf-high boots over what he considered were quite ugly toes. Slowly, deliberately, as if wanting to delay his return to the myriad daily responsibilities, he criss-crossed and then tied off the boots' long thongs. With an emphatic grunt, the king of Clann Ui Flaithimh stood and slapped dirt, grass, and sand from his triubhas—trousers. He bent over, took up his axe and shield, and turned about.

Situated in a grassy hollow, a thousand paces back from the cliffs, a random patchwork of tents formed a good-sized village. They gave shelter to the ships' crews. "So many mouths to feed… and gold to pay," he muttered. His comment was aimed at no-one in particular but was overheard by the small, mahogany-skinned sailor who came into view. Palm forward, Pytheas held his hand aloft. It was a signal that the portly Greek had not quite recovered from the walk up the fairly steep hillside. Conall grinned. "You need more exercise, my friend. Perhaps a stint on the oars of your galley, or I could have Fearghal set you a training regime?"

Partially recovered, Pytheas laughed and stroked a black beard that glistened with jasmine-scented castor oil. "I prefer decadence over austerity." Conall knew the merchant undersold himself. The beard was one of vanity and choice. Unlike many, it did not hide a fragile chin or signal a weak character. Moreover, while in recent years the Greek's flesh may have gained more fat than muscle, he had proven loyal and resourceful in harsh circumstances.

"Are they all necessary?" asked Conall, his gaze once more focused on the village of sticks and skins.

"The crews and rowers of the galleys make up the majority of the population. We have ten biremes—one hundred and twenty rowers for each vessel. Then there are the ships' crews—captain, helmsman, piper,

3

shipwright, bow lookout, and five or six sailors per boat. It all adds up." Pytheas looked along the jetties as if searching for something. Then he pointed to the rugged locally-built ships with their rough timbers and high curved bows and sterns. "On the other hand, *they* only need a small crew—far fewer rowers. They are built for carrying cargo, the biremes for war. You need both."

"How long will it take?"

"The ships are contracted for a year. It will likely take that long—maybe more."

Conall snorted, "So, I'm financing your new partnership with Drostan." He spoke of his onetime enemy and now friend, Drostan Ruadh, the one-eyed king of the Aos na Coille—the Forest People. Drostan had returned to his beloved forests of ancient pine that stretched from coast to coast in his native Northern Albu.

"A happy quirk of fate. It was quite propitious that the ships from the Votod-Daoine fell into our hands." Pytheas looked at Conall's face to gauge whether the king of Clann Ui Flaithimh was truly unhappy. The glimmer of a smile that played at the corners of Conall's mouth was reassuring. "You did get the 'preferred' customer rate," Pytheas said with a huge smirk.

"Ha! Spoken like a true merchant. Perhaps I should have become a partner in your venture. At the least, some of my gold would be returned to me."

Pytheas again scrutinised Conall's expression. Was the young king serious? He had become an accomplished fidchell player. Few could read a face that seldom gave clues as to his thoughts. "Drostan would have no objection—and neither would I."

Conall inclined his head, "Perhaps." His attention was drawn to the vessels once more. "How many warriors can the biremes transport?"

"The shipwrights are adding another deck to the galleys. With that, and reducing the number of rowers per ship, they will each carry fifty warriors."

"Not a lot."

"The galleys are flat-bottomed, fast, and highly manoeuvrable. Much better for beach landings and assaults. An almost full complement of rowers and sailors is needed to cope with the worsening weather that is inevitable between now and the festival of Samhain. We also need to be able to outrun any potential attacks. The coastal Veneti in Aremorio have fast ships and will take to the seas if they see an opportunity for plunder. Plus, there are always Phoenician and Greek slavers looking for easy prey." Pytheas hesitated.

"Well?"

With a cough to hide his embarrassment, Pytheas added, "Then there are the… witches on the island of Andion." Conall raised an eyebrow in disbelief. Pytheas coughed. "Sailors are superstitious. The island is ancient—lots of burial grounds and tall stones. Rumour has it that there is a colony of nine unmarried witches living on the island. They guard a sacred cauldron." Pytheas shrugged and smiled weakly at Conall. "Anyway, the crews will not go anywhere near Andion—especially in the dark."

"Anything else? Huge sea creatures perhaps?" said Conall with a boyish chuckle.

Pytheas glanced nervously out to sea, "It's not good to mock the sea gods. Neither Poseidon nor your own Manannán Mac Lir is known for having placid natures. Who knows what creatures inhabit the deeps?" With a quick change of topic, Pytheas said, "There is one more thing. At least two-thirds of your men will have to train as rowers. It's the only way we can make space for them on the crossing."

"That'll please them," said Conall.

"Sarcasm?" chuckled Pytheas.

"Never!"

***

Conall knew the importance of securing a defensible beachhead in Aremorio. It would determine the mission's success and set the tone and foundation for the wider campaign in Gaul. A strategic blend of captains and warriors was required. Succinctly, Conall explained his thinking to Fearghal Ruad—his battle commander. "They're all sullen, foul-mouthed, foul-smelling eejits… but they're hard bastards who'll get the job done."

Command of the landing rested on the broad shoulders of Lonán Ò Neill. Lonán, the second-in-command of Conall's newest recruits from Ériu's famed Cróeb Ruad—the Red Branch—faced a singular challenge. When he asked for two hundred volunteers, one thousand hopefuls stepped forward. According to Fearghal—himself, a former commander of the Ulaid warriors—Lonán's final selection was a bunch of ugly, toothless killers whose skin had so much scar tissue it was as tough as a boar's hide.

Few were surprised when Conall also nominated Torcán Ò Dubhghaill to be part of the Aremorio landing. Even fewer were surprised at Torcán's jig of glee on hearing the news. Torcán's hundred, as bull-headed as their leader, provided a platoon of the vaunted Clann Ui Flaithimh's shield wall. It was, however, a possible sign of maturity that the bluff warrior was not overly convinced by the profuse assurances of a safe sea crossing from either the tall and beautiful Sidhe—Mongfhionn—or Pytheas. Memories of stormy sailings on the seas and lochs of Northern Albu were all too easy and painfully recalled. So, Torcán flung extra offerings of armour and gold into the sea for Manannán Mac Lir and into a nearby river for the Goddess—better safe than sorry.

The remaining members of the landing party hailed from the mountains and forests of Northern Albu. Armed with clubs and spears, Carmag Mac an t-Sionnaich's cohort totalled one hundred veteran forest fighters. All sported shaggy red hair and bodies covered in elaborate tattoos. It was a sight sure to put the fear of the Hag into the enemy. The women—well, most of them—were distinguished from the menfolk by the lack of bushy, ginger-red beards and whiskers.

The female warriors of the Clann Ui Flaithimh were as aggressive as, some said fiercer than, the men. Hence, the raiding party included Mòrag, the voluptuous princess of the Ravens, and her warband of one hundred spearmen, archers, and slingers. Like many of her tribe—and indeed Carmag's Aos na Coille—Mòrag preferred to fight unrestricted by clothing.

Given her undoubted beauty, few grumbled at her lack of attire. Even fewer queried her inclusion in the assault. If any were foolish to suggest that her addition was frippery, the least they could expect was a fist in the face. Underlying Mòrag's welcoming curves was a core of iron. The Raven's leader could trounce any man in the raiding party.

CHAPTER 2

405 B.C.—North-West Aremorio, Gaul—Mid-Summer

On the cliff edge, Dubnoreix, king of the Venelli, stood legs apace and axe in hand. The tall chieftain's violet-blue cloak flapped in the gusting winds. He was not in a congenial mood. This was due in part to having been stabbed and scratched by the tangle of thorns and brambles that carpeted the dense wildwood that bordered the ancient forest. Not for the first time, he swore. Suspicions about the unnatural movement of the bank of fog he was observing were confirmed when the mist rolled back to reveal ten sleek, amber-red galleys with square black sails. A quick calculation told him he could be facing over a thousand warriors—assuming the rowers took to the field.

The king cursed, and not entirely at the enemy. Around him, a handful of reluctant chieftains and their grudging warriors gathered. Formerly known as great warriors, the Venelli had grown fat and lazy from the taxes and flow of goods between Rome, Aremorio, and Albu. Appeals to their civic responsibility were followed by threats of physical violence. Still, Dubnoreix had raised just one thousand of his tribe's fighters. They were mostly the callow young, looking for adventure and glory, or the old, hoping that a sharp blade would help them escape the helplessness of old age and the misery of depending on others.

There had been no time to enforce the mutual defence agreement with the neighbouring Abrincatui. Messengers were on their way, but reinforcements would arrive too late to help with his immediate problem. Unless Dubnoreix agreed to increase their annual tributes, no help would come from the more powerful tribes to his west and south. Given that the king considered his neighbours already gouged him, it was not a strategy he would pursue with any enthusiasm. Perhaps the many rumours of Roman gold—bribes to curtail the ambitions of the upstart king whose galleys approached—would bring them to the Venelli's aid. Dubnoreix turned. His men milled around on the ribbon of rock-strewn ground between the cliff-edge and the dense forest. He shook his head and bawled out orders.

Dubnoreix spat. A gust threw his saliva back at him. It was not an encouraging omen. The flotilla of ships swept into the shelter of the semi-circular bay. The cove was located on the west side of a promontory that jutted from the northern coast of Aremorio. Filled with the wind, the square sails stretched like pregnant bellies. Ropes and cables cracked like whips in the squalls. At a shouted command, the sails were furled, and oars retracted. The flat-bottomed galleys glided onto the beach propelled by momentum and an incoming tide.

***

Pytheas was well acquainted with Aremorio and its rugged coastline. Bays of gently sloping sand and pebble beaches were guarded by towering, moss-covered, granite cliffs. The few narrow paths that ascended the bluffs were passable only by sure-footed goats and drunkards. Beyond the coast, the landscape of Aremorio was a patchwork of low mountains, undulating plains, rocky plateaus dressed with heathers and mosses, and treacherous marshlands. Vast swathes of pine, oak, alder, and beech covered the fertile land. The main population centres and settlements were further inland and south of the chosen landing location. Hillforts, of rock and wood, perched on the many promontories that defined the long shoreline.

It was late afternoon. The Clann Ui Flaithimh advance fleet had departed the southern coast of Albu at dawn and made excellent time. Once out in the waters of the Muir nIocht, the weather held fair and dry. Light winds and good visibility favoured the vessels for most of the journey. The breezes enabled the rowers to take brief, well-earned rests while their ships maintained their passage with black sails unfurled. The end of their voyage in sight, with burning muscles, the rowers and crews navigated the crescent-shaped cove. Most offered up prayers that the warriors they carried would prevail and establish a camp. None wanted to risk a return journey at night in a sea renowned for its tricky currents and tides—and, of course, witches.

With both hands, Lonán gripped the surf-splashed rail that ran around the prow of the lead ship. Head forward, and neck stretched to its limit, he screwed up his eyes and scanned the cliff top. "At least the sun is behind us," he grunted. It was impossible to tell if they would be greeted by a few curious warriors or an army waiting to throw the invaders back into the sea.

It was more than likely that the Venelli were aware of the massive camp of the Clann Ui Flaithimh in Southern Albu and their intentions. Opportunistic merchants wishing to establish themselves along the growing trade routes between Albu, Gaul, and the nations surrounding Great Sea were only too willing to peddle information for gold and influence. According to Pytheas, the Venelli was a minor tribe. They and their king, Dubnoreix, were considered a nuisance. Still, they guarded vital trading routes and the harbours of Aremorio. Thus, they were wealthy, if annoying, people.

In the best of times, scaling the sheer rock face would be a challenge. The dark bluffs stood between ten and twenty spears tall, were covered in green and orange mosses, and were liberally painted with bird shite. Under fire and with screeching seabirds pecking at and shiting on them, a climb was suicidal. As his galley scraped to a halt on the hard-packed sand, Lonán shouted, "To the cliffs!" and leapt over the side into the foaming waters.

It was a short dash, no more than a hundred paces, to the foot of the heights. Still, the cloud of stones and metal slugs that rained down on the raiders made the distance appear ten times longer. Yelps of pain were accompanied by growls and curses as slingshots slapped exposed flesh. Shouts of "Scíatha - shields!" resonated along Clann Uí Flaithimh's skirmish line, although anyone with a modicum of sense had already raised his defence.

With relief—and just a few stinging bruises—Lonán placed palms against the cold rockface and fought to bring his ragged breathing under control. A glance along the shoreline brought some consolation. Only twenty bodies lay on the wet sand. Hopefully, they were injured and not dead. The ship's crews would tend to them. With his men prone against the rock, the enemy's slings caused fewer injuries. The barrage diminished as it became impossible for the Venelli to target those directly below them. Additionally, any use of their slings now exposed them to Mòrag's archers. This did not, however, prevent the Venelli from changing tactics. Large boulders, rocks, and logs were rolled over the edge. Circling seabirds, protective of their nests, added to the defence of the cliff with raucous cries and liberal splatters of shite.

***

Lonán knew he had to get his raiders moving or face injury and death by attrition. Five hundred paces from their current position two narrow slopes of sand, scree, and rock swept from the cliff top down to the sea. Aeons of heavy winds and crashing seas had collapsed a section of the bluffs. Unfortunately, more massive boulders had tumbled into the sea, making a closer landing by ships treacherous. Lonán's original plan was to edge along the foot of the cliffs until they came to the incline. The increasing volume of rocks and debris descending from the cliff-edge necessitated a change of plan. He pointed at the rise and shouted at Torcán, "Take your men. Secure the slope." Then he signalled Mòrag, "Follow Torcán. Cover him."

The decision was sensible. Torcán's contingent was the most heavily armoured. Leather, inlaid with iron scales, covered their torsos and upper thighs. It was very effective at deflecting slashing blades. At this time of the year, the armour was worn over a thin, woollen tunic to prevent chafing. A leather skirt overlapped brightly coloured, plain, or plaid pants, which were tied at the waist with cord or leather thongs. Most of the warriors preferred soft leather boots, laced up to the top of their calves. In battle and in winter, these were also lapped in thick sheepskin or other pelts. A thick hide could prevent a slash from an opponent's blade from becoming a crippling injury.

Over hips and across chests, broad leather belts and baldrics, inscribed with intricate designs, were secured with bronze, iron, and gold buckles and brooches. All carried an assortment of javelins, swords, axes and daggers. Heads were crowned, and unruly hair confined, with a diverse array of iron and bronze helmets. Few were plain. Most were embellished with gold, silver, and bronze flourishes. Torcán's had a snarling, tusked boar figurine at its crest. The men carried their wealth on their bodies. Upper arms were encircled with rings of gold, silver, copper, and bronze. Heavy torcs of precious metals hung around thickly muscled necks.

Finally, they carried waisted, oblong shields made of wood, which spanned from chin to knee. Most were faced with hide and rimmed with iron. Each had a central protruding boss, itself a weapon that could cause crippling impact injuries. Some were covered in bronze. The bronze-on-wood scíatha allowed for much more individuality in design, which was always a consideration for the artistic Gaels. That said, bronze shields were heavier—a considerable disadvantage in a long battle.

Mòrag's minimally clad hundred took up position behind Torcán and quickly sent a hail of arrows and stones skywards. The slopes were short, only thirty to forty paces from top to bottom, but steeply inclined. Thus, it was not a tremendous strain for archers and slingers to pitch their missiles beyond Torcán as his band laboured toward the clifftop. The men ascended the incline in two groups—one for each slope. Each group of fifty formed up in two rows. The rear row held scíatha above the heads of the front. While the front row's shields absorbed the barrage of slingshots, the rear hoped to reduce the risk of head injuries. Upward progress on the shifting shale and stone surface was slow, steady, and mostly unchallenged.

Meanwhile, on the beach, the remainder of Lonán's raiding party kept tight to the cliff-face as they scrambled over boulders worn smooth by the pounding of ageless seas, and slick with seaweed. Loud curses filled the air as men slipped, bloodying knees and hands. Ankles twisted when rocks slithered from under their feet. The barrage from the cliff-top slowly lessened as the Venelli switched the target of their missiles to Torcán's attack.

"Your bastards will follow in Torcán's footsteps," rasped Lonán to Carmag.

The rust-red-haired warrior dipped his head and grinned broadly at Lonán's orders. Among the Clann Ui Flaithimh leadership, Carmag outranked the Cróeb Ruad captain, but without argument, he accepted Lonán's command of the raid. With a few hand signals, Carmag's men—and women—picked up their pace, quickly overtaking Lonán. Calloused, bare feet gripped the rocks better than boots or bróga.

With laboured breathing, Torcán reached and rolled over the lip of the cliff. Quickly assembling his men into their favoured shield wall formation, he waited, ready to repulse the inevitable crazed barbarian assault. Moments later he snorted with disappointment. "The bastards have fled." Before him, flattened undergrowth revealed tracks leading deep into the forest. Instincts honed by battle felt his men begin to relax. In response, he shouted, "Scíatha—shields!" and heard the reassuring clash of iron rims. He did not trust his first impression. Torcán's caution was justified. From the forest came a shower of stones and slugs. Shields cracked, and helmets rang as the missiles struck. Yelps and curses identified those too slow to raise scíatha.

The barrage was short-lived, dissuaded by Torcán's wall, tramping further into the brambles and the lush tangle of undergrowth that spilt from the wildwood. "Clever arseholes!" The speaker was Carmag, who appeared at Torcán's side. Mòrag's contingent followed Carmag's group and fanned out along the forest edge. Torcán's expression said, *are you going to finish?* Carmag laughed and gestured with his left hand—his right held the great hammer that he favoured. The simple and deadly weapon, with its blackthorn shaft and heavy iron head, was a gift from Conall. "They've retreated into the forest. Do *not* follow them. Leave that to my men."

***

The camp was set up in a semi-circle with the cliff edge as its ragged diameter. The furthest point of the crescent was one hundred paces from the bluff. With a shrug of broad shoulders and roll of his head, Carmag and his command disappeared like ghosts into their natural habitat—the forest. By the time dusk fell, Mòrag's Ravens, wearing little other than the traditional black feather attached to a thin braid of hair that dangled from their scalp, stood in a skirmish line behind the perimeter. The boundary was marked by a string of evenly-spaced stakes. Instead of slings and bows, the Ravens held spears. In the deepening gloom, the warrior princess would not risk injury to Carmag's men.

It was a black, starless night. Cloaked behind slate-grey clouds, the moon's presence was no more than an opaque blue shadow. The silence of the night was broken by the sound of the hunt. Wolves howled, lynxes barked and spat, bears grunted and snuffled. Overhead, the soft wing-beats of owls barely disturbed the air as they hunted. On the ground, in fear of sudden death, prey scurried, hoping to reach the safety of hidden burrows before the talons and teeth of the predators found them. Death shrieks mapped the final resting place of the weak, the too slow, and the unfortunate.

Lonán's orders were for no fires and cold meals. Thus, silent and dark, the Clann Ui Flaithimh camp was an amorphous shadow on the landscape. One half of the party took up guard duty and watched, peering into the gloom. The other half rested and ate, chewing on hard bread, cheese, and salted meat. Fresh water from a nearby spring softened the repast and quenched thirsts. Men drew heavy, woollen cloaks and brats around scarred shoulders that rippled with thick cords of muscle and veins. It was mid-summer. While the days were pleasantly warm, the nights carried the chill of the upcoming autumn.

The cusp between night and dawn was a dangerous time. Lonán, Mòrag, and Torcán constantly moved among their warriors, quietly encouraging and sharing stories. After a long night on damp, rocky ground, the camp was tired and irritable. Eyes were red, strained from the constant searching of the forest. Every flickering shade, real or imaginary, every rustle of branches resulted in a surge of alertness, followed by an imperceptible but real diminishing of concentration.

Carmag sniffed the air. In the gloom before sunrise, only the senses of smell, hearing, and touch were reliable. Like him, his group was well-hidden—in trees, by fallen logs, or under the thick blanket of forest debris. As soon as they could walk, his people were taken to the forest and taught to both love and fear the majestic woods—and how to use its immense strength. Carmag lay under a blanket of pine needles. Even in daylight, his position would have appeared as no more than another velvet wrinkle on the forest floor. He loved the earthy smell of dirt mixed with the sweetness of pine. The occasional scuttling of beetles and spiders over his skin had long ceased to bother the brawny warrior.

It was the abrupt silence that alerted Carmag. The forest became ominously quiet. Blackbirds were absent from the pre-dawn chorus. Predators and prey returned to dens and burrows. The forest floor's carpet of needles and leaves muffled footsteps, providing the perfect conditions for stealth. Carmag felt the vibrations. Trickles of loose soil flowed down his cheeks, coating damp, cracked lips. It was an effort of will not to spit the dirt from his mouth. Tremors of a light, cautious footfall became the thump of leather-wrapped feet as the attackers picked up their pace and jogged past.

His location was a hundred paces east of the camp. He could not raise the alarm. That would betray his position. He hoped the encampment was vigilant. They would get little warning of the upcoming assault. Carmag offered a prayer to the Goddess.

* * *

Dubnoreix stood at the tree-line. Beside him, the young horn-blower nervously licked his lips and sucked on a pebble. His mouth needed to be moist. The last thing he wanted was to disappoint the king with a miserable horn blast. Like wraiths, the Venelli flowed past their king and divided into three groups. They would attack the camp from the east, north, and south.

The king's warriors displayed little uniformity in their dress. A small number wore protection, mostly boiled leather or bronze breastplates, plundered from raids. Only the wealthy and elite warriors could afford to buy a full set of armour. As with clothing, warrior families often passed weaponry down to the next in line. Dubnoreix wore mid-thigh-length mail—a gift from a Phoenician trader. He smiled at the irony. The Gauls had invented chainmail. Most of his warriors wore helmets that varied from a simple iron cap, which sometimes doubled as a food or drinking bowl, to ones that were highly decorated and adorned with horns, feathers, and animal tails. They carried hide and wood shields, round or oval-shaped, and a multiplicity of weapons and blades.

As his men crashed through the wildwood and its verdant, clinging undergrowth, Dubnoreix knew that stealth was no longer necessary or possible. He tapped the horn-blower's shoulder. The young man spat the pebble from his mouth and lifted up the long-necked battle-horn. A baleful, bass wail reverberated throughout the forest. It was quickly followed by others, and by a cacophony of battle cries, screams, and curses as the Venelli broke into a fast lope and zig-zagged towards the Clann Ui Flaithimh camp. From their forest nesting places, a cloud of ravens rose up, adding their harsh voice to the morning.

Torcán glanced at Mòrag and flashed what he hoped was a confident smile. He briefly wondered why, given his widely acknowledged muscular body, rakish good looks, and impressive manhood he had never attempted to coax the curvaceous princess to spread her legs for him. He chuckled. From what he had heard, Mòrag was as promiscuous and lacking in common-sense as he. *A perfect match*, he thought. Instead, he nodded to her. She acknowledged his signal with a grin that suggested she knew exactly what he was thinking. But then, it took no great intellect to discern that most men, and a good few women, wanted to lay hands on Mòrag's enticing curves.

For her part, Mòrag's thoughts were of her infant, Barra Mac Conall. Her son's father was Clann Ui Flaithimh's king. Her brow furrowed. The boy needed a real father. Not someone with good intentions who dropped by when he had the time. Conall's priority was Mórrígan and his son and daughters. Mòrag and Barra often took second place to the needs of the tribe.

For all her adventures, Mòrag was quite conservative and did not entirely hold with the widely held philosophy that children are raised by the community. She sighed. Perhaps it was time to settle down and give Barra a real father. The princess cast a sideways glance at Torcán and wondered. His reputation for womanising was every father's nightmare. But then she was no shrinking violet, and her virginity was a distant memory. She sighed again. It would be her brother and the leader of the Ravens, Brandubh Mac Artair, who would need convincing of Torcán's worthiness.

With a deep-throated voice, Mòrag shouted an order. The Ravens dropped to one knee. Spear-butts were rammed into the dirt, spearheads were held, as Mòrag described, at 'balls' height. Torcán's warriors, spaced alternately between Mòrag's band, tightened shield straps, shuffled booted feet to firm their stance, and hefted javelins.

Lonán's men stood behind the perimeter line. Feet stomped, and arms flexed, driving the cramps and aches of the night from hard-muscled bodies. A few random slams of blades on scíatha became tens and then hundreds. Soon the din was a deafening crash of wood and iron. It synchronised with the beat of their hearts, the crunch of boots on gravel and earth, and the rising war cry of "Conall-Abú!" It was, Lonán thought, interesting that the men's instinct was to shout for Conall and not the old Cróeb Ruad battle cries. His brother, Cuán Ò Neill, the erstwhile leader of the thousand Cróeb Ruad who had recently joined with Clann Uí Flaithimh, would not be pleased.

At the sound of the Venelli horns, Torcán shouted, "Javelins!" The young ceannairí céad—leader of a hundred—reckoned his men, even in the gloom, could pitch two volleys of javelins in the direction of the enemy's shouts before Carmag's warriors entered the fray. Before the sour breath of the attackers filled his nostrils and their phlegm coated his shield. There was a communal grunt as javelins were raised along the perimeter and then released. Familiar cries of anguish told him that the missiles had done their work. With a hand wrapped in iron-studded leather bands, Torcán withdrew his short sword from its scabbard. He smiled as he heard the soft swish of blades along the line. With a wolfish grin on his face, Torcán roared, "Conall-Abú!" This was his environment.

In the half-light, the skirmish fast descended into the chaos of a bloody brawl. Spectral, grey shadows took on substance as they loomed from the gloom, and threw themselves at the camp's human defences. Mòrag stood beside Torcán. Without effort or design, she settled into a stab, block, and slash rhythm with Torcán. Her spear stabbed at shades but found flesh and bone. With each thrust, her arms and chest juddered. Muscle, bone and gristle were a formidable barrier even to a sharp blade. Ere long Mòrag's spear was slick with blood. Torcán's face was a nightmarish mask of red. The wrappings on his hands were soaked in gore. Strings of flesh hung from bloody studs.

*＊＊

Carmag stood, throwing off his earthy mantle. Clumps of black soil and root fibres clung to coarse, red body hair. He shook his long mane of braided hair, grabbed his hammer, and charged the rear of the Venelli. The leader of the forest people was a fearsome sight in battle. Massive upper arm and shoulder muscles strained to control the swinging club with its double head of iron.

In a skirmish, his men tended to give Carmag a wide berth. The enemy was not so fortunate. With a roar that rivalled that of an angry bear, Carmag swung. Three heads became a bloody pulp. It was with some mercy that they had their backs to him. They went swiftly to Mag Mell blissfully ignorant that shards of their skulls and pieces of their brains clung to a large lump of grey metal.

***

The sun rose over the horizon and the eastern mountains—a fiery red ball with a golden-orange corona. It embraced the camp and Clann Ui Flaithimh's battlefield, bathing it in warmth and dispersing the gloom of the dusk. Dubnoreix swore as he gauged the strength of his enemy. His men were more than double their opponent's number. Yet, they had made little headway against the well-ordered defence. Now they were assailed from behind. The Venelli were well-acquainted with fighting in their forests. How had the warriors, dressed only in swirling tattoos and who now battered his men, remained unseen?

Concern deepened for Dubnoreix when he noted the two hundred warriors at the centre of the camp. As yet, they had not entered the affray. Hardly had Dubnoreix given form to this thought than Lonán shouted, "Cróeb Ruad. Ionsaí—charge!" Mòrag and Torcán's lines disengaged and parted with unrehearsed yet remarkable precision. Lonán's men flowed through the gap as the Venelli rushed forward.

It was claimed by the Ulaid of northern Ériu that each man trained as a Cróeb Ruad warrior was worth ten of any other. The assertion was only a mild exaggeration. Under the influence of many jugs of beer, even Nikandros the Spartan admitted he was unsure who he would wager against if it came to a fight between his people and the Gaels. Indeed, because of their fighting prowess, Sparta had used them as mercenaries in the past.

Sandwiched between Carmag and Lonán, the warriors of the

Venelli prayed to their gods and made one final brave challenge. They were bloodily thrown back, many to nurse cracked skulls and broken bones. Honour having been satisfied, the Venelli took to their heels and fled into the forest. Dubnoreix shrugged as his men ran from the battlefield. "The next time we will use wiser tactics," he said to no-one in particular. His shield-bearer and the horn-blower nodded with what they hoped was a grave, yet understanding demeanour.

From his cover, the king continued to observe the Clann Ui Flaithimh as they went about the business of stripping and beheading the dead. He dipped his head in approval as the severely wounded were dispatched with a sharp blade. It was done efficiently and speedily. Furthermore, and unlike his bastard neighbours—the Veneti—the warriors of Clann Ui Flaithimh appeared to take little delight in mocking their prisoners or in torturing them. More than likely they were already well-informed of Aremorio and therefore had no need for information. He wondered if the leaders of his enemy would show mercy to those with injuries that would heal. A sharp blade to the heart or across the throat would be kinder than a life of slavery.

CHAPTER 3

405 B.C.—Samhain

The weather over the narrow Muir nIocht became increasingly capricious as the feast of Samhain drew closer. Strong winds, mountainous waves, and poor visibility made sailing increasingly hazardous. With the high winds came bone-chilling squalls of sleet and snow. For those who lived near the coast, the warm breezes and gentle seas of autumn were replaced with damp, wet conditions that were truly miserable.

Pytheas, however, was in a great mood. His final 'cargo' had disembarked, and he had given the orders for his fleet to set a course for their home port of Massalia on the Great Sea. A winter trading in the lands around the sea's deep, blue waters and warmer climes beckoned the merchant. Most of Clann Ui Flaithimh's army had been transported to Aremorio along with vital tradesmen—the blacksmiths and armourers, and even the cooks and bakers. To the well-vocalised disappointment of the men, there were no whores.

The terrain occupied by the Clann Ui Flaithimh was roughly triangular in shape. It was about four thousand paces in length from the headland's tip and around the same at its widest point. At the centre of the newly acquired territory stood a rust-red pimple of a hill. While the mound was not impressive, it was high enough to overlook the rolling landscape of gentle hills bordered with dense forestland. It was the perfect location. Long sightlines gave early warning of attackers. The land afforded few hiding places. Woods teemed with game, and rivers and seas provided their own bounty. Behind the heather and moss-covered mound, the area offered ample space for the army—and the eventual arrival of the civilian population.

Cúscraid Mac Conchobar, master of Clann Ui Flaithimh's defences, and Nikandros arrived with the fourth landing. Once all had disembarked the Spartan called an assembly of the ceannairí céad and ceannairí na míle—the leaders of a thousand. At the meeting, the olive-skinned Nikandros made it very clear that, in Conall's absence, Cúscraid was commander of the army.

It was a declaration that did not sit well with Cuán Ò Neill. He lost no time in letting it be known that he was of noble stock, and thus it was his right to command. Few took his assertions seriously, and many laughed. Cuán was sensitive about his royal status. Therefore, the mockery did not sit well with him. While Cúscraid minded Cuán's grumblings, his priority was building the defences. Without an adequate stockade and shelter, the army would be overcome and defeated by either the winter or the Venelli and their allies.

Stripped to the waist and with axes and shovels in their hands, the army was put to work excavating and building a massive earthwork of dirt reinforced with layers of rock and timber. The wall ran from coast-to-coast. On its southern slope, the rampart had a deep ditch that ran parallel to the fortifications and was populated with fire-hardened stakes.

Cúscraid's defences were a forbidding and cruel challenge for the native tribes. Timber posts were sunk into the dirt about two paces apart along its broad, flattened crest. Each was linked to its neighbour with cross-braces. The stockade was completed by filling the gaps between the posts with tall stakes. Once finished, the fence was the height of two spears. On the inner face, a walkway was secured to the wall. It formed a fighting platform for the warriors. Steps were carved into the inner surface of the dirt rampart and faced with slabs of rock. Rough, wooden ladders ran to the walkway.

Still, even with an army of over four thousand warriors, it was impossible to adequately man the wall. Sturdy, wooden watchtowers and platforms from which rocks, embers, and boiling oil, water, and pitch could be tipped on the enemy were erected every two hundred paces. Each tower had a complement of twenty warriors, including archers and slingers. Space was cramped, but in the winter the occupants were glad of the communal body heat and shelter from the storms. The stench of sweaty, unwashed bodies was a price they gladly paid. Ten paces from each tower, kindling and wood were stacked and covered with hides. Nearby, braziers glowed incessantly. The wood-pile would quickly become a signal fire visible to the other posts and the main camp.

The earthworks had one main entrance. Wide enough to comfortably allow the passage of two chariots, it was positioned at the wall's mid-point and guarded by square watchtowers on each side. The gateway was set fifty paces back from the line of the ramparts, with each side of the fence curving inwards to meet the gates. Solid oak gates with heavy locking bars secured the opening. A dirt and rock path bridged the perimeter ditch, linking up with a wagon track that led away from the defences. Further along the ramparts, on the eastern and western sides, two smaller gateways were carved into the battlements. Groups of warriors were encamped behind each egress. Their orders were simple. Hold until reinforced.

***

The stone-grey skies of the winter dawn spurned the advances of an anaemic sun. On three sides of the promontory, waves crashed onto pebble and sand beaches. Sea-water flumes splashed against rugged, moss-covered bluffs. Banks of sea fog drifted above the turbulent swell as if waiting for permission to come ashore.

Against the travails of the weather, they stood firm. Spines were held as straight as the barbs from the blackthorn tree. Silver-grey pelts hung from square shoulders and flapped in the gusting winds. Obsidian-black, unblinking eyes stared southwards. On the ramparts that protected the camp, the grim guard stood silent. Four paces separated each from his neighbour.

Winds, heavy and laden with salt-spray, forced Cúscraid to draw his sheepskin-lined cloak tighter to his body. The robe was secured with a fist-sized, gold brooch. It was a gift from his woman. He chuckled to himself as he thought of her. She was proud of her reputation among Clann Uí Flaithimh for her exceptionally sized breasts. Cúscraid sighed and watched the steamy white trails of his breath dissipate. He sorely missed her fragrance and the warmth of her body in the cold nights.

Cúscraid contemplated pulling the thick, wolf-fur hood over his head, but quickly discounted the idea. The swirling winds that buffeted the ramparts would promptly snatch and throw it back onto his shoulders. Instead, he tightened the leather straps of his helmet. Even with its soft leather inner, the headpiece was cold on his head. It did, however, sit easier on his skull ever since he had adopted a cropped—almost shaven—hairstyle. Ruddy-cheeked, eyes half-closed in a permanent grimace, he tramped on. At one of the guards, he stopped, grunted and adjusted the cloak. "That's better. Can't have you looking scruffy."

"You're a disturbing man, Cúscraid… maybe a very disturbed one." Lonán Ò Neill's hazel eyes glinted. In his winter clothes, the tall, broad-shouldered warrior looked twice his usual size.

Cúscraid laughed, "Maybe." He tapped the guard's ivory, wind-blasted skull, "But these 'volunteers' have saved us a good few men. The local barbarians are a superstitious lot." Lonán nodded in agreement. Then he watched as Cúscraid carefully, almost tenderly, adjusted the guard's jawbone. Its clicking back into place seemed to be a signal for its comrades to greet the morning. Along the rampart, five hundred skulls on five hundred spears began to chatter. As if in response, the wind changed direction to challenge the macabre defenders. It only served to enhance their presence. Five hundred jaws gaped. The black maws filled the air with an unearthly howling and wailing.

"The Hag's arse, Cúscraid. The mná-sidhe could learn from these." Lonán shivered—and not from the chill air.

✳✳✳

Dubnoreix scowled and pulled his heavy winter cloak around him. Small, irregular-shaped lumps of ice clung to the bear-pelt that draped his head and shoulders and kept the rain from a head of shaggy, corn-blonde hair. Thankfully, the ash-grey clouds soon scurried away, taking with them the snow and ice. What remained was a dry easterly wind whose embrace was bitterly cold. Despite constant skirmishes and harrying, the Clann Ui Flaithimh had steadily constructed their barrier across his land. Dubnoreix sent countless warbands against the walls. Given the relish with which the 'labourers' grabbed weapons and shields, the sole accomplishment of his attacks was to provide sport and a welcome relief from the tedium of their endeavours.

The king tugged the tails of his long, plaited moustache. They were stiff from frost and the oatmeal he had supped earlier. He grunted. The whiskers were forever falling into his food and drink. Dubnoreix spat as he observed the skulls staked along the wall. Their chattering teeth and wailing mouths had little effect on him save the odd shiver that rippled along his spine. The impact on his people and the more superstitious Abrincatui was much more evident. They quailed as he ordered them into battle as if expecting their former comrades to take up a blade for the enemy.

His neighbours, the Abrincatui, had finally been compelled to join the assault. Better fighters than the Venelli, they also had a custom of hanging several of their latest victims' heads from their belts. *A nasty, if not uncommon, tradition among the Gaulish tribes*, thought Dubnoreix. The skulls tended to stink as they decayed. Still, the Abrincatui were ill-served by weak leaders who squandered the strength of their warriors. They were avaricious and all too easily bribed. As he watched another assault fail miserably, Dubnoreix became resigned to requesting a meeting with the invaders. Perhaps diplomatic efforts, supported by the age-old—and successful—duo of bribery and wine, would yield better outcomes.

So far, and to the king's surprise, the barbarians showed no inclination to raid beyond the wall. The land they occupied was in itself of little value—a knuckle of his territory. The trading ports and mines were much further away. Clapping wind-burned hands together, the king called one of his chieftains to his side.

Nikandros nudged Cúscraid's shoulder and pointed to the forlorn figure that, with his arms held high and palms forward, approached the defences. "Looks like the neighbours want to talk."

CHAPTER 4

404 B.C.—Southern Albu—Imbolg—Winter

On the southern coast of Albu, the vast hillfort of Mai Dún played host to three couples. Conall, Rí Ruirech of Clann Ui Flaithimh, and Mórrígan, his formidable queen and widely known as An Fiagaí Dorcha—the Dark Huntress; Fearghal Ruad and the Sidhe, Mongfhionn; and Urard and Iasg. Much to the amusement of the others, Urard was blissfully unaware of his partner status.

Due to her intense fear of deep waters, Gràinne Ni Fearghal, a lithe and strong Cinn Péinteáilte—Painted One—warrior from North-eastern Albu, also remained with the group. Captain of the tribe's chariot teams, Gràinne was the recently adopted daughter of Fearghal and Mongfhionn. A consequence of adoption was that the Sidhe instantly recognised that Gràinne still suffered nightmares provoked by her previous existence and encouraged her to come to terms with it.

Abused by her father and grandmother, the young woman bore deep mental and physical scars. A web of whiplashes on her painted body was a daily reminder of past tortures. Indeed, the final memory Gràinne had of her grandmother—Diadhaidh, Priestess and Queen of the Na Daoine Tùrsach— was of the queen pressing a dagger to her granddaughter's throat. Gràinne was to be a sacrifice to an unholy spirit. Now, her blood-kin were dead, killed by Conall's forces. On this, Gràinne had no regrets and bore Conall no ill-will. It was understandable that the young woman would seek to draw a line under her distressing past. The problem was, by right of blood, Gràinne was Queen and High Priestess of the Na Daoine Tùrsach, and that was a weighty yoke for slender shoulders.

Together with their caomhnóirí, or personal guards, the Clann Ui Flaithimh leaders were to spend the winter within the secure walls of Mai Dún as guests of the newly crowned king. The civilian population camped within a sling shot of the hillfort's ramparts on its southern side. Taking the lead from his late father, Mai Dún's young king saw Conall and Mórrígan's extended stay as an opportunity to convince them to settle down within his domain. It was a tempting proposition. Land was plentiful. Grain grew abundantly, and the tin, copper, and iron mines provided a constant source of income. That Conall and Mórrígan's destinies guided them elsewhere was perceived as a challenge but not an insurmountable barrier.

Conall's muscled arms enclosed Mórrígan, holding her firmly against his chest. Wrapped in a massive bearskin—the hide of the bear that attacked Mórrígan when she was fifteen summers—only faces were exposed to the blustering winds. Mórrígan fondly recalled the shy young boy she once knew and their innocent dalliances. Now, almost thirty summers in age, Conall's face was etched with lines of responsibility, but his mind was as sharp as tempered steel, and his body was as hard as granite. For now, Mórrígan cherished an all-too-rare moment and enjoyed the warmth and closeness of his body. Although he disguised it well, she felt a tenseness in Conall and knew his thoughts were with the army in Aremorio. It had taken much persuasion, and some threats from the Sidhe, to convince the king that in this instance his place was with his people.

Winter in Albu's coastal south was much less severe than those of Ériu or Northern Albu but could surprise with cold snaps of snow and rain. This evening, as the sun sank below the horizon, the pair stood on the ramparts of Mai Dún. Before them, on the southern side of the hillfort, was the encampment of Clann Ui Flaithimh. A shimmer of blue-grey smoke hovered above the hide tents. Hundreds of campfires glowed red. The mouth-watering smell of meat roasting on spits, stews simmering in giant cauldrons, and baked bread browning on iron griddles and hot stones drifted over the walls.

"They need a home." The statement was to no-one in particular. Mórrígan sighed wearily. It was a topic that monopolised Conall's thinking. A grunt from Fearghal, who stood nearby with Mongfhionn and their well-swaddled infant daughter, Neamhain, suggested that Conall should provide more meat to the bones of his declaration. "Like a tree, the tribe needs a home where it can put down strong roots for the future. The people shouldn't have to move *en masse* each time the army marches to face a new enemy."

"It's our way, Conall. Besides, if they're not with the army, how will we protect them?" asked Fearghal. The king nodded. It was a fair question.

"With a suitable location, Cúscraid can plan and build strong defences. It would have a sizeable garrison." Conall paused in his deliberations. "The people will have to learn to protect themselves. Those old enough need to be trained with simple weapons—slings and spears." Fearghal thought for a moment and stroked his winter beard. Between Samhain and Imbolg it had grown the length of his little finger. Ten summers older than Conall and with a lot more silver in his red hair, the battle commander of Clann Ui Flaithimh smiled. He was proud of Conall. A great warrior, the young king had a deep affection for his people. In turn, the people had a fierce love for their king.

"Perhaps you're right, Conall. We've enough ceannairí céad and veterans in our caomhnóirí to initiate training. A little time spent on practice each day would make quite a difference. The people would likely see it as a welcome break from the chores and boredom of camp life. Leave it to me. I'll get something organised" The tall warrior paused, "As for the new home…"

"Ahhhh." Conall's blue-grey eyes twinkled in the fading light of dusk. "Well, once we have established a base in Aremorio *and*, since Urard loves riding so much, I thought I'd send him and a few hundred warriors, on a mission to identify a few possible places. The chosen location would need to be within striking distance of Rome." Conall thought for a moment. "Maybe I should send Tadhg as well, Brains and brawn." Conall chuckled.

"Shite!" A loud snort and curse were followed by the heavy thudding of over-sized feet as Urard stormed off the wooden walkway. Iasg trailed in his wake. As she caught up with the giant, he was heard to say, "More bloody horses and sore arses." Those remaining on the ramparts roared with laughter.

***

The bonfire roared. Glowing embers and flame-tipped splinters with tails of soot were thrown high into a cloudless, moonlit sky. Waves of heat radiated from the fire, pushing aside the chill of the evening. Flushed from imbibing heroic volumes of beer, faces took on a deeper rosy glow from the fire. The smell of wood-smoke clung to clothes and hair. Under the watchful eyes of parents, grandparents, and friends, children laughed and played games of tag and hide-and-go-seek. Jigs and reels played on bodhráns, harps, and flutes. Those still able to dance endeavoured to conquer impossibly intricate steps. Tall tales and songs of epic battles were greeted with raucous cheering.

What self-respecting Gael could resist the lure of a céili? The feast was established as a regular event. Each quarter cycle of the moon, Conall gathered the tribe together. Free-flowing beer, unlimited food, and an increased probability of friendly thighs was an opportunity too good to miss. For Conall, it was his way of staying close to the tribe and keeping up-to-date with their concerns or, as he put it, listening to the gossip. All nobles or slaves could approach the king during the evening. By his simple act, the dependency between the people of Clann Uí Flaithimh and their king strengthened.

The feast of Imbolg passed, and with it the deep winter. In a cycle of the moon, Clann Ui Flaithimh and their friends would celebrate Bealtaine. Spring rains would refresh the land. The tribe would embark on the ships that were slowly returning to the harbour. Families and lovers would be reunited in Aremorio. The people felt trepidation as well as excitement. Most had never ventured further than their village or farm. Now, they tramped great distances to strange and, oft times, hostile lands.

***

Cathubodua stood at the edge of a copse of slender white birch trees. The wood was on a small rise east of the Clann Ui Flaithimh camp. She watched and listened as she had done on four previous occasions. Wrapped in the shadows of the trees, Cathubodua was well-nigh invisible. Her armour and weapons—helmet, thigh-length mail, arm-bands, a short-handled, double-headed axe, and daggers—were dulled black with ash and dirt. Clothing—tunic, pants, and boots—were dark, almost black, shades of green. Her face, tattooed in curls of indigo-blue sigils, needed no additional camouflage.

A score of warriors stood behind. The band had a contract to fulfil and a reputation to maintain. Their faces were expressionless and silver-grey in the moonlight. All were above average height and heavily muscled without sacrificing speed or stamina. Several had distinctive, hawk-like noses pointing to kinship with Cathubodua. All were dressed and marked similarly to their leader. All carried multiple weapons. None bore shields.

As the fires in the Clann Ui Flaithimh camp faded and the darkness grew, Cathubodua nodded. A single blast of a hunting horn sounded. South of the encampment, on the other side of the narrow stream that skirted the tents, two hundred rose from the recently tilled earth. Inhibitions dulled with beer, they plunged into the cold waters. Some cursed as fingers of icy water grasped their crotches. Weapons held high, they waded slowly through the thigh-high waters. They were loose-toothed, foul-smelling outcasts. Many were mercenaries who still held a grudge from the Battle of Mai Dún. The promise of gold and plunder was enough to convince the gullible that the camp of the Clann Uí Flaithimh would be easy pickings. Fools!

As the first reached the camp-side of the river, a row of torches flared along the bank. Yellow and blue flames flickered, throwing out fluttering light and causing shadows to ripple across the water. One by one, a hedge of spears rose up before the attackers. The weapons were held by men and women with strong arms, and hands thick with callouses from their daily labours. In the torchlight, their faces wore unforgiving looks. These raiders threatened their children.

Several paces behind the line of the newly commissioned militia stood one hundred warriors. They were from Conall's caomhnóirí—his elite guard. Each held a javelin at shoulder height. "None too bright, are ye?" The voice from one of Conall's warriors boomed across the stream. His comrades laughed and together they hurled their javelins in a high arc over their people. Under the watch of a pale cream moon and a canopy of countless stars, the slaughter commenced.

The javelins shattered the resolve of the marauders. Those in the mid-stream cried as the missiles punched gaping, bloody holes in unprotected flesh. Those closest to the bank were pierced with leaf-shaped, iron spear-heads and slipped back into the water. In the moonlight, creeping fissures of blood stained the limestone banks black. Shrieks filled the air until lungs were filled with water. Gurgles of water and blood were the final sounds to escape the lips of the doomed before they sank below the surface. In their last moments, eyes beheld only the chalky silt of the river bottom. Those who could, turned and fled, hoping to find sanctuary on the far bank. For many, the whirr of slings and the smack of stones and metal slugs on flesh were the last earthly noises they heard.

"This will be a bloody mess to clear up in the morning," grumbled one hefty woman.

"We'll have to go farther upstream for clean water. And set guards to prevent the children from using this area. There'll be sickness if we don't," said another.

"The Hag take the arseholes' souls." As their final curses were absorbed by the night, the people turned from the bank and tramped towards the centre of the camp.

Cathubodua snorted. The thieves and outlaws were no more than a diversion, and of no value to her. Whether they lived or died meant nothing to her. They were not her tribe... not her family. She grinned. Moonlight reflected off perfectly white teeth. The smile was as twisted as her profession. Death usually followed in its wake. She snapped a nod at those who waited. Accompanied by her band, Cathubodua set off at a fast lope towards the camp and their targets.

They met no resistance as they flowed past the dark shapes of tents. Only the smell of wood-smoke marked the location of waning campfires. No hounds barked at their presence. There were no people, adults or children, to scream in terror at their passing. There were none to feel the cold bite of their blades... none to bless their axes and swords with blood as they dashed past. Doubts slithered into Cathubodua's thoughts. It should not be this easy... or this quiet. As one, the band's sprint slowed to a crouching, walking pace. Watchful and wary they proceeded.

A corona of light shattered the night's blackness as the camp's bonfire burst into flames. Momentarily blinded, Cathubodua cursed, squinting at the fierceness of its brightness. Were the silhouettes before her real or shadows thrown by the fire? Her answer came as a harsh, female voice called out, "Throw down your weapons." It was an order Cathubodua could never comply with. Death was the only escape.

With a loud yell and blades held high, Cathubodua charged in the direction of the voice. Without hesitation, her men followed. The assassin's blurred vision was almost resolved as Cathubodua launched herself at the closest shadow. She gasped, "Witches!" Before her, stood Mongfhionn, Mórrígan, and Gràinne. The swirling designs on their bodies flowed as molten lead in the light of the bonfire. Mongfhionn's oak staff had the most extended reach. Its ancient, gnarled head met Cathubodua's forehead with a sharp smack. As she faded into unconsciousness Cathubodua's ears rang with the dull cracks of breaking bones and the shrieks of those felled by axe, spear, and sword.

***

Dawn brought no relief for Cathubodua. Thirsty and covered in bites from clouds of sharp-toothed black-flies, her sole consolation was not being savaged by the beasts that roamed the area. Tied and naked, her body wet with the morning dew, Cathubodua sat on a grassy mound facing the rising sun. Her back rested against the cold surface of one of the tall stones guarding the hillock.

She had no memory of how she got to the hill. The fort of Mai Dún and the Clann Ui Flaithimh encampment were visible in the distance. She shook her head. Loosened braids of honey-blond hair slapped her cheeks. Stabbing pains made her wince. Her head pounded from the staff. She likely had a lump the size of a hen's egg and a bruise as blue-black as a fat fly. A numb arse begged for a change of position. She snorted. This was no time to be worrying about her appearance.

Coughs and moans forced her to lift and turn her head. Daggers of pain showed her brain no mercy. Tears ran down dirt-streaked cheeks. A handful of her band was similarly restrained. Some had twisted limbs, others had bones whose ivory-white, jagged edges poked through the skin. A few had cracked skulls; their faces described a mosaic of thin lines of congealed blood. All wept blood from deep gashes when they moved. She recognised her brothers. At the sounds of approaching men and women, Cathubodua looked up in defiance.

Yet, all she saw was a row of heads, the rest of her band staked on spears. Ravens perched on the skulls. Save for the occasional crack of a black beak on a skull, they were silent as they pecked and gorged on the soft flesh. The eyes had been the first target… then the soft tissue of the cheeks. "Barbarians!" Cathubodua's scream echoed off the standing stones. More tears flowed from sea-blue eyes as she recognised the remains of her eldest brother's skull.

"Barbarian is a name better suited to assassins paid with Roman gold." A coin was flipped towards her. In the morning sun, it glinted red as it tumbled head-over-tail towards her, finally dropping at Cathubodua's feet. Its provenance was obvious. "You came to slaughter my children." Conall walked along the line of prisoners. He was accompanied by two females and a huge warrior with a wicked axe. The one called Mórrígan carried a bow. Twin bone-handled long-daggers hung in wood and leather scabbards. Cathubodua started, these she recognised were assassins' weapons. The taller of the women carried only a staff. Cathubodua shivered, neither's eyes held hope of mercy nor hint of forgiveness.

"I see no need to question you. I doubt we'd learn more than we know." The man was of average height. His hair colour was unremarkable save that it had auburn highlights. His face was unshaven, but not bearded, a dark-blue tattoo marked his right temple. Thin white lines of scars stood out on a lightly tanned face. The long, ragged scar from cheek to neck spoke of a leader used to facing his enemies at close range.

He spoke with authority, and his words twisted like a dull-edged knife in her guts, "Gold has no loyalty. It took only beer and the promise of more gold to loosen the tongues of your 'allies'." He paused and continued, "The horn blast was sheer stupidity… foolish hubris. Did you hold us in so much contempt that you thought we would not be watchful?" The king looked at each of the prisoners and scratched a stubbled chin. "The family resemblance is clear." Sadness briefly alighted in his steel-grey eyes, before his demeanour hardened once more.

He pointed an accusing finger at Cathubodua. "*You* have condemned your family." Conall bent over and lifted up her chin so that their eyes met. In a quiet voice he added, "Or should I blame the one who watches from the far hill?"

Cathubodua's eyes widened in terror, "No."

A rustle of cloth alerted Conall to the presence of Mongfhionn. The Sidhe was a sinister creature whose alabaster perfection was often shrouded in a long, grey cloak. She placed her staff under Cathubodua's chin, tilted up her face. "The Roman's call them the Gaesatae. In Gaul, they are known as the Gaiscedach. They come from the banks of the Rodonos and foothills of the Alpes. Murderers, assassins, and mercenaries. They would sell their mothers for gold." Unable to wrench her gaze from the obsidian black eyes that glared from the folds of the hood, Cathubodua flinched at the Sidhe's hissed words.

"The sun is rising. This is a holy place. Sacrifice them. The earth will be better without them. The Goddess will be pleased." A screech from the eagle soaring above seemed to be in agreement with the Sidhe.

Conall shook his head and said quietly, "No."

He dipped his head to the giant axeman who stood close by. "You know what to do." Urard nodded and lifted up his great axe. It was named Breith—Judgment. One by one, the men were led or dragged to the stump of an ancient oak tree. Five times the axe rose and fell. Their deaths were undeservedly quick, and their journey to Mag Mell speedy. Cathubodua sent prayers with each one. She was thankful to the Clann Ui Flaithimh king for this mercy. Stiffly, proudly, she rose and waited her turn.

Conall looked at her, shook his head and spoke softly, "Not for you a warrior's death. Let the watcher on the hill witness my wrath."

He turned to Mongfhionn. "She is yours."

The rider on the distant mound watched and listened. From her vantage point, it was impossible to make out the details of what was happening within the henge. The steady thunk of iron on wood was carried across the gently rolling hills. It left little to the imagination. She too offered up a prayer for each of her sons.

It was the painful and prolonged cries of Cathubodua's agony that grabbed and crushed her heart. In the morning sun, she knew that the raised hand held the still warm heart of her daughter. Gripping the reins, she turned the horse around and galloped south-west to the coast. The rider swore vengeance on the king, the witch, and the Huntress who had destroyed her family.

Mórrígan turned to Conall. She pointed to the distant hill. "My riders can take her. Why risk the consequences of her escape?"

"No. Let her go. She will tell her tribe of this sunset and sunrise. They will fear us."

"I don't agree."

"That's why I'm Rí Ruirech. The decision is mine."

Mórrígan momentarily considered defying her partner, but said, "As you wish." Then she added, "But remember, these people do not behave like the pieces on your fidchell board." The queen exhaled a long sigh. It was time to accept reality. "We have rested in Mai Dún long enough, my love. The voyage will have its perils at this time of the year, but we should go."

Conall nodded, "Duty and a sharp blade."

CHAPTER 5

404 B.C.—NW Aremorio—Late Winter

Dubnoreix stood before the central entrance to Clann Uí Flaithimh's stronghold. He was impressed. The gates, built of split oaks, were at least three spears high and towered above him. Along the curved entrance walls, hard men stood and looked down at him. Their faces were moulded by deep creases, childhood pock-marks, and battle scars. Arrows nocked on bows clearly pointed at him and his companions. Throwing spears were held ready. Dubnoreix cursed the itch that had suddenly appeared under his arm. To scratch might result in a tragic mistake and his unfortunate demise.

His guard of ten warriors, each a head taller than he, glared back at the defenders, fingered weapons threateningly, and stamped cold feet on the frozen ground. Tempers simmered. They were annoyed their king had been made to wait in the bitter cold wind that swept along the defences. The king shook his head. Braided blonde hair threw off the sprinkling of powdery snow. His great horned helmet was carried under his arm. Dubnoreix raised a hand—slowly, to quell his men's irritation.

Behind him, a small voice spoke, "It *is* terribly cold, father." Dubnoreix smiled and berated himself for being an indulgent father to his daughter, Brigindos. She insisted on accompanying him, and he had, with little resistance, acceded. Now, even clothed in a heavy winter cloak and fur-lined hood, she needed him as shelter from the winds.

"Just politics," he murmured. A wry smile flickered on his

weather-worn face. "Just politics."

The scrape of locking bars as they were withdrawn and slammed into the slots on each side of the walls announced the opening of the gates. Accompanied by an unapologetic round of loud curses, the massive gates were first pulled and then pushed open. It took three men for each gate. Shards of ice crashed onto the frost-hardened dirt and were crushed by booted feet. On completion of their task, the men bent over, hands on knees. They breathed deeply and slowly. "New gates. Always a pain in the arse to open," opined one wit. He added, "Need to get our tight-fisted quartermaster, Sárán Mac Craobhach, to part with a few buckets of axle-grease."

The Venelli king chuckled. The accent was difficult to understand, but not the sentiment. Dubnoreix turned to observe the confident stride of the tall, red-haired warrior who approached. The king put his age at around thirty summers. He wore no weapons, save a sword sheathed in a bronze-covered scabbard. The blade hung from a leather baldric that crossed his chest from right to left. A broad belt, with a bronze and gold buckle shaped in the form of two hands clasped, served to gather the apple-red tunic covering his torso and upper thighs.

Beneath the tunic, black and red plaid pants, bound at the waist with a thick cord, were tucked into heavy, winter boots. Twists of wool from the lining poked over the tied neck. A thick woollen cloak lined with sheepskin and finished off with a collar and hood made from silver wolf pelts hung on broad shoulders. The neck of the mantle was closed with a fist-sized brooch of bronze—or perhaps gold.

"Fáilte—Welcome," said the warrior. He bowed and continued. "I am Deaglán Ò Neill, ceannairí na míle of Clann Ui Flaithimh. I am honoured to be your escort and aide for your visit to our camp." Dubnoreix smiled. The warrior had shown respect. The brogue was broad with a pleasant depth to its tone. He strained to understand the words spoken. The king grimaced. Negotiations might be more difficult than he anticipated. Deaglán was puzzled by the frown that appeared on Dubnoreix's face. "Have I said something inappropriate?"

The king smiled and shook his head to reassure his guide, "Your language. It is similar in some words but strange in others. The accent is broader and, if spoken rapidly, is somewhat difficult to comprehend." To Dubnoreix's surprise, the warrior gave a great guffaw.

"Sometimes, we can't even understand ourselves! Lots of beer usually helps." Deaglán pointed to several nearby chariots, "It is about five hundred paces to the ráth. Would you prefer to ride or walk?"

"Let us walk. It is a dry day. We can talk, and I can make a start on better understanding you."

From behind Dubnoreix came a quick retort, "That's fine for you to say, father. I don't have a huge stride like you." Taken aback, Deaglán peered closely at the king and watched as a young woman emerged from the shelter of her father. She came up to Dubnoreix's shoulders. Swathed in her great cloak, Deaglán could tell little about the girl, save that she had a pleasant and youthful voice.

Deaglán bowed once more, "My sincere apologies, my Lady. I was not informed that a princess was in the king's party." He pointed to the chariots. "If you please, one of my men will drive you to the main building."

Dubnoreix huffed. "I present my daughter, Brigindos." As Brigindos took a step in the direction of the vehicles, the king added, "Her legs and feet are as strong as mine. She will walk." Deaglán chuckled as he imagined the pout that likely had appeared on the princess' lips. They halted briefly at the hillfort gates, before proceeding to the centre of the encampment. Dubnoreix shook his head, "Perhaps I should employ you to build my defences!"

Deaglán laughed again, "Our master of defence is Cúscraid Mac Conchobar. Until the recent arrival of our king, he was also the commander of the forces that you see." Dubnoreix frowned briefly. That he now knew who was responsible for causing him so much grief was little consolation. But, on the other hand, the timing of his visit appeared to be quite propitious.

Well set back from the ramparts, the inner defences were affectionately known as Cnocán-Mórrígan, or Mórrígan's Mound. Whether the reference was to the goddess of the same name or the queen of Clann Ui Flaithimh was unclear. That ambiguity would prove useful should their queen be displeased at the naming of the fort. Some wags in muted campfire whispers added a third explanation. The shape of the mound was a pretty fair approximation of the queen's breast and the broch at its centre a stiff nipple. Mórrígan had a penchant for charging into battle naked save for the curling symbols painted on her body. Thus, the comparison was based on actual observation.

Cnocán-Mórrígan was approximately circular, and four hundred paces at its widest point. It could comfortably house three or four hundred. A single dirt rampart reinforced with wood was topped with a wooden palisade and followed the terrain of the mound at its foot. The embankment was edged with a ditch almost as deep as the wall was high. At the fort's centre and apex was a tall, circular stone edifice capped with a steep, conical wood roof. There were no windows, and the east-facing entrance was the only break in the stone walls. Dubnoreix was not familiar with its design, but it looked solid. His impression was reinforced on discovering the building's walls were both very thick and double.

"We call it a broch," said Deaglán. "The design is from Northern Albu. It's mostly a defensive structure and home, providing safety and shelter for those within."

Around the broch, several clusters of circular wooden buildings, cages, and pens had sprung up. The buildings were for both accommodation and workshops. A short walk from the broch and not as tall, a roundhouse of both wood and stone had been constructed. It appeared to have been set aside for the black-cloaked druids. Many of the cages were occupied by wolfhounds. Yet, Dubnoreix saw they were not the rabid, permanently starved dogs so often bred by other tribes. These were well-fed, alert, and appeared to be very attached to their owners. Many happily walked at the heels of their masters.

Within and outside the hillfort there were clusters of smaller round-houses as well as corrals and pens for horses, cattle, and pigs. The presence of hundreds of horses increased the Venelli king's a level of concern. A well-trained and commanded cavalry would be a severe threat. It added another urgent reason why he had to come to an accommodation with Clann Ui Flaithimh. He sighed and, ducking his head to avoid bumping it on the header stone, entered the broch.

"I present, Dubnoreix, king of the Venelli, and the Princess Brigindos, his daughter. He is accompanied by his three sons, his champion and shield-bearer, Divico, and several guards." Deaglán smiled, "Perhaps when we have assured the king that his party will not come to any harm, we can convince him to allow his guard to eat and trade tall tales with our men in the warmth of the barracks." The rumble of agreement at Deaglán's words came to an abrupt halt when Brigindos removed her cloak.

A comely young woman of about eighteen summers with a broad, engaging smile stood before them. Yet what made Brigindos stand out was her hairstyle. She had short, tufted hair that was coloured a mix of blonde and sky-blue. Soon chairs were tossed back as several of the younger Clann Ui Flaithimh warriors leapt forward to offer her a seat beside them. In the end—and to everyone's surprise, it was Eirnín Mac Gabhann who won the prize, and who sat captivated for the rest of the evening. Even more surprising to those who knew Eirnín, Brigindos appeared more than happy in his company.

"An excellent diversion. Your daughter's presence has instantly addled the brains of my younger—and impressionable—warriors." It was Conall who spoke. His tone held a chuckle, and his blue eyes glinted in amusement.

Dubnoreix spread his arms wide and rolled his eyes. "It seems to be my fate to be upstaged by my daughter." In an instant, the room relaxed.

Conall stood and dipped his head to show respect for the Venelli king. "If I may, I will introduce those around the table. I am Conall Mac Gabhann, Rí Ruirech of Clann Ui Flaithimh. To my right is my hand-fast partner and queen, Mórrígan Ni Cathasaigh. She is also known to many as An Fiagaí Dorcha—the Dark Huntress." A frisson of dread rippled through those present. *Thank goodness the Sidhe chose to absent herself*, thought Conall. He quickly continued the introductions. "To my far right is Cúscraid Mac Conchobar, who is responsible for this camp and its defences. To his right is Nikandros of Sparta. On my left is Crum Dubh, druid, and Arbiter of the Law."

At the mention of his name, the tall, sallow-faced druid rose and inclined his head to Dubnoreix. "I am also Leader of the Ériu and Albu Councils of Druids. I expect, in time, to be confirmed as Leader of the Aremorio Council. I have knowledge of your tongue and will provide interpretation and impartial opinion as needed in any negotiations."

"Life is full of surprises." The tone of sarcasm in Conall's voice did not go unnoticed by the druid.

"Perhaps it is I who should bow to you, priest," said Dubnoreix with a contemplative smile.

Conall continued his introductions which, with the exceptions of the curvaceous Mòrag Ni Artair and the striking Bláithín Ni Neill, the hand-fast partner of Cuán Ó Neill, were likely instantly forgotten. The fly in the salve was Cuán, who already had drunk too much wine. His spoken complaint that, as a noble of the Ulaid, he should have been seated at Conall's side drew a sharp look of annoyance from Conall. Sensing impending disaster, Bláithín tapped Cuán's brother, Lonán, on the forearm. A protesting Cuán was bundled from the roundhouse. His absence was no loss to the meeting. Bláithín was a more than adequate substitute.

Red-rimmed eyes smarted and wept as a thick haze of wood and peat smoke filled the broch. Outside, guards laughed at the blue smoke that billowed from the single entrance and held their noses as the level of flatulence increased. The evening stretched well into the wee hours of the morning. Stomachs were filled to bursting with cattle, chicken, and pigs roasted over the central fire. Minds, befuddled by beer and wine—a gift from Dubnoreix, caused tongues to loosen. Any danger of insult or the divulging of confidences, however, were negligible, since conversations were quickly reduced to an unintelligible and slurred babble.

"Perhaps, you would agree to be our guest for another sunset or two." The offer was made by Mórrígan. Still, it was Brigindos' beseeching eyes that tilted her father towards accepting the invitation.

***

The negotiations at Cnocán-Mórrígan lasted over three sunsets and sunrises. As Dubnoreix cantered south to his Venelli hillfort, he mused that the discussions had gone better than he had hoped. The king, his sons, and daughter were well pleased with the gifts of superior horse-flesh from the Clann Ui Flaithimh herds. He had been given assurances that the camp and fortifications were temporary. As Conall put it, the king should view their presence as upgrading Venelli defences for the future. Indeed, so impressed was Dubnoreix with Cnocán-Mórrígan and the fortifications that a plan was already forming in his mind to relocate his home.

Furthermore, Crum Dubh, with Conall's agreement, on behalf of the tribe offered to pay éiric—reparation, to the dead of the Venelli, and assured Dubnoreix that the 'grim guard' would be disbanded. For his part, Dubnoreix mulled over what he could exchange as his part of any deal. The area conceded had water, game, fish, and iron mines. Tin and copper supplies, Conall could have shipped from Southern Albu. The Clann Ui Flaithimh army was mostly self-sufficient and better trained than his. Formally agreeing to the presence of Conall's people on his land was a tad meaningless. They were not moving until they were ready. The alternative—war—was unthinkable. Therefore, as a partial gift, the king promised a steady supply of wine, which was wholeheartedly applauded.

When inspiration came, Dubnoreix gave himself a mental slap on the head. It was an army, made up mostly of lusty men. They had few outlets for their passions beyond exercise and fighting. Thus, when the king stood up and announced that he would send a hundred whores to the camp, his popularity increased immensely. Once gossip spread news of his 'gift', the king was heartily cheered wherever he walked.

However, as he rode away from the ramparts, Dubnoreix the father had other things on his mind. Brigindos insisted on remaining as an ambassador to Clann Ui Flaithimh and a sign of the Venelli's friendship and good intentions. Her knowledge of Aremorio and Gaul would be invaluable to the leaders of Clann Ui Flaithimh. Yet the king knew his daughter well. Brigindos' main intent was to be close to Eirnín Mac Gabhann. The couple had barely left each other's side for the duration of his visit.

As a strategic partnership between two tribes, the burgeoning relationship between his daughter and the brother of the king of Clann Ui Flaithimh had considerable merit. As a father, looking to protect his much-loved child, and only daughter, he was unsure whether Eirnín was good enough. But then, what father thinks any man is deserving of their daughter's favour? Dubnoreix acceded to Brigindos' wishes, but he also agreed with Conall that she have an expanded guard of one hundred Venelli warriors. A side benefit of this arrangement was that it went some way to placate the female warriors of Clann Ui Flaithimh. Slighted by the unfair offer of whores for the men, they chose to perceive Brigindos' protectors as a fresh supply of exotic rutting partners.

***

Eirnín Mac Gabhann stood on the ramparts and watched the group recede into the distance. Beside him was Brigindos. Eirnín was six summers younger than his brother. He had lived most of his life in the shadow of Conall. It was a situation that played on his mind, giving him a sour outlook on life and a sizeable chip on his shoulder. A solitary, introverted figure, most bade him the time of the day. Few considered themselves his friends.

When finally given his chance of command at the battle of Trócaire, a small settlement in Northern Albu, Eirnín survived a shaky start and fought bravely in the blood and gore. Admiration for his leadership grew among those who fought alongside him. After the battle, while it could not be said Eirnín gained more friends, he certainly was respected by many, and few would hesitate to fight at his side.

As he looked at the petite figure beside him, Eirnín, for the first time since the murder of his parents, was on a path to come to terms with the life Fate had set on him. He smiled broadly and saw his smile returned without reservation by a dimple-cheeked Brigindos.

CHAPTER 6

404 B.C.—Rome—The Month of Martius

Cornelia, the beloved wife of Gaius Aurelius Atella, was in a foul mood. Gaius grunted, "With that temper, you should have red hair like the women of Ériu." Cornelia ignored the comment and tightened the straps on her husband's breastplate until he found it difficult to breathe freely. "Do you mean to throttle me? It would be a novel way for a soldier of Rome to reach the Elysium Fields." He stood back a pace and placed hands covered with thin blade scars on his wife's honey-gold shoulders.

"Do *not* treat me like a young girl, Gaius," said Cornelia. "You and I both know that treacherous bastard, Marcus Fabius Ambustus, and his nauseating sons, hope you will be killed on this mission." Cornelia's high cheeks flushed red, and her sapphire blue eyes reflected her anger and turmoil.

"It has been that way since I returned from the debacle in Ériu. Nothing has changed." The memory of the landing in Ériu and the battles with a much younger Conall were ever-present in Gaius' thoughts and dreams. Two hundred Roman soldiers had splashed into the cold surf on a beach in southern Ériu. Only one had returned to Rome. He shivered as he recalled how close he had come to sharing the fate of Spurius, the group's commander. His nightmares were filled with visions of the Sidhe and Mórrígan, and the savage hatred both had for Rome. Yet Gaius could neither blame them nor Conall. Gold from Rome had paid for the slaughter of their families.

"Again, do *not* confuse me with the dull-witted whores your men frequent."

Cornelia wrenched free of Gaius' hands and paced the marble tiles. She wore no sandals, loving the smooth coolness of the floor on her bare soles. Cornelia had a preference for Greek fashion. The simple lines and light fabrics were much more practical in the hot summers of Rome. Her chiton, made of white silk and embroidered with a purple border, swished across her feet as she walked. The dress was gathered at her shoulders with several jewelled, gold pins. On this day, Cornelia's long, black hair, with a sheen almost as blue as her eyes, was braided, forming a circlet on the crown of her head.

Gaius thought she looked like a goddess. He grasped her hand and led her to the balcony of their first-floor apartment. Their accommodation was in his employer's vast complex in Rome. The Pontifex Maximus preferred to keep his captains close. It was another issue that made Cornelia grind flawless, white teeth. She favoured their villa tucked between the eastern shores of Albanus Lacus and the hills south of Rome. As they entered the small balcony, a great cheer arose. Ten centuria stood in the piazza. With a flourish of his hand, Gaius gestured to his men. "See, I have all these burly warriors to protect me."

A shadow crossed Cornelia's face. "More like to die with you," she muttered under her breath. From her father, Marius Furius Camillus—a renowned general and noble of Rome—she was more than informed as to the Gaulish tribes. They were nomadic and numerous. More than two hundred, ranging in size from small warbands to large tribes such as the Belgae, Carnutes, Helvetii, Senones, and Veneti. They were perpetually at war with each other but would jump at the opportunity to band together and attack a wandering legion of Rome.

Gaius' preferred route was to sail with his men from Rome to the Greek port and colony of Massalia. The sprawling, white-walled city was close to where the Rodonos flowed into the Great Sea. It was a route that would avoid having to cross the Alpes, the magnificent mountains that protected the dog-legged peninsula where Rome sat. From Massalia it would be a hard, but achievable, march north over the Cebenna mountains to meet the Liga river. There, they would follow the river valley until they reached Aremorio.

Marcus, however, refused to pay for the transport to Massalia. Instead, he insisted Gaius take a circuitous route on foot through many Gaulish territories. The added incentive of the gold, coin, and jewellery that weighed down Gaius' wagons served only to put an even bigger target on her husband's back. Cornelia's only consolation was that at least on this occasion the journey would avoid the Germani in their dense forests and treacherous marshlands.

A flicker of movement on another balcony caught Cornelia's attention. The silver-haired head of Marcus, the subject of her ire, dipped in acknowledgement of her presence. *Nothing wrong with the old bastard's vision*, she thought.

Age had taught Marcus that anger served little purpose other than to prompt stomach pains and a burning sensation in the throat. Vengeance and retribution were best planned with a cool head. Yet Rome's zealous spiritual leader was irrationally incensed as he looked upon Gaius' men. Even their dress drew his ire.

All his soldiers wore standard uniforms. Only wealth differentiated the quality of materials and tailoring. They wore bronze helmets in the Chalcidian style, which varied from unadorned metal to those crested with high plumes of dyed horsehair. All wore heavy, bronze muscle-sculpted breastplates, greaves, and arm-guards. Each carried a short sword—the xiphos, and a long spear—the doru or sarissa. The spear had a leaf-shaped blade at one end and a sharp spike at the butt. Longer spears were better for the traditional phalanx formation. A large round shield made from wood and leather, and overlaid with bronze, was carried on backs when not in battle. In total, the armour and weaponry added significant weight to a warrior's burden.

Still, it was not the armour that made Marcus hiss with the malevolence of a viper about to strike. It was the colour of the woollen tunics the men wore under the breastplates, and the cloaks they draped over their shoulders. Marcus had decreed that all of his soldiers should wear clothing that was dyed blue-purple. It was, he thought, a much nobler and regal colour. Also, it served as a non-too subtle signal of his ambitions, and a warning that he was not to be trifled with. In contrast, Gaius' men wore tunics of crimson-red. When ordered to change, Gaius had flatly refused. Apparently, the young captain was more concerned about morale and hiding blood stains in battle.

Only in one respect were Marcus and Cornelia in full agreement. Marcus wanted Gaius disgraced or dead, and preferably both. Furthermore, Marcus' patience had been stretched to breaking. His allies in the Senate were of the opinion that, at this time, Cornelia's father, Marius, would not interfere if his son-in-law were targeted. With that in mind, Marcus sent messengers over the Alps to Brennus, leader of the Senones, as well as the tribal chieftains in northern and western Gaul, and the mysterious mercenaries and assassins known as the Gaesatae. For certain, neither Gaius' march nor Conall's landing in Aremorio was a great surprise to the barbarian tribes inhabiting the land.

***

It was cool in the shade of the Aedes Vestae—the Temple of Vesta. This, the most ancient of Rome's temples, was set apart from others by its circular footprint. Twenty tall, white Corinthian columns guarded the inner cella, rising up to meet the marble roof. Gossamer-thin curtains fell from invisible rails. Delicate, they fluttered and flowed around the pillars in even the slightest breeze. The temple was small, at just twenty paces in diameter. It was where Cornelia came to meditate and to ponder her future as Gaius' wife. She could feel the goddess' embrace as she made her way through the temple's sacred grove to its east-facing entranceway.

As she watched the eternal flame at the centre of the cella, the soft rustle of dresses as the temple's priestesses went about their daily activities added to her serenity. A loud voice broke her contemplations. Cornelia swore with venom that would have astonished her husband. It was not that her thoughts had been interrupted. Instead, it was by whom. The voice belonged to Marcus. As the slap of his sandals on the marble floor came closer, Cornelia scampered to hide behind one of the wide columns.

Marcus was accompanied by a tall woman. Her features were hidden by the folds of a pine-green cloak and hood. Her accent was strange. Harsh, like one of the Gaulish tribes. Words from her lips were spat out with anger. A pouch was tossed at the woman. It missed her grasp and fell to the floor with the solid clink of gold. She cursed Marcus, but with one hand gripping the handle of her sword bent to lift the pouch. There was no love lost between these two.

"See to it that you are successful this time," rasped Marcus. "The ballistae parts for the Veneti are in wagons in the woods to the north of Rome. A score of instructors will accompany them. Surely with these, you can defeat the Gaels and their upstart king." The woman snarled a response. Another pouch of gold was tossed at her. "That's to ensure Gaius and his men do not return to Rome."

Blood drained from Cornelia's face at Marcus' final words. He had just paid for her husband's murder.

CHAPTER 7

404 B.C.—Bealtaine—Aremorio

Sat on the cliff's grassy lip, Conall looked down on the crescent-shaped cove and watched as a chevron of galleys crunched onto the sand and shale beach. He tensed as he watched a tall, burly warrior disembark. That he walked with a familiar, relaxed stride bode well. His red mane and beard were untamed, but clean and lustrous. He led two horses. One, a large chestnut-bay, was unmounted. On the other, a smaller, red dun, sat a young, fair-haired woman with an infant in her arms.

Conall stood, stretched his arms and waited. As the warrior approached, he raised up a hand, palm towards the warrior. "Good to see you, Íar. You look well."

Íar breathed slowly and deeply. The walk to the cliff's edge was short but very steep. With a smile, he handed the reins of his mount to his companion. She remained mounted, reflecting her companion's uncertainty. He took a few paces towards Conall. The welcome appeared genuine, but the years had taught both men the art of masking true feelings and intentions. "My father, Ruiri Deda Mac Sin, sends his regards from Curraghatoor. As does Onchú Ò an Cháintigh at Carn Tigherna. During my visit, Onchú was hand-fasted with one of my half-sisters. A good omen for both túatha." It seemed more comfortable for Íar to start the conversation on areas of mutual interest.

"In your absence, the elders at Ráth na Conall have guided the community well. It prospers. They have built a harbour on the nearby headland. Perhaps you could prevail upon Pytheas to include it in his trading routes." Conall nodded. The suggestion made a lot of sense.

"Caher Conri?"

A frown touched Íar's lips, "Not so good." Íar glanced around to make sure Torcán Ó Dubhghaill was not within hearing range. Conall saw the quick glance around and smiled, guessing Íar's concern.

"Torcán is in the main encampment. He was one of the first to arrive."

Íar laughed. *It was*, thought Conall, *a good laugh*, and one that he sorely missed.

"Torcán's brothers, Uallachán and Nuadha, have been causing mischief with their raiding and banditry. So far, my father and Onchú have contained their actions. The garrison at Ráth Na Conall dissuades them from attacking that fort. Still, there's little doubt that the fort is what they covet. Those who live close to Caher Conri think the evil that inhabited Eochaidh Ruad has found a new home in Uallachán."

Conall shook his head. His heart was heavy, and he missed his home. But sadly, there was little he could do. The geis placed on him by the Sidhe made a return to Ériu and Ráth na Conall impossible. His daughters would have to resolve this challenge. Yet, they had never known Ráth na Conall as their home. A sigh escaped Conall's lips. It was time to see if old wounds still festered.

"I didn't think your father would be sending greetings, or is that you just being diplomatic?"

"Me? Diplomatic? There's a laugh." A moment of sadness flashed across Íar's face. "It was difficult informing my father about Áine. The telling helped. It brought things into a better perspective. Also, it turned out that my father had a more realistic understanding of his daughter than her older brother." As if wanting to get past the topic, Íar grinned and pointed to the infant, "My father was overjoyed to meet his grand-daughter, Sorchae. It seemed to him that the Goddess had balanced the scales. I'm glad they spent time together."

"And, the young woman?"

Íar chuckled, "Deda gifted me a wet nurse. Her name is Aoibheann Ni Fionnséach. She was carefully chosen. I'm told she comes from a noble family." Sadness rested in Íar's fern-green eyes, "Her recent life has been troubled. She lost both child and partner to disease. I think having Sorchae to look after helps her manage her sorrow." He snorted. "I also believe that my father is playing matchmaker.

"Deda bears you no ill-will, Conall—and neither do I."

"Are you with me, Íar?" Left unspoken the real question was, *Can I trust you?*

"Am I welcome?"

Conall nodded and smiled broadly. Arms wide, both men embraced on the cliff top. Conall pointed to the harbour and the sleek galleys that knocked against temporary wooden jetties. A steady stream of people and beasts were embarking. One caught his attention, and he smiled. "I see someone prevailed on Gràinne to make the journey."

At the water's edge, Gràinne looked with trepidation on the galley as it rose and fell on the soft swell. Her face, ordinarily pale, held a faint green tinge. She had already thrown up several times on the voyage. Now, her empty stomach begged for food. It was a request she resolutely ignored. She dug long toes into the wet sand as if anchoring herself once more to the land. The happy burbling from the baby in her arms diverted her attention. She smiled, "Fine, Brianag Ni Brion. So ye proved to be a better sailor than yer Ma." Glancing up, she spotted Conall and waved. Then, realising the steepness of the incline and narrowness of the path before her, she breathed deep, held Brianag fast, and strode forward.

∗∗∗

It was an understatement to say that the conversation with her father had not gone well. Cornelia had prevailed on him to take action on the treacherous and treasonous Marcus. He was supportive, but it was obvious that he could or would do nothing to intervene. "There is no evidence of Marcus' wrongdoing. Gaius may be well-liked, but your memory of a conversation overheard in a windy temple is not enough to have the Pontifex Maximus of Rome censured before the Senate."

Angry at her father's impotence, Cornelia stormed from his villa. She feared for Gaius but was at a loss as to what she could do. Now, she found herself on a jetty, staring at the bireme that pulled against its wooden moorings. The captain and crew looked at her expectedly. "The tide is in our favour, my Lady. Will you be sailing with us or not?"

With no firm plans except to aid her husband, she nodded to her maids and the small number of chosen men that Gaius had left as her guard. They tramped up the wooden bridge to the board the vessel. The ship's destination was Massalia. She had heard of Gaius talk of his friend, the merchant Pytheas. Perhaps, she could persuade him to help her. In her mind was one thought: *The enemy of my enemy is my friend.*

CHAPTER 8

404 B.C.—Aprilis—Alpes

It was a barren land of rock and snow. It was a cold and cruel, yet beautiful, panorama. Snow-covered peaks formed a ridge of perfectly white teeth, biting into a cloudless blue sky. This was the land of the gods, for who could scale its summits? On craggy hillsides, grey-brown columns pushed aside great drifts of powdered snow. Wild goats scrambled across rock-strewn slopes. Lynxes tended mewling kittens while waiting for the time to hunt.

The stunning vista of the Alpes sought to enthral, trap, and betray. To the civilisations and barbarians on either side of the range, the mountains were a guarantor of safety. Deep crevasses, camouflaged with ice-encrusted snow, awaited the unwary. Yet the Alpes were as porous as a sieve. It was a challenging but not insurmountable barrier.

Many passes traversed the Alpes from north to south. The great rivers—the Rénos, the Rodonos, and the Donaris, of Gaul and Germania, flowed through its deep, ice-walled valleys. With each passing day, trade between Greece, Rome, and the barbarian tribes increased in volume. Broken fragments of clay amphorae that once brimmed with wine littered the land from the foothills of the Alpes to the rolling plains of Aremorio.

Gaius Aurelius Atella pushed the red woollen scarf from his face. Before turning to face the verdant valley to the north, he squinted one final time at the majestic mountains. He had lost a score of men to the mountains. This was the toll paid to the gods of the Alpes. Still, Gaius knew each man by name, and their deaths pained him. Beside him, red cloak flapping in the wind, Aquila, his grizzled second-in-command, shook his head. He knew what his commander was thinking. Gaius' charity was commendable. One day, it would likely get him killed.

***

Ambigatos, king of the Aedui, stood on the walls of the hilltop fortress of Bibracte and gazed southwards. Bibracte guarded the main pass to the peninsula where Rome lay. Its panoramic views and long sightlines made it the perfect location. The settlement's defences were strong. Earth and rubble filled the main ramparts. Transverse cross beams protruded through the outer grey-white facing stone. Longitudinal timbers were laid on the cross beams and attached with mortise joints and iron spikes hammered into augered holes. Over two thousand inhabited the fort. Just five hundred were warriors.

Few were surprised that the Aedui had become merchants trading with Rome. Sage guidance from the tribal elders guided the transformation from farmers to middle-men, informants, and the eyes and ears of Rome. The tribe, whether from luck or foresight, had attached themselves to the growing power of Rome. In return, they were known as the 'brothers of Rome'. It was likely that this honour meant more to the Aedui than the Romans. As the Aedui's networks with the other Gaulish tribes developed, so they became proficient diplomats and spies. The Aedui were not a substantial tribe, but with the menacing power of Rome at their back, few challenged them.

Fond of his food and beer, Ambigatos' tall frame coped well with a rapidly expanding belly. The Aedui king's mane of ginger hair rose and fell with the winds that swept across the walls of Bibracte. His thumb stroked the sweat-stained butt-end of his war-axe, and he shifted his position to let his shield rest on his hip. Ambigatos' body may have begun the journey to satisfy his more carnal appetites rather than fighting battles, but he remained a respected warrior.

The king stroked long, bushy whiskers. He was perturbed. The meandering, red ribbon of men and wagons that crossed the distant snow-line brought him a problem. He was fond of the Roman, Gaius. At one stage he had hoped that one of his daughters might find favour with the young man. That wish disappeared when Gaius became besotted with Cornelia. Yet he could not bring himself to be angry with Gaius. The daughter of one of Rome's illustrious generals was not a prize to be slighted. Besides, it was a delight for a cynical king to see the love the Roman had for his wife. Today, however, Gaius was a problem that did not have a good solution.

It perplexed Gaius to see the tall, wooden gates of Bibracte remain firmly shut as he and his men approached. By now, he would have expected a welcoming delegation from the settlement and a crowd of dirty-faced children swarming his men, hoping for coin and treats. What greeted him, however, was a wall lined with warriors, with spear-tips glinting in the mid-morning sun. He espied the tribe's leader. Even from a distance, the man appeared to be struggling with some major problem.

"Your gates are closed, Ambigatos. Not a great greeting from a friend of Rome," Gaius called out.

"It is indeed a sad day, Gaius. The Aedui do treasure the honour Rome attributes to us. But messengers have reached us from Rome. You and your men have been designated deserters, outlaws, and outcasts. You are to surrender to me, men and wagons, and await judgment."

Gaius bit back his anger. "I have one thousand veterans, and cohorts of Thracian cavalry and Cretan archers, Ambigatos. I have siege weapons on my wagons. You have at best, five hundred warriors. I could give the order to take Bibracte, slaughter all within her walls, and put your head on a spear."

The king shook his head, "It is not your way, Gaius. Rome knows this. I know this. The tribes beyond the borders of the Aedui know this. You are an honourable man, and you have been cruelly deceived." Ambigatos paused. "I have no power to resist those in Rome, or the

Pontifex." That the Aedui king named Gaius' betrayer was scant comfort. "The Aedui will not attack you, Gaius. But I will defend my people should it be necessary. You may cross our lands without fear of violence. That is all I can do. May your gods protect you." The king bowed and turned to leave the ramparts.

***

"Well, we're in deep shit now." It was Aquila who perfectly summed up Gaius' feelings. "Looking positively, we have wagons filled with gold, jewels, and weapons, including siege weapons. No longer citizens of Rome, we are now the wealthiest and best-armed outlaws in Gaul." Aquila took another gulp of wine. "And we have some pretty decent wine to drink."

"And the other side of the coin, Aquila?"

"We can't go back to Rome. That would be instant death. I hear the Pontifex has developed a taste for a Persian method of execution called crucifixion. Our families are likely already dead." A mix of exasperated sighs and curses resounded around the campfire where the captains of Gaius' legion had gathered. Gaius felt a twinge of guilt. At least Cornelia would have the protection of her father. "We're surrounded by a hundred thousand barbarians, who, with some merit, claim to be the best fighters in the known world."

"The enemy of my enemy…" thought Gaius aloud.

"You can't be serious, Gaius. *He* is as likely to kill us as any other barbarian. Perhaps more so. *And*, from your account of the fighting in Ériu, two other demons would relish a second chance to rip your heart from your chest." Aquila took another gulp of wine. "Besides, there's the minor challenge of crossing the lands of the Senones and Carnutes before we even get to Aremorio."

"We have the best of fighters. One hundred Thracian cavalry, each with two mounts, the same number of Cretan archers, and ten centuria of infantry plus fifty siege weapons and their teams." Gaius paused to reflect on his own words. "Yet, pitched against our enemies, our numbers are small. Our main battle formation—the phalanx, will be useless in the mountains and valleys of Gaul. I know this from bitter experience in Ériu." Gaius paused and looked at each of his captains. "We cannot survive a sustained campaign against us. We need to ally with another army. We are veterans. We are a valuable commodity."

"So we become mercenaries?"

"Possibly. Although, I would hope to be partners. If Conall Mac Gabhann will not have us, then we'll be close to ports that trade with Albu. We could 'disappear' in the land of the Gaels."

CHAPTER 9

404 B.C.—Spring—Cnocán-Mórrígan

Conall supped a horn of spring-cooled, honey-sweetened beer. He savoured the refreshing coolness as the liquid flowed down his gullet. "It will be Eirnín's and Brigindos' decision as to where they live." It was his response to Dubnoreix's observation that his daughter and Conall's brother appeared to be inseparable. That Brigindos' belly appeared to be growing pointed to the closeness of their relationship. "My brother is insufferably happy these days, and that is no bad thing," Conall paused to order his thoughts. "Eirnín's life has been difficult since our parents' deaths, and I am guilty of not being the brother he needed." A slug of beer presaged Conall's next words, "I'll miss him if he chooses to remain with the Venelli. But, if that is what he decides, then he goes so with my blessing."

Dubnoreix shifted his plaid-covered arse on the stump of the tree. An unseasonably warm sun caressed his naked torso. Beer dripped from the tips of his braided moustache onto a chest sparsely covered in blonde hair. The king grunted in resignation. He was a father faced with the potential departure of his only daughter. Yet Dubnoreix knew it was a good union politically, but all the more so for his daughter's happiness.

"Has either indicated a date for the hand-fasting?"

"No, but I'm going to suggest the feast of Lugnasad. Clann Ui Flaithimh will be officially celebrating the coming together of the tribe at that time. I thought we could incorporate the hand-fasting at the festival, providing Eirnín and Brigindos agree."

"Seems appropriate. Are the Venelli invited to the feast?"

Conall laughed, "I could hardly refuse. Just bring your own wine."

"Cheap Gaels." Both men chinked their horns of beer, emptied them, and called for more. "Perhaps, now that we have concluded organising the lives of our loved ones, we could enlarge the party?" Conall looked quizzically at Dubnoreix and then nodded. He called for his aide.

"Ask the Queen, the Sidhe, the ceannairí na míle, and Crum to join us." With a quick dip of her head, the aide dashed off.

***

"Let me tell you about a gold mine."

Located on Veneti land, and east of the Venelli border, the mine was overlooked by a small hillfort. The fort perched on a hill at the mouth of a river estuary on the northern coast of Aremorio. It was guarded by a thick wooden palisade, but Dubnoreix maintained that its defences were not of the same standard as an active stronghold. There was a small garrison of fifty warriors whose primary duty was to protect the gold ore as it was shipped from the mine to a nearby harbour. Their other task was ensuring that the slaves who laboured in the pits were productive.

"It's a soft target. If you agree to raid the mine, I'll provide scouts who know the area. The Veneti will be ignorant of my involvement and blame Clann Ui Flaithimh for the raid. We'll split the gold evenly." Dubnoreix smiled, sat back, and looked around, "What do you think?"

Conall's eyes sparkled, "I think that there's no chance of us splitting the gold evenly." A round of laughter was followed by more rounds of beer before the Venelli king retired to his quarters. Due to his frequent visits, he had been provided with a large roundhouse within the ráth. Conall looked around the circle of his commanders and advisers. "What do you think?"

"It's too good to be true. Plus, do we want to piss off the Veneti? I hear their king is a nasty piece of work." It was Mórrígan who spoke first.

62

Fearghal interjected. "We need the gold. The treasury is exhausted. Until we find a permanent home, we won't be able to grow crops, raise cattle, or work our own mines. Better raiding the Veneti than Dubnoreix's lands."

"Do we have a view from our spiritual advisors?" Conall turned his head to face Mongfhionn and Crum.

"Technically since it is theft, and likely that blood will be spilt, then I should counsel against the raid," said Crum. "Yet, the Veneti are not of our tribe and, let's be honest, raiding, whether for cattle or gold, has been a source of wealth for the kings and queens of Albu, Ériu, and Gaul for countless generations. My druids will not take part in the raid. Should you choose to go ahead, conduct yourselves honourably. We will pray to the Goddess for your safe return."

"Make the proper sacrifices to the Goddess. Kill as few civilians as possible. Every drop of innocent blood spilt will have its consequences. That is my advice." Mongfhionn rose and with a swirl of her cloak walked from the gathering.

"Well, that was really helpful. Have you not been taking good care of the Sidhe recently, Fearghal?" Nikandros winked knowingly and slapped his friend on the back. Fearghal growled and pondered whether the Spartan was right.

"According to Dubnoreix, the gold mine is about one sunset's ride or five sunsets march from here. Íar will take five hundred horses and lead the assault on the mine. Five hundred of Carmag and Brandubh's warriors will depart at the same time. They can travel faster than those in the more heavily armoured shield wall, although not as quick as the horses. They will provide a defence for the cavalry on the return journey." Íar began to protest, but was halted by Conall, "If the Goddess allows, you'll be returning with wagons heavily laden with gold. The speed of your horses will be of scant use to you."

Conall paused and smiled at Íar. It was a smile that sent a chill down the strapping warrior's spine. "Take Gràinne and half of her chariots with you. They could be useful."

"No. Please no," whispered Íar, as if not wanting his words to ride on the breeze to the nearby training square. For there, Gràinne was honing her long-sword skills. "She's wild, like a feral cat."

"She's enthusiastic and a bloody good warrior," growled Fearghal. Being both a mentor and adopted father, he had a soft spot for Gràinne.

"Bah! Women have no business with swords or fighting." No one would ever accuse Íar of being a misogynist and live. But deep inside, Íar had a very traditional, some would say straight-laced, view on the role of the female in society. That his cavalry still remained all male was unsurprising.

Another smile ghosted across Conall's lips. While enjoying Íar's discomfort, his attention was drawn to the training square. There, Sorchae's wet-nurse, Aoibheann, approached Gràinne. After a brief conversation, the nurse discarded her léine. Underneath, she wore yellow plaid pants to her knees and a leather harness that went some way to cover her breasts.

A quick flurry of dexterity—Conall never understood how women did this—her long, fair hair was piled up and secured with several wooden pins. She lifted up a wooden training scíath and sword and approached Gràinne. The two touched weapons. This was followed by a furious round of swordplay. It was not in Gràinne's nature to give ground or go easy in training. From what Conall could see, Aoibheann had little need of either. Conall nudged Nikandros, for the Spartan had also observed the duel.

"I suppose you think all women should be like Aoibheann, quiet, reserved, good in bed, a good mother, and a good cook," said Nikandros with a broad grin.

Íar's face reddened in discomfort. "Nothing wrong with that. Aoibheann has been well brought up," retorted Íar, "And, no, I haven't bedded her." The Spartan roared with laughter and slapped Íar across the back. "I think your father has a great sense of humour as well as a great eye for women."

As the final touch to Íar's misery, Conall added, "By the way, I think you should recruit females to your riders. We'll talk more when you return." Íar's visage was crestfallen. His friends were doubled up in laughter.

***

Tadhg Ò Cuileannáin groaned. No matter how slow he walked, the broch came closer. He had been summoned by Conall, and that usually pointed to trouble. Gifted with a sharp mind and a dogged nature, the young man was well-known as Conall's 'investigator-in-chief'. While this meant he was highly valued by Conall, in Tadhg's mind, it also meant that he got the shitty missions and tasks.

With a sigh, he ducked his head and entered the broch. To his surprise, already seated around the oak table were Conall, Mórrígan, Mongfhionn, Íar, Cúscraid, Nikandros, Crum, and Fearghal. At the far end of the table sat a scowling Urard. His friend, Iasg, stood behind him. Her small hands were in constant motion as she attempted to ameliorate the warrior's mood by massaging knotted shoulder muscles. Standing to the side and entirely taken up with each other were Eirnín and Brigindos.

Conall smiled. "Welcome, Tadhg. Take a seat. Mórrígan and I have not seen enough of you lately." Tadhg's stomach flipped. This was a terrible sign. In Tadhg's experience, a pleasant Conall was a devious Conall. The beaming grins around the table and fulsome expressions of best wishes for his health and well-being succeeded only in making him more anxious.

"I have a mission for you."

There it was. Six words that will surely mess up my life, thought Tadhg.

With resignation in his voice, Tadhg smiled wanly and said, "What crime am I investigating? Who's been murdered? Who needs 'monitored'?" There was a moment of silence, and then Conall slapped the table and roared with laughter. He was soon followed by those around the table. It was not the reaction that Tadhg anticipated. He frowned. In this, he was not the only one in the building with a look that would sour milk. Urard was plainly not amused, and this was puzzling.

"Am I really that bad in the tasks I give you, Tadhg?" It was the sort of question, which should never be asked and could never be answered truthfully. Tadhg may have been pissed off, but he was not stupid.

"Of course not," Tadhg responded. He fooled no-one.

"You and Urard," a grunt from the giant caused Conall to pause. "As I was saying, you and Urard will leave as soon as it can be arranged. Your job is to find a suitable location for Clann Ui Flaithimh. The people need a home. You will find it. You'll take three hundred warriors with you. I leave it up to Urard and you to decide on the mix of fighters." Conall stopped and then waved at the others in the room. "Each of these has a different perspective on the lands you will travel through and suggestions as to the directions that may be productive in your search. Listen to them well. Ask questions now. You'll not have the opportunity once you have commenced your journey."

Tadhg was smiling as he exited the roundhouse and blinked in the intense sunshine. He turned to Urard, who was still scowling and said, "That wasn't too bad."

Urard looked at him with cynical, ocean-green eyes, "You think?"

CHAPTER 10

404 B.C.—Late Spring—Aremorio

It was, thought Íar, *a pleasant journey, so far.* For the most part, the land-scape was a mix of coastal plains, woods, and rolling hills that challenged horses and riders without presenting insurmountable barriers. The land was a palette of late spring hues. Rich, subdued purples, greens, and rusts from the heathers and mosses formed a solid canvas for the striking pri-mary colours of yellows, blues, and reds from sprouting wildflowers and gorse bushes. Dense forests of pine, birch, and oak teemed with game and provided cover for the conspiracy of ravens that followed. As he encouraged his chestnut bay to stretch its legs, both man and beast were in harmony. Even the ever persistent horse-flies were tolerable.

At the end of the first sunset, they had covered two-thirds of the distance to the Veneti gold mine. Still within the borders of the Venelli, the troop dismounted and brushed down sweat-flecked, velvet coats. Each rider had his own routine, usually worked out by trial and error between man and beast. Some used straw, others carried with them a variety of cloths, brushes, and combs. While a quick glance would show little difference in the final outcome of the brushing, the presentation chosen for each horse's mane and tail was unique.

Neglect could cause a horse to go lame. Thus, particular attention was paid to ensuring bony hooves were cleaned and free of stones, cracks, and disease. Fetlocks and lower legs were inspected for cuts and bruises. Finally, the horses were fed and watered. Thick dillats were thrown over silky backs. The nights still held a chill. From a practical perspective, most riders took good care of their mounts. Their lives depended on a healthy beast. Yet the relationship between man and beast was much more profound—even spiritual. Besides that, none wanted to face the anger of Íar over a mistreated horse.

It was meán lae—mid-day—when the raiding party led their mounts down the gentle, wooded incline that formed the eastern bank of a slumbering river. Íar signalled a halt and then proceeded alone, emerging from cover to catch a first glimpse of the settlement that guarded the mines. Situated in a picturesque river plain, its setting was idyllic. The hillfort was small and built on a rocky crag that erupted from the mostly flat valley floor. Strategically, it also secured the nearest ford. The outcrop was not overly elevated, but its steep sides and the double-timbered stockade that formed its crown suggested that a small company of defenders could resist a much larger force. Egress from the hillfort was via a single narrow gateway on its northern side.

The sound of whips cracking, harsh voices, and shrieks of pain and despair caught Íar's attention. Five hundred paces north of the hillfort were the mines. Hidden by the shadows of the forest, the burly warrior guided his horse in a slow trot toward the clamour. A more striking contrast in fortunes could not have been envisaged. Ragged and torn tents, shabby and tattered clothes, and insufficient food summed up the slaves' predicament. The camp sat a hundred paces from the mine openings. Íar snorted. The land around the mine had been cleared, but the Veneti left a ribbon of trees to partially obscure the pits from the hillfort. Apparently, the occupants of the fort did not want their vista spoilt. *Fools*, thought Íar, *the cover will be useful.*

Gold is an ancient metal usually uncovered in its pure state. Whether found in rivers, bogs, or mines, the metal glitters enticingly, encouraging the worst in men. Indeed, gold had inspired greed, lust, and violence in man since the beginning of time. From dusk to dawn scrawny, haggard slaves of all ages worked, stopping only for a mouthful of tepid water or a meagre lump of mould-stained bread. Hair and skin were covered in a ghostly crust of mine debris. As they walked past torches or in the sunlight, many sparkled with the wealth they could never spend. The lash of whips echoed across the valley. The cries of the raped rose up, but going unheard, dissipated with the racking sobs of the violated.

In the dark, dimly-lit mine passages male and female slaves followed the threads of gold. Young children carried the chippings outside where they were pounded into smaller fragments by elderly slaves. Finally, the powdered ore was spread on inclined tables where streams of water separated dirt and rock from the heavier gold. Buffed and then bagged, the gold was dragged to sturdy wagons ready to be driven to the river estuary and onward via transportation by ship.

**

Cingetorix was a vain, cruel man. His vanity had no foundation. The king was neither tall nor short, his appearance could aptly be described as ugly and his gait ungainly. While some scars add character and a rakishness that many women find attractive, the blemishes on Cingetorix's pock-marked face conferred a permanent sneer on it. An aversion to bathing left his hair lank and his body odour rancid. Were he not the king, Cingetorix would have been avoided like the plague. Perhaps in recognition of this, Cingetorix ruled his tribe with casual and quixotic brutality.

Perhaps it was a coincidence, or fate, that at this time Cingetorix chose to visit this particular hillfort and mine. Always suspicious of his subjects, a rumour had come to his attention that his loyal subjects were syphoning off part of the gold production to enhance their own wealth. The gossip was, of course, correct. Its source was a disgruntled noble who thought that he should be the hillfort's commander and that it was his turn to increase his prosperity in a similar manner.

Sadly for the originator of the tales, Cingetorix brought with him men he could trust, promptly executed all the hillfort's leaders, including the rumour-monger, and gave orders that their families should work, and die, in the mines. Unfortunately for Íar, Cingetorix having little trust in his people's loyalty also brought five hundred warriors with him, including one hundred mounted warriors. Íar cursed the Hag for his misfortune.

***

In the sky above, Fate and the Goddess soared on warm updrafts. Both looked forward to the upcoming entertainment. In the forest, the rustle of blue-black feathers increased as ravens preened for flight.

The river was not deep, barely rising above the horses' shoulders. Its already muddy waters showed little sign of disturbance as Íar's cavalry stepped into it and slowly crossed to the far bank. Slipping a long-handled axe from the leather loop attached to his mount's girth, Íar nodded to the rider alongside him. The warrior smiled, licked his lips, and raised a bronze horn to his lips.

Several short blasts of the horn rang out across the valley. Uttering shouted battle cries, the Clann Uí Flaithimh horses galloped towards the mines. The distance was covered rapidly. It would seem that the slaves had a heightened sense of survival. At the sound of the horn and thundering hooves, many slaves abandoned the task in which they were engaged. Most either ran for cover or dropped to the ground, hoping that the heavily-muscled beasts would leap over them. Their actions were unfortunate for their Veneti sentries. Confused, the guards remained standing and were instantly recognisable.

The score or so mine guards responded to the attack with all of the fortitude that they had shown in their dealings with the mine-workers. They turned and ran. The few that were not cut down by the riders found themselves dragged to the dirt and beaten to death by captives bent on revenge. Inside the mine, freed slaves shouted to those still working. Pick-axes and hammers were turned on the remaining guards. The skirmish was over in less time than it takes to bathe. Control of the mine was in the hands of Íar.

Pointing to the line of trees between the mine and hillfort, he shouted, "Four hundred take up position in the woods along with the chariots. The rest secure the gold wagons." Thirteen wagons sat already loaded, waiting for the teams of oxen to be hitched to the yokes. As Íar trotted towards the carts, he noticed that while the vast majority of the slaves had grabbed a handful of gold and fled the site, a small group remained. An elderly man walked towards Íar, his hands held up.

"Can you understand me?" he called out. Íar nodded. "That's a relief." The man's parchment-dry skin had the ghostly pallor of someone who had not seen the sun for many days. Skin-draped bones testified to the lack of nutrition. Wasted muscles on skeletal arms made it an effort for him to direct Íar's attention to those standing near the wagons.

"Like me, these men are slaves. It is your good fortune that they are also the ones who haul the wagons of gold to the coast. They are skilled at their jobs and know the teams of oxen. They wish to drive the wagons for you."

"What do they expect in return, old man?" asked Íar.

"A home for their partners and their children." The elder laughed. It was a dry cackle that rattled the bones in his throat before whistling through gaps in his remaining teeth. "Observe the bulges in their pockets and the pouches that hang from ropes around their waists. Most are quite wealthy now. They will not be a burden to your tribe." Íar took off his helmet and scratched his sweat-damped head. The man pointed to Íar's riders.

"Please don't take this the wrong way. Your men are skilled in war and fierce in battle, but they know shite about hauling heavy wagons with stubborn oxen. Or how to avoid being impaled on those big curved horns."

Íar laughed. His booming voice carried to the fort on the hill. "You make a good argument, old man. Tell your men I agree, but also tell them this. The gold on the wagons belongs to Conall, king of Clann Ui Flaithimh and their oath-lord. I'll cut the hands of anyone who steals *that* gold." Íar's tone became more urgent, "I want the gold wagons, and any others you need, ready to roll before the sun touches the treetops. This will not be an easy flight. We'll use the crossing east of the fort."

The old man shook his head. "The wagons will not make it up the slope on the eastern bank. But there's a wagon track a hundred paces south of the crossing. It follows a cleft in the hillside and rises gently to a plateau." Íar dipped his head.

One hundred of Íar's riders were assigned to protect the wagons. For men used to the speed and power of their mounts, and even though each cart was pulled by a pair of the broad-shouldered beasts, the pace of the wagons was agonisingly slow. The oxen were undoubtedly strong and bloody-minded. Possibly their unpredictable temperament had something to do with the fact that they had been castrated. Few men would be happy with such treatment!

From the walls of the fort, Cingetorix fumed as he watched the line of wagons trundle towards the river crossing. The pace was slow but steady. "Throw this dog in the ditch," he rasped. The 'dog' he referred to was the sole surviving member of the mine guards. The man, possibly hoping to curry favour, had avoided Íar's cavalry, which in itself was no mean feat. As he stood before Cingetorix, he described in detail the raid on the gold mines. After, confirming that the guard had related all he knew, Cingetorix nodded to the warrior who stood behind the man. The guard's chin was grabbed, his back arched, pushing his belly outwards, and a long blade eviscerated him. There was logic to Cingetorix's action. Who wants in their employ an idiot whose judgment is so obviously poor?

Few trusted Cingetorix's word or his temperament. Still, even the most truculent of his nobles and chieftains acknowledged that he did not shirk his duty in battle. The king led from the front, and the rank and file warriors followed enthusiastically. Mounted on a sturdy, dark-liver chestnut bay, the king directed his cavalry and infantry at a fast jog down the fort's slope and towards the river crossing.

In normal circumstances, Cingetorix first would have sent his infantry into battle. His riders' role was to protect the foot warriors' flanks and cut down the enemy once their lines had been broken. On this day, the king knew that even at a fast run, his men would not reach the ford and wagons in time. Thus, he roared commands and his one hundred mounted warriors charged through the ranks, scattering from their path those too slow to jump aside. Had Cingetorix considered his strategy with a cooler head, it is unlikely he would have proceeded as he did. One hundred horses against five hundred is never a favourable wager.

With Íar at its apex, those not protecting the wagons formed a wedge and charged towards Cingetorix. Each horse carried three javelins in a sheath strapped to their flanks. A fourth spear was held in every rider's hand. Shouting insults and profanities, the two sides were twenty paces apart when the Clann Ui Flaithimh hurled their missiles. Given the speed of the horses and their uneven gait, the likelihood of actually hitting a chosen target depended more on the fickleness of the gods than proper technique. Yet accuracy was not Íar's goal. Sowing confusion was.

On this day, Fate looked kindly on the Veneti king. His horse, hit by several javelins, first reared up and then stumbled, throwing the ruler to the ground. A glancing blow from a muddy hoof cracked against the king's winged headpiece. The chin straps snapped, and the helmet rolled away. Stunned, Cingetorix rose up on his knees. It was then he heard the swish of a blade cutting through the air. Fortunately, it was the flat of the blade that slapped against the king's thick skull. Nonetheless, it opened up a flap of skin from chin to temple. Rendered senseless, the king collapsed. It was a short and not terribly consequential skirmish for Cingetorix. The same could not be said of his men.

The Clann Ui Flaithimh wedge sliced through the Veneti cavalry like a knife through goat's cheese. There was little to secure riders to their mounts save a grasp of the mane or bridles, and feet wedged into girth belts. In pain from multiple javelin strikes, horses screamed and tossed riders from their backs. Many riders, dazed by the fall, suffered the indignity of being kicked by their mounts. A small number fell to the slashing blades of Íar's men as they bludgeoned their way through the Veneti.

Leaderless, the unhorsed took what cover they could find. Those still mounted—about half of the original band—looked at the line of cavalry that guarded the wagons. All had javelins ready to throw and the time to pick their targets. Outnumbered, Cingetorix's riders took a collective decision and fled the field.

With the Veneti mounted force in total disarray, Íar's riders galloped towards Cingetorix's infantry. Wide-eyed with fear, and caught on an open plain that was perfect for cavalry tactics, the Veneti advance faltered. Those at the rear pushed and screamed, calling for the cowards at the front to step aside. It was not long before they appreciated the reluctance of their comrades. Faced with thundering hooves, their bravery leached away.

A high-pitched blast from a hunting horn succeeded in raising the level of their terror. From the trees between the mine and the hillfort, five chariots broke cover. Flags and banners flapped in the breeze. Iron-rimmed wheels crushed grass and gravel as the gaily coloured chariots gathered speed and prepared to rake the Veneti flank. That they were led by a naked apparition, screaming like a bean-sidhe, piled agony on top of misfortune.

The Veneti warrior did everything right. As the chariot passed, she jumped clear of the reach of the rotating scythes, turned to face the rear of the vehicle, and hurled her spear. The throw was good. It was too good. Only the small, round scíath strapped to Gràinne's back prevented the spearhead from burying itself between her shoulder-blades and precipitating a journey to Mag Mell. As it was, the spear glanced off the metal boss. The point raked Gràinne's shoulder and upper arm. Surprised by the missile, an unbalanced Gràinne tumbled from the chariot. Luckily, she had the presence of mind to roll clear of the chariot's wheels, but was unable to avoid a moss-covered rock.

In another battle… another bloody melee, the Veneti warrior would have triumphed. On this day, she found that Fate was capricious and the Goddess in the mood for cruel drama. Hunting knife in hand, she ran towards her enemy. Dazed, Gràinne fought to rise. Her sword lay several paces away. Confused, she struggled to draw her knife. Both warriors looked at each other. The Veneti warrior was surprised at how similar they were—height, build, and hair colour. Even their eyes had the same golden hue.

She started to raise her hand in friendship and then realised that it held a knife. This was her enemy. Almost reluctantly, she stepped forward. The wide-eyed look on her opponent's face should have been a clue. The sound of wheels filled her ears. An excruciating, throbbing pain travelled upwards. Torn like paper, her lower legs tumbled to a bloody halt, resting a body's length from her. "No!" she screamed. Her thoughts were not of dying, but of being crippled. She had a child to raise.

"No!" she cried as with failing strength she used a discarded spear to pull herself upright. The frayed stumps of her legs seeped blood into the rich soil. She glared at the warrior before her, wondering what was wrong with her vision. It was then she realised she was much shorter than before. "Bitseach!" she shouted, although she put no blame on the warrior.

Gold-flecked eyes held her enemy's. "End it. Please." She did not beg. It was a request from one warrior to another. A longsword flashed, in the pre-dusk sun. A head rolled to the side. Gràinne cried for an orphan child she would never know.

CHAPTER 11

404 B.C.—Spring—Alpes

Brennus, king of the Senones, stood, rested scarred hands on the table, and peered around his Council. He farted, scratched his crotch, and announced to no one in particular, "How did I end up with this worthless bunch of arse-lickers?" The Council looked at each other, wondering whether the correct response was to agree with the king or risk protesting. In the end, they took a curious interest in the dirt ingrained into cracked and yellowed fingernails.

A tall man, Brennus was considered muscular with little visible fat. His chest was broad, his waist trim, and his arms and legs rippled with muscles marbled with thick blue veins. Wide-set, hazel-green eyes glared from a square face. A shock of unruly red hair crowned his head and was usually barely contained by a battered iron and bronze helmet decorated with long, curling horns. Today, however, his hair fell across his shoulders and was set off by four thick plaits of whiskers that settled on his chest.

The king appeared much burlier than his build suggested. Brennus had an affliction. He always felt cold. Thus, even in the warm days of summer, he wore several layers of pelts and heavy fleece-lined boots. Typically, his hands were swathed in ribbons of soft leather, enough to hold back the cold without restricting his grip on weapons. The ensemble looked uncomfortable, but not to Brennus. Additional layers of clothing had saved his life on several occasions. It was difficult for an assassin's blade to penetrate with enough force to make a killing wound. He snorted. The clothes also hid the mail shirt the king was rarely without. Brennus was a hard man to kill.

Now, he cursed and tossed aside scíath and spear. They fell clattering to the paved floor of the royal roundhouse as Brennus stomped out the doorway. Yet the king was not without weapons. A sword was sheathed in a bronze-faced, wooden scabbard. The sword's blade was nine hands in length, the width of Brennus' little finger at the hilt, and tapered to a rounded tip. It hung from an ornately engraved and studded broad leather belt, which was closed by a fist-sized bronze and gold buckle. A dagger, the size of a small sword, also hung on the belt and slapped against his right thigh. At his back, a throwing axe was wedged between belt and garment. Of course, these weapons were only those that Brennus chose to show.

A small drainage ditch was his destination. As he approached it, his nostrils flared in disgust at the smell of piss, shite, and carcasses in varying states of decay. The cadavers were mostly those of animals, although a few skulls picked clean by ravens and vultures testified to the unfortunate demise of tribal members. The smell did not, however, prevent him from adding his pale, straw-coloured stream to the foul mix.

To Brennus, it seemed that these days he drank and pissed more, but never quite enough. The healers—a worthless bunch of charlatans in his opinion—informed him he had 'honey-sweetened piss'. They could not tell him, however, what that meant or how to get rid of it. Their cures amounted to little more than old hag's tales—leeches, blood-letting, and eat more fruit and vegetables.

Alone, albeit briefly, the king found himself with time to think as, like a small boy, he playfully directed his flow. He had over thirty thousand restless and belligerent warriors under his command. Many of his chieftains and nobles thought they could do a better job and were forever plotting his demise. Brennus' strategy was to provide them with a constant range of 'diversions'. Opportunities for raiding were accompanied by a diversity of rewards—plunder, slaves, ransom for captured nobles and, of course, rape.

Approximately half of his forces were scattered along the Rénos. The river was the border between his territory and the Germani. Both sides were forever raiding each other's lands. For a rebellious noble, a command posting on the Rénos was a clear signal that they had come to Brennus' notice, and likely his displeasure. Yet, it was also a good way to blood younger warriors. Five thousand warriors were quartered in and around Brennus' main fortress, and the settlement of Sens. These were the most loyal, gathered from his extended family, although that in itself was no guarantee of fidelity.

The remaining ten thousand Brennus considered Gaul's rapid deployment security force. According to Brennus, their mandate was to enforce the law, protect property, and limit civil disorder. This was much to the annoyance of his neighbours. With few exceptions, the other Gaulish tribes correctly saw the force for what it was, a means of Brennus extending his territorial borders. It was no secret that Brennus' ultimate ambition was to rule Gaul. Recently, he had dispatched five thousand to Aremorio. Officially, they were to support the north-western tribes in dealing with the invading Clann Ui Flaithimh and their bastard king. Unofficially, they were to foment dissent among the tribes *but* without losing any battles with Conall.

Brennus sighed. Without assigning men from his loyal battalion in Sens, he was left with five thousand poorly led men to remove the problem of the Roman from his territory. Were it up to him, he would allow Gaius and his men to cross his lands and make his way to wherever he wanted. They would be a thorn in the side for the other tribes, and an excuse for Brennus to demonstrate his influence. However, Brennus had a weakness for gold and a willingness to be bribed. The king had been paid well by Rome and given license to slaughter ten centuria, which hitherto was unheard of. In fact, it had been made crystal clear to Brennus that total eradication of Gaius' force was the only acceptable outcome. It was an extraordinary request. That said, Brennus was no fool and had no doubt that Rome would just as quickly betray him when the opportunity presented.

He huffed, wiped pee-soaked hands on his pants, and called for the commanders of the five thousand.

***

Since the dawn of time, fast flowing rivers had washed away dirt and stone, leaving steep-sided gorges. Cascading waterfalls swollen with melting winter snows pounded grey rock faces. Clouds of spray shimmered with rainbow colours in the morning sun. This was the southern lands of the Senones, and the panorama was breath-taking. The forests were less dense and comprised a wide range of soft and hardwood trees. Soils were rich tones of rust and black. The surrounding terrain, bursting with vibrant spring colours, added its impact to an already stunning vista. The drone of bees gathering water, nectar, and pollen increased in volume with each day.

To traverse the glens and ravines was to seek trouble. Opportunities for ambush were numerous and irresistible to the barbarians. Therefore, Gaius chose a longer route, journeying along the relatively flat land of low, rolling hills that skirted eastern Gaul. Even here, they were persistently harassed by small warbands led by young chieftains eager to impress. This was familiar to his men and a mark of previous missions in Gaul and Germania. Most of the attackers died from arrows and heavy darts long before they could close on Gaius' meandering column of wagons and infantry. Their bodies were left where they fell, welcome food for flies, fowl, and animals. A valuable purpose was served by the skirmishes. They kept the Roman centuria alert in the open plains.

Now, having reached the mid-point of Brennus' domain, Gaius turned his watery gaze to the west. He was in a foul mood. The past few days had witnessed snot flow relentlessly from his nose. The brightly coloured silk squares that Cornelia gifted him were dark and sodden. Inflamed nostrils matched the red of the cloth in his hand. Broken, raw skin was a constant irritation. Sneeze, cough, and spit. Sneeze, cough, and spit.

His head pounded. The fog that shrouded his brain meant he was barely capable of coherent thought. Goblets of hot wine infused with honey and spices offered some relief. The chewing of raw garlic cloves only served to further diminish his sociability. Once more he hacked up a great glob of phlegm. To his relief, it was yellow-green, not clear. A hopeful omen that his torment was coming to a close.

Gaius gently tugged on the reins of his patient mount. The grey came to a stop, choosing a spot where spring-sweet meadow flourished. It dipped its head to rip a clump of the grass. Rays of sunshine rippled over the silver decorated bridle. A broad, thickly forested valley stretched as far as the eye could see. At its far end was the river that marked the boundary of the Senone territories. Gaius sighed. Mounted, and at a fast canter, the valley could be crossed in a day. On foot, with the wagons and their weighty cargo, it would take at least eight days.

Escarpments rose up on either side of the valley. To the south the bluffs spread like a ragged piece of torn cloth; to the north, they rose up, a solid wall that was topped by a rock-strewn plateau covered in mosses and heathers. Brennus' main fort of Sens lay on the north-western corner of the plateau. A broad trail, wide enough for two wagons or chariots to pass comfortably, carved a reasonably straight path through the forest ending at the far river. It was ordinarily busy with merchant caravans, especially those carrying wine for the barbarian tribes. Today the road was ominously deserted.

Gaius smiled grimly. "I think we're expected." Aquila nodded.

On either side of the avenue, tall, ancient oaks rose up. Their trunks were wide. Three men encircling them would barely touch fingers. Like lovers, they reached for each other. Wooden fingers first felt, then grasped, and then drew closer. As their embrace deepened the gnarled trunks inclined toward each other. Firmly entwined, the limbs formed an archway above the road. It protected the path from rain and kept the surface of the trail reasonably firm. At the boggier patches, rocks and logs had been used as fill, ensuring a solid footing. No one wanted to disrupt the passage of trading caravans or Brennus' armies.

"We have no choice, Gaius," Aquila spoke of the need for the wagons to travel on the forest trail.

The trees of the old forest were more widely spaced than those of the wildwoods and the uncontrolled new growth that edged the woods' perimeter. These magnificent trees had staked out their places generations past, starving rivals of food and water. "It was," Gaius thought, "like walking through a never-ending temple." Living columns of brown rose to touch the sky. They drained the soil around them of sustenance, discouraging all but the most basic ferns, mosses, and lichens from growth.

Above the gloom, the canopy pulsed with life. The insistent chatter of birds gave a running commentary on Gaius' men's passage. On the thick floor of pine needles, the snuffling and snorting of prey and predator ignored their presence, if from a respectable distance. To travel through the woods would be to suffer delays as the wagons encountered boulders, fallen trees, burrows, and small rivers. Broken wheels were a certainty.

"Assign a centuria to guard the wagons. The rest will divide and move into the forest. The cavalry will ride ahead, *but* will avoid confrontation." Aquila's eyebrow lifted. Gaius raised his hands in acknowledgement. Romans were not known for their riding prowess. Therefore, they hired skilled mercenaries to address that weakness. The Thracian riders who accompanied Gaius were highly valued for their proficiency in battle. They were also notorious for their love of plunder and appetite for women. Whether the females were willing was of little consequence.

Thracians preferred to fight unencumbered by armour, although increasing numbers were succumbing to the wearing of leather corselets covered with overlapping bronze or iron 'fish-scales'. Their principal protection remained their oval shields. Some were made of wood, others of wicker. Each rider and horse was a repository of ranged and close combat weapons—bows, spears, long two-edged swords, short swords, narrow-bladed battle-axes, war picks, daggers, maces, and heavy darts.

"Have the archers split into two groups. They will form skirmish lines in front of the infantry. The main body will form up in two ranks one hundred paces behind the bowmen. Our long phalanx spears may give some advantage if we're attacked in the forest."

Aquila grinned, "You don't really think Brennus will attack in the woods. Do you?"

"No. Unlike the Germani, the Senones are uncomfortable forest fighters. Brennus will wait until we reach the only sensible river crossing point. His main force will be positioned in the woods on the far side of the river. A smaller division is probably tracking us. When the battle commences, they will move to cut off our retreat.

"Once we commit to the crossing, he'll attack." Gaius paused. "That's what I would do."

***

Wet boots that were rapidly disintegrating clung to feet that had been damp for days. The stench of accumulated fungi, mould, and rotting skin wafted upwards as Matres squelched her way through the muddy slop and small ponds left by the recent rains. For many reasons, Matres was not looking forward to this meeting.

The avenue to the Great Hall, and the quarters of Concolitanus, king of the Gaiscedach, was deliberately narrow, and abruptly widened out into an expansive open area before the building. The Hall was built on a massive mound of dirt and stone. The platform was level and the height of a tall man. On all sides, for a hundred paces, the ground had been levelled and was bare of any barrier that would offer cover for an assassin or group of attackers. The rectangular building towered over the settlement, providing commanding views as well as an excellent defensive position.

Once dusk fell, braziers burned to radiate heat and light. Hundreds of lamps and rushlights around the perimeter threw out a smoky, yellow light and filled the air with a rancid fragrance. Guards patrolled the boundary day and night. Others ringed the Hall itself. They each stood five paces apart on a wooden walkway that skirted the building, shield and spear in hand. Their loyalty was guaranteed, since members of their families enjoyed the king's hospitality.

Concolitanus was the leader of the Gaiscedach—a tribe of thieves, mercenaries, and assassins. As such, his position was forever precarious. For the right price and opportunity, there was no shortage of those who would attempt to take his place. Thus, periodically, the king would announce the uncovering of a disloyal guard or noble. The accused and his family would be brought before the king and denounced in public. Eager witnesses would swear to their guilt.

It was a sham. Most knew that the king's choice was arbitrary, having little to do with blame or intent. The punishment was cruelly final. Any female old enough to bleed was repeatedly raped by loyal guards. Then all were executed, usually slowly, painfully, and with much screaming. The accused was always the last to be killed, and often his demise matched Concolitanus' sadistic tendencies. It proved an effective way to dampen ambition and ensure fidelity.

Two at a time, Matres ascended the steps to the Hall's entrance. Water and mud oozed from her boots, leaving wet footprints on the oak boards. She bent over, and removed her footwear, exposing water-wrinkled toes. A pungent smell of damp, encrusted sweat briefly assaulted her nostrils. The guards reflexively lowered and pointed spears at her, but recoiled at her harsh stare and bare-toothed snarl. All knew that Matres had a very long memory, no pity, and thousands of fanatical followers. Furthermore, she had once been Concolitanus' queen. Wooden doors slammed against the inner walls. She snapped a curt "Thanks" to the guards and crossed the threshold.

Piquant odours of the previous day and night's feasting—unwashed bodies, rutting, spoiled food, grease, old beer, vomit, and piss—assailed her senses. The smells were carried on waves of shimmering heat. Three fire pits, located along a central aisle and spaced equidistantly between the entrance and the high table, were always kept lit. Blue-grey ribbons of smoke from the wood-burning fires curled upwards and clung tenaciously to the eaves. Sides of beef, venison, and pork, impaled on iron hooks, hung from blackened roof and cross-timbers.

The building's walls were a double-layer of wooden posts. The inner layer was pine and cedarwood. Resin oozed from the timbers. Together with the fragrance of cedarwood, it lent a sweet and antiseptic scent to the building. The outer layer was oak. The roof, once a thick, dark-brown thatch, now was a faded grey-brown from the winds and rains. The Hall could hold five hundred with reasonable ease and serve as a feasting room. It also housed the king's quarters and a smaller chamber for greeting guests in private. In the winter, it was a store of heavy sacks of grain and a refuge for hundreds of rats and mice.

Through the rippling hot air that rose from the fires, Matres caught a first glimpse of the king and his latest consort, Genovefa. Concolitanus relaxed on the thick pile of furs that covered an imposing throne. Matres huffed. The size of the throne matched the king's ego. That he, and Genovefa, were naked was not unusual. He was the vainest man of a vainglorious tribe. In itself, this was a considerable feat. A peacock among peacocks, Concolitanus was immensely proud of his body and his manhood. Matres grudgingly conceded that the man was in the prime of his life. The thick staff between his legs had satisfied her on numerous occasions. His stamina was legendary.

Concolitanus was a head taller than most of the tribe, and an accomplished fighter. His skin was deeply tanned and glowed with smoky-scented oils. Thick, well-veined arms and legs were effortlessly muscled. His abdomen was as flat, and as hard, as slate. New and faded lines of scars tracked across most of his body. Few were on his back. Concolitanus never turned his back on enemies or friends.

Genovefa kneeled on the floor between Concolitanus' legs. A thick wolf-pelt saved her slim, softly rounded knees from the indignity of splinters. The bobbing up and down of her head was accompanied by over-zealous sucking noises. Concolitanus was a man who enjoyed loud and vulgar demonstrations of lust.

The young woman was less than half the king's age. Her pale-skinned body was crowned with dark, almost black, hair. Thin tresses of auburn-red, the colour enhanced with dyes made from local plants, were interwoven within the long hair. She was young and artless in the use of weapons, save possibly for the poison-coated dagger strapped to her right thigh. Genovefa's sublimely curved body, dark bushy triangle, and full breasts were her weapons of choice. Gossip abounded that she was a demon who had seduced Concolitanus. She did nothing to discourage such rumours.

Yet, strikingly beautiful as Genovefa's body undoubtedly was, it was cast into the shade by the indigo-blue snake inscribed onto her ivory-white frame. Its tail curled around her right ankle bone, coiled around her leg and wound its thick scales around her torso. The serpent's head rested on Genovefa's left shoulder. The up-and-down movement of her current activity attributed an unnerving animation to the tattoo. All who looked upon the snake were mesmerised by it. It had a mystical quality. Many swore it was real and, that its coils moved with the young queen.

Matres shivered. To her, it seemed that the snake's eyes, two rubies implanted on the young woman's shoulder, watched as she drew closer. "Not a demon... a witch," Matres muttered under her breath. She strongly suspected that her replacement once belonged to the coven of degenerates that lived high in the Alpes. How else could this child have taken her place with such ease?

The royal couple chose to ignore Matres as they indulged their primal urges. Genovefa skill with her mouth prolonged the king's climax— and Matres' annoyance. Still, all pleasures eventually end. A loud, prolonged orgasmic moan escaped the king's lips. Matres rolled her eyes in disdain, and a modicum of envy, as she listened to the wet sounds that signalled the gulping down of the king's seed. To Matre's relief, at last Genovefa ended her worship of the king's manhood. Without turning to look behind her, the young woman said, "We have a guest, my Lord." She then rose and sat her softly curved and petite frame on the throne beside the king. Less than half the king's size, she was dwarfed by his physical presence.

Concolitanus opened deep, teal-green eyes and inspected Matres. He wondered what he had ever seen in her. To say that she was lean would be an understatement. She was tall, although less than he. Long cords of muscle sculpted her limbs. Little bigger than half of a ripe apple, her breasts paled in comparison to Genovefa's. And, her arse was bony.

Yet Matres had been an ardent lover and very fertile. She had given him a daughter and five sons and could fight better than many men. As if knowing what he was thinking, Genovefa stretched and, with her breasts, caressed an arm that was sparsely covered with red hair. She had no need to divert his attention. The thoughts of his sons and daughter tightened the king's lips into a thin line as he snarled.

"*My* sons and daughter are dead, led into a foolish trap by *you*."

There was little Matres could say, so she stood silent and wondered if this were the day she would lose her head. "Did you deliberately set out to deprive me of my heirs? Did that decrepit Roman, Marcus, fill your head with fanciful ideas of reclaiming the throne of the Gaiscedach, *my* throne? Or perhaps it was enough for him to spread your whore legs and rut you?" Matres squirmed at the venom in his voice but said nothing. It would serve her little to make any retort, particularly in anger.

"Worse. You underestimated the barbarian, Conall. Were your informants so lacking in intelligence that they missed that at seventeen summers Conall Mac Gabhann destroyed two Roman centuria, that he defeated Eochaidh and then marched north to battle Ailill and Medb of the Connachta to a standstill, *and*, not content with this, he humiliated Macha, the High Queen of Ériu? In Albu, his army held off Drostan of the Aos na Coille, while he went raiding north and, apparently with the sanction of the Goddess, exterminated the Na Daoine Tùrsach and their hideous Priest-queen. Then, and now allied with his former enemy, Drostan, he hunted, chased, and vanquished the forces of that demon, Kartimandu.

"By all accounts, Conall is a cunning, brave, and ruthless king, surrounded by seasoned leaders. Even I have heard of the vaunted shield wall, his cavalry, and the several thousand Cinn Péinteáilte who follow him. And, if that were not bad enough, a Sidhe is among his closest advisors, and a score of druids accompany him. As for his queen, the less said about the Dark Huntress, the better. If half the horrors told about her are true, she would make a worthy queen of the Gaiscedach."

A growl from his side brought a fleeting smile to Concolitanus' face. "No, I'm not thinking of replacing you," he reassured Genovefa, squeezing a full breast and circling a nipple with a calloused thumb until it became erect. She purred and pulled his hand between her thighs.

"Am I to conclude your stupidity was deliberate, and that a slow death should be your reward?" Matres stood straight, defiantly holding Concolitanus' gaze. It was not in her character to beg for mercy. She had her pride. "I have heard rumours of a gathering of the tribes in Aremorio. You will take five hundred of your warriors from Lugudunon and five hundred of mine. Finish your mission. Kill the Clann Ui Flaithimh king, his queen, and his children.

"You will also set the tribes that gather against each other. I do not want them united. It reduces their need for our services." Matres nodded, holding back any expression of relief. The king pointed a finger at her, "Fail me this time, and you will not return. At least not in one piece." He turned his head from Matres in dismissal. The accusing finger had duties elsewhere.

CHAPTER 12

404 B.C.—Spring—The Senone Border

Sat astride the grey, Gaius absent-mindedly rubbed his shoulder. Many years had passed, but the deep wound taken in the battle with Conall still throbbed, especially between changes in weather. The nightmares and bitter taste of defeat in Ériu were always with him. The Roman phalanx, a formation adopted from the Greeks and Etrusci, had been out-manoeuvred and defeated by a young and inexperienced barbarian. To a man, two centuria of Rome's best were slaughtered. He had watched his commander gutted by the Sidhe. Spurius' heart, still beating, was torn from his gaping chest. His cooling corpse was left as food for the birds and wolves.

On his return, Gaius frequently argued with his father-in-law that Rome should abandon the phalanx and build on the example of the barbarian shield wall. Marius' haughty retort was blinkered but unsurprising. "The Republic of Rome has nothing to learn from barbarians."

A blink of his eyes cleared the gloomy thoughts from Gaius' head. He observed the slow-moving river before him. It marked the western border of the Senone lands. The river was only about one hundred paces wide. Steep sides were held in place by a tangle of bushes and roots from trees and shrubs. Thousands of eyes peered at him, and he felt every one.

On the near side of the river, the forest had all the appearance of having been bitten by a mouthful of huge teeth. The flattened, scalloped edge of the treeline enclosed a river plain one thousand paces in breadth for most of its length. Low ridges rippled the land. Green shoots of spring crops planted in impossibly straight drills broke the surface of fertile, dark soil. A rash of small farm-holdings pock-marked the landscape. It was a windless day, and smoke curled up lazily from hundreds of cooking fires.

The other side? It was forested. The chaotic, but vibrant, wildwood ran along the western river edge. Beyond this, the ancient forest's canopy spread westward to the middle of Gaul. "Obviously the Bituriges and the Carnutes do not like farming," Gaius mused. The river crossing, its waters burbling over rocks and stones long smoothed by the undercurrents, was located where the borders of all three tribes met.

"More like, they want a barrier between them and Brennus. He's made no secret of his ambition to be Dictator of Gaul," said Aquila.

Gaius dipped his head in agreement, "In that, Brennus has much in common with Marcus—and a good few of Rome's generals."

The snort of a horse drew Gaius' attention to the leader of the Thracian contingent. There was a pleading look in the heavily-armoured and darkly-tanned warrior's brown eyes. Gaius shook his head and was rewarded with a snarl, and what he assumed was a mouthful of Thracian curses. In response, the Roman glared at the mercenary leader. For a moment both men's hands hovered over the pommels of their swords. Then the Thracian flashed a mouthful of impossibly white teeth, slapped his hand on his moulded breastplate in salute, and moved to rejoin his men.

"Surly bastards," said Aquila. "Not far removed from the barbarians we'll soon be fighting."

Gaius nodded. "They'll get the plunder they yearn for soon enough. Or they'll be dead and rutting all the celestial virgins they can lay their hands on." Gaius laughed. "Either way, they're winners." Gaius pointed to the far side of the river. "What do you think?"

"At least five, maybe ten thousand behind the treeline. Brennus' strategy will be to overwhelm us quickly. In battle, barbarians, both men and women, are unwashed, loud, and generally drunk. The females are vicious, the men are braggarts. But they're good fighters. Many use them as mercenaries." Aquila stopped briefly. A fat, blood-engorged fly had chosen to alight on his arm for its next drink. A curse followed by a sharp smack smeared both fly and its previous meals over Aquila's tanned arm. "They… the Celts, that is, have a weakness. They're like a bowman who has just one arrow. One shot and they're done."

"Obviously, they would like us to cross the river. It's not deep. Knee level at the crossing, but it would slow us down."

"We need something to make them attack us."

Gaius nodded and called Amodocus to him. "Divide your Thracians into two groups. Burn the farms to the north and south. Take the farmers, and their families, hostage." The Roman looked at the sky. "Make sure you're back in camp before dusk. The mercenary smiled broadly but falsely. Gaius was as enlightened as any Roman could be, regarding barbarians. Yet even he perceived non-Romans as uncivilised and closer to being property than human. It did not enter his head to question using them as pebbles on a latrunculi board. Still, as the Thracian turned away from him, Gaius had a moment of conscience and called out, "You will *not* rape the women. I'll cut the balls of any who disobey."

***

The morals of his employers never ceased to amaze Amodocus. Their claim to being civilised was a thin, transparent veneer. If they really looked at themselves, they would see a tribe as barbaric as the worst of the Gaulish or Germanic tribes. In fact, quite a few tribes were more enlightened than Rome. Genocide, organised rape, and dissolute behaviour were weapons to be used according to circumstance. To the Roman nobility, the end—domination—justified the means.

The Thracian tugged sharply on the rope that trailed from a rough-skinned hand. That it suddenly tightened, informed him that a few of the captured had stumbled. Amodocus chuckled. *A man had to get his fun somewhere*, he thought. The prisoners were naked. If Roman sensitivities did not permit his men to enjoy the women, at least they could leer at, squeeze, and slap their pale bodies. He sighed. Some had very desirable breasts and arses. Perhaps later?

Fibrous, black soil clung to the knees and shins of the women. While Gaius had explicitly ruled out rape, Amodocus made an 'in-field' decision that this did not preclude the use of the captives' mouths. Frequent retching sounds interrupted the women's wailing and sobbing as they attempted to expel foreign fluids. Curses from their menfolk were met with the flat side of a blade or the lash of a whip. Shrieks from the prisoners made Amodocus grin. His men were sadistic bastards and very precise as to where the whiplash was laid.

As he approached the camp, Amodocus was impressed. Like worker ants, Romans were a tireless and efficient people. Their diligence in constructing temporary defences akin to small forts was impressive. A shoulder-high dirt wall stretched for about two hundred paces on each side of a rough square. Its top was flattened. Short, spear's-length timbers were laid side-by-side along its length. They were held in place by stakes hammered into the dirt every ten paces. The west, north, and south sides were reinforced with trees from the nearby woods. Felled by axes, the trunks lay with tops pointing outwards. Sharp branch-ends faced the enemy. It was a quick, simple, and very effective barrier.

Before the sun rested, the camp's yard was a hive of activity. Commands barked out, urging the assembly of the legion's complement of field ballistae. Thirty faced forward; the remaining twenty were divided between the northern and southern walls. One hundred Cretan archers took up position between the ballistae. Their long composite bows did not have the range of a recurve bow or a slingshot, but their rate of fire and accuracy was legendary. Amodocus snarled a greeting at the group's commander. There was no love lost between the mercenaries. Both tribes claimed superiority with the bow. That the Cretan bowmen were plainly sighting their weapons on him made Amodocus shiver. A lapse in concentration or tremble of a tired finger would see him despatched into Zalmoxis' arms.

Dawn greeted the Roman camp with the usual raucous chorus of birds in the forests. Men stirred and shook the heavy dew from uniforms and cloaks. Bones cracked, muscles and joints resisted movement, and stomachs called for food. Campfires were rekindled and the first meal of the day prepared. Men slaked overnight thirsts with spring water and fresh milk. Gaius discouraged drinking beer or wine before battle. Amodocus' men had brought back sizeable herds of livestock. Warm, creamy liquid slapped the sides of bronze buckets and splashed the dirt as they were carried across the camp.

Their bellies satisfied, the men belched and farted, then pissed and shit against the berm. The pungent aroma of bodily waste contained within the confines of the dirt walls soon caused the men to call for battle outside of the camp. Gaius had little sympathy for his men's pleading. With a stern look on his unshaven face, he reprimanded his captains for permitting their men to "Shit in their own yard." He pointed out that the forest was only several hundred paces from the camp, and added, looking at the rising sun, that the stench would increase as the day became much warmer.

Gaius climbed the rampart and gazed to the west. He wondered if his enemy would take the bait. To fight his way across the river was not an attractive option. The loss of men and wagons could be crippling.

***

Behind the tree-line, on the western bank of the river, the commander of the Senones sniffed the air and cursed the smoke and resin fragrance that clung to his nostrils. The barbarian's senses were besieged. The freshness of the morning air was tainted with the foul odours of pillage, and the orange-pink hues of a perfect dawn smudged with trails of soot and ash that continued to rise from burning farmsteads. Now, as he gazed across the river, he also heard the cries and pleadings of men, women, and children as they were paraded in naked helplessness. He felt his men's rising anger and sympathised with the demands for vengeance.

Gaulish parents could be unimaginative when it came to naming offspring. Fathers and mothers held faint hopes of influencing their off-spring's future with the flattery of a noble name. Thus by a quirk of fate, in command of the force was Brennus. The poor man was a very distant cousin of the king of the Senones. In fact, so tenuous was his claim of kinship to the king that the poor man was often referred to as 'Brennus the Ignored'. Today was his chance to change his future, to impress his king, and to foster a closer relationship. The rewards of power and wealth would be considerable. With the back of his hand, he wiped specks of drool from an unruly moustache.

But Brennus the Ignored had a problem. Aside from a natural tendency to vacillation, his king's instructions left little room for interpretation. "Stay on the western bank. The Romans must cross. They have no choice. Do *not* attack until they are in the river." The king also added, "Put one toe in the water, and the rest of your life will be short and full of pain." Behind him, however, increasingly strident and mutinous voices urged immediate action. His king was far away in Sens; his men's spears were at his back.

Fate, not fortune, favours the brave. Events have their own momentum. Choice was removed from Brennus the Ignored. The rage of his men reached a crescendo as the Senones watched the male captives separated from the women and children by the Thracian horsemen and herded towards the river. The deep resonating sound of multiple Senone war horns reverberated throughout the forest. It was accompanied by a cauldron of hoarse screams, battle-cries, and cursing. Few held any spark of hope for the prisoners.

Similar to a club or hammer, but unlike swords, bows, or axes, there is nothing overly fancy, stylish, or beautiful about a mace. It is basically a ball or lump of metal fixed to a handle that varies in length from six to ten hands. Mounted warriors tended to prefer a more extended shaft. Many of the Thracian designs reflected the brutal nature of their wielder. Studs and flanges enhanced the weapon's ability to rend flesh in addition to its usual delivery of blunt trauma.

Over one hundred men and boys ranging in age from ten to fifty summers met their death. But not by the clean cut of a sword or axe. Their skulls were crushed by swift downward strokes of the blunt weapons. Clumps of hair and skin adhered to mace-heads. Only a fistful of bone shards and pulped flesh remained of a head no longer recognisable to loved ones. Gore and pink-grey brain matter splattered the river-bank. Spouts of blood splashed riders and horses. Twitching with the last spasms of mortality, the corpses tumbled into the muddy waters. A trail of blood marked their journey as they floated downstream.

The victims had little opportunity to cry out. Their death was unpleasant, yet swift. It was left to their kin to mourn. In helpless rage mothers, sons, and daughters collapsed on the dirt. They pounded the soil that their men had tilled. That it now sprouted green shoots of new growth seemed an insult. Cries for revenge and justice reached up into the skies. On this day, the gods were deaf to their pleading.

On the far bank of the river, the howls of the Senones were unrestrained. Yet, they held their position. It was a small boy that provided the catalyst for bloody mayhem. Stick in hand, the child, who was no more than six or seven summers, wrenched himself from his mother's grasp and dashed to where he had last seen his father.

The flicker of movement caught the Thracian rider unaware. His vision was restricted by his helmet. Without thinking, he lashed out. There was no scream when the child's face disintegrated. An awful realisation wrenched the Thracian's gut as he looked down upon the wretched body, jerking spasmodically in the dirt. Uttering a loud curse, the rider leapt from his horse. A sword hissed as it was withdrawn from its scabbard. Skewered through his small, faltering heart, the boy ceased this life. It was an act of mercy. It was also the straw that broke the ox's back.

Unleashed, the Senones swept into the river. Brennus the Ignored tried in vain to hold the mob back. His shouts and pleadings were ignored. Without ceremony or respect, he was shoved aside. Soon the river was cloudy with mud and silt. The Senones were almost mid-stream before the Thracians realised the danger. Spears were lofted. Slings whirred. A dozen of the Thracians fell before Amodocus gathered his wits and shouted the retreat. Dead or injured made little consequence. The fallen Thracians were violated, relieved of their heads and genitals, and stripped of anything of value. Then they were trampled into the dirt as, full of wrath, the angry barbarians charged forward.

Jaw set, Gaius watched the remaining women and children prisoners herded back through the camp's entranceway. Globs of spit hit any Roman within distance. Few retaliated. "Well, that achieved the desired result," said Aquila. The distaste in his tone was not disguised.

"Barbarian lives for Roman lives. I can live with the consequences." Gaius looked at the group of prisoners and shouted to one of the centuria captains, "Bind their ankles. Keep them out of our way. Those that live will make useful slaves." Gaius then turned to those manning the ranks of ballistae. "Stand ready for my signal." To the archers on the berm, he shouted, "Send volleys into the barbarians as they come within range." As Amodocus cantered into sight, Gaius called out, "Take your men to the trees. Your job is to protect our flanks."

As he surveyed the camp, Gaius was confident in his tactics. The barbarians had relinquished the security of the forest and the advantage of the river. The front line of the howling, unwashed horde had already covered half of the distance between river and camp. Volleys of arrows and bolts from his ballistae would break their resolve. In the ensuing confusion, he would march his phalanx into their midst. Long sarissas would stab the hearts of the barbarians. *Yes*, he thought, *it was a good plan.*

It all seemed so simple, so straightforward. Everyone knew barbarians had no patience for long battles. Once repulsed, they would flee. The Roman turned to his cohort of field ballistae. Hand raised, the order to commence firing was on the tip of his tongue. Alas, Gaius had not reckoned on the gods blessing Brennus the Ignorant with a single flash of inspiration. About to drop his hand, Gaius heard a familiar sound—the rolling snap of skeins loosed and the juddering of wood. It was followed by the whoosh of air being pushed aside followed. Yet, his ballistae still stood ready, waiting. Realisation almost came too late, Gaius dropped to the dirt. He was fortunate. The bolt that kills is silent.

Bolts as thick as two fingers and the length of a short spear swept upwards, following a shallow arc over the heads of the stampeding barbarians. In their frenzy, it was unlikely they were aware of their presence. A bloody aerosol formed over the west wall as the first volley swept Cretan archers and ballistae teams from the rampart. Long, three-sided, pyramid-shaped iron sharps punched effortlessly through flesh and exited to continue their path of death. Men skewered by the missiles were flung like rag dolls from the fortifications.

Other projectiles with leaf-shaped heads carved bodies like a dagger slicing meat from a boar on a spit. A young man cried as he stared at where his legs should be. They lay beside him. A bolt had neatly sheared limbs from the torso. In shock, and his spine severed, he felt little pain. He died swiftly as his blood gushed out, washing over the wooden defences.

A second volley followed hard on the heels of the first. As they galloped along the line of felled trees, Amodocus' men bore the brunt of the early barrage. Some deemed it a judgment from the gods. Horses screamed as they trailed headless riders, feet trapped in belly straps. Others, propelled by the force of the bolts, found themselves thrust onto the sharpened tree branches. Some were joined for eternity. Rider and horse skewered together like pieces of meat on a spit.

In the camp, men screamed. Their armour was as much use as the linen shrouds used to swaddle the dead. Thick-shafted bolts tore gaping holes in their flesh and severed limbs and heads. There was no escape. Shields were useless. Blood and body parts were strewn randomly across the camp. The prisoners did not escape. A mother pulled her baby and daughter close to her. The embrace provided comfort, but not protection. Bloody tears flowed down her cheeks as she slumped over. The bolt-head that entered her back ripped a bloody gash in her belly, impaling both mother and child.

A groan to his left made Gaius turn. Aquila slumped to his knees. Streamers of flesh hung from his shoulder. Bright blood soaked his uniform. His arm lay several paces distant. The fingers still twitched. Gaius shouted at the legion' surgeon. Both surgeon and assistants were overwhelmed by the unexpected swiftness and destruction. The smell of burning flesh told Gaius that Aquila's wound had been cauterised. He prayed to Apollo that his friend would survive the shock.

Gaius' mood quickly went from shock to rage. Who had supplied the barbarians with heavy ballistae? Who had trained them in their use? To stay in the camp was suicide. He roared out orders. "Ballistae. Rapid fire! Ten volleys." To the men, he shouted, "Phalanx formation. Fifty men wide. Sixteen deep. The rest guard the rear gateway. We march on the last volley." That he no longer had one thousand men did not occur to Gaius.

It was yet another perfectly reasonable assumption on Gaius' part. No sane commander would fire on his own warriors. As he led his men out of the gateway and between the tree-lined defences, the Roman anticipated that the ballistae from the Senones would cease. His Cretan archers would continue to shoot into the horde of unarmoured savages. At a rate of one arrow per count of ten, this alone would have a devastating impact. The Thracian cavalry, seeking revenge, would meet savagery with savagery. Mounted on tall, hardy horses, they held a lofty advantage and could retreat and attack at will. The phalanx, with its bramble of long sarissas stabbing high and low, would move slowly and inexorably towards the river, painting the land with the blood of the barbarians.

High above, the gods laughed. As Roman phalanx and barbarian horde clashed, the rolling crack of heavy ballistae continued unabated. The missiles showed no partiality. In Brennus the Ignored's fractured mind, this was justifiable revenge for years of sneers and snide comments. The nobles and men who had mocked and pushed him aside bore the brunt of his wrath. On this day, at last, they would fear him. Columns of men, barbarian and Roman, were culled by successive broadsides of bolts. Lines of blood, bone, and sundered limbs lay as straight as crop drills. Nevertheless, it did little to sate the Ignored's twisted fury. He strode along the rank of missile-throwers urging quicker reloading.

Blood welled from new cuts. His spear-arm burned with the constant stabbing. Slick with gore, the sarissa was firmly bonded to his hand. His bronze-faced shield no longer glittered in the sun. Covered in a film of battle debris, it bore the marks of spears, swords, and axes. Gaius groaned as he rebalanced the heavy scíath. He felt the pain from the deep track the shield's wooden rest carved on his shoulder. The ringing in his ears from many strikes on his helmet added the annoyance of a permanent headache.

Once more he ducked. It was a reflexive move based on an instinct to survive. He briefly felt guilt as the bolt passed over him and swept another group of his men from this life. Another harvest for the Elysian Fields. Gaius railed at the threat from the skies. Sarissas, broken by long Gaulish swords wielded two-handed, littered the ground. Hoarse shouts of "Stab high! Block! Stab low! Block!" continued to resound from the centurions. Their weapons were the splintered ends and butt spikes of shattered spears.

The enemy, slavering, howling, spitting, pressed the phalanx. Weapons—spears, axes, and daggers—were hurled. Grey swords, splashed with crimson and held in blood-encrusted fists, slashed at flesh and shields. In close combat, the barbarians used their bodies to good effect. Heads smashed noses. Teeth tore ears. Knees rammed crotches. Hands grabbed balls. The constant stream of bloody saliva spat into an opponent's eyes was disgusting but effective. The rank smells of sweat, piss, and blood were a second line of assault.

Uncharacteristically, the Senones showed little sign of flagging enthusiasm for the fight. In contrast, the Roman phalanx stumbled to a grudging halt. Surrounded and heavily outnumbered, the situation had become a grave concern to Gaius. He sensed the rising exhaustion of his men. Many, weakened by the unrelenting tiredness and loss of blood, had succumbed to wounds. Those that fell outside the phalanx were lost. Helpless to protect them, Gaius' ire was written on the bloody mask that was his face.

Yet, there was an increasing rumble of angry voices from the Senones. They were losing more warriors to the fire from Brennus' ballistae than to the Roman formation, or the skirmishing cavalry and archers. Finally, a great cry arose from the Senones. Frustrated and spitting blood they turned to face the missile launchers across the river. At first only a few charged towards the river. Soon, they were joined by scores more and then the main force. Brennus the Ignored cackled and called for more bolts to be loaded.

***

Gaius shook his head as he appraised the line of heavy ballistae. There were one hundred of the machines. Before the Senone warbands scattered into the forests, they disembowelled the operators. To each ballista, the retreating warriors nailed the hapless ballistae teams—loaders, winders, and spotters. Most were still alive. Their moans and cries for mercy filled the air. Unsurprisingly, they found the Romans unsympathetic and in no mood to relieve their suffering. Eventually, Gaius ended their misery, but also added his own personal flourish. His fury at the loss of his men was undiminished. Oil and pitch were poured over the ballistae. Human torches burned brightly into the evening.

Wood-smoke is a comforting fragrance, thought Gaius. Kindled under a grey, cloudy sky that threatened rain, hundreds of dawn fires brought the promise of a warm first meal of the day. Still, the taint of burnt, human flesh from the previous day's executions fouled the air. Before him stood a trio of mercenaries. Amodocus glowered with barely restrained rage. The commander of the Cretan archers, Sarpedon's face bore a mask that was unreadable. The Greek surgeon and slave, Alkaios, had the haunted air of a man who had seen the bloody debris of too many battles and would likely see many more. Gaius' second-in-command, Aquila, survived the action and the loss of his left arm but was too feeble to attend the meeting.

"Well?" asked Gaius.

"I have only half of my men fit to ride and barely enough horses for them to mount. How many more survive is in the hands of the Greek." Amodocus snapped a quick look at Alkaios, who merely nodded. *He's an annoying bastard*, thought the Thracian.

Gaius looked at Sarpedon. "Much the same story. I lost one-third of my archers. Those remaining are not happy. There is talk of seeking an alternate employment option."

The Roman glared at the mercenary leaders, "You have, and will be, well paid. Death is as much a part of the contract as gold and plunder."

"Being named an outcast and outlaw of Rome wasn't in the contract," spat Amodocus. Sarpedon nodded in rare agreement with the Thracian.

Gaius paused briefly, as if considering what his options might be. "Settle your men, or I will." The threat in the last three words was clear. A cough from the Greek surgeon brought everyone's attention to the central question: What was left of the army? Gaius dipped his head, and Alkaios spoke.

"Just over five centuria remain fit for battle." There was a sharp intake of breath from his audience, but Alkaios smiled and held up his hand. "That is not the full story. The dead number around one hundred and fifty. The remaining are the injured. The badly injured and those who lost limbs will be offered a quick death with a sharp blade. I guess that about half will take the path to the Elysian Fields. Likely, you will be left with seven centuria, *but* only five will be battle-ready. The rest will take a full cycle of the moon to regain full fitness." Alkaios paused, "We will need a lot of wagons and the favour of the gods."

Gaius rubbed his jaw. It ached. Lately, he had taken to grinding his teeth during his sleep. "We march tomorrow at dawn. On the move, we'll be less of a temptation to the other barbarian tribes." He looked at Alkaios, "You have the rest of this day to use your blade. Speak with the quartermaster about re-purposing the captured wagons. Anyone who can walk *will* walk."

***

Those of the Senone army, who returned to Sens, faced the fury of Brennus. For disobeying the king's appointed commander, the nobles and chieftains were staked before the tribe. In his mercy, their families just had their throats cut.

The ordinary warriors were not overlooked. No matter the provocation, infantry could not disobey orders and expect to go unpunished. Brennus decimated the remaining command. Over four hundred men died, although their end was at the sharp end of a sword or axe.

As for Brennus the Ignored, he was 'fortunate' to have died at the river. The rest of his line was terminated.

CHAPTER 13

404 B.C.—Spring

On a thick slab of blood and piss-stained wood, Cingetorix roared and thrashed against the restraints. He felt each sharp stab of pain as the needle punched holes in his flesh. Each drawing of coarse catgut through cheek and scalp was a slow torment. Two score stitches knit the hoof-shaped flap of skin. It was a hideous wound that made an ugly face worse.

The healers had no illusions as to their fate. Cingetorix would never be happy with their work. The moment they began their sewing of his ruptured face, their lives were forfeit. Precautions were necessary. Immediately following their ministrations, Cingetorix would be too weak to assail them. Thus, they had a brief window of time. With a 'gift' of gold, they came to an understanding with the king's guards. A liberal dosing of the king's food and drink with hemp would assure he remained oblivious of their flight until they were long gone.

Unsteady on his feet, suffering from severe headaches and blurred vision, it was several days before Cingetorix's heavy footfall was heard on the walkways of his fortress. His normal unpleasant and quixotic temper reached new heights of cruelty. Nobles and chieftains found themselves grasping at slippery entrails or with their throats slit because the king claimed they stared at his face. Others met a similar fate because they averted their gaze.

A raiding party of one thousand warriors was despatched in pursuit of Íar and his thieves. Less than eight hundred returned, bloodied and many with wounds from which they would not recover. They bore tales of a battle in the forests, with wild, red-haired demons who crushed heads with huge hammers and naked female warriors who disembowelled with a flick of their spears. Cingetorix was unconvinced of the veracity of their tales. The nights that followed were filled with mourning for the dead—from the king's justice.

For Cingetorix, this was a time when he could show no mercy and no weakness. The raid on the gold mine, his defeat in the forests of Aremorio, and his physical weakness served only to encourage conspiracies and increase the flow of rumours of his imminent demise. Still, and as much as he would like to, he could not slaughter all his nobles and chieftains. He needed them and their warriors. His mind roiled, but it was his gut that set his direction.

Cingetorix looked to the east and the land of Dubnoreix of the Venelli. "Sound the war horns," he bellowed.

* * *

As members of the Ò Neill clan, Cuán and his hand-fast partner, Bláithín, had been part of Northern Ériu's aristocracy. Yet, of the two, it was Bláithín who carried her regal upbringing and bearing more assuredly. Indeed, she was also the more politically astute. Many also claimed she was the better warrior. The Cróeb Ruad tattoo on her right shoulder bore witness to that assertion.

It was past midnight. A cool spring breeze teased the ends of her long hair as Bláithín lay on her cot. She breathed deeply, inhaling the pleasant fragrances of meadowsweet and lavender that permeated the paillasse. Anxious thoughts would not allow her the unbroken sleep she desired. Bláithín was perturbed by the recent and increasing frequency of her partner's laments that he was not given his due place among Clann Ui Flaithimh. In this, he chose to ignore that both he and Bláithín had been offered, and had taken up, seats on the tribe's governing Chomhairle.

While she could indulge and gently laugh off Cuán bemoaning his lot in the privacy of their quarters, lately he had been too vocal—in public. He was fortunate that his outburst of petulance when the Venelli king visited had been overlooked by Conall. Oft times her partner imbibed too many cups of wine, a recent introduction to Clann Ui Flaithimh's palate.

Wine was a deceptive beverage with a pleasant golden-green colour and a smooth, sweet taste. The liquor, however, was a much more potent brew than the beers and ales to which Cuán was accustomed. It was said that only barbarians drunk wine undiluted. Bláithín sighed. Watering wine was one custom they should learn from the Romans.

On occasion, with lips set free by his over-indulgence, Cuán would expound on his disbelief at how a low-born blacksmith's apprentice could be the Rí Ruirech of Clann Ui Flaithimh. His none-too-subtle inference was that one of nobility should be the ruler. And, of course, that should be him. Cuán considered himself a religious man, and this served only to imbue him with an unwarranted zeal for his precarious supposition. In his eyes, he had a divine right to reign.

It was fortunate that Cuán's older brother Lonán was also his drinking partner. Lonán, as he put it, "had a belly-full of politics" in Ériu and was totally disinterested in the political shenanigans of the tribe or indeed his own links to the nobility of the Ulaid. He was a plain-spoken warrior who recognised the dangerous words that flowed from Cuán's wine-loosened lips. For the most part, Lonán was able to drag his brother away from the drinking dens with a slap on the back, a hearty laugh, and gold for the next rounds of drinks.

Yet, both Bláithín and Lonán knew that they could not guard Cuán, or his mouth, from sunset to sunrise. Separately, they had come to the same conclusion. One day they may have to choose between Cuán and Clann Ui Flaithimh. Both also knew the time for this drew closer.

Bláithín listened to the snorts of her partner. She rolled her eyes. Wine made Cuán's rasping snores much louder. What once was a humorous foible was now just irritating. The beverage did little for his manhood either. She sighed heavily. They had no home in the land of the Ulaid. Macha Mong Ruad, Ard-Righan—the High Queen of Ériu— had persecuted them and their followers for years. The politics of Ériu were complicated and brutal. It was only the gold of the Ò Neill nobility, and the threat of a violent uprising from friendly Cróeb Ruad generals, which offered an escape route to Albu.

There, they and one thousand warriors and followers joined with Clann Ui Flaithimh. They were accepted by the tribe and fought with them against the mad queen, Kartimandu. This was not a situation that Bláithín wished to jeopardise. She had the future of two young boys to consider. Both had been accepted as friends among the youngest generation of the tribe.

Thankfully, so far, her husband's drunken rantings had gained no credibility among the army. No leader, whether ceannairí na míle, ceannairí céad, or veteran, paid them much attention. All were fiercely loyal to Conall. Still, there were always malcontents and the weak-minded to be found among any tribe. Now that the full clann, civilians and army, was encamped on the headland of Northern Aremorio, the situation was a fertile ground for Cuán's promises of better times were he to wear the crown.

Bláithín frowned. Her husband's myopia blinded him to the high regard in which the tribe held Conall. He was truly adored by the people. More important, he had the allegiance of the army, the druids and, not insignificantly, the Sidhe. Indeed, this loyalty often sparked off another bout of petulance from her partner. With each passing day Cuán's thousand Cróeb Ruad, *his* men, became more integrated into the army of Clann Ui Flaithimh. More specifically, they had become part of the shield wall, and that was a brotherhood of warriors unto itself.

Notwithstanding this, from the telling of the stories of his battles and judgments, Conall was ruthless, especially when it came to disloyalty. And so was his queen, Mórrígan. Even if Cuán's men stood with him in his sedition, Bláithín considered the chances of success against the army of Conall to be unfavourable. Perhaps even non-existent. Although it was a warm night, Bláithín shivered. The retribution, which would follow any attempted coup, would be swift and severe. It would, she thought, be much harsher than their persecution at the hands of Macha Mong Ruad. And, in Aremorio, they had nowhere to run.

Bláithín moaned and prayed to the Goddess for wisdom and a night's rest. For a moment, she ran a finger along the cold metal of the blade that was never far from her reach. "Please no," she whispered.

✳✳✳

Cornelia acknowledged that she had two flaws—limited patience and an impetuous nature. Both were a constant irritant to both father and husband. As she disembarked onto the bustling dock in Massalia, Cornelia shivered. It was not cold. In fact, it was a warm late-spring afternoon. The sun was high, and the blue sky was ribboned with long wisps of cloud. The tremble was an acknowledgement of a fear that possibly she had been precipitous in her behaviour.

To Cornelia's way of thinking, she had tried her best at persuasion. She prevailed upon her father to use his influence to counter the scurrilous accusations of desertion and treason the Pontifex levied at Gaius and his men. Most honourable men in the Senate recognised that the young soldier was the victim of a longstanding undercurrent of distrust and envy. That said, none—including Cornelia's father—were willing to oppose Marcus. It was deemed to be politically dangerous, at this time.

An exasperated Marius bluntly told his daughter to keep her nose out of politics and military matters. Fuming at her father's perceived impotence, Cornelia purchased passage on a seaborne galley. She was accompanied by her guard, ten veterans hand-picked by Gaius to ensure his wife's safety. Cornelia's last sight of the harbour was of an irate father, red-faced and shaking his fist at the departing ship.

Cornelia's destination was Massalia. Situated on the coast, east of the Rodonos delta, Massalia was a major trading port of the ancient world. It was a little Greece in a mostly uncivilised land. The seaport sat on fifty hectares surrounded by a high, stone wall. Its multinational, multicultural population had grown to about six thousand. With no particular effort at town planning, Massalia was a sprawling maze of narrow chaotic streets lined by stone houses with plastered exteriors and frescoed interior walls.

Unsurprisingly, Massalia's docks were the centre of brawling, drinking, and every conceivable form of debauchery. Sailors, thieves, whores, spies, and mercenaries frequented its panoply of brothels, inns, and run-down shacks. Slaves shackled at ankle and wrist awaited their fate. Most had despairing eyes and cowering demeanours. Few chose defiance.

The city was a hive of economic activity. It thrived as a trading link between an inland Gaul hungry for Roman goods and wine, and Rome's apparently limitless need for new products and slaves. Its fleet traded across the Great Sea, along the coasts of the dark continent of Alkebulan to the south and Gaul to the north, as far as the islands of Albu and Ériu.

Massalia was the home of Pytheas, friend to her husband and the barbarian king, Conall. Fate was no friend to Cornelia. When she arrived, she discovered that Pytheas had departed several days earlier. His servants were unsure as to when he would return but did offer Cornelia and her men accommodation within the safety of the merchant's compound. Weeks later, Cornelia's patience once more wore thin. While a great admirer of Greek culture and architecture, the attractions of Massalia's marble and limestone temples of Apollo and Artemis, its open-air theatres, public squares and markets, stoa and stadium, paled quickly.

***

In truth, Cornelia did not have much of a plan or stratagem apart from somehow finding Gaius. Furthermore, she significantly underestimated her husband's ability to extricate himself and his men from unfortunate circumstances. Nor did it occur to the somewhat spoilt and indulged daughter of one of Rome's leading families that her actions might complicate matters further.

To Cornelia, an overheard conversation between Pytheas' servants concerning a caravan soon to depart for Aremorio appeared a gift from the gods. With little thought, Cornelia decided to join the convoy. Gold and the presence of her guard overcame any objections of the caravan's leader. In her mind, Cornelia decided that she would travel north and meet with the barbarian who haunted her husband's dreams. She hoped to convince him to help her find Gaius. That she had nothing to bargain with was swept quickly from her thoughts.

It was an imprudent plan fraught with danger and more holes than a sieve. Sitting cross-legged by the doorway to Pytheas' home was a beggar. He was missing one hand, a sure sign of a thief. With a bowl raised up in his remaining hand, the unkempt vagrant stayed from dawn to dusk. Through a mouth of decaying and missing teeth, he slurred, "Alms. Please have charity on a veteran." Cornelia had no doubt that the dust-covered man was no warrior. Still, she dropped a few coins in his bowl each time she passed, covered up her nose at his stench and hurried on her way.

Cornelia should not have been concerned about the man's well-being. His remuneration from begging was much less than the gold he received from several groups of thieves and slavers. His job was to listen, watch, and report on gossip from Pytheas' household and the comings and goings of guests. In Cornelia, he had found a fruit ripe for picking.

CHAPTER 14

404 B.C.—Cnocán-Mórrígan —Near Lugnasad

Lugnasad was a cycle of the moon hence. The land flourished under the warm summer sun and mild rains. Grasses, heathers, and wildflowers bloomed. For many, their skin lost the ghostly pallor of winter and sported attractive hues from golden to deep brown. Those with red hair, however, suffered. At best, they developed thousands of freckles. At worst, they burned pink. Flurries of flaking skin scurried like snowflakes on summer zephyrs.

A bellow at the main gate drew the attention of those in the guard towers. At the far end of the dirt path that led to the gates stood, legs apace, a tall, massively proportioned warrior. His barrel chest and fat belly glistened in the meán lae sun. Only squinting eyes and swarthy cheeks were visible in a face framed by a long, shaggy mane of nut-brown hair. His mouth was concealed by an unruly beard whose beaded and braided tips rested on his chest. In a hand the size of a bear-paw, he gripped an axe. Notched but well-oiled, it was a warrior's blade and glinted golden-red in the sun. In his right hand, he held a rough sack.

He roared again, "I am Cingetorix, king of the Veneti. I bring you greetings... and a gift."

"That's not Cingetorix." It was Íar who spoke. He stood next to Conall in the watchtower.

"I guessed as much. Let's see how this plays out."

Contemptuously the man strode closer to the gate. With as little effort as tossing a pebble into a pond, the burly warrior hurled the sack. It arched over the gate and landed with a sickening thud in the mud beyond the oak gates. Neither fate nor the gods favoured Eirnín that day. The entrance's ramparts and guard towers were in his command. Watched by his men, he splashed through pools of muddy water to investigate. As he drew closer, patches of dark, red stains and irregular, spherical shapes constrained by the sacking pointed to an unhappy outcome. He sighed and prodded the bag with his sword. The drawstring did not yield.

Resigned, he gripped the bottom corner of the sack with one hand. With the other, Eirnín slashed through bag and twine. Freed, the contents rolled into the mud. He staggered back with a cry of anguish. Before him lay the heads of Dubnoreix, king of the Venelli, his queen, and their three sons. But that was not all. Eirnín stretched out a hand, praying that the sight was an illusion. He knew it was not when his fingers touched the soft, tufted, blue and blond hair of Brigindos, daughter of Dubnoreix.

Conall's younger brother sank to his knees in the mud. Nursing Brigindos' bloody head, Eirnín rocked to and fro and sobbed. Pain and grief poured out in great rivers of tears. Slowly, still holding her head in hands forever stained with his love's blood, Eirnín rose. He screamed until hoarse. He cursed Fate, he cursed the Goddess, he cursed his brother, and swore vengeance on all who had cruelly shattered his dreams. Those who looked upon Eirnín knew that he was as dead as Brigindos.

Taking the steps two at a time, Eirnín soon stood on the stockade's walkway. In his hand was a javelin torn from the hands of one of his men. "Tú!" he bellowed. The word carried an intensity that surprised the warriors around him. Eirnín was known as a dour, undemonstrative man. Proven in battle, he did not form friends or relationships easily. He shouted again, "Tú!" It was a voice of command. This time the subject of his anger hesitated and turned around.

The javelin left Eirnín's hand as the giant's face came into view. It was doubtful if the warrior knew much about his death. Possibly, he did. Onlookers spoke afterwards of seeing slitted eyes widen as the missile bore down on him. The charcoal-grey spike that tipped the javelin seemed to pause tantalisingly as it touched the man's eyeball but only for the tiniest fraction of time.

A viscous tear rolled slowly down the warrior's cheek as the spike burst through the cornea. The javelin's tip proceeded to carve a path through his brain, emerging in a gush of pinkish-grey gore and ivory-coloured shards of bone. The corpse, for the man was evidently dead, staggered for a moment. Several more spears and a handful of arrows launched from the wall punched into his torso spinning him towards the ditch. As he stumbled into the ditch, his final repose was to dangle from the stake upon which he had been impaled with agonising slowness. Painted crimson with heart-blood, it removed any scintilla of doubt that the warrior had passed beyond the veil.

A hand on his shoulder prompted Eirnín to turn. His brother stood beside him. "I'm sorry." Conall knew his words were inadequate. He had no salve for the grief that Eirnín suffered. His relationship with his younger brother was like a crop sowed in a stony field. With little depth of soil, there was little hope of a good harvest. He put his arms around his brother and pulled him close. Hot tears soaked Conall's neck as sobs wracked Eirnín's body. Instead of hand-fasting and joyful celebrations, they would build a funeral pyre. Conall also cried. Yet, his tears were hot with anger for vengeance and for a brother he had lost a long time past.

The brothers' mourning was short-lived as Eirnín pushed Conall away. "Bastard! It was your raid that brought this on us. Brigindos is dead because of you." At that, Eirnín turned and stormed from the ramparts.

"At least we know why Dubnoreix didn't come to collect his portion of the gold," Fearghal had appeared at Conall's side. He pointed to the track, "Another visitor?"

Bile soured Conall's mouth as, grim-faced, he looked down on the chariot that halted an arrow's distance from the gateway. The two-wheeled vehicle was well-regaled and the horse that pulled it was an impressive beast. The metal fittings of its tack glittered gold, bronze and silver in the noon sun. The warrior had a similar build to, but was much more impressively armoured than, the previous one. That he was also accompanied by a guard of five score men added to his credibility. He undid the chin strap of a helmet, which was remarkable by having a life-size metal bird perched on its crest. Even more so when the wings of the bird flapped and clattered in the wind.

The glimmer of a smile crossed Conall's face as one of his men muttered, "That's one ugly face. When we kill him, the helmet is mine." It was followed by a round of, "Not if I get to it first."

The Veneti warrior passed the helmet to the driver, gripped the rail of the box and called out, "Barbarian invaders. Thieves and murderers."

"Now there's the cauldron calling the griddle black."

There's always one wit in the company, thought Conall, although he found it impossible to disagree with the sentiment expressed.

"Leave this land. Return the gold you stole," the warrior continued.

"Now that would be difficult." Conall raised his eyebrow at the wag. The man smiled, "Well, how do we return the gold if we have left the land?" Conall shook his head. The man likely had a future as a Brehon or a druid.

In a clipped, but loud voice, Conall asked, "And who would you be? Insulting us and making demands." The glacial look returned to Conall's demeanour as he glared at the warrior.

"I am Cingetorix, king of the Veneti."

"There would appear to be many kings of the Veneti. We just bade farewell to your predecessor." Conall nodded in the direction of the ditch.

Cingetorix paused as if searching for an appropriate rejoinder. He grinned broadly, exposing a mouth missing half of its teeth. Those remaining were ghoulish shades of yellow, green and black and gripped diseased gums with tenuous roots. Hands wrapped in leather straps slapped a highly polished breastplate. "*I* am the one and only king of the Veneti. He was a dupe. A worthless messenger." In this, the king's words were supported by a round of cheers and the rattle of spears on shields from his guard.

Conall turned and dipped his head almost imperceptibly to Mórrígan. Along with her brothers, Bricriu and Beacán, she stood at his side. "Can you kill him from this distance?" he whispered, his tone cold and devoid of feeling.

Mórrígan smiled and, in a voice that matched the chill of her partner, replied, "Of course. His life is not beyond my reach." Then the queen added, "His guard too?" Conall nodded, and then took a deep breath.

"I am Conall Mac Gabhann, Rí Ruirech of Clann Ui Flaithimh and Hand of the Goddess. We will not leave. You will not receive any tribute from us. You have murdered our friends. Depart. Or the next time I look upon you will be at your death." Cingetorix cursed and raised his sword in the air.

It was unlikely that Cingetorix meant his action as a signal to attack. That would have been foolish. Nonetheless, the gesture was open to interpretation. Behind the stockade of the Clann Ui Flaithimh came the whisper of arrows loosed. Black shafts sprouted from Cingetorix's throat and his eyes. A final gurgle of bloody saliva stained the blonde moustache of the king of the Veneti. He tumbled over the chariot's cret. His driver soon followed. In confusion, the guard of one hundred milled around. They were easy targets for Mórrígan archers and Brandubh's slingers.

"Quick!" Conall shouted to Torcán who had arrived at the gate. "Take their heads. Stake them before the ditch." As the gates swung open the scream of horses and the crack of a whip were heard. Torcán swore as his men scattered to the sides of the causeway, narrowly avoiding the chariot's iron-rimmed wheels. The vehicle was driven by Eirnín. *At least*, thought Torcán, *he hadn't time to fit the battle scythes.*

Springs crashed, and wheels bumped across rutted mud and grass, as the vehicle came to a juddering halt at the body of Cingetorix. In stunned and curious silence, those on the walls watched as a vengeful Eirnín leapt from the cret. A rope was quickly looped around the Veneti king's ankles; the other end was tied off to a metal ring at the rear of the chariot.

"This is not going to end well." It was the voice of Fearghal. The battle commander stood beside Conall. He was clothed in full battle armour.

"He's mad with grief," said Conall with a shrug of resignation. "Who can blame him? Brigindos had become everything to my brother. I had hoped that he would enjoy a long life enriched by her presence." Conall gestured at the receding chariot. "My brother deserved better. Instead, I see death. I have no wish to stand by my brother's funeral pyre. Yet, it does not take the powers of the Sidhe to know his life will be short. Who is to say that a warrior's death and a meeting with Brigindos in Mag Mell would not be a better end than a life of lost love and the canker of bitterness?"

The body of Cingetorix bounced and bumped, rolling from side-to-side as it was dragged behind the chariot. Many times it slammed against the wheels and cret of the chariot, or the rocks that lay in the way. From the distant forests to the south, came a great wailing. The Veneti horde emerged from the edge of the woods. They watched in horror, stunned at the desecration of their king.

Yowls of sorrow and howls of anger rose from their ranks. They watched, helpless, as the corpse was dragged parallel to, but safely out of reach of, the line of warriors. A collective sigh of relief was exhaled as the blood-splattered chariot finally stopped. The Clann Ui Flaithimh warrior jumped from the box, and with his sword slashed the rope that snagged the king. The Veneti's relief was short-lived.

Eirnín's sword glinted as it caught the rays of an inappropriately glorious sun. He hacked at the neck of the corpse and, after several attempts, finally severed the head from the body. The chariot bounced on its springs as he hopped back onboard and proceeded to spike Cingetorix's head on one of the chariot's banner poles. The act was greeted by more, and louder, shrieks of anguish and shouted promises of revenge from the Veneti. In response, Eirnín spat on the head and turned his chariot team around.

As he sped away towards the Clann Ui Flaithimh encampment, the chieftains of the Veneti recovered the slab of meat that had been their king. Behind the fortifications of the Clann Ui Flaithimh, Conall and his commanders prepared for war.

✱✱✱

The larger of the eagles bumped the other, sending the bird into a tail-spin towards the earth. "Why?" she screeched at the rapidly receding raptor. It was not overly challenging to correct his flight path, and a bonus was spotting a young boar. The wild pig squealed as long talons sunk into flesh. It struggled limply when dropped into the nest. Its fate was clear.

The Goddess shrieked again, "I liked Eirnín and the girl."

Fate looked up from disembowelling lunch. "Their fate was sealed with the first kiss. Brigindos' geis was called. She knew more happiness… more love… in her time with Eirnín than many in a lifetime. She understood and accepted her fate."

"And what of Eirnín? Did he have a choice?"

"That was sad. Perhaps Brigindos told him… maybe not. There are some veils we cannot see through."

"And *his* fate?"

"That is for me to know, Goddess."

CHAPTER 15

404 B.C. —Cnocán-Mórrígan—Lugnasad

"I see you've brought a friend."

Cúscraid chuckled at his friend's observation. Fearghal shook his head in mock disapproval. "Lonán was right. You've developed a strange affection for the company of the dead, Cúscraid."

Cúscraid stood next to the head of Cingetorix. The skull had been rescued from Eírnín after a group in his céad—his hundred—got him drunk, took it from him, and mounted it on a pole on the stockade. Ravens had picked the head clean after first pecking out the juicy eyeballs. Several birds circled in the sky above the skull. They watched for the wriggling maggots, which would emerge from the putrefying brain.

"Do you think they'll send another king to negotiate? If we keep killing them, we could delay the battle until we all die of old age." Laughter rippled across the stockade.

Cúscraid grumbled, "Smart-arse," and looked along the defences.

One thousand stern shield warriors lined the ramparts of Clann Ui Flaithimh's defences. These were the veterans. All mean bastards and killers to a man or woman. They expected and gave no quarter. Retreat was not in their lexicon. They would prevail or die. Even if they were slain, the cost would likely cripple the enemy.

Each had a diverse array of weapons, all oiled and honed on whetstones to the sharpest cutting edge. Javelins, spears, swords, axes, clubs, and daggers rested against or were stuck in the wooden fence. Most leaned on the rim of their signature scíatha, the face painted with a swooping black raven on a crimson field. While deadly in their profession, the raucous laughter and craic shared along the stockade was a sure sign that few took themselves seriously or placed much value on their lives.

Those close to the platforms, where smouldering braziers and cauldrons of boiling oil and water sat, coughed and cursed the thick smoke and acrid fumes. Water was splashed and ladled over faces darkened with fine black soot. Rubbing stinging eyes, they prayed for a breeze to sweep the air clean. Or for the battle to begin. Blood splashed on flesh was always an antidote to minor complaints.

Interspersed with the shield-men were a thousand of Brandubh's Ravens. Each had a sling and a bag of stones and slugs. Shallow pits dug behind the ramparts overflowed with pebbles scoured from nearby rivers and beaches. Several hundred were also expert archers. Their wood and bone recurve bows were already strung. Quivers of black-shafted arrows with red and white feather fletchings hung on their belts. They sent two test flights, each time noting the location of the arrows' feathers as they fluttered in the light morning breeze. One marked the farthest distance their missile would travel. The other, roughly midway between the bowman and outer arrow, set the range for a targeted kill.

Behind the wall, the remaining two thousand five hundred of Conall's shield-wall waited. These were a mix of gender and age, from fifteen to fifty. Those veterans not on the ramparts stood in the front ranks. The youngest was kept to the rear. If they had to fight, Conall knew he was in trouble. Shouts from their ceannairí na míle and ceannairí céad scolded and encouraged.

Alongside, Carmag's forest fighters stomped bare feet in the dirt. As usual, they were restless for the fight. Naked as the day they were born, they revelled in the warmth of a perfect late-summer day. Male and female were not shy about flaunting their bodies. Catcalls and lewd suggestions from the watching civilian population and other warrior brigades were met with shouts of, "Ye'r just repressed!"

Behind the shield-ranks were rows of box wagons. Each was filled with stores of javelins, arrows, and replacement weapons, as well as basic necessities such as food and water. Barrels of beer stood alongside the wagons, although Sárán Mac Craobhach, the army's quartermaster, frowned at what he considered a frivolous item. Many of the fighters disagreed with him on this issue. Dressed in his usual bright orange, plaid pants, boots and tunic, it was hard to miss the skilled warrior. And gifted Sárán was. Not the best fighter in the army—although his expertise with a staff was much improved—his grasp of the logistics needed to keep the Clann Ui Flaithimh army fully serviced was unmatched, and well-appreciated by Conall and the army's commanders.

The mounted warriors were divided into two under Íar and Nikandros and waited at the eastern and western gates. It was as well that the two leaders were kept apart. It was widely rumoured that Nikandros had not entirely forgiven Íar for what he considered gross disloyalty to Conall. That said, since his return, Íar had the ear of Conall. Camp gossip was that Íar had argued that the Spartan was not worthy of the king and queen's trust.

Glowering looks between the two men foretold an imminent reckoning. It seemed the only thing the former friends had in common was their love of horses. Sensing a battle, the beasts snorted and stamped hooves impatiently. Metal tack chinked constantly and melodically; ornate bridles decorated with gold and silver glinted in the sun. The sound contrasted with the dull clacking of the small, overlapping iron scales sewn onto the boiled leather plates, and which protected their foreheads and chests.

By necessity, the cavalry wore modified armour. In the warm sunshine, most gave up their thick, red leather shirts, preferring moulded leather breast and back plates strapped to their naked torsos. Bracers of bronze and leather and metal rings protected their arms. Their leather pants had iron scales sown between the layers of leather, protecting thighs and calves. From the crests of utilitarian helmets dangled bushy fox tails.

Strapped to the horses' shoulders, leather sheaths and loops held javelins, long-handled axes, and long-bladed swords. Each mount and rider was a walking armoury. All weapons were checked for ease of withdrawal. Booted feet were settled into the loops of girths and belly straps. Small adjustments for comfort were made to the thick, brightly coloured dillats on which they sat.

Gràinne's squad of chariots faced the main gateway. Unlike their comrades in other sections of the army, the chariot teams had no dress code. The ten chariots had closed sides, and open fronts and rears. Each was painted with individual colours and sported an array of tribal and clan banners on long poles. Pairs of powerful, matched horses for each vehicle pulled against their harnesses and the high, curved shaft to which they were attached. The drivers knew their horse teams well and guided them with the reins and a foot on the shaft. Whips were frowned on unless to strike an enemy.

Long quivers attached to the cret sides held javelins. Normal-sized quivers carried a supply of arrows for those proficient with a bow. Not unexpectedly, given her heritage, Gràinne's preferred armour was the tattoos etched and painted on her skin. However, she now also put faith in the long-sword strapped to her back. The vehicles were already fitted with the long battle scythes. Hence, they kept a respectful distance from the foot warriors.

Banners of red, black, and gold, for tribe, clan, and king, were fixed to long poles on the perimeter wall and the ramparts of Cnocán-Mórrígan. They flapped in the wind. The beat of bodhráns and blast of horns from the hilltop fort melded with the thump of boots on the walkways and the crash of blade against shield. It could have been a festival were it not for the armies arrayed before them.

***

The brawny, blonde-haired man next to Conall pointed to the horde

119

emerging from the distant forest. "Quite a collection of banners. I don't recall that many tribes on the same side for a long time." He thought for a moment, "Well, actually never." Conall's eyebrow lifted as if urging the warrior to continue. "Veneti, Venelli, Senones, Carnutes, Bituriges, Abrincatui, and…" the man stopped to hack up a glob of bitter phlegm, "…Gaiscedach whores."

"You and your men don't have to be here," said Conall. "You're free to go. If you stay, you'll be fighting against your tribe."

Divico heaved a long sigh. There were sadness and anger in his answer. "We have no tribe. I was Dubnoreix's champion. The hundred with me is known for their loyalty to Dubnoreix. It is probable that our families are already dead. We would be executed, slowly and painfully, should we return." He chuckled blackly, "As would the whores that the king gifted the camp." The man kneeled on the wooden walkway and offered his sword hilt to Conall, "On behalf of my men, you have our oath of loyalty—if you accept it."

Conall smiled, "I accept." That said, behind the smile was uncertainty. Despite his oath, Conall thought it likely that Divico's estrangement from his tribe would be set aside if he delivered Mórrígan or his head to the Venelli's new leader. Mentally Conall chastised himself for being cynical. *I'm getting more like Mórrígan… or the Sidhe*, he thought. With a wry grin, he asked, "But what of the whores? Where does their loyalty lie?"

The Venelli warrior laughed, "You'll have to negotiate with them. Their leader, Dufach, is tough, but realistic. Your gold is good. They've been treated well. I see no great issues that would deprive your men of the comfort of their thighs."

***

Further along the stockade, Torcán's scheming and manoeuvring positioned his centuria next to Mòrag and her group of Ravens. It took promises of beer and wine, the names of women who were certain to rut, and suffering none too subtle inferences about his intentions. His only consolation was that the cherry-red blemish on his throat, a 'gift' from Mongfhionn, had not flared up at his foolishness. That he took as a positive omen. In an attempt to clear and lubricate his throat, he sipped from a water pouch. It was not wholly successful, and in a cracked voice he asked, "Would you like some water?"

Mòrag's well-known reputation for wild behaviour belied a sharp, pragmatic mind. She had made some inquiries and knew that Torcán's recent conduct was not his usual custom or practice. By reputation, he was much more of a 'get them drunk and spread their legs' man. Even so, she heard few complaints from his 'victims' regarding his performance or treatment. Many recalled that Torcán was both an ardent lover and generous by nature. The princess was pretty sure that the bunches of wildflowers that had started to appear at the entrance to her round-house came from Torcán. The flowers were obviously chosen with care for their pleasant fragrances, and that pleased her.

"That would be nice. Thanks." She could almost feel relief radiating from Torcán. Being an inveterate flirt, there was little chance that Mòrag could resist raising her suitor's temperature. With deliberation, she bent her head backwards, arching her back. Long tresses of waist-length, copper-red hair dangled freely. Black raven feathers attached to the tips of the braids almost touched the wooden walkway. Her ample breasts strained against an inadequate leather harness. Inwardly, she chuckled as she sensed Torcán struggle to contain the moan that wanted to escape his lips.

The Ravens, as with many of the Cinn Péinteáilte tribes of Northern Albu, preferred to fight naked in their spiritual armour of curling body designs. Mòrag would have happily thrown off her harness and the skin-tight triubhas. Although they left few details of her body to the imagination. In fact, the partial dress only added to her allure. Her brother, Brandubh, constantly pleaded that, as a princess of the Ravens, she should dress more modestly. Mòrag longed for battle. It would not take long for her chest harness to sunder under the strain of battle.

Torcán, and it has to be admitted, a good percentage of the warriors around them, watched as Mòrag drank. He watched her throat undulate as she gulped the liquid down. He wondered how on earth she managed to let a single trickle of water flow down her chin, neck, and finally between her breasts. For once in his life, he considered the possibility that fighting may not be everything.

He had to break the hypnotic scene. There was an uncomfortable stirring in his pants that might get quickly and embarrassingly out of control. Another gulp and Mòrag ceased drinking. "Thanks. That was delicious. So cool. You must have got it straight from the spring." What Torcán noticed was that her thanks actually appeared genuine.

Oh well, he thought and then spoke, "I was wondering if Barra would like a wolfhound pup. I know of some excellent stock with good temperaments. Lively without being annoying…" His voice trailed as Mòrag's lips puckered.

"Conall, his father, gave him a pup. One from a recent litter."

"Oh." The one word and the crestfallen look on Torcán's face almost caused a tear to fall from Mòrag's emerald-green eyes.

"But…"

"Yes…" There was a boyish eagerness in Torcán's tone.

"Someone will have to help train the hound and teach Barra how to control it. Perhaps you could do that?" There was no 'perhaps' in the speed of Torcán's reply.

"A lamb to the slaughter." Deaglán Ò Neill sighed as he observed his friend and the scene that was playing out.

"What?" It was Tadhg Ò Cuileannáin who responded and then grasped what his friend was alluding to. He grinned, "This might make a good tale for me to write. We should start a wager. To be or not to be?" A groan, from behind, made them turn around. Brandubh was also taking in the tableau.

From his lips, they heard a prayer of, "Please, no," offered to the Goddess. The Goddess, having a sense of humour and quite enjoying the behaviour of the erstwhile lovers, soared on an updraft and answered.

"Let the children play!"

***

No rain had fallen for several cycles of the moon. The land was dry, cracked, and parched brown in large areas. It trembled. Dirt ran like fine sand into cracks and gullies as the Gaulish tribes advanced. Only the front row was visible. Behind that line, the tramp of thousands of feet stirred up an enormous dust cloud of limestone and dirt particles that seemed to hover above the horde. Even the sun struggled to penetrate the thick miasma.

The wooden gates of the defences swung inwards on iron hinges and then slammed shut as Mórrígan and her hundred galloped through the entrance. The Huntress' warband had been two hundred but had lost half of their number in the battles with Kartimandu. They were specialists in what Conall termed the darker arts of warfare—terror and assassination. Their use of blade and bow rivalled any in the army of Clann Ui Flaithimh. Indeed, they were as much feared by the tribe as the enemy. On this morning they returned from reconnaissance.

Mórrígan steamed with perspiration. Horse sweat from the sodden dillat soaked her pants, making her grimace with disgust. She slapped her hip-length mail, and a cloud of dust almost choked her. A similar action on her triubhas was less successful, since they were saturated with moisture. As she removed her raven-crested helmet and flicked dust from the long black plumes, there was a burring belly laugh from one of the chariots. She growled, her eyes focused in the direction of the laughter. It was Gràinne, perched on the rail of her chariot. "Nice facial mud pack. It and the white border tones in well with your red hair."

It was then that horse and mistress decided to sneeze. Mórrígan followed this up by hacking up a great glob of spit. "Ewww!" said Gràinne. "Not very regal."

"Take care, young woman. Don't ever think that Fearghal and Mongfhionn will protect you from my justice," smiled Mórrígan. After ducking her head in a barrel of rainwater, Mórrígan took a long drink of fresh spring water and then ran up the steps to join the Chomhairle. While the water may have made her face presentable, it did little for the rich smell of horse sweat, shite, and piss. The noses of those she passed twitched, echoing Gràinne's sentiments.

Good job I'm a benevolent queen, Mórrígan thought, *or I'd have this lot strung up.*

"I make it about twenty thousand. The good news is that the tribes don't seem overly friendly. They remain in their separate formations. I saw fights break out. Not much integration, apart from the Veneti, the Venelli, and the Abrincatui, which is not surprising. It's almost as if someone doesn't want the clans and warbands to be united. They have cavalry and chariots. Bows too, and slings likely."

The queen held Conall's gaze, "I saw the Gaiscedach watcher. From what I saw, she appears to be the leader of that contingent. We should have killed her when we had the chance." Conall grunted at the unsaid "I told you so". He was more concerned that their advantage of horses was no more. Until their arrival in Aremorio, Clann Ui Flaithimh's riders had little competition. Soon, he would find out how good they were.

It was meán lae, and the sun was high in the sky. The enemy's warriors advanced to within five hundred paces of the walls of Clann Ui Flaithimh, just at the limits of a slingshot. The timing was strange. Why start a battle in the middle of the day, when the sun was at its hottest? Conall felt the heat of the burning orb pound his head and shoulders and was glad that they had many springs to provide water. The enemy would need to continually refill barrels and pouches if the battle lasted any longer than a skirmish. For a while, the two sides did little more than yell curses and obscenities in a variety of tongues at each other. Conall turned to Mórrígan, "Have Divico join us."

On hearing Divico's footfall on the wooden boards, Conall pointed to the enemy and asked, "Where will they find water?"

"There are three or four small rivers to the south and east of the horde as well as a similar number of springs. The Venelli will know where they are."

"Can your men ride?" Divico smiled and nodded. "Find Íar. Ask him to find you suitable mounts from the herds." Conall looked at Mórrígan. "Destroy access to the water. Cripple their wagons. Smash the barrels. Kill the beasts who haul the water. I want them to fight with parched throats." He paused. "But, not yet. I will tell you when the time is right."

As Divico strode off and was beyond hearing their conversation, Conall added, "We should not overly trust our new friends until they have proven their loyalty. When you make the assault on the supply lines of the Gauls, let Divico take the lead. Watch him. If you smell a trap or betrayal, kill them all."

The Dark Huntress nodded and smiled. "I note you do not seem to be concerned about my ability to slay them all."

"Should I be?"

The queen snorted, "Of course not," then added, "Gràinne has been impatiently kicking her heels at a lack of action. Perhaps, her chariots could provide additional insurance?"

Conall smiled, "I have no objection."

***

"Something's going on with our friends." A lone voice called out.

Nikandros, Cúscraid, and Fearghal stood alongside Conall and watched with deepening curiosity. The forward lines of the Gaulish tribes stretched for about a thousand paces on either side of the main gateway. Even twenty thousand warriors, if two thousand wide and ten rows deep, takes up relatively little space. Disturbingly, the massed horde showed little sign of advancing further.

A ripple of movement permeated the body of the Gauls, and corridors opened up within the ranks. Warriors trotted forward, coming to a halt just beyond arrow and slingshot range. Conall cursed. The warriors carried long spears and held them at waist height, tip pointed towards the ramparts. More troubling was the rumble of solid wheels as hundreds of wagons, drawn by teams of oxen, forced a path through the ranks. Fighters cursed as they were brusquely knocked aside. Some stumbled. Limbs were crushed underneath the solid wheels. The wagons came to a rolling halt behind the line of spears. Men scurried to unload the cargo. Others stood by directing the operation. Soon the sound of hammers striking metal and wood resounded across the landscape.

It was dusk when the hammering finally ceased. The half-light and distance obscured details from those on the Clann Ui Flaithimh defences. The squeals of unwilling wheels and the grunts of men gave little clue as to what was going on. Still, it seemed there would be no fighting on this sunset. The Clann Ui Flaithimh army relaxed and watched as hundreds of campfires flickered into life on the open plain. The enemy settled down for the night.

Nikandros, the tall, olive-skinned Spartan, paced up and down the walkway. In the sunset, his bronze breastplate glowed a burnished red-gold. The Spartan still preferred the armour of his native land, cuirass over an indecently short red tunic, bracers and greaves. Under his arm he carried a bronze Corinthian-style helmet with long, red horse-hair plumes, trailing from its crest. His armour was completed with a large, round, bronze-faced shield.

He pulled at the braids of shoulder-length, black hair and rubbed the nape of his neck in a state of increasing agitation. Unintelligible words were muttered in his native Doric. The Spartan had not slept during the night, and in the morning Conall and Fearghal found him rooted to the same spot, staring southwards. Lips moved repeating one phrase, "De bastardis—the bastard. I counselled against this."

"Perhaps you would inform us why you are so agitated?" Conall's tone was light, but there was an edge to it.

"Duck," came the response.

"What?"

"Duck!"

This time Nikandros screamed the order with as much volume as his lungs could manage. And, he kept shouting until his voice gave way. It said much about the tone of authority that most of those within range heard and acted on the Spartan's command. Others quickly passed on his entreaty. There was a moment of silence, followed by the swish of air. Some with sharper ears thought it was the sound of many volleys of javelins or flights of arrows. They were almost correct.

Short and long bolts with wicked iron heads crashed into the stockade. Several watchtowers disintegrated. Cauldrons of boiling water and oil and braziers were knocked over. Shrieks of pain from those splashed with the scalding hot liquids resounded along the ramparts. Fires broke out but were quickly quenched. Other missiles soared over the fence, causing havoc among the assembled warriors and beasts.

Within the Clann Ui Flaithimh defences, there was a period of stunned silence. Outside the ráth, what remained of the morning's tranquillity was shattered by the sound of cheering. Levers were cranked. Skeins of animal sinew and rope shrieked as they were twisted. The clunk of missiles being placed in the launch grooves was ominous. Another volley of bolts was flung at the defences of Clann Ui Flaithimh. The pattern was repeated from dawn until dusk.

Conall, the commanders, and the Chomhairle retreated to the safety of Cnocán-Mórrígan's broch to discuss the unusual battlefield tactics of the enemy. Meanwhile, Fionnbharr Ò Cuileannáin, his team of healers, and a score of druids made cautious rounds of the defences. Fionnbharr's immediate concern was determining what and how severe were the injuries from the bombardment. He expected burns, gashes, broken bones, and splinter wounds. In this, he was not disappointed. He also hoped for few deaths. In this, he was.

"What's the damage?" snapped Conall. His jaw ached from grinding his teeth, and his head thumped as if his brain was attempting to escape his skull.

"Several guard towers, including the gate towers were demolished.

Most of the rest are in need of repair. Many sections of the fence need to be strengthened. The entrance gates were unaffected. They're sunk back into the defences. Thank the Goddess, there was no fire, beyond a few braziers knocked over." Cúscraid paused, "Fionnbharr will have a report on the injured and dead, by early morning." Then he asked the question on all their lips, "The Hag's skinny arse. What was that?"

"I believe Nikandros can throw some light on our predicament. Is that not so?" Conall's stare at the Spartan was severe.

Nikandros exhaled and adjusted his position on the narrow bench. "Ballistae—armour-piercing bolt-throwers. Bloody great big javelin throwers. Siege weapons. It's rumoured that the Greeks invented them and the Romans stole the designs. Now it appears someone has sold them to the Gauls. I guess that Marcus Fabius Ambustus has begun a profitable trade in heavy weapons. He must be doing a good job of keeping his actions secret. Arming the barbarians will not win many friends in Rome. Even for the Pontifex."

"And you neglected to inform your *friends* about this type of weapon because?"

Exasperated, Nikandros threw up his hands, "There was supposed to be an agreement not to trade these weapons with the barbarian tribes. It was to be an edge the civilised nations would always have in battle."

"In a pig's arse. Didn't bloody well work out too great. Did it?" Fearghal's face flushed pink with anger. "How do we counter the weapons before they reduce our defences to wooden splinters and rubble?"

The immediate proposal by Cuán Ò Neill that they should send him as an envoy to open negotiations was met with cries of derision by all present. A few, however, volunteered to saddle a horse for him. On realising how foolish, and personally dangerous, his proposal was, Cuán slumped back on his seat and sulked for the remainder of the meeting. Yet, in his mind the twisted stirrings of opportunity surfaced. To Cuán, Conall had underestimated the enemy and put the clann in jeopardy. The higher the death and injury total, the better would be Cuán's case.

"Well there's no lack of trees or rocks, so they're not likely to run out of ammunition to toss at us. We can't just sit behind the wall and absorb the barrages." Cúscraid felt he was stating the obvious, but it had to be said. The master of Clann Ui Flaithimh's fortifications was already mulling over how future defences could be constructed to mitigate the impact of siege weapons. *More rocks*, he thought, *much more rock*.

"Horses?" Conall looked at Íar. The huge warrior supped on a jug of milk, a large portion of which flowed down his beard. He shook his head, "They're clever. Not acting like barbarians at all. It's bizarre. Anyway, horses will not cross the line of spears that protect these weapons." He glanced at Nikandros with the glimmer of a tight smile that said, "you've messed up." The Spartan growled but inwardly acknowledged the sudden precariousness of his situation.

"They have Roman advisors." The stark words were uttered by Mórrígan. "Nikandros and Íar's descriptions have helped me piece some things together. When I was scouting their lines, I saw a score or more of men who just didn't look right. They wore local clothing, but their demeanour and hairstyles cried out 'stranger'."

"Evil bastards—the Romans," interjected Fearghal. No-one disagreed.

"We have two immediate priorities: destroy the weapons and kill the Roman advisors." Conall looked at Mongfhionn. "Any suggestions, my Lady Sidhe? A lightning strike along the line might lack the subtlety of your previous work, but none of us would object."

"I think not, Conall, although, perhaps you are on the correct path to a solution." Conall looked at the Sidhe with a look of exasperation. She smiled and said one word, "Fire."

CHAPTER 16

404 B.C.—Massalia—Late Spring

Drawn by lumbering oxen and broad-backed horses, the trade caravan trundled along rutted paths that crossed the landscape of southern Gaul. At its centre were Cornelia and her guard. The merchant was more than pleased. The young woman paid well and in gold, and he had experienced warriors in his train. The region's forests, valleys, and mountains were ideal for ambushes by outcasts, outlaws, and slavers. Patting a belly that showed his appetite for food, the trader allowed himself to breathe easier. For once, this should be a safe and profitable journey to Aremorio and its ports. He might even be able to escape the need to bribe the various outlaw bands for safe passage. The merchant chuckled. More profit for him.

It was daytime. Cornelia was uncomfortable. Every pore seemed to leak profusely. Unseen insects with razor-edged teeth persistently fed on her. The relative luxury of her carriage afforded her little relief. Bounces of the vehicle gave her bruises on her ass and a pounding headache. Cooler nights that carried winter-touched winds were a welcome relief. The journey also provided ample time and solitude to review her actions. Increasingly, these seemed foolish. More like the conduct of a petulant child. Locked into a path of her own making, Cornelia shrugged her shoulders in resignation.

Socially, Cornelia and her guard preferred to remain separate from the rest of the caravan. This evening was different. It was to be a celebration of the merchant's birthday, and it would have been rude to refuse the invitation to a feast that had been prepared with lots of care. Food and wine flowed. Music and entertainment were provided by members of the merchant's family and retinue. Evening stretched into the night. Minds became dulled by wine.

Golden streams of light pierced the mist that hovered over Cornelia's eyes. She attempted to rise, but bindings on her hands and feet constrained her movement. It was then she realised that she lay on the dirt and not her soft bed. She was also naked. Her mouth was parched, and there was a terrible back-taste. Slowly her eyes regained focus, and she turned her head. Several of her guards lay close by. Their throats had been slashed almost to the bone. Blood, now black and dry, pooled beside their heads.

"The Roman bitch is awake." Cornelia vaguely recognised the voice. It belonged to Aveta, one of the merchant's female servants. Roughly, Cornelia was pulled up by her arms and held between two men. They were part of the 'protection' that the merchant had hired. His judgment had clearly been amiss. Cornelia bent over and vomited. The meal and wine of the previous evening splattered the ground. She yelped as one of the men cuffed her ear. It was his response to the puke that coated his boots. She tried to snarl at him, but it came out as a pitiful whine.

Dragged to the centre of the camp, she saw more bodies scattered in the dirt. All were dead. Most with their throats cut. Flies buzzed around garish, red wounds, and settled to feast and lay eggs on the pools of dried blood. A harvest of squirming maggots would appear by the next sunrise if the bodies were not dragged away and devoured by scavengers. Cornelia was surprised to see few signs of resistance. Anger filled her thoughts. Why had her guard not fought? She coughed and grimaced at the sour taste of puke in her mouth. Again there was a harsh, bitter taste at the back of her mouth. Then she understood—poison. They had all been drugged at the feast. Probably by the whore that was strutting about the camp, bellowing out orders.

Only eight, including Cornelia and her two younger maids, survived. All female and young, they would fetch a good price as slaves. Tied to each other and to a ring on one of the wagons, they staggered and stumbled as the caravan once more moved on. This time, by the position of the sun, it was heading east and certainly not in the direction of Aremorio. Whips cracked, lashing bare flesh. Men with swarthy, pock-marked faces and dirt-encrusted hands grabbed soft round ass cheeks and groped breasts. Leering faces got much too close. Their breath smelled of rotten cabbage and old eggs.

"Enough of the whips!" shouted Aveta, who clearly was the leader. "I don't want them scarred. They won't fetch as good a price on the blocks at Lugudunon." Like a snake, a dissatisfied grumble slithered between the men—there were about twenty now. The woman laughed, "You can spread their thighs and asses, and rut all you want. But I'll slit the throat of any man who leaves them marked where it can be seen." The men cheered. The captives sobbed. The journey to the Gaiscedach settlement of Lugudunon was many nights of degradation away.

***

Normally, Pytheas was known for a calm disposition, which he claimed came from a lifetime on the seas. Today, the merchant was apoplectic. He had learned of Cornelia's visit and abrupt departure. His tongue flayed the head of his household. The servant who had been with Pytheas for over twenty years bowed his head. His master's anger was understandable. In his defence, he declared, "I could not restrain her. She was very set in her ways. And, she had a formidable guard."

In a calmer tone, the merchant replied, "I know. The girl is as stubborn as her father… and her husband. But we must discover the direction of her journey… for her sake." Several days later, after questioning all who had come into contact with Cornelia, Pytheas noticed a common theme. That of a one-handed beggar who sat all day long at his door. Pytheas guided his servant to the front gateway and with a flourish of his hand asked, "Where is the beggar?"

The servant thought for a moment and then answered, "He has not been seen recently." He considered once more and, in a subdued voice, added, "Not since the young lady departed."

"Find him." The servant nodded.

In Massalia, few had a better network of informants than Pytheas. The merchant was known to be generous and paid well for useful information. In time, the beggar was delivered protesting to Pytheas' doors. "Why do you no longer find my doorstep profitable?" The beggar blinked rapidly and feigned ignorance. "It seems you spent your days begging at my gates while my Roman guest was present. Now that she is gone, so are you. I find this a strange coincidence."

The beggar squirmed. He was guarded by two burly men with expressions that spoke of their desire to cause him pain. "I know nothing, Master. I'm just a beggar."

"You are indeed a beggar. But one who is the eyes and ears of the Gaiscedach in Massalia." Pytheas turned to the men holding the beggar, "I have no time for talk and negotiation. Cut off his fingers one at a time. Then his hand. If that does not loosen his tongue, then use your knives lower." The beggar was loyal to the Gaiscedach, but only to a point.

"Perhaps with some gold, I might remember…" A high-pitched scream escaped from the man's lips as a finger dropped to the gravel.

"I have neither time nor patience for arbitration." Pytheas' face was implacable. One more finger emphasised the merchant's position. The beggar's tongue loosened, and the sad tale of Cornelia and her kidnapping was told. Agitated, Pytheas ran his hand through plaited black hair. Should he sail for Rome and an audience with Cornelia's father, Marius, or for Aremorio and Conall? In the end, Pytheas chose to plead his case with Conall. A sizeable barbarian raiding party likely could be despatched quickly. The snake-pit that was the Republic's government and its nobility, even if they took the word of a Greek merchant, would jostle for advantage for a year and still do nothing. He turned to walk away.

"What shall we do with the beggar?"

"Take him to the docks. Cut off his remaining hand. Cut out his tongue. Throw him into the waters. Poseidon's sharks will judge if he lives." The screams of the beggar as he was dragged away were the last sounds he would ever utter.

CHAPTER 17

404 B.C.—Cnocán-Mórrígan—Lugnasad

"Given our discussion on the wall at An Balla Leac, I'm reluctant to suggest where you should stand on this particular stockade."

"There's an unspoken 'but' in that sentence."

Bláithín Ni Neill smiled at the warrior beside her. Brocc Ò Cathasaigh, older brother to Mórrígan, sported a finger-wide tress of white hair that swept back from his forehead. It was in stark contrast to the red-auburn shock of curls that otherwise covered his head. Impetuosity had been forcefully driven from the warrior by the death of his friend, Labhraidh. The unusual plait of hair was a constant reminder of loss and grief.

Brocc was of average height and wiry, but muscular. His body was marked with numerous battle scars, including a thick, curved one that ran the length of his left forearm. Sharp facial features did not lend themselves to a description that included the word 'handsome'. Yet Bláithín thought there was an attractive intensity about the warrior. When he smiled, his green-flecked hazel eyes sparkled.

Sheepishly, Brocc smiled and dipped his head. "There is, and yet I am hesitant to risk either your displeasure or a matching scar on my right arm from the axe you carry." Bláithín was slim and tall—almost a head greater than Brocc. The woman's beauty was enhanced by the rare combination of fire-red hair and deep blue eyes. She was several summers younger than Brocc yet seemed to have accrued an astuteness that belied her age.

On this day, Bláithín had foregone the dress of a noble and stood in battle apparel. Well-padded on its interior surface, the bronze breastplate that protected her chest and abdomen had obviously been moulded to her body. Although functional, it also served to emphasise a trim waist and delightfully rounded breasts. The armourer had also added final flourishes of navel and nipples.

Tied with a matching cord of the same colour, red triubhas accentuated her waistline. The trousers were tucked into soft, leather boots. Bláithín's battle outfit was completed with a leather belt that rested on her hips and a small, round scíath. The shield, its diameter no more than five hands length, was carried on her left arm and gripped in her fist via a central handle. As well as a favoured short-handled, double-bladed axe, the belt held a variety of daggers. Brocc noted that she had knives slipped into her boots as well. Bláithín was not a woman to be trifled with.

"First, I have a gift. Then a suggestion."

Bláithín blinked in surprise. Unlike his friend Torcán, Brocc was known neither for flippancy nor casual rutting. She coloured slightly, finding herself flattered by his attention. "I hope this is a good size. The armourers can alter it or add some more padding." Bláithín gasped at the beauty, and appreciated the functionality, of the helmet that was offered. Made of iron and bronze, it was decorated with intricate, curling designs in gold. Conical in shape, its apex was a raised central knob shaped like a small pinecone. From the pinecone sprouted several large fistfuls of horsehair. The plumes were dyed blue and were an almost perfect match for her eyes. Each strand was about two hands in length. Finally, the helmet had a protruding neck guard as well as hinged cheek plates to protect the sides of Bláithín's head.

"I observed that you had no helmet. I hope you won't think me forward."

It was not often that Bláithín found herself lost for words. She just about stammered, "Noooo. Not forward. Very thoughtful. Thanks." Then she coughed and recovered her composure slightly. "You had a second suggestion."

Brocc grinned, "Ah, yes. Until repairs are made, the place where you now stand is protected only by a single row of posts. I have witnessed that the heavy javelins thrown by the barbarian ballistae can breach this. If, however, you move a little distance to either side, the fence has a double barrier. No sense in getting injured or killed by a stray missile." Bláithín nodded. As Brocc turned to continue his round of the stockade, Bláithín held a hand out. It touched the scar on his forearm, and he stopped. With a quick glance around, Bláithín guided him closer, and their lips met.

The kiss was short, little more than a quick brush of lips. Disinterested onlookers would see it as no more than a parting of friends. For Bláithín and Brocc, the caress was long enough to signal that neither would have objected to its lingering.

"Shite! As if life isn't complicated enough."

Lonán Ò Neill was neither disinterested nor unobservant. He shook his head as he watched Bláithín and Brocc break from the kiss before both took up their assigned positions on the rampart. The burly warrior cursed his brother's recent attempts to undermine Conall. Not only was that dangerous, for Conall was neither blind nor a fool, but Cuán's neglect of Bláithín was sheer folly.

***

Once again, the day began with the crack of ballistae and the taunts of an enemy who were beyond a killing strike. Thousands of bolts rained destruction on the Clann Ui Flaithimh defences. Impotent and frustrated by the tactic, the army of Conall could do little but hunker down and wait for the long-range assault to stop. The patience of warriors used to the death, and the ebb and flow of battle, was their shield. Not so for the civilian population. Many, curious about the new weapon and sceptical of its range, stood outside their roundhouses. The bolts showed no mercy. Children, bored with the constraints placed on them, escaped from their kin. They were soon to realise their folly, orphaned by barbs that showed no partiality. The cries of the tribe stabbed deep into Conall.

It was a breeze. A zephyr of relief on a hot summer day. Mongfhionn sighed, "Ahhhh," as she felt the wind's fingers lift up her hair. She stood and looked to the horizon and smiled.

"Get down, woman. Even a Sidhe can lose her head to an iron blade." It was a plainly exasperated and increasingly short-tempered Fearghal who spoke. Inaction did not sit well with the tribe's battle commander. Beside him, Conall peered with curiosity at Mongfhionn.

"I think the Lady Sidhe may have some news for us."

Mongfhionn chuckled, "What, now you can read my thoughts? A dangerous weapon." She pointed to the horizon. "A light wind is pushing clouds in our direction. It will rain before sunset. On the following sunrise, the dew will be much heavier than usual." Conall looked with a raised eyebrow at the Sidhe. She smiled, "Bundles of skeins are needed to achieve sufficient torsion for the launching of the ballistae. If they are wet, they will not function efficiently." She sighed at the blank look on Conall's face. "Put simply. The weapons do not work when wet. They are, after all, merely large bows."

Conall clapped his hands in glee and jumped up. The bolt that thudded into the tall post beside him was a sign that his move was rash. "Sunrise, fool!" rasped Mongfhionn. "Sunrise!" The Sidhe's solid oak staff hit Conall squarely behind his knees and left him sprawling on the guard-post's floor.

✳✳✳

Centurion Crispus Galerius Donatus tugged at the tight black curls that crowned a well-sunburnt head. The sides of his head were shaved. It was a practical hairstyle and suited him. In the early-morning, sweat was already forming beads on his broad forehead. He felt uneasy in civilian clothing. Only the weapons hanging from his baldric and belt gave him any comfort. The centurion looked with barely concealed disdain on the barbarians surrounding him. They stank, were vulgar, and fought like feral cats and dogs. Even the presence of a common enemy and gifts of siege weapons and gold did little to constrain their in-fighting. Indeed, several of the tribes seemed to be encouraging the continual discord.

As Crispus walked the long, ragged line of silent ballistae and the fence of spears that protected them, his temper was uneasy. The hackles on the back of his neck were stiff. He looked to the sky in the hope of a good omen, but only saw two great eagles and a flock of ravens circling the battlefield. What were they waiting for? His sense of unease intensified. It would be a while before the weapons were functional. An unearthly shriek from the ramparts of Clann Ui Flaithimh spurred Crispus to self-preservation. He ran.

The Sidhe's ear-shattering yell was the signal for the Clann Ui Flaithimh cavalry to gallop through the main entrance. The earth trembled as four thousand bony hooves beat on the compacted dirt. A safe distance away and relegated to a helpless bystander, Crispus turned to watch. The Roman admired the horseflesh. He had a small stable outside of Rome and recognised quality. A few of these stallions and mares would significantly increase the value of his stock. He exhaled. That assumed that he would return to Rome.

Íar's riders stayed just beyond the range of the long lances of the barbarians. Keeping a safe distance between horses and the line of spears and ballistae, they tossed small, round clay pots. Once the jars were exhausted, his men pulled javelins from their sheaths and hurled them. In Íar's wake, those under Nikandros followed. They carried flaming brands that soon followed the arc of the terracotta jars.

From the smell, it quickly transpired that the vessels were filled with a mixture of pitch, oil, and sand. The grit was a cruel enhancement. It increased the mixture's adhesive qualities, especially on flesh. Fire-pots smashed against the siege weapons. Along the row of spears and ballistae, men and women cursed as they were splashed with the sticky brew. There was little the spearmen could do to prevent the coming storm.

Many, realising their enemy's intent, turned and fled. That day, the ones who fell to Clann Ui Flaithimh javelins were considered fortunate.

The morning was still. No breeze of any significance. Yet, as soon as the fires were started, a stiff north wind arose. The breeze fanned the inferno, which consumed all before it. As the flames roared, they were accompanied by more nightmarish ululations from the defences. Crispus shuddered. What creatures walked the stockade of Clann Ui Flaithimh?

Crispus recalled advising the barbarian leaders to build a berm before the weapons. It would have provided some protection against the riders. His advice had been ignored. In the recriminations that would undoubtedly follow, no-one would remember his words. They would only remember that he was a Roman and not one of them.

The sun was high in the sky, as Crispus walked the charred, smoking ruins of men and machines. His ears still rang with the terrible screams of men and women engulfed by fire. Human torches, they spun and stumbled wildly until shock and smoke rendered them senseless. The brimstone odour of burning hair and the sickening, cloying smell of scorched flesh hung suspended in the air. It would be in his nostrils and visit his nightmares for weeks. If he lived that long.

He walked along the charred remains, kicking the odd ballistae that had not been entirely destroyed. Some could be refurbished, but not nearly enough. New ones could be built. There was plenty of wood in the forests. Iron nails and fittings had not perished in the flames and could be reused. Crispus knew that would not happen. The tribes were impatient for battle. The chieftains were already plying their warriors with unlimited beer and wine. False courage for the idiots who would provide a screen for the wiser veterans.

The centurion cursed his misfortune. He had lost half of his men in the attack. Most he executed to end their suffering. In anger, he kicked a smoke-blackened ballista. It was not all it seemed. His sandaled foot split open the scorched black crust and plunged into the tender pink interior. A tipping point was reached. Crispus threw up. Puke hissed as it splashed on burning embers. A groan caught his attention, and he tramped with no great enthusiasm to its source. The blackened shape was vaguely human. Lidless blue eyes held his own, beseeching. As he had done on a score of previous occasions, Crispus took his dagger and sent the poor bastard to his or her gods.

Crispus had a nose for trouble. He was well aware that he, and what remained of his squad, were in trouble. Their utility had been consumed by the flames. He planned to slip away when the barbarians attacked. The problem was where to go? His mission had failed, and his employer, Marcus Fabius Ambustus, was not known for his forgiving spirit. Crispus was wise enough to know that he and his men were witnesses to Marcus' plottings and as such were loose ends. They had neither friends in Rome nor among the Gaulish tribes.

***

"I doubt they'll attack today."

Conall agreed with his battle commander and was relieved. An aura of shock cloaked the Clann Ui Flaithimh. The destruction meted out by the riders was a glimpse of the Otherworld. Íar had returned, immediately bathed, and strode off to find somewhere he could be alone. Likewise, Nikandros washed but then proceeded to get very drunk and seek a woman willing to spread her thighs. Still, water, beer, or womanising did little to remove the charred, smoking scar before the walls. The people of Clann Ui Flaithimh were thankful the mysterious north winds continued to blow. The strong breezes rolled much of the choking smoke, and the stench of cooked flesh, back on the Gaulish camp.

Mongfhionn was both a part of, and apart from, the small group of leaders who stood on the ramparts. As usual, she wore her cavernous grey cloak and gripped her oak staff. It was a lighter summer cloak, and she had foregone any inner garments. Yet, its weight was almost unbearable in the current warm weather. Jealous of the Ravens and Carmag's people who happily wandered about naked, at least in the warmer seasons, the Sidhe sighed wistfully. It seemed that she was only ever nude when performing something terrible or when she lay in Fearghal's arms. She much preferred the latter.

The cloak's hood hung over pale-white shoulders. Golden-blond tresses streaked with fire-red highlights fell freely down her back. It was rare for the Sidhe to braid her waist-length hair. Even in battle, she preferred it natural. Lifted by a breeze, it formed a golden corona around her face. To the people, this, and her manic screams, were iconic symbols of her powers.

Mongfhionn knew of the unease among the people and their suspicions that the winds were her doing. She snorted, of course they were. Most refused to meet her eyes, although that in itself was not a very good measure. In normal times few could or would hold her dark stare. The Sidhe was an ancient figure of power and awe. An ability to make friends was not a prime job requirement. She was their nightmare as well as their protector.

"At least we're on even terms with the bastards," said Fearghal.

Cúscraid slapped him on the back and laughed, "What have you been drinking? We're outnumbered four- maybe five-to-one."

Fearghal returned the slap. "I have total faith in your defences. But, failing that, our leader has a plan." The silence from Conall prompted Fearghal to add, "You *do* have a plan?"

"In the morning they will throw themselves furiously at our walls, hoping to overwhelm us. With their numbers, they may succeed."

"Not exactly a rousing call to battle," growled Fearghal, "You should consider a more positive approach."

Conall smiled. "The 'plan' is to make it too costly for them to continue. The tribal leaders know there is a limit as to how much blood they will wish to leave in the earth. A weakened clann or sept will fall prey to its neighbours."

CHAPTER 18

404 B.C.—Cnocán-Mórrígan—Summer

"Where's Eirnín?" Conall turned to address Deaglán. The sharp tone held notes of a brother's anger, concern, and frustration. The king in Conall, however, pointed to the warriors formed up below and behind the rampart. "I do not see my brother with his céad."

Deaglán looked uncomfortable. "I believe he may be with Cuán. They spend quite a lot of time in each other's company." Conall's face darkened. *It was*, Deaglán thought, *difficult to discern whether the Rí Ruirech was angrier at Cuán, Eirnín, or himself as the bearer of the news.* "Befriending Eirnín appears to be a priority of Cuán's since Brigindos' death." At the sight of Conall's glowering demeanour, Deaglán bit his lip to curtail further conversation.

"Send men to my brother. His place is with his men. See that he is armoured and escorted to them with all speed." Deaglán dipped his head sharply and turned about.

Conall's gaze searched the stockade, spotted Lonán Ò Neill, and called him over. "Find your brother. Impress on him that I expect his immediate presence on the battlements. He will fight with his men. If necessary, he will die with them." Conall's gaze fell on Bláithín who, hoping to remain unseen, hovered close by. Her expression told of her fascination with the conversation. She was startled and blushed furiously when the king pointed her out to Lonán, "The Lady's bravery shames her partner and your brother." Lonán spluttered with rage and, with a parting glare at Bláithín, stomped off. Yet his anger was not at Conall's words or Bláithín's example. It was because the king spoke the truth.

Cuán was deep in conversation and oblivious to his brother's approach. To Lonán, the company that his brother kept was deeply troubling. The small group contained well-known malcontents and troublemakers. Most had been disciplined and ejected from the army and the Cróeb Ruad as not being fit for service. Given the many unsavoury traits and personality flaws of the individuals in Clann Ui Flaithimh's army, to be designated not 'fit for service' was a damning indictment. Worse, this group were notorious fomenters of strife. Only one woman, more a child, sat with the group. It was the whore, Laoise. She appeared to be in thrall to Cuán.

Lonán swore, and then strode into the centre of the group. "Your presence is requested on the ramparts." Startled, Cuán dropped the pouch he was about to hand over. It hit the dirt with the clink of gold. Lonán's black look cowed his brother. He heard the soft scrape of a weapon drawn. Lonán's sword was unsheathed, silently and swiftly, as he turned to face the threat. In one smooth, backhanded movement, the blade eviscerated the man. Silent in his shock, the conspirator fell to his knees. A dagger was cast aside as he attempted to prevent his guts from unravelling on the dirt. He looked up with beseeching eyes. In return, Lonán kicked him in the head. The dying man sprawled on the ground as Lonán spoke, "A mercy blade is not for the likes of you. Die slowly and in pain."

It was the pouch of gold that caused the rest of the group to hesitate rather than flee. Stained by the blood of their comrade, they were snared by the wealth that lay on the earth. Their eyes were unavoidably drawn to the bag. Lonán's mirthless laugh sent shivers of ice up their spines. "Touch the bag, and I'll sever hand from wrist." At that, the group scattered, shouting oaths and promising retribution.

Regaining some composure, Cuán railed at his brother, "You've ruined everything and put me in danger."

Lonán shook his head, "You can pay off your wagers another day, brother. Now, you have a battle to fight."

"No. You don't understand. You don't understand." Shoulders slumped and muttering incoherently, a disturbed Cuán followed his brother.

***

Dawn was heralded by the rumble of wheels and the scream of axles that needed grease. Hundreds of wagons, pushed by burly warriors with bulging thigh and arm muscles, edged closer to the perimeter ditch. Behind them, in managed chaos, the Gauls marched in tribal groups. Distinguished by flushed cheeks, the drunk and the eager pushed forward. The veterans stood aside, putting up token resistance. They knew the real battle would commence when the foolish were harvested, and their bodies lay broken and bleeding on the ramparts.

"It was," mused Cúscraid, "not my finest defence-work." The outer face of the earthwork gently sloped to meet the ditch. Had he time, the trench would be mid-way up the slope and would be both broader and less shallow. The rampart was, however, substantial. A latticework of rocks and timbers permeated the construction. Tough grasses and heathers, even in the short period since its erection, had taken root. They spread across the rampart, binding the surface dirt. Atop the embankment was a tall wooden fence.

Cúscraid adjusted the chainmail to sit more comfortably on his shoulders. To prevent chaffing, he wore a soft leather tunic between mail and flesh. A light, hip-length, red over-tunic protected the armour from dust and the sun. The suit was new, and Cúscraid was having doubts as to the wisdom of wearing it on this particular morning. Like a new pair of boots or bróga, he suspected that it would take time for him to be entirely comfortable with the equipment.

Thick, yet not stubby fingers tightened the leather straps of his bronze and iron helmet. Being a practical man, Cúscraid had foregone the more exotic decorations that enhanced his friends' helmets. Instead, from the spiked crown, there hung a single, yellow-gold ribbon—a memento from his long-time cot partner. A gust of wind blew the precious cloth across his face. Cúscraid smiled. Her distinctive fragrance heavily impregnated the fabric and aroused his senses.

He sighed and hoped the battle would be short. In this, Cúscraid would likely get his wish. This was a fight between hot-tempered Gaels and Gauls. It would be furious and unrelenting. Not at all like the massed battles, tactical formations, and lengthy sieges of the Greeks, the Macedonians, and the Persians that Nikandros frequently recounted around the evening campfires.

A great shout from the Gauls commanded the attention of all behind the fortifications. It was followed swiftly by Fearghal's roar of, "Raise shields. Slingers target the wagon-drivers. Archers prepare fire arrows. Target the carts." The orders were echoed along the wall by each cohort's leader.

***

Sweat trickled from weather-burnt skin as the Gaulish wagons built up momentum. They were not empty. Inside the boxes were logs, rocks, and straw. Behind and alongside the carts, thickly muscled arms and thighs bulged. Human oxen with calloused hands gripped rough wood and pushed and pulled. They swore as splinters pierced their flesh. Once beyond the Clann Ui Flaithimh markers, a barrage of slugs rained down. The man-beasts cursed the sharp slap of stones on exposed skin.

With eyes raised, they marked the charcoal-grey trails but were helpless to evade the fiery barbs. Flaming arrows thudded into the wagons. Some found flesh. The slow build-up of fires stung eyes and raised blisters on scorched hands, drawing more oaths from the men. Still, they held to their task, and the wagons trundled steadily forward.

Shouts and grunts of defiance were thrown at the defenders as each vehicle was upended at the ditch edge. Wood shattered and splintered. Wheels spun uselessly or rolled into the depths of the trench. Fires spread. Along the ramparts, each cart did its part. The gulley was bridged in many places. The brave who had dragged the vehicles forward found little time to savour their victory. Few would appreciate or even hear of their sacrifice. Their reward was to be pinned to the dirt with javelins or to stumble into the ditch, clutching the black-shafted arrows that sprouted from perforated chests. Their bodies were the final contribution to filling the channel.

A huge roar arose from the Gauls as they charged forward. Disunity was their weakness. Like a clutch of brightly-coloured balls of yarn, the tribes tumbled and jostled each other as they dashed towards the walls. Each skein was a different tribe with a different target. Even warbands within the same clan clashed.

Thousands of slingers halted and loosed showers of stone and iron at the Clann Ui Flaithimh defences. Like a winter-grey cloud, the hailstorm cracked indiscriminately against shields, wood, and skin. Under the fierce onslaught, the Clann Ui Flaithimh defenders could do little but suffer patiently, sheltering behind any cover they could find. Those who risked a head above the parapet felt the ring of rocks striking helmets. A stunned few fell to the walkway. Blood seeped through cracked skulls. Some never rose again.

Thankfully, the barrage could not continue. Supplies of stones were quickly exhausted, and the slingers dared not risk striking their own. As the staccato clatter receded, Clann Ui Flaithimh warriors stood. Scíath rims clashed as the red wall formed along the ramparts. Additional spears rested against the fence. Black cauldrons of agony simmered on glowing braziers. Defiant battle cries of "Conall-Abú!" resounded along the wall. With a hoarse *kraa kraa*, from the forests to the shores, a great cloud of ravens swooped in support of their brothers, whose eyes glared from painted shields.

It was impossible for Conall and his commanders to adequately man the long dirt and stone rampart. Even had they been able to, numerically the besiegers had the upper hand. Yet, rather than flowing like a wave over the stockade of rough timbers, the Gauls scrambled across the fence in small bands. They had no plan, save to kill anyone in their path, rape the women—or men if that was their preference—and accumulate plunder and slaves. They were always at a disadvantage. The Clann Uí Flaithimh fought for each other and their kin.

Conall hoped the assault would be on one central front, but in their disunity, the Gauls attacked along the full length of the defences. "Another thousand scíatha to the eastern ramparts and the same to the west. Íar is to command the east and Nikandros the west. Carmag will remain in reserve." A roar of disappointment swelled up from Carmag's warriors. Conall turned to the shaggy-haired commander, "Silence your warriors. They will see enough blood before we're done."

Along the wall, the screaming horde scrambled across a ditch that was now an inferno. Smoke stung eyes and flames licked at flesh, hair, and clothing. Javelins rained down on the Gauls as they struggled up the rampart's slope. Soon the incline was slick with blood and gore, and littered with the injured and dying. The press behind pushed the front ranks forward. The horror of their plight was sobering, but they could do no more than forge ahead and die.

A tumultuous roar ascended from the Gauls as they reached the stockade. Grappling hooks thudded against wooden posts, embedding in the soft pine. Hastily constructed ladders crashed against the fence. Warriors were propelled upwards with cupped hands or used the backs of comrades as springboards.

As their riposte, the defenders tipped cauldrons of boiling oil and water, and of hot sand and burning embers over the enemy. The least offensive was the dropping of rocks and logs on those sheltering in the lee of the fence. Bludgeoned by falling boulders, scalded by boiling oil and steamy water, and caressed by millions of grains of hot sand that trickled into every orifice, the attackers suffered. No relief was offered to the fallen. Considered a hindrance to the assault, the best they could hope for was to be trampled on. Most times they were grabbed and hauled aside. Many ended up in the ditch they had fought to cross.

The blue-crested helmet bobbed up and down as Bláithín crouch-walked along the walkway. She winced as an iron barb embedded itself into a nearby post, narrowly missing her shoulder. The rattle of hundreds of ladders slamming against the wall made her jump. The roar from thousands of Gaulish throats had neither form nor words. It was a primal scream and was getting closer. In her head, Bláithín knew the besiegers would likely overwhelm the stockade. There were too many to hold back.

Yet it was a shock when she saw a horned Gaul helmet appear above the fence. It was followed by two dirt-encrusted hands placed on the posts. Remarkably, she observed that the backs of the hands were quite hairy, as were the stubby fingers. *Hopefully, it's a man.* Instinct and Cróeb Ruad training took over. The boss of her shield slammed against the attacker's face crushing his nose and letting loose a gush of snot, blood, and tears. She swung her axe. It missed the warrior's head, and she saw his taunting, toothless grin. The blade of her axe continued its path and bit into the wooden post's flat top. Blinking away the splatter of hot blood on her eyes, she glanced down. The screaming warrior fell back, crushing those beneath. His hand remained twitching on the fence.

Since they were not in formation, the men and women of the shield-wall had the freedom to choose with which weapons to fight. Many retained a last javelin, using it to stab and punch holes into an enemy whose armour held little resistance to the spikes of iron. When the spear finally snapped or was wrenched from their hands, trapped as the victim's final act of defiance, the warriors switched to their favourite blades. For Torcán that presented a problem. His chosen weapons were his head and his fists.

Thus, it was with a sigh of resignation that he drew a battle-axe from the securing loop on his belt, gripped his scíath firmly, and swung at the head that made its appearance before him. The face had a wash of grey-black soot and dirt. Several missing teeth and scarring marred its finer features. A voice like a broken axle, and enough to make Torcán cringe, screeched at him. Still, before she could swing bruised legs over the fence, Torcán added to her countenance. The axe cleaved her skull from eyebrow to chin. Her face fell apart, spilling brains and blood. It was one wound that would never knit.

Further along the fence, Conall paced to and fro like an animal in a cage. He was angry, but not at the bloody, frenzied chaos of battle that was raging around him. His ire was directed at the ten men from his caomhnóirí who killed anyone who got close to him. Hence, Conall's axe blade remained unbloodied and in pristine condition. He shouted his disagreement at the men. The response from their leader was, "You'll fight when we say you fight."

"So much for being king," he growled.

***

It was not often that the Ò Cuileannáin brothers—Craiftine, Fionnbharr, and Tadhg—fought side-by-side. Since the death of the fourth brother, Labhraidh, in a senseless chariot accident, the remaining brothers were rarely seen together on the battle line. On this day Fate conspired to bring them together.

All were tall and wiry with shocks of unruly sandy hair. Fionnbharr, at twenty-six summers, was the oldest. The man had outgrown his boyhood shyness but retained a charming reticence. He was a warrior of renown, as affirmed by his many scars. Under Mongfhionn's tuition, Fionnbharr had become Conall's personal physician and was in effect the surgeon-general of Clann Ui Flaithimh. Healing was his passion. Still, he was a very proficient swordsman who, while not in favour of the blood and guts approach of Torcán, efficiently dispatched opponents with a disturbing lack of compassion.

The youngest of the brothers, Craiftine was acknowledged as the most accomplished harpist among Clann Ui Flaithimh and beyond. Even at rest, his long, callous-tipped fingers twitched involuntarily as he imagined new melodies. In an age of cut and slash, Craiftine Ò Cuileannáin was an artist when it came to swordplay. Craiftine, the warrior, favoured the use of twin swords. Unsurprisingly, Craiftine's greatest fear was not being able to play. Thus, his one indulgence was the commissioning of a pair of mail gauntlets. This created good-humoured covetousness from Torcán, who quickly envisioned using the gloves for fighting rather than protection. This day on the ramparts, the gauntlets were encrusted in the grime of battle.

The third brother was Tadhg. Tadhg was the tribe's seanachaí—poet, raconteur, and chronicler of Conall's story—and had a brain as sharp as the best edge of any blade. Like a dog with a bone, Tadhg would pursue a mission until its resolution, and a mystery until it had revealed its secrets. Not the best warrior of Clann Ui Flaithimh, his resilience in battle was based on his unmatched powers of observation and an ability to quickly home in on an opponent's weaknesses.

As the Gauls flowed over the western section of the ramparts, the brothers united in a terrible slaughter. Like a golden-headed Cerberus, they pounced, danced, and killed until their length of the walkway was awash with blood and scattered with limbs and guts. They fought together, heart, mind, and hands, untempered by compassion. Mercy would have been Labhraidh's contribution.

The eagle swooped and soared, delighting in the brothers' butchery. She screeched in ecstasy with every sword thrust that tore flesh and delivered spirits to Mag Mell. The Goddess spat in anger as Crum Dubh shouted for the brothers to cease and rest.

"I will have them," screamed the Goddess. "They will entertain me."

"You will not!" Fate's wings smacked the other's head bringing her out of her euphoria. "Their fate remains in my hands, not yours. And, I have not finished with them." The Goddess would have snarled in anger if it was possible for an eagle to do this.

"Where is your Dark Huntress? I do not see her in the battle."

Uncloaked, the Goddess was all-powerful, but an eagle's brain is little bigger than a chestnut. It could hold focus on only one topic at a time. The golden eyes blinked. "She has a mission to complete." Fate smiled. He had successfully diverted his companion's attention and now followed in her wake as curiosity led her to find Mórrígan.

CHAPTER 19

404 B.C.—Aremorio—Summer

In the distance, the sound of battle rumbled under an opaque, dirty pink cloud of blood and dust. Mórrígan gently tugged on the reins of the mustard-yellow mare. It came to a halt beside the narrow, fast-flowing river. Taking advantage of the stop, the horse dipped its head to feed on the lush riverside grass. The Huntress removed her helmet, wiping the back of her scarred hand across a forehead beaded with sweat. Salt stung her eyes. Slowly, she swung her right leg across her mount's back and slid to the ground. The cold waters were irresistible.

Her men had already dismounted and, having taken care of their horses, washed trail dirt and dust from raw throats. Hair dark with sweat was dipped in the water. Some simply threw themselves into the river. The scene was followed by impossibly prolonged and forceful streams of piss. Sighs of relief accompanied the unrestrained bladder relief. Loud sneezes as plugs of snot exploded from dirt-encrusted nostrils added a final touch to the tableau. There was no modesty shown by the men. Mórrígan wondered if they thought of her as a woman. Should she be pleased or angry if they did not?

"They certainly know Gràinne is female," she huffed as her eyes picked out the Cinn Péinteáilte warrior. Naked—of course, Gràinne stood beside her chariot. Sword in hand, she religiously practised the moves taught to her by Fearghal. In an age of slashing and bludgeoning opponents into submission, there were few actual artists with a blade.

Gràinne was a member of that elite group. Even at her young age, she was a master of sword-play. Sensing, that she was observed, Gràinne turned and looked at Mórrígan. Her head dipped, not in recognition of Mórrígan's position, but in guilt. The queen shook her head. The girl needed to get over the accident that maimed Mórrígan's brother, Brion. There was no fault or blame to assign.

Mórrígan gave a sigh, looked around and gave a long low whistle. It was the signal to mount up and was greeted with an irreverent round of farting. According to Divico, their destination and the first of several springs was a morning's canter downstream. His men were already scouting ahead. There were few signs of friendship between the two warrior groups. The Venelli kept their own company and watched their new allies with furtive glances. For their part, the Clann Ui Flaithimh stared back with hard, untrusting eyes and kept their weapons close. Mórrígan wondered whether her men had picked up on her wariness or whether they too sensed that something was not quite right.

Fully aware of the chill between his men and the Clann Ui Flaithimh, and between Mórrígan and him, Divico conceded that their suspicions were legitimate. They could not possibly know for sure of the price on each of their heads. Yet, it would be a foolish person who did not consider this. Neither Mórrígan nor her band were fools.

Delivery of Mórrígan's head to the new kings of the Venelli or Veneti would undoubtedly see him accepted, ostensibly with open arms, by either tribe. His reward would be enough gold to last a lifetime. Still, Divico was not dim-witted. He and his men would be looked upon with suspicion by the Gaulish tribes. How long they would enjoy their new-found wealth was uncertain. Kings gave away gold with profound reluctance. A knife in the back from another wishing to curry favour, and who would settle for a much smaller reward, was a distinct possibility. Divico had much to think about, but not much time.

***

Meán lae passed. The sun approached its zenith in a clear, celestial-blue sky. Battle had been joined with the birth of the new day. No water had crossed the besiegers' lips since the battle started. Throats were red raw, scratched with the debris of battle. War cries were hoarse. A communal thundering growl not unlike thunder and unintelligible to any who took time to listen.

On the Clann Uí Flaithimh side, a host of young boys and girls ignored pleadings from parents and grabbed buckets of water. During lulls in the battle, they scrambled along the stockade, slipping and sliding in pools of gore, strings of grey-pink guts, shite, piss, and limbs that seeped blood. Every warrior on the rampart cheered the gift of water and the bravery of the children. They half-heartedly cuffed the young ones as they passed and told them to get back to safety.

The Gauls' numbers were their advantage. They could afford to throw bodies at the wall. Losses were an acceptable price for victory. Now, the veterans entered the field. The besiegers' grip was tenuous on fence posts slick with their comrade's blood and gore. Splinters vied with blades to stab exposed flesh. Those who successfully surmounted the fence landed in the bloody slop that coated the walkway. Momentarily unsteady on their feet, they were vulnerable to a spear thrust or the slash of sword and axe.

Eventually, the frenzy of the assault descended into a grim clash of shields and slashing weapons. Blades no longer held their keen edge and were useful only as clubs. More effort was needed to deliver a killing stroke. Along the wall, small groups battered and hacked at each other with grim resolution. Chests heaved and muscles burned. Armour and weapons became intolerably burdensome. Movement became clumsy as exhausted minds failed to send orders to legs and arms. Instinct and experience won over enthusiasm. In the sky, Fate selected the harvest.

On the eastern wing of the battlements, the Gauls poured over the fence only to come face-to-face with a nightmarish creature. It wore the face of one who haunted their dreams. Had she stood before them as the Crone, wizened and ancient, the vision would have been more

155

acceptable. Instead, they were confronted by the awful beauty of the Sidhe. Blood seeped from shattered eardrums as she shrieked, calling out to the Ancients for power. Her cloak was long gone. Naked, save for the black ribbon fastened around her throat she slaughtered without mercy. The fabric hid a scar that was as deep as her soul and was never removed.

She stood before them. A tall, porcelain-skinned apparition. Like a newly sculptured statue, her skin was marble smooth and unblemished. No hair adorned her body, save the golden cloud that crowned her head. Her face, with its obsidian eyes, full ruby lips and fiery red cheeks, seized her victims' attention and froze their blood. Hearts felt as if they were clenched in a monstrous vice.

Symbols of power etched on her milk-white body glowed black and gold in the sunlight. In her right hand, an oak staff as hard as iron cracked the skulls of those around her. In her left, a curved sacrificial dagger dripped blood. As she whirled and danced, delivering death, it seemed that not the tiniest droplet of blood adhered to Mongfhionn's immaculate body.

Bouquets of fruit and honey mixed with sour breath wafted into Bláithín's nostrils. A hand touched her left shoulder. Instinctively she turned and lashed out with an axe that was bloody and pitted with blade strikes. Only a wine-soaked cry of surprise and the sight of Cuán stumbling backwards and over the edge of the walkway forestalled the blade's downward curve. A curse rose up from beneath the parapet. Her partner did not seem to appreciate his narrow escape from being cleaved from brow to breast. Furious and battle-tired, Bláithín screamed at the prone but unscathed, either from the fall or the fight, noble. "Why are you not with your men?" Left unsaid but clear to all nearby was the word "Coward."

By her side since dawn, Lonán grunted, "Well, that'll not help improve your relationship." The tall warrior shrugged and turned to meet two of the enemy as they scrambled over the fence. Gripped in two hands, his longsword swung, tearing a ragged gash across the throat of one. In one of the coincidences with which battles are replete, and which Fate loves, the sword cut the warrior's artery. The ensuing gush of bright blood blinded his companion. He felt but never saw Lonán's blade open up his stomach, almost cleaving his spine with its force.

Bláithín was in no mood to consider Cuán's feelings. She had fought on the wall since dawn. A multitude of cuts wept and mingled with the fluids of her victims. If a blade did not end her life, then poisoned blood might. When she walked, she felt the crust of gore that adhered to body and raiment resist and crack, sending dark flakes into the air. Her arms and legs ached. Her hand was permanently cramped grasping an axe shaft thick with gore. Her head throbbed, and her ears rang. The latter brought a quick smile to her lips and a flush of heat to her cheeks. It was a quick reminder of Brocc's gift, which had already saved her life many times.

Now, to cap it all, her bladder was bursting. She cursed the men around her. "Men have it easy," she hissed. Even in battle, they could quickly slip out their manhood and pee against the fence. From the pungent smell of urine, many thought even that too onerous and pissed as they fought. Men! A shouted warning made her duck and turn. She felt a breeze lift up a stray, damp strand of hair and the scrape of a blade as it slid along the neck guard of her helmet. She grunted at the sting of another cut.

Crouched and blade raised, she swung her short-handled axe in a vicious tight arc. Her opponent screamed and fell backwards. Blood pumped from the stump of a leg severed below the knee. The screaming did not last long. A spearman turned and with an economy born of experience stabbed downward. The young woman's flailing ceased as her head flopped to the side. Only tendons and gristle kept it attached to her torso.

With a quick nod and a hoarse, "Thanks," Bláithín turned to face her next opponent. "Shite!" she shouted and then clapped her hand over her mouth. Under the mask of battle-dust and blood, her face burned a deep shade of pink. Lady Bláithín's bladder had surrendered, and she had peed her pants. Around her, some chuckled. Many cheered.

CHAPTER 20

404 B.C.—Aremorio—Summer

It was the third river. The setting was idyllic. The stream, overflowing from the melting snows of spring, gurgled pleasantly. Silver-scaled fish leapt out of the water trying to catch flies. On a canvas of blue, sheep-shaped clouds touched the peaks of rust and purple-shaded mountains. The valley floor was level for about one hundred paces on either side before it climbed gently to grassy knolls fringed with leafy trees. Beyond the foothills, vast swathes of forestland were broken up only by farms and crops.

Nonetheless, to Mórrígan, there was something amiss about this particular scene. Unlike the sweat and industry of the water gatherers found at the previous rivers, these labourers seemed to undertake their task with nonchalant ease. Unguarded, horse and oxen teams lolled about, eating riverside grass and lapping up fresh water. Some cooled their legs in waters where tall, heavy-headed bulrushes swayed in the gentle breeze. Mórrígan dropped her hand and the band charged.

At the whooping of the mounted warriors and the sound of pounding hooves, the Gauls fled. But not before tossing sticks into the wagon carts. Mórrígan's nose wrinkled as she smelled smoke. Streamers of dense, dark soot rose into the air. Bricriu and Beacán Ó Cathasaigh pulled their horses to a halt alongside their sister. "The wagons are filled with straw, rags and kindling soaked in oil and pitch. It was fire-brands that were thrown into the wagons."

"It's a trap," snarled Mórrígan. In the same breath, she unslung her bow, knocked an arrow, and swivelled in her dillat to face Divico. The arrow sped from the bow. The fleeting look of sadness, resignation, and innocence in Divico's eyes told the Huntress she had made a grave error. Still, an arrow, once it has left the bow, cannot be recalled. The barb sunk deep into Divico's throat, cutting off any protest and erupting from the rear of his neck. Two more arrows thudded into his chest. They pierced his heart, instantly putting an end to his suffering. The shafts were Mórrígan's apology.

Confused, the remainder of Divico's men fell to arrows and blades. Only a handful escaped. They joined the false water-hauliers who ran to horses tethered nearby and galloped towards the crest of the hill on the west side of the river. "The Hag forgive me," muttered Mórrígan as she watched her men repeat her error. Too late, she realised that those riding for the hilltop were the guilty ones. Divico had been betrayed by his own men.

Frantically, Mórrígan scanned the surroundings. The trap had been sprung. Where and who was the hunter?

***

Crispus scratched his head and looked around him. Satisfied that no one was watching, he dipped a hand into the spring and cupped the cold water. He relished the refreshing liquid as it trickled down his throat. Once more he plunged his hand into the spring. This time the water was splashed over his head. Four men travelled with him—the remnant of his command. They too supped the waters cautiously. The reeds and rushes at the river's edge only gave partial cover. A few paces back from the spring, and river the grass was a waist-high, verdant sward of green with splashes of wild-flowers. Nevertheless, it provided little conceal-ment for the men.

The small band made their run for freedom when the Gauls be-gan the assault on the walls of Clann Ui Flaithimh. While not prisoners, they were encouraged to remain within their tents, and watched closely by a mix of Senone and Gaiscedach warriors. To their advantage, their guards appeared to trust each other even less than they did the Romans.

War-horns blasted out across the Gaul encampment. Their deep reverberations were felt as much as heard. There was little order to the advance on the Clann Ui Flaithimh defences. Chaos and distraction followed the massing of the tribes and continued as they lumbered forward. Internecine fights broke out as warbands jostled for position. Well before the Gaulish tribes had cleared their camp, a trail of the dead and injured littered the ground. In the confusion, Crispus and his men overpowered their guards and took possession of their weapons. Escape was not without a price. He lost men to the spears of several alert Gauls.

In reality, Crispus had not given much thought to the future beyond escaping from the Gaul encampment. His life had been one of service and following orders. Tactics and strategy were not a requirement. Only the ability to kill without remorse. The Roman's plan, if it could be called a plan at all, was to strike out east from the Gaul's camp. Once sufficiently distant, they would turn northwards either to the coast of the Muir nIocht and onward to Albu or keep more to the northeast and the lands of the Belgae. Life as a mercenary was the most optimistic outlook.

"Time to move. We'll cross the river here and keep travelling east. Stay alert. Keep your swords in your hands." His orders were met with a truculent grunt. The men were unimpressed with Crispus' leadership and probably would abandon him as soon as the opportunity presented. To their thinking, good fortune had been lacking under his command. That said, no one objected and they stepped into the slow-moving river. The group crossed the river without incident, emerging on the far bank with sighs of relief.

The riverbank swept up a long incline to a grassy crest, where stands of beech and ash stood as leafy sentinels. From the ridge, the panorama was breath-taking. In the far distance, mountains provided the border for a patchwork landscape of rolling hills, farms and farmlands, forests and marshland. To cross the land would be hard work, but not impossible.

And to their advantage, the terrain now provided lots of cover.

It occurred to Crispus that their journey would be much easier and swifter if they were mounted. From his hilltop perch, he spied a farm that was a short march distant. White smoke curled up from the scattering of buildings, signifying that the farm was inhabited. Hopefully, the occupants would have some horses and be open to selling them. If not, they would steal them. Crispus' hope for a stealthy approach was in vain. They were spotted by the men of the farm who ushered their women into a sturdy roundhouse, barricaded the doors and then grabbed whatever weapons were to hand—axes, hammers, pitchforks, and sickles. A solitary rider sped from the farm.

The ensuing skirmish was short and bloody. The Romans' battle training eventually prevailed over men more used to ploughing fields. No farmer survived the brawl. This was more due to the Romans' frustration and anger at a needless fight. Among the bodies that lay on the blood-soaked dirt were two of his men. Delayed by the men of the smallholding, the only horse and its rider were far in the distance, and likely heading at a fast gallop to the nearest hillfort. The alarm would be raised shortly. Crispus and his diminishing group would become the hunted again.

He cursed, "Let's see what is inside the home." His men grumbled sullenly and dismantled the hastily erected barricades. There was little in the farmhouse beyond food, beer, and women. A while later, having used the females to assuage their anger, Crispus ordered his remaining men to grab anything useful and meet him in the farmyard. As he crossed the threshold and left the gloom of the roundhouse, Crispus squinted at the bright sunshine and shaded his eyes with a hand. A shadow fell across him. A horse whinnied. Had the young rider foolishly returned?

Amodocus grinned maliciously at the man who stood in the entranceway. He was apparently a Roman, yet curiously not in uniform. Crispus looked desperately around him for an escape route. The Thracian shook his head. "There is nowhere to flee Roman. We are mounted and outnumber you." Amodocus gestured to his left. "One false move and, with their arrows, my Cretan friends will happily separate your balls from your shaft." Amodocus stared harshly at Crispus. "And yet, instinct tells me that you have more than us to fear."

At that, the Thracian cavalry parted, and a grey horse slowly cantered forward. Horse and rider were covered in a thick layer of reddish-white dust. It made both look as if they had come from a potter's shop. Their ghostly appearance sent shivers along Crispus' spine. His hands automatically went to his sword. Red lips, a garish contrast with the face, drew apart. "That would be an ill-advised move, Crispus Galerius Donatus, Captain in the army of Marcus Fabius Ambustus, Pontifex Maximus of Rome. *And*, if I am not mistaken, a specialist in siege weapons, especially ballistae."

"You're…" stammered Crispus.

"Dead?" snapped Gaius. "Is that the word you were searching for? I think not. Never trust a barbarian to finish the job."

Screams from the house diverted Gaius' attention. Two men struggled to exit the roundhouse while attempting to gather themselves together. Several arrows thudded into wooden posts supporting the roof, and they stopped. Gaius spoke to Amodocus, "Check the situation inside." The Thracian nodded to several of his men, who slipped from their mounts and strode inside. They were met with shrieking and screams.

Soon, Crispus and his men, together with the remaining residents of the farm, were lined up in the courtyard. For vastly different reasons each group looked anxiously at Gaius. "I can see that we will have a good long talk, Crispus. You likely have much to tell me." Crispus made to protest but was cut off with an imperious wave of Gaius' hand. "You *will* tell me what I want and need to know, with or without encouragement. I have men exceptionally skilled in loosening reluctant tongues. Many of my men have lost comrades and friends due to your treachery. I will have no shortage of volunteers."

Gaius looked to Crispus' companions. Their beseeching looks caused not a glimmer of mercy in Gaius' cold, red-rimmed eyes. With a gesture of contemptuous dismissal, he said, "These I have no use for." The dismay in the men's eyes increased when Gaius ordered them bound to the farm's fence. "They have had much pleasure without pay or permission. I'm sure the women of this household will reward their endeavours."

***

Mórrígan ordered her troop behind the water wagons. It provided some cover, although that assumed an attack would come from the west. Perched on a sweat-stained wagon-seat, she studied the hilltop looking for clues. A line of tall, spindly birch crowned the hill. The Huntress appreciated their silver beauty against the skyline, yet cursed their presence. She looked to her rear. Perhaps, they should make a dash for the other side of the river. The stream was broad but had a stoney bottom. Slow-moving waters came level with a horse's belly, so it was passable.

Matres adjusted her arse on the horse. Her smile was broad as she observed the activities of the queen of Clann Ui Flaithimh. Frankly, she was disappointed that the Huntress had fallen into her trap. Maybe her reputation was exaggerated. A ghoulish sneer settled on her face as she counted the dead Venelli. She admired the ruthlessness of the queen, even though she had been wrong and had reduced her force by half. She nodded to her second-in-command. Appointed by Concolitanus, he was her watcher and probably her executioner. He walked his mount to her side.

"Your men will flank them on the north and south. Mine will attack them directly."

The squat Gaiscedach warrior sat uncomfortably on a broad-backed dun and scowled at Matres. "One thousand against one hundred. This is not a worthy use of the king's army. Leave five hundred. The rest can join the assault on Clann Ui Flaithimh." Matres sighed and then breathed deeply. Without so much as a glance in the warrior's direction, the knife that had miraculously appeared in her hand was buried in the man's throat. He tumbled from his mount, clutching the knife and attempting to stem the gush of blood from the wound. His efforts were in vain. Had he managed to stop the loss of blood, the poison on the dagger's edge ensured his entry to Mag Mell.

"Any other objections?"

Mórrígan's options were reduced rapidly as the horns of the Gaiscedach signalled the attack. "Pick your targets. Make every arrow count." She nodded to Gràinne and instantly three chariots with spinning scythes drove forward. Horses galloped, and foot-warriors charged down the slope before her; others splashed in the river waters. Only a few hundred. The Huntress breathed easier. They had faced greater odds than this before and triumphed.

Bows now set aside, Mórrígan's cavalry hefted swords and axes. From their positions on the wagons and chariots, they slashed at the mounted Gaiscedach. Surprisingly, they had both a height advantage and a stable platform to fight from. Soon the carts ran crimson-red with the blood of her enemies. Mórrígan's twin bone-handled daggers flashed unceasingly in the spring sun. Her long arms seemed to rotate continuously in a circle, dealing out death to all who came within her reach. Blood splattered her from head to toe.

A second round of horns blew. The Gaiscedach gathered up the lightly injured and retreated. The badly maimed lay on the slush of blood and soil and cried out for mercy. The dead lay still, the last painful grimace on their face frozen forever. Mórrígan breathed harshly and tried to spit. She failed. She looked at the water barrel beside her and swore. It was empty. "Incompetent bastards," she muttered. As she watched the Gaiscedach withdraw, she prayed that they would not return. Her men and Gràinne's chariots had fought well. So far none had died, but many carried fresh wounds and gashes that would add to their scars. They would also constrain their ability to fight. A tired, bloodied band would not fare well if there were repeated assaults.

Matres chuckled. She had tested Mórrígan's resolve and dangled the glimmer of hope before her eyes. Now it was time to make the bitseach pay for her family's deaths. A raised arm dropped. The Gaiscedach horde crested the hilltop, and galloped or ran towards the river and their enemy.

"Shite!" moaned Mórrígan as she saw the Gaiscedach horde stampede down the long slope towards them. Most were on foot, which was something to be thankful for. The Huntress cursed, promising to make Conall pay for his charity when she spotted the female Gaiscedach assassin leading the charge. In an instant, Mórrígan recognised the situation was hopeless. Unless the Goddess came down and fought beside her, they could not hope to survive. She shouted, "Mount up. Ride for the other side of the river."

***

"Gaiscedach scum." Amodocus spat. No disagreement came from Gaius or Sarpedon. The Thracian had been impressed with how the Clann Ui Flaithimh queen had fought off the first wave of the Gaiscedach. He had been even more impressed when she quickly assessed her situation and ordered the retreat. Now the Clann Ui Flaithimh warband was midway across the river with the Gaiscedach only several hundred paces behind.

"You know what to do?" said Gaius.

Amodocus and Sarpedon nodded. "Keep the queen alive."

Gaius inclined his head to the queen. "Her life will be our gift to Conall. If Jupiter allows, it may be enough to prevent our immediate execution."

Mórrígan slapped her mare and kicked its sides with her booted feet. She felt terrible about doing this. Íar would not be amused. Yet she needed every ounce of effort and strength from the horse. Surrounded by her riders, muddy river water splashed her, soaking clothes and dillat. The eastern bank was tantalisingly close, but the screams of the Gaiscedach seemed closer. Mórrígan offered up a silent prayer to the

Goddess. In the skies above an eagle shrieked in response.

A nudge to her back drew a snarl from Mórrígan, and she swung around. She became aware that her men had stopped and shouted, "No! Keep moving." A tug on her shoulder elicited a sharp, "What?" It was then she noticed the warrior pointing to the riverbank. "Kiss the Hag's arse!" She exclaimed as she saw the Thracian cavalry and Cretan archers. A sharp ring on her helmet from a Gaiscedach slingshot snapped her back to her predicament. With a deep breath, she summoned up all of her strength and shouted, "Forward. There's only a hundred of them. We can break through."

Amodocus grinned. He could imagine the confusion in the Clann Ui Flaithimh queen's mind. He ordered his men and the Cretans back a hundred paces from the river's edge. The space would allow the Clann Ui Flaithimh to climb from the waters and regroup on the bank. As the first of Mórrígan's band clambered up an increasingly slippery bank, and onto the grassy verge, Amodocus' men dismounted. Together the Cretans and Thracians slipped bows from their backs and nocked arrows. Mórrígan shuddered and crouched to present a smaller target. This did not look good.

With a loud gulder, Amodocus shouted, "Down!" Out of self-preservation, Mórrígan slid from her horse. She was followed by the rest of her men. In the face of the Thracian and Cretan arrows, they would be slaughtered, even with the armour they wore. Eyes closed, Mórrígan prayed that the Goddess would watch over Conall and her children. She heard the familiar twang of bowstrings released, and the swish of air as arrows were guided to their targets. Then she heard the screams of the Gaiscedach. Caught in the river and lightly armoured, they had little defence to the barbs of their unknown attackers.

The Thracian jogged to stand beside Mórrígan. "We have sown confusion among the Gaiscedach. You need to follow us. Even with our arrows, they will breach the riverbank. We don't have the numbers to prevail."

"Why?"

"Later. We must withdraw *now*."

Mórrígan nodded and signalled to her band. Unsure about the motives of her new benefactors, she was caught between Scylla and Charybdis. She smiled. Her knowledge of Greek history had clearly improved with Nikandros' story-telling. A high-pitched shriek of anger drew Mórrígan's gaze back to the river. Midstream, a visibly annoyed and frustrated Matres screeched at her forces, cajoling and threatening them with the promise of severe punishments if they did not capture the Clann Ui Flaithimh queen, and gold if they did. Around her, beasts screamed as arrows plunged deep into velvet hides. Men were tossed from crazed mounts. Others tumbled backwards. The force of several arrows thudding into exposed chests propelled them into the river's blood-stained waters.

An arrow was nocked to Mórrígan's bow. She settled her stance, and with a grunt, she pulled the bowstring taut. Shoulder muscles tensed as the Huntress held her posture, waiting for the right moment. The black arrow sighed as it was released and sped towards Matres. Fate intervened. A fateful zephyr made its red and white fletching flutter. Matres' horse chose at that moment to rear up, stung by a Cretan arrow. The Huntress' arrow sunk not into Matres' chest, but into her thigh. It tore through muscles, pinning the Gaiscedach's leg to the flank of her mount. Rider and horse screamed in anger and pain.

"That bitseach has more lives than a cat," snarled Mórrígan as she leapt onto her horse and followed Amodocus up the long slope. Amodocus grinned. He was beginning to warm to the Clann Ui Flaithimh queen and wondered what her face looked like behind the battle dirt and ornate gold and silver decaled helmet. Only the deep green eyes and red hair gave him a clue. He pointed to an ancient oak that sat imperiously on the crest of the slope.

"Tell your band to ride for the oak. Do not veer much to either side." Mórrígan looked at the Thracian curiously. Did the man ever stop smiling? "We have a few more surprises for the Gaiscedach. They are persistent bastards. A few volleys of arrows and the river alone won't discourage them from their attack."

It was as they approached the crest of the hillside that Mórrígan's suspicions rose to nightmare levels. In the shadows of the sparsely populated line of beech, oak and birch trees familiar shapes were pushed forward to clear the treeline. Ballistae! She turned to Amodocus, a mix of fear and anger in her emerald eyes. Her jaw stiffened in a reasonable semblance of Conall. She opened her mouth to demand an explanation but was cut short as the ballistae pitched a rapid series of arms-length bolts at the Gaiscedach.

The shock of having once again underestimated her foes silenced Matres but only momentarily. The ballistae missiles cut through her ranks like a knife slicing honeycomb. Yet it was the confusion sowed that threatened Matres' attack. She rode through her warriors, now gathered on the riverbank. Commands were shouted to her captains. Threats were hurled at them, and in turn, they cursed and bullied their men to action. Once more the Gaiscedach moved forward and up the long grassy slope towards Mórrígan.

"A determined bunch. You must be worth a lot to their leader," said Amodocus. Mórrígan noted that the ballistae had ceased their furious volleys. "Perhaps your men should stand aside." Mórrígan, feeling atypically helpless, nodded and signalled to her band. A long, mellow blast from a horn sounded.

"No!" gasped Mórrígan. Her hands immediately went to her long knives.

From the treeline marched Gaius at the head of three rows, each of two hundred men. Commands of "Spears!" were shouted along the ranks and the long sarissas dropped, presenting a hedge of iron to the Gaiscedach.

"Romans! We are betrayed," shouted Mórrígan. She immediately found herself surrounded and Amodocus' dagger at her throat.

"Watch." He growled while not releasing the pressure on the blade.

Anger rumbled in the ranks of the Clann Ui Flaithimh as they watched their queen apparently taken captive. All veterans, most stayed their hands, looking for an opening where they might rescue Mórrígan. That is, apart from Gràinne who, longsword flashing in the sun, drove her chariot across the ranks of the Romans and towards the queen. The lithe apparition stormed towards the Thracians, who quickly moved to protect Amodocus. Mórrígan screamed, "No!"

It was uncertain who her command was aimed at—Gràinne or the Thracians, who were readying bows and heavy throwing darts. In the end, neither took heed. Gràinne continued her charge. The Thracians threw a volley of missiles at the oncoming chariot. The horse team bore the brunt of the darts and arrows. Pierced repeatedly, they collapsed. Likely as they finally stumbled, they were already dead. As they fell, the chariot pole dug into the soft earth, pitching the vehicle into the air. Driver and Gràinne were thrown from the cret. Dazed, Gràinne scrambled for her sword, only to feel a sharp pain in the back of her head before she lapsed into unconsciousness. Her driver was not so fortunate. He lay where he had landed, splayed across a large boulder. His neck and spine were broken.

Matres swore as she watched the Roman phalanx march down the slope. She outnumbered the Romans, but not by enough. The bastard Cretan archers continued to pick off her leaders. Her thigh ached. The flow of blood had stopped, and the fact that she was not dead suggested that no vital blood vessel had been severed. To face the Romans would be to further court disaster. Raising her bow above her head, Matres accepted the unpalatable truth. "Withdraw!" she shouted. She would retreat and lick her wounds in her fortress at Lugudunon and face Concolitanus' wrath at her foolishness.

***

Great deep-sounding horns reverberated across the battlefield. Slowly the Gaulish tribes disengaged and began the weary trek back to their camps. Feet dragged across the bloody earth, shoulders slouched. They were sullen-faced, for they had not tasted victory. That evening there would be few cries of camaraderie or tales of great duels fought and won.

Few gave a thought to the injured they passed and the plaintive cries for succour. They just wanted a good meal in their bellies, many horns of beer, and a quick rut with the camp whores. Hopes of an undisturbed night's sleep, however, were quickly dashed. Wolfhounds bounded towards the Gaul camp. The snuffles and growls of the ghost-grey hounds of Clann Ui Flaithimh as they prowled the encampment brought no rest.

Yet it was the terrors inhabiting their dreams that kept many awake. From the ramparts of Clann Ui Flaithimh, the monotonous drone of druidic chanting travelled far in the still night air. On the stockade, the Sidhe stood, oak staff in one hand, the other raised to the dark sky. Her dark, unblinking gaze held the camp in her mind. Soft yet ominous invocations continued from sunset to sunrise.

***

Across the campfire, Mórrígan and Gràinne simmered, looked sullenly at each other, and then at Gaius, Aquila—pale and missing his left arm—Amodocus, and Sarpedon. Gaius was plainly displeased. He stared at Gràinne and then, with a bite in his tone, spoke, "Your foolishness caused the death of a fine team of horses *and* your driver. Perhaps, for everyone, it would have been best if you too had gone to your Goddess." Gràinne avoided Gaius' gaze as she examined her toes, and herself. She had been stupid and rash in her actions. The death of her driver prayed on her mind. Worse, as she looked at Mórrígan, she saw the seed of doubt in the queen's eyes. Mórrígan had never held her responsible for her brother's accident. After today, would there be hesitation in her unconditional support?

"What do you want, Gaius Aurelius Atella?"

"I know your Law, Mórrígan, Queen of Clann Ui Flaithimh," said

Gaius. "You are in my debt."

"Our Law is not for Romans—or Thracians or Cretans," spat Mórrígan. The Huntress had still not thanked Gaius for the rescue of her band. It rankled that she could not be as pragmatic as Conall, who undoubtedly by now would be passing around the beer and wine and slapping backs. As queen, she knew it was her duty to thank, even reward, the Roman and his men.

"My men and I are outcasts from Rome. This is due in part due to my defence of Conall and my knowledge of the goings-on in Ériu that Marcus would rather not have broadcast. Now, I have discovered that Marcus has been trading heavy siege weapons with the barbarians. I cannot go back to my home until Marcus has been destroyed. Conall and I have a common purpose and enemy."

Mórrígan stood. In the flickering firelight, she gathered her thoughts. If her words were forced, her voice was steady as she spoke, "I thank you, Gaius Aurelius Atella, and your allies, for your intervention this day. Without it, we would undoubtedly have suffered grievous losses." She paused and then continued, "My men will depart at sunrise to re-join the battle with the Gauls. I will be agreeable to you accompanying us. I will leave it to Conall and the Chomhairle to decide your fate."

The Huntress smiled at Gaius. It was an unnerving smile. "You will, of course, need to make your peace with the Lady Sidhe. Since you have not rescued *her*, it will be interesting to hear what sacrifice she demands and whether you are willing to pay it." Mórrígan pointedly glanced at Gaius' crotch. "Perhaps, she may find your manhood an acceptable sacrifice." The men around the fire grimaced at the image and watched as Mórrígan and Gràinne strode away.

"Nice ass," said Amodocus.

"Which one?" asked Sarpedon.

"Both, I suppose." There was a rumble of agreement around the fire. Gaius was unusually quiet. He was thinking about the Sidhe and how his companions had no idea of what may lie before them.

CHAPTER 21

404 B.C.—Aremorio—Summer

Conall watched with barely contained amusement as his fierce guard were brushed aside. It was as if they had no more weight than a feather in a whirlwind. At the same time, Clann Ui Flaithimh's king reassured himself that his axe was within reach. These were dangerous times. Assassins were rarely obvious. Before him, hands on her hips, stood a small—she would reach his shoulders if she stood on tiptoes—black-haired woman. The hair was lustrous, waist-length, and tied back with a red ribbon. Scars on her hands and taut muscles on her arms told that she was not one to retreat from a fight. She had a full figure. *In her youth*, Conall thought, *she would have been very desirable*. Now, her brown eyes brimmed with anger and, if she could, she would be spitting fire from her full, red lips.

In her wake, the woman dragged a reluctant, slightly built, young woman. Around fourteen summers, Conall guessed, although he could be wide of the mark. She was tiny, a hand smaller than her companion. Unwashed, copper-red hair darkened with sweat hung limply on narrow shoulders. Her eyes, deep pools of shimmering blue, were already tainted with the realities of her chosen profession. Today, they were set off by a blue-black background. A quick glance would have suggested that she, like many of the women, had used a combination of plants and dyes to enhance her eyes. That would have ignored the bruises that emphasised her high cheekbones and the congealed scabs of blood on her lips.

"Put that bloody axe away," barked the woman. There was authority in her tone, and Conall instinctively made to obey. Then he laughed.

"To what do I owe the pleasure of your company, Dufach—*in the middle of a battle?*" Dufach was the unchallenged leader of the camp's whores from the Venelli tribe as well as those from Albu and Ériu.

"Bah! Men fight, and women wail," retorted Dufach. She tugged on her companion's hand propelling her forward to stand between them. "Take a look at this." She spat the words in a tone as bitter as wormwood. Her rage simmered. With a quick twist, she loosened the drawstring on the younger female's white léine. It fell to the wooden walkway, leaving the girl standing naked. "This is Laoise. Observe what one of your brave men did to her."

To many, Laoise had an enjoyable body. No hair graced the mound between her thighs. Her breasts were small, no more than the size of one of her clenched fists, and her nipples and areolae dark. She was almost boyishly slender. Conall quickly took this in as his own anger rose. Had Laoise been standing in the burning red glow of the morning sun, her body would have seemed painted in bright colours. In the shade of the stockade, it was a mass of ugly red, purple, and green-yellow bruises and bites. Fist and boot marks were visible both back and front. Long, thin red lines criss-crossed her torso—as if a knife-point had been dragged over her skin.

"Being a whore is a tough life. No one needs abuse like this."

Dufach spoke from experience. Sold by her family when she was barely thirteen summers, it was the only way to escape their debts. Her owner raped her and beat her daily. It was his way of educating her as to her future path. She was soon put to work for him. With her youth, big breasts, and firm arse, Dufach was very popular and made a lot of gold for her owner. She was later to reflect that being a whore did not require much training. Three positions—on your back with legs spread, bent over and skirt raised, and on your knees to suck—were all a good whore needed to master. There was a career path of sorts. After all, she now had a large stable of whores.

"I agree," said Conall. "Do you have a name?"

"It was Cuán Ò Neill. That man has a mean streak in him."

"I will speak with Cuán. The druid, Crum Dubh, will decide on the appropriate restitution." Conall turned to Laoise. "I am sorry for your pain. Go to Fionnbharr or Mongfhionn. They will provide any salves that may heal you faster, at no cost." Thankful to escape, the young woman said, "Thank you, sir," grabbed her léine, made an awkward curtsy, and dashed off. On her way, Laoise bumped into a tall woman as she sped away. She mumbled, "Sorry, my Lady," but did not stop.

Cheeks flushed with anger, Bláithín Ni Neill turned to Lonán. She had overheard enough of the conversation. "Did you know about this?" she said through clenched teeth. Lonán did not have to answer. His inability to meet Bláithín's gaze told her all she needed to know. "Brothers. Bastards, the both of you." She turned and stormed off. She had taken only a few paces when she recalled the colour of the girl's eyes and hair. They were the match of hers. "Bastards!" she screamed.

Lifted up by a gust of air, a thin tress of hair fell across Dufach's face. She rubbed an arm across her brow. Conall noted the streaks of dried blood on Dufach's arm and hand. "How goes it with the wounded?" The king was acutely aware that without the assistance of the camp whores, the healers would not be able to cope either during or immediately after battles. In a strange twist of life, whores made excellent carers. And they were not at all squeamish.

It was with sad eyes and resignation that Dufach replied, "Some are beyond healing. There are ones who can't face a future without an arm or a leg. Others fear to be a burden for their kin." She sighed and tapped her leg. Strapped to her thigh, concealed by her dress, a dagger rested in a bronze-covered, wooden sheath. "We keep our knives sharp. One final suck of their manhood or the sight of a pair of full tits eases the pain as a blade slips between ribs. They enter Mag Mell with a smile."

***

Bláithín was furious. She was dirty, sweaty, and smelt of stale piss. She needed a bath to sluice the bloody grime of battle from her body but knew that was a faint hope. Yet, this in itself may have been bearable. After all, her state was no different from the thousands around her. None raised an eyebrow or crinkled a nose as she stomped past. What most did not have was a hand-fast partner who had been whoring around, and who apparently liked abusing one who, on the surface, partially resembled her.

"Sick bastard!" she screamed to no one in particular. It raised a cheer and round of agreement from her men. The sound of feet pounding the wooden walkway behind her made her stop and turnabout. Thinking it was Lonán, she shrieked, "Stay away from me." An instant later she realised her error as she saw Brocc hold up his hands in mock surrender. Like her, he was covered in the dust and bloody debris of battle. Yet, he also looked strong, handsome, and available. Like many on the ramparts, the bulge in his crotch signalled that he had not quite recovered from the excitement of the fight. Some would find a whore… others would relieve themselves with a steady hand.

Brocc found his hand seized and he summarily dragged along the walkway, although not unwillingly. Feverishly, Bláithín looked around for some cover. A small piece of privacy. In the shadow of the walkway steps, she pulled Brocc down to the dirt. Her hands slipped under his pants and grabbed his firm arse. "Take me. Please. Take me." She flinched, ashamed at the begging tone in her voice. Yet, she could not bear the thought of him refusing. He lifted up his arse. Her hands undid the tyings of his pants, and she held his manhood. It felt warm, pulsating as she stroked it. She looked into his hazel eyes and begged, "Please."

He smiled, "Perhaps I should remove your helmet." Bláithín nodded, but she was not about to release her hold on his throbbing staff. As her helmet rolled to the side, he pressed his lips against hers. Tongues fought a mock battle in which there were only winners. She felt her pants tugged down and a warm breeze caress the thick, fire-red hair of her mound. Her legs parted. She still held him tight, afraid that he might change his mind. That he would see the madness, the folly, of their passion.

"Please. Take me. Take me hard. There will be other times for gentleness." In the dirt and mud, Brocc penetrated Bláithín. She felt the cool mud cover her arse as he thrust in and out of her. She imagined herself a naive girl, convinced by the local stud to spread her thighs for the first time. It was wicked and dirty. She cried out as he burst inside her. Their rutting brought a rush of deep, satisfying pleasure as she orgasmed.

They lay in each other's arms, panting, trying not to overthink what had transpired. She had never been unfaithful. Her lovemaking with Cuán at its best had been timid. It was her duty to give him children. Pleasure was secondary, if even that. Bláithín felt her breastplate fall away as Brocc unbuckled the straps. She could not prevent the smile forming on her lips, and moaned as his hand slipped under the light shirt that protected her skin from the chaffing of the armour. He enfolded her breast, and his fingers teased her nipple. Engulfed by the desire to have him inside her again, she stroked his cheek.

"I may not be very good at this," she said, her voice hoarse from the battle and husky from her lust. She had never had a man's shaft in her mouth. Now she bent over and took the semi-erect manhood in her mouth. Her head bobbed up and down as she sucked and licked. The reward for her endeavours was not long in arriving, and she once more pleaded, "Please."

CHAPTER 22

404 B.C.—Cnocán-Mórrígan—Summer

Curses and the noise of breaking pottery and splintering wood warned Bláithín that there was at least one intruder in the roundhouse. She guessed the target. The locked, iron-bound chest held the substantial dowry she had received from her father. Her father was a wise man, and suspicious of the persona presented by her chosen partner. Thus, the dowry was given with restrictions. The primary constraint being that none of the wealth could be used without her permission. It proved to be a constant source of conflict with Cuán. Bláithín turned to her children and whispered, "Run. Fetch Lonán."

A wise course of action would have seen Bláithín wait outside until help arrived. But in threatening situations sometimes folly precedes wisdom. Bláithín slipped the dagger from its sheath, edged inside, and crept slowly across the wooden floor towards the din. Anger replaced apprehension when her eyes, having grown accustomed to the gloom of the home, saw that it was Cuán who was furiously attacking the chest.

"By the Hag and the Goddess. Have you lost your mind?" she screamed.

Startled, Cuán swung around, advanced towards his partner and, with menace in his voice, snarled, "I need gold. Give me the key, bitseach."

Holding the dagger steady, although her arms still ached from the battle, Bláithín drew herself up. It did not cross her mind that Cuán could be violent to her. "The dowry is for our children and our old age. I will not allow it to be frittered away to settle your wagers." For a brief moment, the anger in Cuán's eyes was replaced with pleading and desperation. It almost moved Bláithín to sympathy for whatever predicament into which her hand-fast partner had fallen. She hesitated, and her blade lowered. That Cuán could move so quickly caught her by surprise. The backhanded blow struck her forcefully on the cheek. Stunned, and with the metallic taste of blood in her mouth, she crashed to the floor.

"Wagers. If only it were that simple." An unpleasant sneer took command of Cuán's voice as he bent over and, with both hands, ripped Bláithín's light, under-armour shirt. A stream of drool flowed from one side of his mouth as he gazed on her exposed breasts. The violence stirred his passions. Perhaps there was time. He shook his head as if to clear his thoughts. Gold was the priority. Reaching down he grasped the brass key that hung from a gold chain around her neck.

"Step away from Bláithín. *Now!*" The tone brooked no refusal. Cuán hesitated.

"The gold is mine by right. The bitseach has no right to refuse me its use."

Disgust overlaid the anger on Lonán's lips. "You dishonour the *Lady*. Release your grasp on the key. Step away." With less belief, Lonán added, "We can resolve this as a family." Cuán looked into his brother's hard eyes and then to the sword held firmly in his hand. "You are not good enough or fast enough, brother."

"You and she have conspired to hasten my death." With a cry of anguish, Cuán ran past Lonán and his sons, and away from the stone and wood house.

***

Men and women, exhausted and bloodied, slumped against rough wooden posts or lay down on walkways still wet from the gore of battle. They would rest, some would sleep, and then they would eat. In a short while, the half-light of dusk would make way for the inky blackness of night. It gave further respite, for who but assassins and murderers fight at night?

At the centre of the clann's encampment, away from the battle lines, and a good one thousand paces back from the main defences, stood the mound and small—a thousand men standing shoulder-to-shoulder could encircle it—hillfort of Cnocán-Mórrígan. The cultural and spiritual centre of Clann Ui Flaithimh, it was a pleasant and peaceful location and a refuge from battle. Strains of flute and harp music drifted over its walls, joining with the chants of the druids to wash the tiredness from weary limbs and spirits. Noted for being home to the royal family as well as many members of the Chomhairle, it was also the healing quarters and residence of the druids. In the many small buildings that surrounded the grey-stone broch at its heart, skilled craftsmen and artisans plied their trades.

A high wooden stockade and ditch ran along the mound's perimeter. This evening, as the barbarian tribes retreated from the main defences, five hundred nervous warriors heaved a sigh of relief, set their shields against the fence, and relaxed a little. The hillfort was manned by the newest recruits. Most were callow, being aged between fourteen and fifteen summers. They looked uncomfortable in their armour. Many had not learned to view their weapons as part of themselves.

Still, theirs was not a trivial command. During times of trouble, the offspring of the hierarchy of the tribe dwelled within Cnocán-Mórrígan. Yet this evening the young men and women on the stockade stood confidently. In the unlikely event of the main defences being overrun, their place would be taken by the veterans of the army. There was no reason to fear anyone within the greater encampment. They were of the tribe. They were Clann Ui Flaithimh. And the clann was united with Conall.

They were mistaken.

A prolonged shriek of agony disabused them of their security. The grappling hook snared shoulder flesh and bone before pinning the unfortunate to the soft pinewood stake. His friends looked on in shocked silence as their comrade writhed in agony and bled out on the walkway.

Soon they heard hundreds of irons rattle against the fence before biting in to secure a grip. The clunk and thud of ladders soon followed. Unseen, the rebellion had percolated through dark alleys beyond the hillfort to reach the dark shadows at the foot Cnocán-Mórrígan's ramparts.

Panic struck and fear grasped young hearts. In danger of being overwhelmed, only the roar of a great bear, or in this case Urard, averted disaster. "You are the shield wall. You will hold or die. Lock scíatha. Heft javelins. Give no quarter. Those with torches—thrust the flames into the bastards' faces. Let them fight with their hair on fire." Battle-axe, Breith, in hand, the massive warrior prowled the catwalk, carving meat with impunity. In his wake followed his partner, Iasg. Her forte—throwing knives sheathed in two leather belts that crossed her chest—quickly found homes in lightly armoured torsos. When her blades were gone, she turned to the pair of small axes that hung at the rear of her belt.

Cries from the entranceway's guard-posts drew Crum Dubh's attention. The Lawgivers and healers were also well-known for their skill with the sword. Thus, it was with unsheathed blades that Crum and his score of druids dashed to secure the gateway's two stations. A similar number of the camp's whores, who, during battle, nursed the injured to health or death, followed in the wake of the priests. Their primary skills may have been carnal, but they also were artists with a knife.

The entrance was the main point of attack, and hence was where the most experienced rebels, many outcasts from the army, were concentrated. Heavy oak gates shuddered as makeshift rams slammed against them. The leader of the rebellion swore as the give in the wood resisted the battering and held the besiegers at bay. The guard towers were awash with blood. Caught by surprise, their young sentinels were no match for veteran soldiers or brawlers. Dropping to the dirt, the attackers ran to withdraw the gates' large locking bars and give their comrades access to the fort. Their tactic was logical but ill-timed. Confronted by an implacable Crum Dubh, the men, more used to backstabbing and brawls in the camp's drinking dens, fought without order and fell to the druids' swords. The whores quickly scampered up the posts' ladders. Besiegers screamed as wickedly sharp blades sliced across eyes and throats.

The blare of horns from Cnocán-Mórrígan alerted Conall to an, as yet, undefined danger within the encampment. His first thoughts were that the barbarians had left people behind and one of the smaller gateways had been breached. With each step towards the small hillfort, his anger rose. In the flickering light of torches, fires and braziers, before him was a scene from the Otherworld. Brogues from Clann Ui Flaithimh fines brayed with malice as the rebels scaled the stockade or attempted to smash and overrun the gateway. "Find Carmag," he shouted to one of his caomhnóirí. The faithful two hundred had followed their Rí. "Tell him to put down this rebellion. No quarter is to be given."

Once the intent and force of the rebellion were known, the reckoning was swift. Conall led his veteran caomhnóirí against the insurgents who attacked the main gateway. In numbers, the sides were approximately equal. Yet, the attackers had no answer to the spears of a shield wall that stabbed them. Cornered and without hope, like vermin they bared teeth, only to wish they were as small as rats and could scuttle away into the darkness. Those attempting to scale the stockade found themselves bludgeoned with clubs. Carmag's forest people took out their frustration at not having participated in the main battle by reducing bodies to a bloody pulp.

***

Dawn's light swathed the dead in garish beauty. Of the hillfort's garrison, only half had survived, and many of those had grievous wounds. Overseen by the druids, the dead lay in neat rows within Cnocán-Mórrígan. They waited in peaceful silence. Soon they would be washed by the tears of distraught mothers and sisters while the fathers and brothers called for justice and bloody vengeance. Of the thousand or more who rebelled, fewer than four hundred were alive at sunrise. They were guarded, outside the walls of the fort, by the grim-faced Cinn Péinteáilte from Northern Albu.

"Mercy," croaked the rebel leader. On his knees, he briefly looked up into the cold, cruel eyes of Conall and shivered. Yet his eyes flickered constantly from side to side, searching for the faintest opportunity to escape. Perhaps he could inspire his followers to one last act of idiocy. With their sacrifice, he might slip away in the chaos. Did he have information sufficient to trade for his life? Did the king know of Cuán Ó Neill? His hope was in vain.

"Mercy?" Conall looked to the Sidhe. "The Lady is not noted for compassion, and you sought to do harm to her offspring, and to mine, and to the sons and daughters of the Chomhairle. There is no forgiveness in this place." Conall unsheathed his sword and tossed it on the ground before the rebel leader. "Here is my justice. You have two choices. Fall on the blade or fight me." The man looked at the sword. He licked cracked lips. His shoulders slumped. His chin fell to his chest. "Coward," spat Conall. Behind the rebel, cries and sobs arose from the bloodied insurgents. Any hope of final glory was ephemeral.

"Bind and nail him to the gates of Cnocán-Mórrígan. Disembowel him. He can watch his followers staked and listen to their death cries while he rots." A great wail arose from the kin of the rebels crowded on the ramparts. "Quiet! Or join these traitors." roared Conall. "Many brave young warriors are in Mag Mell because of your kin. My mercy is that you live. Do not make me regret my kindness."

CHAPTER 23

404 B.C.—Cnocán-Mórrígan—Summer

It started with a pleasant and welcome pitter-patter. The parched terrain exhaled and gurgled as it supped the refreshing rainfall. Senses tingled, invigorated by the earthy smell of a refreshed land. On the battlements of Cnocán-Mórrígan and along the long rampart wall, deep lungfuls of air were gulped. Smiles creased the faces of the besieged as they listened to the gentle drumming of raindrops on wood. Conall looked to the skies, enjoying the water washing over his face. It was a pleasant interlude.

Dark, dense clouds rolled in, bullying the weaker threadlike filaments. The pale sun was quickly banished. Thunder followed. Bright daylight flashes of lightning seared eyes. Rods of liquid iron pounded the earth. Hail the size of quails' eggs thrummed and cracked against the stockade. No eyes could penetrate the wet curtain beyond one hundred paces.

In their camps, the barbarians wailed and cried out in pain and anger. The gods showed no partiality or mercy to Gaul or Gael. Driving winds plucked the tents of the Gauls from the earth. Hail punched through the flimsy coverings. In Cnocán-Mórrígan and its surrounds, sodden thatched roofs collapsed. Furious torrents streamed off the mound to collect in great pools at the foot of the ramparts.

The stockade and walkways were long deserted. Warriors trembled. Only the Sidhe stood on the ramparts, naked and with hands stretched high towards the roiling skies. Mongfhionn revelled in the power of the storm. It sustained her. Above the roar of the wind, all could hear the Sidhe's chants.

Water flowed into the trench that ran along the Clann Ui Flaithimh wall. It was not long before the channel overflowed. The land sloped gently away from the ditch. Bloated bodies, previously trapped, escaped their snares and rose to the surface. Cadavers floated morbidly and slowly towards the far edge of the trench, seizing a final opportunity to escape. Rats, fat on feasting on the dead and unwilling to surrender their feast, sunk sharp teeth into the corpses. They could offer only feeble resistance to the will of the waters.

For seven sunsets the rain demonstrated to the warring Gaels and Gauls the puniness of their campaign. Now, in a calm dusk of flushed gold and orange, Conall looked first to Mongfhionn and then to the sight that confronted him. The Sidhe was draped in her usual grey cloak, although normal was a matter of opinion when it came to the Lady. Both looked with awe on a land transformed. It was as if the gods had resculpted the landscape.

Torrential rains had washed away light soils, leaving deep veins of clay and rock. Bogs, long since dried up with cold winters and hot summers, now stretched black, deep, and ominous. Large pools of stagnant water dispersed across the land reflected the morning sun like mirrors. Trenches gushed with new river waters. Under the sun's growing heat, the terrain was verdant and splashed with blooming wildflowers. Small copses of oak and birch surveyed their new demesne with equanimity.

Pale white-green corpses were scattered aimlessly over the ground. They still moved. This time they heaved with maggots, gorging on dead flesh. The stench of rotting meat rose up on steaming vapours. The smell was intensified by those of rotting wool and leather, and unwashed feet. Piles of clothing lay randomly discarded. It was fortunate that the season was not winter. The Cinn Péinteáilte laughed at the forced, uncomfortable nakedness of their comrades.

"Well, póg ma thoin!" exclaimed Conall, partly in wonder, partly in frustration.

Beside him, the Sidhe smiled. "A change of battlefield. A change of tactics."

Conall nodded. The quagmire before him would be a nightmare for his cavalry and a challenge for the shield wall. "There remain wide tracts of land for fighting. They are just not close to the ráth. Our margin for retreat is diminished." Conall called to Deaglán Ó Neill, who hovered nearby. "Ask the Chomhairle and the ceannairí na míle to meet in my broch. We need to plan a battle."

* * *

Hunted and haunted, he lived in the comforting embrace of the gloom. This night, with a clay wine goblet gripped unsteadily in one hand and a wineskin held in the other, a plainly drunk Cuán zig-zagged along a walkway shrouded in deep shadows. He stopped at a firing platform. That he avoided falling over the edge was more luck than design. Slippery in patches from the lichens and fungi that sprouted after the rains, the boardwalk's surface was treacherous. Vermin, gorged on human flesh, lumbered along the walkway.

Cuán's mind seemed incapable of focus. *I am bewitched*, he thought. What other explanation could there be for his recent behaviour? He had become a bitter man, full of regrets and unfulfilled dreams. He drank too much. Foolish ambitions had spawned a rebellion, although even that had spun out of his control. He was estranged from Bláithín. He had struck out at her. The blow was hard by intent. Branded a traitor by Conall, the Lady would never tolerate Cuán's presence. An outcast of the tribe, revenge or retribution was a certainty.

His brother, Lonán, infuriated by his behaviour, had disowned him. He had pissed off Eirnín Mac Gabhann with his continual snide remarks about his brother. Eirnín, it turned out, was mightily angry at Conall, but blood was blood. The Cróeb-Ruad warriors brought from Ériu were no longer loyal to Cuán. They had assimilated into the shield wall, and their allegiance was to Conall, the clann, and the comrades who stood with them. Rumours circulated about Bláithín and Brocc Ò Cathasaigh. Cuán dismissed this as camp gossip. Bláithín was of noble birth. Brocc was a mere commoner.

A plague on Conall Mac Gabhann, he thought.

Finding himself at an impasse, he flailed around for a solution, a rationale, but his mind continued to light upon those he deemed to be disloyal or could accuse of mischief. If indeed he was bewitched, then that put the blame on the Sidhe and Mórrígan. Perhaps, even Crum Dubh and his accursed band of druids. He cried out in despair to the Goddess. She ignored his self-indulgent whining. He drained the dregs of wine from the skin and tossed it and the goblet into the ditch.

He wanted to inhale deeply, but the stench from the ditch was overpowering. On his knees, his hands rested on the platform. Nauseous from too much wine and the cloying smell of death, his belly heaved and disgorged its contents. Wiping vomit from his mouth, Cuán rose unsteadily. He attempted to grip the stockade, but instead, his hands fell on the shoulders of a tall warrior.

"Fool," hissed a vaguely foreign accent. It was a night with few clouds and many stars. Cuán looked into eyes made blacker and more malevolent by the silver moonlight. The coldness of fear made his body shiver. Frantically, he looked around for help. "No one will come to your rescue. You have no friends, no allies. Even your enemies hold you in contempt." The assassin paused, "Still, your amateur bumbling cannot be allowed to foil plans that have been laid by those with power."

Cuán felt the point of the sword press on his belly. He should have cried out at the sharp pain, but wine dulled his senses. The shock of the twisting motion of the weapon silenced his vocal cords. Thrust into Cuán's abdomen, the blade followed a straight line parallel to the walkway. Its bloody exit was hidden by Cuán's cloak. He gasped as the edge cut through his stomach before it was withdrawn.

The alcoholic haze dissipated with the pain. Forcing himself to remain standing, he faced his assailant. The attacker was shrouded in a dark cloak. A metal breastplate glinted in the moonlight. As the moon emerged from behind a cloud, it bathed the face in silver light. Cuán coughed, "Bastard," in grim recognition. It was of little help or consequence. His only satisfaction was in the spray of blood that spotted his murderer's face. The wound was mortal. His guts already lay coiled on the walkway. He lurched towards his assassin. It was a well-intended, even a brave, act. He could only grip the cloak. *Perhaps, he could hold on until someone passed by.* A hand was placed firmly on his chest. Cuán tumbled over the platform's edge and into the ditch.

***

Barely recognisable, the bloated shell that was Cuán Ò Neill was discovered several days later by one of the burial and scavenging teams. A trail of maggots and clouds of blue-black flies marked the path of the body as it was dragged from the foul-smelling ditch. Mid-morning, Tadhg Ò Cuileannáin was summoned to the king's broch. He approached with a heavy heart and strong suspicions. Rumours of Cuán's demise had spread like wildfire throughout the settlement. Conall, Mongfhionn, Fearghal, Crum, and an ashen-faced Bláithín sat around a solid wood table stained with grease and beer. Their countenances were etched with worry and sorrow.

Conall spoke first, "Cuán Ò Neill has been murdered. A sword thrust to the belly. The weapon has not been found." Tadhg nodded. There was little to say. It was unlikely the blade would ever be found, and there were very few uniquely-shaped weapons in the camp.

"Suspects?"

"The list is long."

"You wish me to investigate?"

"I know this displeases you Tadhg, but you are the best to get to the bottom of this heinous and tragic act. For what it is worth, you are now raised to the rank of ceannairí míle with the full authority of that status."

Tadhg dipped his head, "Thanks, my king." He paused and then asked, "The body?"

"You have until dusk to examine the remains." Conall nodded in the direction of the druid. "Crum will take you to where the corpse is resting and will ensure that all respect is paid to the noble." Tadhg shrugged. He doubted that a corpse would be much interested in proprietary.

At sunset, the funeral pyre for Cuán Ò Neill, Rí Clochar and captain of the Cróeb Ruad, blazed high into the night sky. Conall and the Chomhairle stood alongside the Ò Neill family. They were ringed by the thousand Cróeb Ruad who had followed Cuán from Ériu.

***

As he walked away from the fire, a hand pressed on Conall's forearm. "You play a dangerous game, Conall Mac Gabhann, Rí Ruirech of Clann Ui Flaithimh. You already know who murdered the foolish Cuán Ó Neill. I saw it in your eyes when *you* examined the corpse and when *you* removed that scrap of cloth from Cuán's grip. The threads are fine, resembling those you have carried since the day your Ma was defiled at the hands of Cassius Fabius Scaeva but are of a deeper red. Yet Cassius is dead—executed by your own hand. And Marcus has never travelled far from Rome."

Jaw set, Conall made to wrench the hand from his arm. Instead, he held it firmer, as if needing the strength it represented. "You and I both know that there was always more than one agent of Rome in Ériu. I think, however, that only one remains. He watches me, and I watch him."

"You put Tadhg in peril. He is not experienced enough to face this enemy. Yet, he will pursue relentlessly and regardless of the cost."

"It has to be. My enemy will expect an investigation. *We* will pull Tadhg back from the edge when needed."

"You place too much reliance on my powers, Conall. And, too great a responsibility on me. I am Aes Sidhe. From our underground palaces, we devise plans, we meddle, and we guide the affairs of men to our own ends. We are not allowed to become involved."

Conall gave Mongfhionn's hand an affectionate squeeze and looked upward. Two eagles circled. "You have suffered for us. If the Aes Sidhe do not approve, I know the Goddess does."

CHAPTER 24

404 B.C.—Cnocán-Mórrígan—Early Summer

In armour of burnished bronze, crimson plumes trailing from the crest of a helmet that enclosed most of his face, there was no doubt that, sat astride his jet-black horse, the Spartan cut an impressive figure. Nikandros shifted his arse on the thick, purple dillat, and gazed along the assembled ranks of the Clann Ui Flaithimh army. Then he snorted. Several raised eyebrows queried his 'comment'. The Spartan laughed and pointed to Carmag and Brandubh's Cinn Péinteáilte arrayed on both flanks of the shield-wall. "Not long ago *I* was mocked for wearing scant clothing. Now, *I'm* the modest one among thousands of warriors, male and female, who rush into battle as naked as the day they were born."

He shrugged. "Strange times."

Battles are the bloody meat sandwiched between the celebration of life and remembrance for the dead. As with all mêlées, there is a festive atmosphere before the slaughter. Brightly coloured flags and banners of king, tribe, clann, and fine flapped in the morning breezes. From the ramparts of the Clann Ui Flaithimh ráth, trumpets and pipes sounded, and bodhráns pounded out a low, chattering rhythm. Shouts and songs were raised by young and old.

The Goddess had been given her due. Rivers, bogs, and deep pools gleamed with sunken treasure and suits of armour. Within the ranks of the warriors, good-natured craic and insults were traded. Final adjustments, borne of custom, habit, and superstition, were made to armour, scíatha, and weapons. The wealth of the tribe was on display as heavy torcs and armbands of gold, silver, and copper glittered in the sunlight. It was more than understandable why bodies were thoroughly searched after a battle. Families could gain wealth more than sufficient for many seasons.

After the fight, the survivors would drink copious volumes of beer and wine. Fallen comrades would be remembered with a fondness that often belied reality. Tall tales of heroic duels were recounted, becoming part of the tribe's inheritance. Thankful to be alive, or not severely maimed, warriors would engage in bouts of feverish carousing and rutting. Bloody hand- and fingerprints would be left on pale breasts, arses, and manhoods.

Eventually, alcohol, while intensifying desires and lusts, would leave the flesh unable to consummate. Like a rash, arguments and fights would break out, only to be subjugated with more beer and curtailed by the need to void stomachs and bladders. In the morning they would wake with pounding heads, thick fur-covered tongues, sour mouths—and more bruises. But they would thank the Goddess. For at least they were alive.

***

"She's a warrior, a leader of her tribe, and a beautiful woman." Torcán's words elicited a sigh of pity from Brocc. "That obvious, is it?"

His friend smiled, "That you convinced Fearghal our céadta should stand as a fence while the slingers and archers of the Ravens shower the Gauls with missiles was an accomplishment—if not a very clever one. Our chances of survival are not good. Nonetheless, you cannot protect her from all harm, and she would not want you to. That path only leads to disaster… for both of you."

Torcán gazed over his shoulder at the assembled ranks of the Ravens. Each sported a single black feather that hung from a long, thin, tight braid of hair. Like a flock of birds, the feathers rustled in the morning breezes. For most, the feather was the only compromise to their nakedness. The swirling, indigo-blue designs that covered their bodies were the armour of the Cinn Péinteáilte. Spear-butts were rammed into the soft dirt. Small shields lay face-down beside them. At this time, the Ravens unwound the slings that rested around their waists and felt the weight of pouches of river-smoothed stones. Among them, two hundred archers tested the strings of their bows.

The pugnacious warrior lofted his sword and shield and roared, "Conall-Abú!" His battle-call was taken up by his and Brocc's céadta.

From the Ravens, a loud and instantly recognisable female voice rang out, "Torcán-Abú!" It was both compliment and embarrassment. To his chagrin, it was taken up by the mass of Mòrag's warriors. Brandubh, Mòrag's brother and prince of the Ravens, shook his head at his sister's impetuosity. The sound of hooves drew Torcán's gaze to the black beast that towered over him. Toirneach snorted, pawed at the damp ground, and dipped his head several times as if to give the prologue to his Master's words.

"Do I need to be worried, Torcán?" asked Conall, his face grave and eyes unblinking. "Perhaps, you're looking for promotion—ceannairí na míle? Perhaps even Rí?" Torcán felt the purple blemish on his throat throb. Eyes on the ground, his mouth opened to protest his innocence, but only a frog's croak emerged. On the point of dropping to his knees, the bluff warrior heard a ripple of chuckles from behind. Risking a look at his king, he was confronted not with a grim visage, but with a king barely able to stop himself from laughing.

"*Aon ghéilleadh*—no surrender, Torcán," said Conall as he bent over Toirneach's broad shoulders and reached out a hand.

"Aon ghéilleadh, my king," replied Torcán as he grasped his Conall's forearm.

As Conall rode away, Torcán breathed a deep-felt, "Shite!" And then, with more bravado than he felt, muttered, "Bastard's eyes must have been inherited from the Hag." It was then a second dark shadow fell across Torcán. The hulking figure of Urard stood before him, his giant axe Breith resting in bear-paw sized hands.

"Beware Torcán. The king has a sense of humour. "*I don't.*""

Bláithín stood on the ramparts close to the gateway and scanned the field for a sign of Brocc. Several sunsets had passed since Cuán's funeral, and Brocc had kept a respectful distance. Yet the rising panic and pounding in her heart were a testament to both her need for Brocc and a fear that the death of Cuán might drive them apart. Furthermore, it did not take a genius to figure out that she was a prime suspect in the murder of her hand-fast partner. The fading bruises that accented her high cheekbones were motive enough. And then there was her nascent affair. She regretted her dalliance with Brocc, but only because it placed him equal with her as a suspect.

A movement to her right caused Bláithín to turn her head. The tall figure of Mongfhionn was in an intense discussion with Cúscraid. As usual, Cúscraid had been given charge of the defences—and the people. In the event of a retreat, it would be up to him, his five hundred, Crum's band of druids, and the embryonic Clann Ui Flaithimh militia to hold the walls until what remained of the army was safe. As if sensing Bláithín's gaze, the Sidhe looked up and smiled. It was a smile of recognition. Not the least, and given her protectiveness over Conall, Mongfhionn was also a suspect in the murder of Cuán. Ironically, the one thing in the Sidhe's favour was the lack of ritualistic disembowelment and that Cuán's heart remained in his chest.

To put her distractions aside, Bláithín examined Conall's chosen battlefield. The army had staked out their positions in the half-light before dawn. The striking raven-formation had as its wings the cavalry and the Cinn Péinteáilte contingents of Carmag and Brandubh. At its centre was the vaunted shield wall. Three thousand warriors strong, it was divided into four divisions located at each angle of a flattened diamond. At the head, Conall stood with one thousand men stood. Behind and at each of the two flank points seven hundred and fifty were arrayed. The trailing position of the diamond had five hundred men. These were the very young—untested apprentices of war. They were a reserve. If they were called upon, the battle was most certainly lost.

All stood in two rows. Ceannairí na míle and ceannairí na céad tramped up and down, bellowing orders. At this time, the ranks and rows were relaxed, allowing room for javelins, bows and slings to perform. Once the missiles had been exhausted, or the enemy had closed on them the ranks would tighten. Four double-walls of blood-red shields emblazoned with black ravens would lock. Bláithín shivered, the sight was impressive. Hopefully, it would strike the fear of the Hag into the Gauls.

On each flank, but offset and slightly back, was the Clann Ui Flaithimh cavalry—the talons of the formation. Chainmail protected the horses' chests. Brightly-polished metal fittings on bridles, harnesses, and tack chinked as the mounts shuffled, dipped heads with braided manes, and bumped against each other. As the sun rose in the morning sky, thousands of glints revealed the cavalry's positions. Signature red fox tails hung from the crests of conical helmets and bobbed as men patted their mounts broad shoulders and velvet necks. The cavalry's helmets were both light and basic. Their main requirements were unobstructed vision and hearing, and to divert the path of a sweeping blade or arrow. Only the helmets of Íar and Nikandros were more ornately dressed.

Forward of Íar, Carmag's thousand warriors milled and stomped callous-soled feet. The wing was impatient, eager for battle, but uncertain about the lack of forest cover, which was their natural habitat. Clubs and axes lay in restless, scarred, and rough hands. It was to this band that Gràinne gravitated. Her chariots were useless on this battlefield with its maze of trenches and deep holes that would smash spoked wheels and break horses' legs. Neither she nor her men were trained for the shield-wall. With her skill wielding the longsword, it seemed that joining Carmag's warriors made the best sense.

Behind the rearmost shield-wall, dozens of supply wagons lined up in precise order. It was a mark of Sárán Mac Craobhach's penchant for detail and organisation that even in the chaos of battle he knew precisely how many and where each item was placed. Often a figure that bore the brunt of many jokes, in the midst of a skirmish the sight of his bright orange plaid clothing was greeted with cheers and deep sighs of relief.

At last, Bláithín's eyes fell on the far-right wing of the battle formation and on Brocc. The Ravens, led by Brandubh and Mòrag, were positioned on a gentle rise. Brandubh and Conall hoped it would provide some advantage while the stones and arrows flew. Bláithín breathed in sharply. Her hand went to her mouth to muffle the sound of her anguish. The wing was further forward than the rest of the army. It was evident that this division would join battle first. Worse, while the Ravens launched their arrows and stones, Brocc and Torcán's men would bear the brunt of the Gaul attack.

Bláithín hoped that the Goddess heard her prayer for Brocc's well-being. "He is an accomplished warrior." Bláithín started at Mongfhionn's words. It was unnerving how the Sidhe had sidled up to her without a noise *and* how she knew Bláithín's thoughts. Bláithín nodded. Mongfhionn chuckled, "It doesn't take an oracle to understand the apprehension on your face." The Sidhe brushed a hand over Bláithín's bruised cheeks, "*He* would not have done this. Neither, I think, would he kill a rival in the shadows of the night." Mongfhionn pointed to the distant wing, "Your helmet is distinctive with its blue horsehair. It would not be amiss for you to wave it in his direction."

Above the mound, a screech of eagles compelled Brocc to look upwards and then towards the ramparts. He smiled.

***

Exposed by the heavy rainfall, a limestone ridge skirted the length of the eastern edge of the battlefield. It ran almost from the defensive ramparts of Clann Ui Flaithimh to the tents of the Gauls. Ranging from one to two spear-lengths in height, the ridge was little more than a long, ragged scar in the landscape. Its uneven summit was carpeted in a thin layer of mosses and scattered tufts of grass. Thickets of ash, oak, and hawthorn provided cover for man, beast, and fowl. On its western side, a sheer drop of a sword's length melded with a bank of shale and limestone and sloped gently towards the battlefield.

On the far side of the ridge, the argument as to tactics had cooled from boiling to simmering. Mórrígan railed at Gaius, imploring him to join the ranks of Clann Ui Flaithimh. All could see Conall was well outnumbered. For his part, Gaius pragmatically asserted that his six hundred fit men—seven, if he counted the Thracians and Cretans—and Mórrígan's one hundred would make little impact unless they had the element of surprise on their side. Much as Mórrígan hated to admit, Gaius was infuriatingly correct. Nevertheless, watching Conall's forces brace for the impact of the Gaulish assault was unbearably frustrating. Helpless, the queen of the Clann Ui Flaithimh, whose face toned perfectly with the colour of her ginger-red tresses, stomped to and fro.

Thus, the Huntress was astonished to see Roman wagons driven to just below the top of the ridge, still out of sight of Gauls and Gaels. Mórrígan watched as, with practised efficiency, mobile ballistae were removed, assembled and dragged to the crest, along with supplies of the vicious, iron-tipped bolts. Soon, along the ridge a line of ballistae waited, ready to bring the Otherworld to the battle.

"Why?" she stammered, her face flushed in anger. "The Gauls will see the weapons. You've thrown away any advantage."

"People only see what they expect," answered Gaius with exasperating and rather smug confidence. He turned to the Aquila, Amodocus, and Sarpedon. "See that your men know their places." Briefly, he looked to the sky. It was clear apart from some wisps of fragile clouds. A good day for battle. Then his gaze fell on Alkaios the Surgeon. "This will be a long and bloody day. I think you will be the busiest of us all." The tall, thin healer sported a pale gold tone to his skin which perfectly blended with deep brown eyes and light, ash-brown hair. He dipped his head while maintaining an otherworldly aspect. It was as if Alkaios observed but did not participate in the activities of men.

***

"Not as many as we feared."

Conall nodded in agreement with Fearghal's appraisal, watching the Gauls approach at a fast walk. "About half, I'd guess. Not surprising. The remoter tribes likely got bored and left when the rains fell. Mostly it's the Abrincatui, Senones, Veneti, and Venelli and who are left. There'll be mercenaries while there's gold to pay their wages. The Veneti and the Venelli have more to lose and a harsh future if they do not defeat us. Still, that leaves around fifteen thousand against our six. Five, if you discount Íar's riders. The ground is still soft. I'm not sure how much use the horses will be. At least our opponents will be similarly constrained."

Fearghal's nose wrinkled at a gust of a southerly wind. "Pig shite smells better. You'd think all the rain we've had would have washed away the stink of these barbarians." Conall laughed. He suspected that they didn't smell much better. Dismounting from Toirneach, he watched as the horse was reluctantly led away before he took his place in the shield wall. At least, in the wall, his guards could not prevent him fighting. On the ramparts, the bodhráns kept up their insistent beat, but the trumpets fell silent. Until the fight was over, only those on the battlefield would sound. In the distance, the great war-horns of the Gauls reverberated their deep *barrr-ewww*. The horde's pace increased to a brisk jog.

At the front of the Gauls' attack were the young—many not more than fourteen summers—the foolish, and the drunk. Male and female competed in the loudness and vulgarity of shouted battle cries. They hurled themselves forward in a slavering frenzy. Truthfully, their only advantage was that of the reasonably firm ground. Behind the front ranks, trampled by thousands of feet, the land progressively became a muddy quagmire, sucking the last vestiges of rotted leather boots from feet and enrobing them in a thick evil-smelling slime.

Veterans filled the middle ranks. The backbone of the assault, these were the hard men—and women. Warriors scarred in body, with souls, if not immune to violence, then certainly inured to the bloody tapestry they would create. Survivors of many clashes, they were determined that they would eat this evening. Among this echelon, small groups of champions scanned the Clann Ui Flaithimh ranks for any advantage. They chose their locations wisely and, with ne'er a thought, would sacrifice the fools before them as their shield. In their wake, trudged the reluctant. This group's sole ambition was to avoid fighting or severe injury.

Signal horns from Clann Ui Flaithimh blasted out. Their tone was both sharper and higher than the Gaulish horns. Brandubh and Mòrag shouted orders. Torcán instinctively ducked as a storm-cloud of projectiles arched high into the sky above his and Brocc's men. Stones and metal slugs from whirling slings were flung at the Gauls' western flank. Then, as the mass drew closer, arrows sprang from two hundred bows, seeking unprotected flesh.

From the Gaul ranks arose shrieks of anger and pain. Some tried to halt and use their slings but were knocked aside by the throng. With howls and curses, a score of warbands from the assailing army broke away. Their path curved towards the rise. A final layer of missiles—Torcán's squad's javelins—were thrown at a much closer range, but with equal devastation to flesh and bone. The thud of bodies against scíatha quickly followed.

On the ramparts, the people fell suddenly silent. From their advantage of height, they had spotted the ballistae on the ridge. Many looked for cover. Recent history made them expect the worst. Warnings were screamed at the defenders. Arms were frantically waved and pointed to the ridge. A communal growl of "Bollocks!" resounded along the ranks of the shield wall and the Cinn Péinteáilte formations. Shields were raised with little hope that they could accomplish any good against the anticipated bolts. With anxious eyes, Conall looked forlornly towards the limestone ridge to the east.

The cry of twisted sinews was swiftly followed by the snap and crack of wood. An eerie wail of disrupted air was heard as fifty ballistae hurled their missiles. Painful memories plagued Clann Ui Flaithimh minds. A residual vision of wood smoke and burning flesh pervaded the nostrils of the people. Caught in the open and with little cover, Conall was faced with two unpalatable choices. Absorb massive losses from the ballistae until they ran out of bolts or make a hasty retreat to the safety of the ramparts. In desperation, he sent a prayer to the Goddess.

She and Fate were watching above with ill-concealed amusement.

Only a burst of cheering from the walls and the ululating cry of the Sidhe forestalled what would have been a fateful and disastrous set of orders. The first salvo from the ballistae poured death from the ridge, but not on Clann Ui Flaithimh. Conall studied their flight and watched as they ploughed into the Gauls' right flank. Salvo after salvo flayed the Gauls. Screams swelled. Bodies, pommelled by the bolts, twisted and were flung aside to crash into comrades. Leaf-shaped bolts cleaved arms and legs. Razor-sharp, pyramidal iron spikes made heads disappear in a spray of brains and bone shards. Severed arteries crafted lurid fountains.

"Whoever our ally is, he knows battle tactics," said Fearghal. "The bolts are aimed at the mid-ranks—where the veterans are."

"I wonder *who* our ally is…" replied Conall, "and what will be his price?" A long, baritone note from a horn beyond the ridge gave the king of Clann Ui Flaithimh his first clue. Painful memories roiled his mind. "The Hag's arse, Fearghal. It can't be." Horses appeared on the crest of the ridge and jumped downwards onto the sloping scree. Their leader's helmet glinted in the sun. Its trailing raven feather plumes flared in the wind. "Mórrígan!" exclaimed Conall. His voice was a mixture of surprise, relief, and questioning.

"Aye, but who're the riders with her? Strange armour and skins darker than Nikandros." Conall was about to respond with a "Who cares?" when once more there came the sound of the horn. Once more memories of long-past battles and slaughter rose to the surface. With disbelief, Conall watched as the Romans crested the ridge. Mórrígan's riders took up positions on the right flank as the troop fell into a square phalanx. In the front four ranks, tall sarissas dropped as they marched towards the Gaul's flank.

"Shite!" exclaimed both Fearghal and Conall.

The scene unfolding before them had more elements of fantasy than reality. A sharp clang of a slingshot on his helmet reminded Conall the charging horde before him was real. "Javelins ready!" he roared. Then turning to his young horn-blower, he said, "Sound orders for Carmag to join with Mórrígan." Then he added, "When you've done that, get to the back of the shield wall." There was disappointment, and somewhat of a pout, on the girl's face. "No argument," Conall added sternly, dipping his head to those behind. The girl was unceremoniously grabbed by the shoulders and hauled, shouting curses, to safety.

"Where did such a young girl learn so many swear words?" commented Conall. "Maybe the druids need to spend more time with our youth."

***

Eirnín's countenance was as bleak as the mist-shrouded moors of the Penn-inus. Eyes, red-raw from nightmares, tears, and the grit of battle, rarely closed. From sunrise to sunset, he was haunted by images of the bloody head of Brigindos, tumbling from the hessian sack. Wine provided no release. And now it appeared neither did the violent monotony of battle. Along with the front rank of the shield wall, his cohort rebuffed the first wave of the Gauls in a welter of blood and gore.

"Children," he raged to any who would listen. "They send children against us."

It crossed Eirnín's mind that perhaps Conall had deliberately placed his céad in the forward thousand as a means of keeping a watchful eye on him. The more cynical view was that his brother had set him at the front of the battle in the hope that he would fall and be dispatched to Mag Mell—a legend of Clann Ui Flaithimh. Eirnín shook his head at that thought. If anything, Conall was too honourable for his own good. *A pity*, he thought. For indeed Eirnín was, to all intents and purposes, an empty, haunted shell.

He gazed at the berm of corpses strewn before the shield-wall.

Blood seeped from still warm, twitching flesh, forming dark pools at the edges of the human bank. Sated, the land could not drink anymore. A bellow of defiance followed by an arm-numbing strike to his scíath roused Eirnín from his reverie. Lank-haired and, from their stink, un-washed for many sunsets, the Gaul veterans announced their arrival in an exuberant style. These warriors fought with measured fervour.

Each was the height of a thrusting spear. Faces, pockmarked from their youth and tight with the scars of numerous battles, held grim ex-pressions. Frozen forever, the rictus was a macabre mirror to each soul. Slabs of muscle on gnarled arms were held in place by thick blue veins and bands of gold, silver, and copper. Legs, covered with coarse mat-ted hair, had the appearance of great fleshy tree trunks. Most had aban-doned the plaid, woollen pants that had rotted in the torrential rains.

To these warriors, the rampart of the dead was an opportunity from which to launch their attack. Air, expelled from the fallen, voiced a pitiful foul-smelling protest as muddy feet stomped on bellies that would never again transform food to shite. In death, these corpses had one final use as a springboard for the fighters who used the bank to hurl themselves against the red shields of Clann Ui Flaithimh. Others paused, and with little apparent effort, lifted bloody bodies and tossed them at the wall.

"Is nothing sacred?" inquired a Clann Ui Flaithimh warrior. The corpse of a child-warrior released its gory grip and, sliding down his shield, paused briefly at the protruding boss before coming to a final rest on blood-soaked boots. "Can a man not get slaughtered and rest in peace?" The irony of him furiously kicking the deceased aside was lost on him, if not his grinning comrades.

On the eastern flank, Torcán grunted. Slowly, but surely, his line was being pushed back. The Gauls were attempting trying to run around him to attack his rear. Already he had reduced his shield-wall by a score of men. Their purpose to discourage the flanking attacks. The ragged breathing of his men told him that they were close to the limits of being able to defend themselves, let alone take the battle to the enemy. Any exposed area of skin glistened red with sweat and blood.

He glanced at Brocc. The sharp-featured warrior slashed at the helmet blocking his vision only to see his dull blade skim off the smooth iron and crunch through muscle and bone to lodge firmly in his opponent's shoulder. Momentarily joined by a wedge of metal, both men stared at each other. A large spit of blood and saliva splattered against the top edge of Brocc's scíath and sprayed his face. Torcán laughed at the look of disgust on Brocc's face. He watched as his friend, frustrated at his waning strength released his grip on his sword, pulled a dagger from his belt and slammed the point into his opponent's eye. A single spurt of eye fluid caught Brocc on the bridge of his nose and brought a shout of, "Pig!"

***

It would be inaccurate to assert with any confidence that the battle raged. Apart from an initial period fuelled by hot-headed passion and beer, soon, and as with most large-scale confrontations, the fight descended into a grinding, and increasingly laboured stand-off between two relatively equal armies. The Gauls had numbers on their side; Clann Ui Flaithimh had a plan and the leaders to execute it. Toe-by-toe, foot-by-foot, the blades of the shield wall took their toll. Submerged in cloying mud and gore, feet and ankles were stained a dirty-red as both sides fought to a standstill in a bloody quagmire.

Unexpected, but welcome, relief was provided by blasts from the Gaulish war-horns. With a final slash, spit and curse, the Gauls disengaged, retreating to about one hundred paces from the battle lines. *It was*, Conall thought, *a surprisingly orderly falling back.* Along the front, the piteous cries of the wounded replaced the sound of the horns. Feeble arms lifted hoping for a friend to pull them from the morass. Few were granted their plea. The Clann Ui Flaithimh king roared, "Hold!" His grateful army sent silent thanks to the Goddess. It was followed by, "Drag our wounded to the rear. Close up ranks. Reserves forward."

"What are they up to?" The question was posed by a gore-splattered

Fearghal. The commander of Clann Ui Flaithimh's army would have preferred to trot along the shield-wall's ranks to his king. In the end, all he could manage was a tortured shamble.

"I think we may be about to find out." Conall pointed to a disturbance in the Gaul ranks. A path opened up as an impressive warrior strode clear of the barbarian army. He stood a score hands in height and seemed to be as broad as he was tall. Long braids of blonde hair trailed from beneath a helmet decorated with a pair of antlers. It matched the deer theme engraved on the warrior's oblong shield. In a massive hand, he gripped a thick-shafted spear. He wore only a broad, brownish-coloured loin-cloth. The choice was perhaps deliberate, as it drew attention to a trunk that was as thick and solid as an oak tree. Hanging from a thick cord belt were three skulls in various stages of decay.

The warrior came to a halt midway between the opposing armies, set his feet a pace apart, and bellowed his challenge. "I am Albiorix, champion of the Veneti, the Venelli, and the Abrincatui. Send out your finest warrior. Let us settle this battle with honour in single combat."

"We can't refuse. Single combat is a bit of an archaic notion, but it's in the tradition of the Ériu, the Cinn Péinteáilte and, apparently, the Gauls. We'd lose face if we refuse the challenge." Fearghal removed his helmet as he spoke, shaking shoulder-length hair. From the scabbard on his back, he unsheathed his famous longsword. "As your battle commander, I'm also your champion," Fearghal smirked at Conall.

"If we win... if *you* are the victor. Will the Gauls honour the result?"

"Not a chance," laughed Fearghal. "They'll attack no matter who wins." Conall shook his head. "Honour is for Tadhg's epic stories. It will not put gold in pouches or a meal on the table." Another bellow from the Gaul challenger brought their discussion to a close. "I should go..." A great cheer from the shield wall startled both men. As they looked to its source, they saw a solitary figure emerge from the ranks and stride towards the Gaul.

"Shite!" Both men shouted simultaneously.

CHAPTER 25

404 B.C.—Cnocán-Mórrígan— Summer

Eirnín Mac Gabhann, Prince of Clann Ui Flaithimh and brother of Conall, Rí Ruirech of Clann Ui Flaithimh, trudged through the mud and slop of battle. He came to a halt several paces from the Gaul. His opponent laughed, "You mock me. Are you the best your tribe can offer?" Both men held a spear and scíath. Eirnín, wearing a mail shirt to his mid-thighs, was technically better armoured. There the similarity ended. Of average build, Eirnín was a stalk of straw compared to the tree that was the Gaul.

"You didn't rate a fight with our champion," snarled Eirnín. "Let's get on with this. Or are you afraid to fight?" His ego bruised, the Gaul roared at the insult and stepped forward. The great spear cut the air before Eirnín. Fortunately, Eirnín leapt backwards and thrust his shield forward. The tip of the leaf-shaped spearhead gouged a thin trail across the scíath. Otherwise, the contest would have been over almost before it started and Eirnín's guts spread over the muddy grass.

It was, Eirnín knew, a foolish... a hopeless task, borne from a yearning to be with Brigindos. His one advantage, one sliver of hope, was that he did not care if he died. The combatants circled each other, again and again, looking for gaps in each other's defence. Both had drawn blood, but no wound was mortal. Eirnín sensed the Gaul was toying with him and playing to the gallery of raucous supporters. A feint to Eirnín's left was quickly retrieved, and a flash of pain told him that the Gaul tired of

205

the games. The razor-sharp blade carved a deep, long gash on Eirnín's upper arm. Without looking, he felt the sticky trickle of blood.

Resolutely, and with a set jaw that Conall would have been proud of, Eirnín, to the cheers of his men, did the unthinkable. He attacked. Shoulders crouched, scíath raised, and spear firmly in hand he pressed forward. To the surprise of the Gaul warrior, he kept advancing. Boisterous cheers from the Clann Ui Flaithimh army drew a wry smile from Eirnín. Had he ever been so popular? His enemy retreated a dozen steps in the face of Eirnín's determined attack. Like a wasp's stinger, the spear struck again and again. Uncannily, Eirnín appeared to know precisely where to hit. Hope rose in the breasts of the army.

The Gaul turned and ran. Jeers and shouts of *"Cladaire*—coward!" rose up from Clann Ui Flaithimh. Mystified, Eirnín halted. He should have kept going. His opponent stopped and turned, his spear raised for throwing. The distance was still close. A half-competent spearman could hurl the missile and expect success. Propelled with the strength of the Gaul, the shaft flew true, piercing Eirnín's shield. The spearhead continued its path snapping ribs and grazing Eirnín's heart to emerge in a gush of gore from his back.

"Cheating bastard!"

A roar of disgust welled up from Clann Ui Flaithimh. The Gaul warrior grinned, spat, and closed on Eirnín. A small axe, pulled from his belt, was gripped in his hand. His intent was clear. Eirnín had shown no respect for Cingetorix. Thus, the Gaul intended to extract as much pain from the Clann Ui Flaithimh prince before he finally died. Eirnín coughed raggedly as he released his grip on the scíath and struggled to push spear and shield away from his body. The bubbles in the blood that flowed from his mouth showed that the spear had cut through his lung. Axe in hand, the sneering Gaul towered above him as he finally was free of the weapon. The axe descended.

As the tide of his life ebbed for the final time, Eirnín looked to the skies and smiled. The face of Brigindos smiled back. He was happy and unafraid of the blade. This infuriated the Gaul, causing him to hesitate. The sound of disturbed air brought a smile to Eirnín's face. "Thanks, my Sister," he whispered. Then to the surly warrior, he spat, "Die you bastard." They were the last words of Eirnín, hero of Clann Ui Flaithimh.

The Gaul warrior's face took on a look of bewilderment as he swatted at the vicious swarm that attacked him. A full quiver of arrows sprang from his torso. Several tore the flesh from his throat, slicing through arteries. He was dead on his feet. Still, for a time his massive body, rooted in the mud, stood defiantly. Inevitably gravity won and, arms spread wide as if asking, "Why?" the Gaul tumbled face first into the mud. On the western flank of the Clann Ui Flaithimh army, the olive-skinned Sarpedon, bowed to Mórrígan. "Your skill with a bow is impressive. Perhaps you have Cretan ancestors?"

Mórrígan smiled, "I doubt it." She smiled and nodded to the Cretan's quiver. It was half-full. "As I recall, you matched me arrow for arrow."

Sarpedon smiled. "The Gaul was a big target. Even at this range, the worst of my men could hardly miss."

In the skies above two eagles soared. "The face in the clouds was a nice touch," remarked Fate. "Was it really her?"

"He thought it was, and that's what counts," replied the Goddess. "Now we watch and see how the battle finishes."

***

From the heights of the skies, the bean-sidhe wailed and swooped to seize Eirnín's soul. The apparition was his guide to Mag Mell. The cry was echoed by a sorrowful howl of, "Eirnín!" from Conall. The Rí Ruirech of the Clann Ui Flaithimh tossed scíath and sword aside and ran to where his brother lay. Two hundred men and women of Conall's caomhnóirí immediately followed in the king's steps.

Mischance often decides the fate of battles—a misheard command or misperceived action. Such is the edge of capriciousness on which battles are won or lost. Thinking that Conall was about to attack the Gauls, the rest of the shield wall unsheathed their favoured weapons, took up a war cry of, "Eirnín Abu!" and rushed forward. It was inevitable that they would be swiftly joined by Carmag and Brandubh's Cinn Péinteáilte, as well as Íar and Nikandros' riders. Cretan and Thracian mercenaries joined with Mórrígan's band and rode into the fray. A bemused Gaius watched as the charge gathered momentum, shrugged his shoulders, and marched his phalanx towards the Gaul lines.

Barely recovered from the shock of seeing their champion cut down, the front ranks of the Gauls were assailed by thousands of warriors who appeared to have totally lost their minds and took no heed of personal safety. The men and women of Clann Ui Flaithimh hacked, clubbed, and pommelled the Gauls with a ferocity hitherto they had not experienced. They looked into the blood-crazed eyes of Torcán and snarling teeth of Brocc, seeing only their death.

The front row of the Gauls put up a futile resistance before collapsing under the bloody assault. The rear ranks, manned by lesser warriors, crumpled and fled, hoping to avoid the blades of their enemy.

CHAPTER 26

404 B.C.—Cnocán-Mórrígan—Summer

The people of Clann Ui Flaithimh looked on in brooding silence as Gaius marched his men through the entrance of the ráth to their allocated quarters. To minimise potential conflicts, the Romans, as well as their Cretan and Thracian mercenaries, were housed distant from the main centres of population. A sizeable minority remembered the massacre at their home settlement in southern Ériu and the battles for Ráth Na Conall vividly. All undertaken and paid for by Romans and Roman gold. Most of the clann were appreciative of the help the Romans gave in the battle but very wary of the motives or the eventual price to be paid.

Several sunsets and not too many brawls later, Conall and Gaius sat down with the clann's Chomhairle and Gaius' captains. It was a strange and strained meeting around the long table in Cnocán-Mórrígan's Great Hall. Mórrígan sat uneasily beside Mongfhionn and Fearghal. That she owed her life to Gaius' timely intervention upset her carefully nurtured hatred of all things Roman. Like a predator cheated of its prey, the Sidhe glared at Gaius. In this, she was almost matched by the smouldering rage emanating from Crum Dubh. The druid also had a deep enmity for all Romans.

As for the rest in the Hall, they prayed for someone to break the ice so that they could get down to some serious feasting. An audible sigh of relief was heard when Conall finally rose from his throne-chair. "We have been enemies in the past, Gaius Aurelius Atella. We may be ene-mies in the future. But, while you and your men are under the thatch of Clann Ui Flaithimh, you will be treated with respect as honoured guests, friends, and, perhaps, allies. As Rí Ruirech, you have my personal thanks for intervening to extract my Queen from a very perilous situation and for your timely presence on the battlefield." As he finished, Conall reached out a hand to Gaius.

The Roman stood, bowed and gripped Conall's hand. "My thanks Conall, Rí Ruirech of Clann Ui Flaithimh and Hand of the Goddess. And to you Mórrígan, Queen of Clann Ui Flaithimh and the Dark Huntress." Gaius took a deep breath and faced Mongfhionn. "And thanks to you my Lady Sidhe, for without your agreement this evening would not have taken place." The Roman paused and then continued, "My men and I are outcasts. No longer welcome in Rome and estranged from our loved ones. We are very grateful for the sanctuary you have offered and gratefully accept."

Gaius smiled, "Now that the solemn speeches are done. Perhaps we could break open the casks of beer and wine and sample the bread and roasted meats. Their aromas have made my belly growl constantly. But first a toast." Gaius raised a horn of beer and shouted, "To Conall and Mórrígan of Clann Ui Flaithimh." The resounding cheers around the table confirmed that Gaius had chosen his words well.

The night waned. Ears buzzed with the fluctuating volume of hun-dreds of conversations. Throats, hoarse by shouting, were refreshed by beer. It was during a lull in the discussion that Gaius drew closer to Conall. "You choose strange advisors," he murmured, nodding momen-tarily in the direction of Nikandros. As if aware of the attention on him, the Spartan glanced up, smiled, and raised his tankard. To those nearby, it seemed a friendly gesture—a greeting between estranged comrades.

"Like you, he once saved Mórrígan's life," said Conall, "He has been a good teacher. *She* still favours him." Gaius noted the inflexion in Conall's tone.

"The Spartan's reputation was… perhaps still is as a ruthless mercenary and assassin. He is stained by Marcus' gold. That is a hard taint to cleanse and shackle to unlock. Be careful friend."

***

Ascendant in the sky, the sun commenced its leisurely descent towards the western horizon. The blueness of the firmament was reflected on the usually greyish-green waters off the northern coast of Aremorio. Two men stood at the cliff's edge. Both were deep in contemplation. Conall sighed heavily at the cost in men and women from the recent insurrection and the battles with the neighbouring Gauls. In his heart, he knew that neither the boils of hatred nor rancour would have been lanced by the bloody skirmish. Celts and Gaels of all origins had long memories and a taste for vengeance.

Still, he shared Pytheas' joy of the sea. The perpetual slap and splash of waves was a soothing balm, and a means to put his cares into perspective. The cry of the two golden eagles soaring high above brought a smile to his face. "I know you're there," he said.

"What?"

"Sorry, Gaius. Just thinking out loud."

The Roman nodded, but his mind was also far away. His nights and days were tormented by thoughts of Cornelia. His emotions ran from abject misery at their estrangement to irrational bouts of jealousy at the mere idea that she might forget him or assume him dead and take another lover. He knew his divergent passions were ridiculous but could not shake free of the shackles with which they bound him. And there were his men. No matter how often Aquila told him that he was ridiculous, Gaius blamed himself for his legion's fate and the loss of almost a third of his force. It was his duty to ensure their well-being, and to Gaius' mind, in this, he had failed.

Gaius' turmoil was profound and understandable for anyone with an ounce of compassion to see. "You can remain with Clann Ui Flaithimh. Become part of the tribe. Make it your home as many others have done. It will not be an easy path, for some still hold Rome, and by inference you, responsible for many deaths. Also, are you and your men prepared to fight against Rome and its armies? For that is one outcome to this journey." Conall paused, "Can you kill your former comrades? That is not a choice that I would like to make."

Gaius sighed, "Is there another option? Do I have any choice?"

"There is." Gaius' attention was snared. With an eyebrow raised, he gestured Conall to continue. "Take ships and go to southern Albu. To the king at the hillfort of Mai-Dún. I'll send an envoy with you. With my declaration of friendship and recommendation, I'm sure you'd find a warm welcome. The land is good and plentiful. You could make a good life there and would be a valued resource for Mai-Dún."

"You would do this?"

Conall dipped his head, "In another life, we could have been friends from the beginning, Gaius."

"I will speak with my men and the mercenaries."

A flicker at the edge of his vision caught Conall's attention. Curious Gaius looked in the direction of his gaze. Gliding across a placid sea were two black-sailed biremes. The splashing waters glinted in the sunshine as oars cut through shallow wavetops. There was something about the urgency of movement that caused Conall to frown as he watched the ships sweep into the cove and run aground on the shingle beach. At the sight of a small, dark-haired man jumping into the surf, both men spoke one word.

"Pytheas."

CHAPTER 27

404 B.C.—Cnocán-Mórrígan—Summer

"The Hag's arse, Tadhg. You can't be serious. Brocc, a suspect in the murder of Cuán?" Tadhg was taken aback by the vehemence of Torcán's defence of his friend and scrambled backwards as the bluff warrior rose from his seat with clenched fists to defend Brocc's honour. Only Deaglán's firm hand on Torcán's shoulder restrained the angry warrior and prevented bloodshed.

"Of course, he doesn't, ye eejit. But he has to consider all possibilities." The five friends—Craiftine, Deaglán, Fionnbharr, Tadhg, and Torcán, sat around a crackling fire of wood and peat. Somewhat mollified but still glowering at Tadhg, Torcán resumed his seat and ripped a leg off a slightly undercooked fat chicken. The action suggested that Tadhg's limbs would be similarly separated from his torso if he continued with his nonsense.

Grateful for Deaglán's intervention, Tadhg nodded. In truth, the young man appointed by Conall to determine who killed Cuán looked miserable. The list of possible assassins with motives was long and included Conall, Mongfhionn, and Urard, as well as Brocc and Bláithín. With a dismissive wave of his hand, Fionnbharr disposed of three. "Conall is too honourable; Mongfhionn would have left a bloody mess with those curved knives of hers and likely carried out the deed in public; and Urard's sole choice of weapon is that bloody huge axe, Breith." All nodded in agreement.

According to Tadhg, that left a second group that included Bláithín and her lover, Brocc, Dufach, the leader of the whores, and Laoise, the victim of Cuán's temper. All had access to weapons, a reason to harm Cuán and a variety of opportunities. "Whoever did this knew how to kill." Tadhg looked beseechingly at his friends. "I don't think it was Laoise. She's so skinny. I doubt she'd have the strength to use a sword in such a manner."

Craiftine rubbed his chin thoughtfully. "You're judgment's suspect there, Tadhg. Whores are resourceful." The other friends looked curiously at Tadhg, whose face, even in the glow of the fire, had visibly reddened. "It's rumoured that she's the striapach you've favoured since Dubnoreix brought the group to the camp." The harpist chewed on a lump of bread, took a gulp of beer, and continued amid the background noise of mashing teeth. "Her anger at Cuán's treatment might just have given her the strength she needed. That said, the question of who could wield a weapon with such efficiency does throw up a few additional suspects." Tadhg groaned, but his friends urged Craiftine to explain.

"You have to include Lonán Ò Neill. He wasn't overjoyed at the trouble his brother was stirring up between the Cróeb Ruad and Conall. And, he too has an eye for Bláithín. Brocc needs to watch his back. It would have been simple for Lonán to have taken Cuán aside and plunge a sword into him."

"Shite!" exclaimed Tadhg. "Anyone else on your list, brother?"

"Yes. There's two hundred of them," smiled Craiftine.

"The caomhnóirí," exhaled Deaglán.

Craiftine dipped his head, "Not one of those bastards would hesitate to stick a blade in anyone who they deemed to pose a threat to Conall or indeed, Mórrígan and the children. Cuán was an arsehole with a big mouth and a love for wine. It wasn't as if he hid his intentions."

The atmosphere around the fire was subdued as the group mulled over Tadhg's challenge. "I have no weapon and no hope of finding it. There are no witnesses or at least none that have come forward. And, I have a growing list of men and women with sufficient motive and ability to carry out the murder."

The young man sighed, "It's hopeless. Unless…"

***

To Tadhg, the request was tantamount to an invitation to the inner sanctum of a ravenous beast. His stomach churned as he ducked under the lintel and entered the gloom. Not even the tightness of the straps on his cuirass—a measure he had adopted after his previous investigation when an assassin placed an arrow firmly between his shoulder blades—gave him any comfort. At the open fire sat Fearghal. Tadhg glanced around nervously. Perhaps only Fearghal was in the dwelling. His hopes were dashed as Mongfhionn emerged from the gloom.

"Good morning Tadhg. I am glad you could join us." In reply, Tadhg could only swallow hard and attempt a weak smile. "Sit down. Eat." To Tadhg, his movements were painfully slow and exaggerated, but with a final effort he sat down. "I hear that you have eliminated me from your list of suspects." Tadhg dipped his head. "My blades are curved like an eagle's talons. They are designed to rip, tear, and excise. To prolong the sacrifice's agony. The blade by which Cuán Ò Neill met his end was, from what I hear, a short sword. Too merciful by far. At least for me."

Tadhg swallowed hard. He got the impression that Fearghal was enjoying his discomfort. What on earth was the reason for him being here? His musings were soon answered. "I have been speaking with Conall. He and I are in agreement that you should cease your investigations." Tadhg rose to protest but was summarily arrested by a stern look from the Sidhe and Fearghal's firm hand on his shoulder.

"Just let her speak her mind. It's usually the best course of action," Fearghal spoke quietly with a touch of humour in his voice.

After a brief glare at Fearghal, Mongfhionn continued. "First, none of the Chomhairle, including Conall and those present, wish to see you adorn a funeral pyre. We would prefer that you abandon this commission. Assuming, however, that you will ignore good advice from your betters, then here is a gift for you." The Sidhe glanced at Fearghal. The tall warrior rose, walked to a shadowy corner of the broch and returned with a package wrapped in what appeared to be a beautiful, pale yellow lambskin shirt. That the package thumped heavily when dropped onto the table gave some hint of the contents.

Fearghal opened the parcel to reveal a gleaming, chainmail coat. "I prefer my fish-scale and boiled leather armour, but there's no doubt that mail will turn the point of a blade or at least limit the damage from a murderous thrust."

Tadhg was dumbfounded at the prescience and thoughtfulness of the gift. It was a vast improvement on the cuirass. As he made to thank his hosts, he was halted once again by Mongfhionn. "Be very careful, Tadhg. The suit will not protect you from a dagger after the nakedness of rutting."

CHAPTER 28

404 B.C.—Summer

Lugudunon's white walls were bathed in soft tones of pink and orange from the morning sun as the orb rose above the horizon. At the meeting of the Rodonos and Souconna, the hillfort sat on the loftier of two hills. The fort's tall ramparts appeared to grow organically from the earth. Influenced by Greek and Roman architecture, earlier timber, dirt, and rock fortifications had been replaced with walls constructed of carved stone blocks. Within the fort, the chaos of transition between the Gaul's traditional rock and wood roundhouses and the newer cubic-style of white-painted brick and plaster laid down in a grid of parallel streets was evident. Matres' capital was a formidable edifice, having long, glowering sightlines across the valley's settlements, farms, and mines.

Positioned, like a prize cow, at the front of the line of slaves, Cornelia lifted despondent eyes. She thought it obscene that the fortress looked so beautiful. That it drew exclamations of awe rather than fear and disgust from her shackled companions made her want to scream. Only their constant sobbing carried on morning zephyrs assuaged Cornelia's undisguised contempt. The last faint hopes for rescue, for escape, receded with each trudging step towards Lugudunon and the slave block in the market-place. Mocked by their captors, who promised one more night of violent rutting and groping with dirt-ingrained hands, any expectation of delivery evaporated quicker than the morning mists.

The fires in the final camp crackled. Hobbled like a horse and with wrists that bore the burns of rough shackles, Cornelia listened to the screams of her fellow victims. She raised her head, straightened her shoulders, and in true Roman patrician style, gazed upon both captor and captured with disdain. After a few nights, the slavers had ceased to use her to satisfy their carnal lusts. She had quickly recognised that they needed fear, needed to hear the cries of terror, and needed the resistance to fire their violent passions and stiffen their manhoods. Thus, with admirable determination, Cornelia fought her own battle. She refused to give them what they desired. In those first nights, as they held her down and thrust into her, she offered no resistance, showed no emotion, and took no part.

In their frustration, they swore and called her a cold fish. Unable to comprehend her strategy, and commanded by their leader not to beat her, they grew sullen, taking their frustration out on the other women. Only three of her captors broke Aveta's rules. Their bodies lay on the trail—food for scavengers, and a lesson to the others.

The other slaves cursed her, but only because they could not follow her example. On occasion, the men still pushed their manhood into her as if to assert their dominance. It was to no avail. Once more, they grew angry at her lack of response and their impotence. To punish her they tied her to a stake at the centre of the encampment so that she had commanding views of the nightly debauchery. So that she could savour the fear of the abused, the raped. They did not, however, understand the Roman capacity to consider those beneath them as having no value and unworthy of concern. Inwardly she wept. For herself and for Gaius.

As she drove the slaves to the gates of the Gaiscedach fort, Aveta licked sun-cracked lips in anticipation of receiving substantial compensation. She dreamed of purchasing a 'normal' life with the gold earned. Under her stern eyes, the women and girls from Massalia came to the gates of Lugudunon largely unblemished—at least on the outside. The purchase of aloe vera and milk was a costly expense but was effective in protecting the Roman bitch's pale skin from the burning summer sun.

A hand dragged across Aveta's forehead swept the fast-increasing volume of sweat away. At the sound of marching feet and the rattle of spears and shields, the slaver turned. She gulped and dropped to her knee. It was never a good idea to look Matres, ruler of Lugudunon, in the eye. Matres approached. There was a drag to her step. The wound from Mórrígan's arrow had healed but left Matres with a limp. The queen's visage reflected her profound annoyance at the continual reminder of another defeat at Mórrígan's hands.

"Well?" she snapped.

Aveta rose slowly, palms open and still avoiding eye contact. Of the many qualities with which the Gaiscedach queen was endowed, capriciousness was not one. Instead, she was quite constant in her cruel ways. To those deemed to have disappointed her, a quick death was a welcome, if unlikely, outcome. Aveta gestured to the group of slaves. "A prime selection from Massalia. They should fetch a good price on the trading blocks." The slaver paused and nodded to her men. Cornelia was pushed and pulled forward. "And, I have this precious gift for you."

A sneer slowly crept along Matres' thin lips, and she walked forward to stand before the Roman noble. Cupping Cornelia's chin in a calloused hand, she forced her head up. Barbarian and Roman locked eyes. Neither retreated from the other's stare. "Cornelia, daughter of Marius Furius Camillus, General of Rome, and wife of Gaius Aurelius Atella, recently *disgraced* soldier of Rome." Matres smiled at the look of shock that briefly crossed Cornelia's face. "I saw your husband recently." A spark of hope flickered in deep blue Roman eyes. "He was responsible, in part, for this," Matres snarled, rubbing the puckered pink scar on her thigh.

Cornelia shuddered as Matres' fingers combed the Roman's long hair black hair. It had lost its lustre in the sun and was lank with sweat and the dirt of travel. She shrunk as Matres' hand grazed her nipples before the queen turned to face Aveta. "She is a fine piece. A collector's item. With lighter hair, she would remind me of my daughter," said Matres. Aveta looked around her warily. There was a tone in Matres' voice that sent a chill down her spine. "She has no value... except as a pet to amuse me."

Aveta's mouth opened. Uncertain how to protest or argue her case for compensation, she stood nervously shifting her weight from foot to foot. In her anxiety, she missed an almost imperceptible signal from Matres. A sharp pain in Aveta's back was followed by a gush of blood as a spearhead erupted from her belly. Skewered, her life ebbed from the wound. Trickles of blood and air bubbled from the edges of her mouth. Trying to understand in her last moments, she uttered a plaintive, "Why?"

"You were foolish to bring her to Lugudunon. No-one can know she's here," said Matres, as if it should be obvious.

Eyes dimming, Aveta watched Matres take a dagger from her belt. She felt the cold metal of a blade bite the soft flesh of her neck. "Your band of outcasts is already dead," hissed Matres, drawing the knife slowly across Aveta's throat. With a mouth full of blood and no strength to curse or spit, Aveta could only gurgle in response.

Cold eyes smiled at Cornelia. The Roman shuddered at the relish with which Matres had disposed of the slave leader. Blood dripped from the knife's point as it was slowly wiped across Cornelia's breasts, smearing them with gore. She held her breath, expecting a painful death. Instead, Cornelia heard an awful cackle from the Gaiscedach queen. "There is no, nor will there be, an easy end for you." Matres drew Cornelia's attention to the other female slaves. They stood nearby, crying and burning in the noon sun. "As for your travelling companions, they will not be so fortunate. Death for them will be slow and very painful. You will watch each one die. You will hear them curse you. For your presence decided their fate." Cornelia's head dropped. It was an attempt to hide the tears that flowed down her cheeks.

***

It took Conall, Pytheas, and Aquila, as well as a hammer-fist to the jaw from Fearghal to restrain Gaius. That no-one blamed Gaius for his behaviour was understandable. He had just been informed that his wife, Cornelia, had been kidnapped and was either a slave of Matres in Lugudunon or dead. He railed against her father Marius, against that bastard Marcus, and against Pytheas for not stopping her from leaving Massalia. The kidnappers, if still alive, he would see roast in a special place in Tartarus—after he flayed them alive.

Now his ire turned to Conall. Distraught, he paced the wooden floor of the broch in Cnocán-Mórrígan. Hoping to get him drunk, he was continually passed pottery chalices brimming with wine, some of which were liberally laced with a gut-rotting concoction known euphemistically as uisge beatha—the water of life. His anger though appeared to turn the drink into water. Eyes red-raw from crying and anger, Gaius turned on Conall.

"Give the command to march. We must destroy Matres and that snake pit called Lugudunon and rescue Cornelia."

As obdurate as Gaius was angry, Conall shook his head. "The tribe will not march to rescue one person, no matter their status. My people have just recently fought major battles. They have had no time to rest or recover from their injuries. Many still mourn the death of loved ones. Without preparation, a trek such as you are suggesting would be both exhausting and dangerous. The Gaulish tribes, smelling weakness, would descend on us like wolves." Conall paused. He had great sympathy for Gaius' plight but greater responsibility for his clann. "No. Speak to me about this after the feast of Imbolg, and we will see what is possible."

"Bastard! Coward! You owe me. I saved your queen. My ballistae turned the battle in your favour."

The Roman's anger controlled his thoughts and his words. In a less tolerant environment, his head would already lie separate from his body. A one-armed Aquila held out his palm to Conall. A silent plea for mercy for his commander. "He is not in his right mind. Let him drink. Let him mourn as if she has already departed for the Elysian Fields. His rationality will recover. He is a good man."

Ignoring an increasingly inebriated and maudlin Gaius, Pytheas drew Conall and Fearghal to the side. "Lay to one side the merits or otherwise of mounting a rescue for Cornelia and whether you owe Gaius a favour for supporting you. You should, however, consider this. Clann Ui Flaithimh and its people need a home. The stronghold of Lugudunon and the valley it stands sentinel over would make an excellent choice as the tribe's home in Gaul. The valley is guarded by mountains, served well by rivers, and is rich in resources—farmland and mines." Pytheas paused for emphasis, "It is also within striking distance of Rome. Furthermore, the Gaiscedach are despised among the Gaulish tribes. Conquering the hillfort might gain you some allies."

"I agree, Pytheas. Yet, it is also certain that the path from Cnocán-Mórrígan to Lugudunon will be long and bloody. Without the protection of the fort, the clann will be exposed to those we recently defeated, and to the full might of the Senones, the Carnutes, and the Gaiscedach. I will not begin the journey until the tribe is fully prepared." Pytheas dipped his head acknowledging Conall's argument. Yet the small, swarthy merchant was burdened by guilt at letting Cornelia slip from the safety of his home. He looked at Conall with pleading eyes that reminded the Rí Ruirech of his wolfhounds.

Conall grasped his friend's arm. Pytheas' flesh was less firm these days, yet there was an underlying strength in the clasp that was returned. "The clann will march after the feast of Imbolg, but before Bealtaine." Pytheas sighed with relief. "I will also suggest to Gaius that Mórrígan with, and assuming they are agreeable, the addition of the Thracian and Cretan mercenaries, are sent in advance as soon as they can ride. They will gather intelligence and be an assassin's blade in the side of the barbarian tribes."

Pytheas' face showed his relief and thanks. He looked at an unconscious Gaius slumped over the table, "I will inform Gaius when he has recovered."

✳✳✳

"Have you taken leave of your senses?" The intensity of Marcus' anger made Matres recoil. Her hand automatically went to her daggers. She would kill if necessary. "You keep the daughter of Marius, the most senior general of Rome, a prisoner—a pet for your amusement." Marcus crossed the marble floor to stare into Matres' eyes. "Madness! Lunacy!" Their noses almost touched. Flecks of spittle spattered her face as he spat, "Kill the girl. Bury her in the deepest crevasse in the Alpes. Should even a rumour of her capture reach her father's ears, then nothing will prevent the might of Rome marching on Lugudunon and the Gaiscedach. You may have already sealed the doom of your tribe."

Shocked at the vehemence and vitriol of Marcus, Matres stood, uncertain as to her next move. "Go!" Marcus pointed to the side entrance of his chambers. "Go! No-one saw your entrance. Let no-one see you depart." Stiff with rage, Matres bowed and turned. She was stopped by the Roman's rasping voice, "*Never* set foot on Roman soil. *Never* come here again. Like a rabid dog, you will be killed on sight."

As the limping figure of Matres disappeared from his vision, Marcus called for his eldest son. Tight-lipped with rage, he instructed Quintus. "Send a messenger to Concolitanus, king of the Gaiscedach. Suggest strongly that he terminate Matres, raise Lugudunon to the ground, and slaughter anyone who may have seen Marius' daughter. Then, and if Cornelia is not dead already, he is to cut the bitch's throat." As his son turned to depart, Marcus grasped his arm, "Also, send messengers to Brennus of the Senones and Ambigatos of the Aedui. Impress on them the danger of allowing Concolitanus to live after he has seen to the demise of Matres. Suggest that Concolitanus has ambitions in which both kings play no part." Quintus smiled at the duplicity of his father. The old man's rasping voice spoke one more time, "You will, of course, kill the messengers when they return."

As his son departed from the chamber, Marcus slumped into a well-cushioned chair. Skeletal, liver-spotted hands trembled as he reached for a goblet of wine. This time they shook, not in anger, but in fear. His plans and his future rested on thin ice.

CHAPTER 29

404 B.C.—Cnocán-Mórrígan—Autumn

At just two springs old, Sorchae Ni Íar was a delightful child and much admired for her amazing resilience to what life thus far had thrown in her path. Sorchae had fine fly-away hair that defied all attempts at control. Her determined right-foot stomp as she marched across the hillfort of Cnocán-Mórrígan brought a smile to all. Everyone in her path was greeted with a broad grin and a throaty laugh.

Wherever Sorchae walked, her suitors were never far behind. Aodán Mac Conall and his half-brother, Barra, were rivals for Sorchae's affections. Being the elder by three years, Aodán had informed Barra that he was too young for Sorchae and he should go suck his thumb elsewhere. Barra just roared with laughter and ignored his sibling.

At the centre of the camp, the threesome was joined by Neamhain Ni Fearghal and Brianag Ni Brion. The same age as Sorchae, Neamhain and Brianag were never far apart and had quite contrasting personalities. Brianag was a charming and thoughtful child who favoured the temperament of her father, Brion Ò Cathasaigh, king of the Na Mèadaidh in northern Albu, rather than her mother, Gràinne Ni Fearghal, the wild, painted warrior who led Clann Ui Flaithimh's chariots.

As for Neamhain, much to her father's dismay, she was in every way her mother's daughter. She had a willowy frame topped off with long strawberry-blond hair that wrapped itself around her face in the breeze. Her favourite activity was to find a high vantage point and, with hands stretched upwards, scream into the wind. The ululations sent shivers down the spines of nearby adults. It caused her father, Fearghal, to raise an eyebrow and her mother, the Lady Mongfhionn, to roll her eyes and shrug. As for Neamhain's friends, they merely laughed or joined in her shrieking.

The group met daily to watch Brighid and Danu, now ten summers old, practice their fighting and weapons training. The twins were much older than the quintet but not nearly as old as even the youngest of their mothers and fathers. Thus, they had been adopted by Sorchae's group as more appropriate role models. From their seats on some fallen tree trunks, they watched. Later, they would remember and practice. As for the objects of their admiration. Brighid and Danu were outwardly disdainful of but secretly pleased by their followers.

It was not uncommon for Urard, Iasg, and now Torcán to be present at the training sessions. Urard was not only one of Clann Ui Flaithimh's fiercest warriors, but also the guardian of Brighid and Danu. On this day, however, his interest and thoughts were drawn to the slender figure of Iasg. She had just finished her knife-throwing lesson with the twins. A flash of Iasg's deep green eyes was enough to make Urard's heart skip a beat. He growled, "Stupid old man," and watched as Iasg walked across the training field.

She had, Urard thought, *a surprisingly beautiful gait*. Her style of walking was curious and mostly due to the combination of being pigeon-toed, knock-kneed and slightly bow-legged. It was a mix that should have spelt disaster and sparked off cruel humour. Instead, the traits had blended seamlessly into a walk that earned admiring glances and indelicate invitations. The gentle roll of her firm, round arse caused Urard to reflect that maybe the age difference between them was not insurmountable. The poor man did not realise that Iasg had discounted age as a barrier quite some time past.

Urard scratched the day-old stubble on his shaven head. The ridge of skin that formed the finger-length scar on the back of his head was a reminder of the kidnapping of the twins by the agents of Kartimandu and of the axe that almost ended him. Life was tenuous. Perhaps it was worth risking rebuttal. The giant warrior stood, grasped Breith, and tramped off to intercept Iasg.

***

As the training session came to an end and the young friends bade farewell to one another, Torcán stood, holding a braided rope loosely. Attached to the leash was Barra's wolfhound. It sat patiently at Torcán's heel, although the steady thump of its tail on the ground was a clear signal that it was looking forward to playing with its young master. Carefree, man, child, and dog strolled to the roundhouse where Mòrag and Barra resided.

Mother and child had recently moved from the protection of Conall's broch. Mòrag knew her independent streak would eventually cause problems. Furthermore, she was not naïve. The constant, if unintentional, reminder that Conall was the father of Barra already tested Mórrígan's forbearance. Thus far, Mòrag had resisted the pressure from her brother, Brandubh, to share his home. Fortunately, Mòrag had a strong personality, a sharp tongue, and the fists to support her arguments.

It was Torcán's unspoken opinion was that it was good for Mòrag to have her own home. Nevertheless, the tight confines of the Clann Ui Flaithimh encampment and the even smaller hillfort of Cnocán-Mórrígan where they both lived could still be stifling. Furthermore, the tradition for families to, if not reside together in a single roundhouse or compound, then certainly to be within spitting distance, meant everybody knew everybody else's business. Modesty and privacy were rarely high on anyone's list of priorities.

Torcán waved to Mòrag as they approached. She stood, hands on hips, framed by the entrance timbers of the roundhouse. *A fierce woman*, he thought. He handed the leash to Barra. Dog and master bounded—or more accurately, the hound dragged Barra—towards his mother.

Torcán scratched his head ruefully as he advanced on the house at a slow walk. It had been several cycles of the moon, and still he had not been invited inside. During the same time, he had not been with a woman either, which was remarkable in itself. It was also the source of unrelenting merriment and teasing from his friends.

"Perhaps you will stay and share a meal with us, Torcán?"

The bull-necked warrior had said his usual 'Hellos' and 'Goodbyes' and was already turning about. "What?" he stuttered. He immediately wanted to kick himself.

Mòrag laughed, "No matter what you may have heard. My cooking is not that bad."

"No. No. It's not that." Torcán found himself looking at his feet. They seemed unable to stay in the same place for more than an instant. He felt the purple mark on his throat burn and throb—a sure sign he was about to embark on something foolish.

'Well?"

In truth, Torcán's reaction was not what Mòrag anticipated. For a moment she thought she may have kept him at arm's length for too long. Perhaps he was no longer interested. Maybe he had another woman. Her face flushed and her pulse raced. The thought of a rival made her want Torcán even more.

"Of course, I'd love to eat with you. The invitation took me by surprise. A delightful surprise."

In truth, Mòrag could have served up cow-shite, and Torcán would have said it was the best food ever. Barra rolled his eyes and giggled at seeing his large friend so captivated by his mother. Even the hound seemed to give Torcán pitiful looks. The interior of the roundhouse was hot. It was a pleasant evening, and the central fire was blazing. Sweat formed a lustrous coating on his naked upper body. He felt his pants damp and clinging to his body.

"Time for you to go, Barra."

The young child nodded to his mother, grabbed a small sack and raced across the floor to hug her. "Be good." Barra nodded, kissed his mother, and then dashed past Torcán and out the entrance. In the half-light of the roundhouse, Torcán looked at Mòrag with a somewhat puzzled expression. She laughed, "He will be staying with Conall this night. I know Barra and you get on well, so I hope you are not disappointed."

"No. Definitely not." Torcán desperately tried to think of all sorts of clever conversation pieces, only to have his tongue trip him up each time. *The Hag's arse*, he thought, *I haven't been this nervous since my first rutting. Worse, I think she's enjoying this.*

For her part, Mòrag found that Torcán's uncharacteristic shyness made him much more desirable. The sight of his hard-muscled chest glowing red in the firelight tightened her throat. Between her legs, the growing dampness was making her skin-tight triubhas uncomfortable. "It's quite warm in here. Don't you think?" Torcán nodded his head. He watched as she stood and stretched her arms above her head. The strain of her breasts against the leather was only eased as she slipped the harness off.

"Magnificent," gasped Torcán.

"Why thank you," said Mòrag coquettishly as she clasped hands behind her head. The gods had amply endowed Mòrag, and now, before Torcán, her breasts hung like a sumptuous feast. The upward curve presented dusky-pink nipples as big as cherries. They sat temptingly on large rosewood-shaded rings of slightly puffed up areolae. Torcán stood and held her in his arms, relishing the warmth of her body pressed against his chest. Her arms wrapped around him and she nuzzled below her ears. It seemed that they held each other for what seemed a long time. Likely it was mere moments.

Mòrag grinned as she felt a scarred, hard-skinned hand slide tentatively under her pants and softly squeeze her ample round cheeks. "I'm not a delicate wildflower. You *can* squeeze harder." The hand gripped her firmly. Hard fingers dug deep into the soft flesh. "Much better," she moaned. With well-practiced ease, Mòrag slipped out of her pants and resumed Torcán's embrace. He smelt good. A blend of smoky, sweaty, and musky fragrances. None were overpowering.

"Fair is fair, Torcán. Time to lose these—unless you're shy." A quick tug on the waist cord and Torcán's trousers fell to the stone floor. Mòrag's voice was husky with passions that were increasingly challenging to control. It was all she could do not to throw Torcán to the ground and straddle him. She felt his hard, warm manhood against her well-trimmed but full bush. Her hand slipped downwards and caressed the throbbing manhood. *The rumours were not exaggerated*, she thought.

The princess of the Ravens did little to resist as Torcán pushed her down on top of a pile of soft pelts. She moaned at the hot breath on her breasts and breathed in sharply as his mouth found her erect nipples. Long fingers grabbed his hair and held him hard against her breasts. A hand drifted downwards, stopping briefly at her mound. His grip on her thighs attempted to spread her legs wide. It met the resistance of smooth, but well-muscled thighs.

There was a snort in the half-light. "If you think you're going to get away with a quick suck on my tits, before you spread my thighs, and thrust into me, you're sadly mistaken, Torcán Ò Dubhghaill. I can find hundreds of men who can do that. I want a real man." Torcán's lips pursed half-way to a pout before lifting into a smile.

"Mòrag, you know me well. I'm not good with words and my manner is considered by even my friends to be unrefined." Torcán swallowed, "I'm impetuous and inflamed, even confused, by your beauty. Perhaps, you would instruct me as to your needs?" He felt his head held gently but firmly and guided down.

She paused at her mound, "Just take time to know me. Smell. Know my fragrance." Then she pushed his head between her widely spread thighs. Drawing her knees back she presented her lips to him. "Taste me. Lick me. Caress me. Learn what pleases me. Drink deeply from my spring. You will know the right time to enter me."

Torcán proved to be a quick learner. And, much appreciated by

Mòrag, he turned out to be an ardent lover. Previously, he just had never been asked to extend himself. Torcán grinned. Mòrag was quite vociferous in her demands and appreciation of her lover's attention. Their neighbours were likely kept entertained by her screams as she orgasmed under his mouth and fingers. Entering her, knowing she had climaxed, added to is enjoyment. That said, she nearly broke his spine when she wrapped firmly-muscled legs around his waist and shouted, "Thrust deeper. Harder. Faster!"

Glowing and slippery with sweat, the two lovers lay on the pelts. Chests rising and falling, they exhaled and inhaled deeply. Mòrag purred at the pleasant throbbing between her legs. She revelled in the pulsating, crushed, and bruised lips that now layered butterfly kisses over Torcán's face and chest. They kissed deeply, devouring each other, fighting for supremacy. Torcán had won that battle, but only, he knew, because she allowed him.

Mòrag cleared her throat. Torcán's immediate thought was a panicked, *what have I done?* He watched as she moved, enjoying her luscious curves and the movement of her breasts in the firelight. Now he found himself looking at her incredible arse raised in the air. *Is there anything about her that isn't wonderful,* he mused and then moaned, "I am so lost." She giggled. It was a child's chortle from the mouth of a woman and was powerfully intoxicating. She wiggled her arse and looked over her left shoulder.

"I like it this way too."

It was an invitation that Torcán was never going to refuse.

***

The rising sun sent shafts of light streaming through the roundhouse's single entrance. Gold and silver motes of dust glittered and danced in the beams. At times like this, as he gazed on the naked body of Mòrag sprawled on top of several furs, Torcán wished he had even a small portion of Tadhg's gift for words. He sighed, "At least I can make myself useful." Carefully, he covered Mòrag's form with a soft, woollen brat.

Her eyes opened briefly. She grunted her thanks and slipped back into sleep. *Not a morning person*, thought Torcán.

After re-kindling the fire, Torcán pulled on his slate-grey plaid triubhas and grabbed a couple of pails. His first stop was the spring to fetch some cold water; his second was to one of the cow pens for a bucket of creamy milk. He hoped he was still in credit with the lady who oversaw the milking.

Torcán was quite proud of himself as he neared Mòrag's home. He spilt little of either water or milk and had fended off the amorous advances of the milk-maid. Yet, pride goes before the fall. As he made to cross the entrance stones of the roundhouse, a hand was placed on each of his scarred shoulders. He heard the five words that many fathers and more than a few hand-fast partners had spoken to him, "I think we should talk." With a wry smile, Torcán turned. Before him, stood a stern-faced Conall and Brandubh.

The young warrior held up the pails of milk and water. "May I deliver these?"

CHAPTER 30

404 B.C.—Aremorio—Autumn

Tadhg's shoulder itched. It was a constant, nagging irritation, which he could do nothing to ameliorate. The chainmail was impervious to both fingernails and curses. He grumbled that he could not even scratch his arse without a major exercise in logistics. Footsteps on the wooden walkway behind him caused Tadhg to abruptly turn around. He crouched, and his hand went to his sword. These days, the weapon always rested in the scabbard without its leather safety loop. A passable swordsman, Tadhg had prevailed on his friend and acknowledged sword-master, Deaglán, to give him lessons. Deaglán knew little about defensive swordplay. It showed in Tadhg's reaction.

"A bit twitchy, aren't we?"

The grizzled veteran looked with amusement on the young man. Tadhg recognised him as one of Conall's guard. The observation did not make him any happier. "Take my advice. A sword's not much use in unexpected close combat or a brawl. Takes too long to unsheathe. Use a dagger. By the time that sword cleared its scabbard, I could have put this blade between your ribs." It was only then that Tadhg saw the knife grasped menacingly in the man's right hand. A bead of sweat tracked down Tadhg's cheek. He could feel his heart pounding in his chest. Fight or flee seemed two unattainable options. He licked dry lips and waited.

The veteran's posture relaxed, he smiled and shook his head as he returned the knife into his belt. "It's not me, son. And, for what it's worth, I don't think the person you're looking for is a member of the king's guard. Lucky for you, I guess. Cuán was all mouth and wine. Few of my mates saw him as a threat to the king." The man thought for a moment. "*But* there is a rumour of a tall warrior, shadowing Cuán on the ramparts that night. If the gossip is true, then you'd be wise to walk away from this." The veteran sidestepped Tadhg. As he passed, he pointed to Tadhg's throat, "Wear a thick torc around your neck. Chainmail is good. It won't stop someone cutting your throat."

Tadhg nodded and muttered a hoarse, "Thanks," to the man's receding back. Hand on a stockade post, he gazed without really seeing anything across a landscape bursting with autumn rusts and golds. With a rare moment to think he considered the state of his current investigation. Twice he had been warned to let the investigation drop. It was too late. Thanks to some judicious words whispered in receptive ears, gossip spread quickly throughout the encampment, and hillfort, that Tadhg had a witness to the murder. "Now," he murmured, "all I have to do is wait until the assassin tries to kill me!"

Above the ráth, a pair of beautiful eagles swooped and soared on kindly updrafts. To anyone watching, the birds were a picture of graceful, effortless movement. Keen, yellow-gold eyes picked out the lonely figure of Tadhg. "Has he taken one risk too many?"

"Perhaps," replied Fate.

"It would be a pity. He's a wonderful seanachaí. Who will remember us without the telling of his stories?" said the Goddess.

***

"Irrumatores!"

For a while, that was the only word that Gaius could utter through chattering teeth. That he was the butt of much frivolity and jests from those seated around the campfire did nothing to improve his demeanour. His friends prepared a fire of driftwood so that Gaius could get some warmth into his body while his clothes dried.

Many sunsets had passed, until Gaius' self-pity and attempt to drink

234

himself into oblivion were ended by his second-in-command, Aquila. With the complicity of Amodocus and Sarpedon as well as Alkaios, the Greek healer, Gaius was dragged to a nearby cove and without ceremony thrown into the sea. The waters off northern Aremorio never warmed even in the hottest summer's day. Hence, it was a frigid and sobering experience for Gaius. After being tossed back into the cold saltwater for the third time, Gaius pleaded for mercy.

It was inevitable that the group should exhaust its repertoire of inane topics with which to fill the social void and avoid addressing the issues that hung over them like the sword of Damocles. Gaius broke the awkward silence, "I have made up my mind. We will march for Lugudunon immediately. Provisions for the journey will be purchased from Conall. Once there, I will devise a strategy for rescuing Cornelia."

"No! He has learnt nothing." Amodocus threw up his hands in despair and stood. It was a Prince of Thracia who spoke, not a mercenary. His tone brooked no argument. "You tell him," he said looking at Aquila.

"Tell me what? I am your commander. You serve under me and will obey my orders."

The one-armed Roman looked at Gaius and spoke. His tone was soft and understanding, yet there was iron in his voice. "There is no command, Gaius. We are no longer a legion of Rome. We are not even counted as Romans. Outcasts and outlaws that is our lot. The men sympathise with your plight and Cornelia's predicament, *but* their families, and mine, are likely dead, executed on Marcus' orders and carried out by our former comrades. He will want no witnesses to his treason." Aquila looked to Amodocus and Sarpedon. "Our friends' kin will not have been as fortunate. Likely, they were made to suffer as entertainment and crucified on a tree. Food for fowl and beast." Aquila shook his head in sorrow at the thought of the suffering of the men and at the shock on Gaius' face.

Anger and despair crept once more across Gaius' face as Aquila continued. "You are our leader. We accept that, but no longer can you take decisions without consulting those around this fire. Especially those that concern only your misfortune." Gaius stood, his mouth trying to form words to match his thoughts. Aquila raised a hand, "Please sit friend. Hear us out." Gaius slumped down on the shale.

"As a tactician you know Conall is right. It would be foolish to set out for Lugudunon. It is autumn. If we are lucky and avoid too many skirmishes with the barbarian tribes along the banks of the Liga, we would reach Matres' stronghold around the festival of Saturnalia— mid-winter. Where would we find shelter and forage in the snows and storms falling from the Alpes or the cold and violent north-western winds that flay the Rodonos valley?

"Further, the Gaiscedach can put ten, maybe twenty thousand war-riors into the field. Matres alone probably has five thousand warriors quartered in and around Lugudunon. Our legion numbers seven hun-dred. Less when the hundred who wish to start a new life in Albu leave. We will die gloriously, having achieved nothing."

A sob of anguish escaped Gaius' lips, "I cannot leave her with-out hope. I will go. Alone, if needed. Perhaps the gods will grant my petitions."

Aquila rose and laid his hand on Gaius' shoulder. "I had not fin-ished. Hear me a little longer." Gaius shrugged not believing any succour was at hand. "Conall has agreed to journey with his people to the domain of Matres. Pytheas has convinced him that the area would be a good location for Clann Ui Flaithimh. He will march south from Cnocán-Mórrígan to meet the Liga and follow that great river to the Rodonos valley and Lugudunon. *But* they will not depart until the spring. Think on this Gaius, he has ten thousand people to get through the winter and to prepare for a very long journey through the territories of many barbar-ian tribes. It is impossible for him to move quicker."

"Summer, Aquila. It will be summer before I set eyes on Lugudunon. How can Cornelia possibly survive?" Aquila's heart ached to see his friend in such pain. Yet there was little solace he could deliver. Their lives were in the hands of Fate and each of their gods.

Aquila spoke again, "Conall has agreed to send an advance force, under Mórrígan's command to Lugudunon. Amodocus and Sarpedon have petitioned Conall to join this force—*permanently*." The Roman looked at the two men who nodded their agreement. "The Dark Huntress' mission is to bring terror to the tribes along her path. Once she has reached Lugudunon, she has agreed to search for Cornelia and ascertain her condition. She will rescue Cornelia if possible. At worst, she will maintain a watch on your wife."

***

The autumn sun, high in a cloudless sky, pounded the earth with waves of balmy heat. Conall watched Mórrígan inspect the riders cantering through the gates of Clann Ui Flaithimh's defences. Between the Battle of Cnocán- Mórrígan and this day, he relished the company of his partner and his children. For a brief time, they were a complete family. In the night, he had held and enjoyed Mórrígan. Inwardly, he cursed. It would be Bealtaine before he saw her again. Still, as he stood on the ramparts, he smiled proudly at his hand-fast partner sat astride her pale, golden horse and chuckled as she adjusted the thick, emerald green dillat to the curves of her arse. As it moved to and fro, Mórrígan's mount glittered in the sun. Its halter, bridle, and girth-strap were inlaid with silver and gemstones.

Long tresses of red hair fell on a sleeveless, burnished chainmail shirt. Even though much of her body was unclothed, decorated only by swirling sigils of power, the queen would be sweating under the mail. The ornate helmet that usually protected her head was strapped to her belt, its long, black plumes trailing from the small, gold raven at its apex. Her earthly weapons were minimal. A pair of bone-handled blades and a recurve bow with several quivers of black-shafted arrows. To Conall, she looked magnificent—perhaps as impressive as the Sidhe. Conall snorted. Before the Huntress was out of sight of the ráth, she would be covered in dust and dirt, and smelling of horse-shite.

Mórrígan considered her regenerated warband. With the addition of the Thracians and Cretans, it would be a much stronger, fiercer, and larger force, but only if she could combine its disparate parts. Two hundred and fifty strong, the core remained the veterans who had survived the skirmishes with Kartimandu. To them had been added, almost in equal numbers, the Thracians and Cretans. Her men, she did not include the mercenaries in this group as yet, were lightly armoured. Most wore boiled leather breastplates, some inlaid with iron scales, and greaves. An increasing number were switching to chainmail. Although more weighty than their traditional armour, it was more flexible and could stop a sword thrust or arrow. The tribe's blacksmiths with knowledge of mail had increased in number, which meant the armour was widely available and less costly. All carried a selection of bows and blades—swords, daggers, and axes. Helmets, conical-shaped with little embellishment, made of iron and bronze and tied by thongs, dangled from horse-tack. The final piece of armour—small, light wooden scíatha—were strapped to their backs.

The mercenaries were as different as they could be in their choice of armour and weaponry. The Cretans, under Sarpedon, carried a longer composite bow, several slings wound around their waist, and as many quivers of arrows that their horses could hold. All brought a long, narrow-bladed sword, and several knives. All, however, aimed to kill their enemy well before he or she got within sword range. Sarpedon's men carried roughly spherical, bronze helmets with no crests, but as with their swords, the wearing of a helmet was almost an admission of failure. Typically, if anything, they wore a simple boiled leather cap. Small wicker shields were slung from a belt.

The Queen of Clann Ui Flaithimh sighed as she watched Amodocus flirt outrageously with every and any woman or girl he trotted past, including her. She could almost see Conall's jaw tighten and hear his teeth grinding. The faint heat rising in her cheeks, she accorded to the sun. While her men, and the Cretans, were built for lightning attacks and long-range tactics, she wondered whether the Thracians could pack any more armour or weaponry on their horses. And while each of the Cretan archers and her warband had a spare mount, the Thracians had the equivalent of a pack-horse, which carried even more armour and weapons.

Amodocus' men favoured their traditional short, curved swords, or sica, as well as the longer, vicious slashing rhomphaia, whose blade was slightly curved, and the skull-crushing mace. In Carmag Mac an t-Sionnaich, whose treasured weapon was a heavy hammer, Amodocus had found a kindred spirit. The Thracians wore breastplates, arm-bands, and greaves. Most were leather, a few were bronze. A light, round wooden shield was slung on their back. A traditional hemispherical domed helmet enclosing the head with protective nose and ear guards was favoured. Amodocus' helmet, as expected, was much more flamboyant than those of his men.

About to remonstrate with herself at the low number of females in her band, a loud battle-cry uttered in a thick Northern-Albu brogue drew Mórrígan's attention back to the gateway. It was followed by the sound of iron-rimmed wheels crunching over the dry earth and charioteer whips cracking. From the gates thundered Gràinne's gaily coloured chariot teams, banners flapping in the light breeze. The queen looked up at Conall, her eyebrow raised. In return, she received a smirk and a shrug of his broad shoulders. Gràinne had pleaded with Conall and Fearghal to be allowed to join, and they had acceded to her request. It was a sound decision. The rolling hills and plains of northern Gaul and the banks of the River Liga were ideal for chariots.

A whistle brought a huge smile to Mórrígan's lips. To her left, in the long grass, the massive grey shapes of a score of wolfhounds rose up. The hounds were as paradoxical as the Gaels. Gentle and playful with their owners, they were ferocious beasts in battle, with jaws that could tear a throat or crush a skull with consummate ease. The queen cantered to the head of the warband. Flanking her were Bricriu and Beacán, her brothers. At her back were Amodocus and Sarpedon. Mórrígan lifted her arm to give the signal to advance when a single note was blasted on a horn within the ráth. Curious, she turned around. Even stranger, she watched as the druid, Crum Dubh, trotted through the gateway on a bay horse that stood at least sixteen hands high. He came to rest alongside the queen.

"My dreams inform me that I should accompany you," the sallow-faced druid said in response to Mórrígan's quizzical look. The queen shrugged. It was well-known that the spiritual leader of the clann was very proficient with a sword. Once more, she went to signal to advance, when an irreverent voice rang out.

"Shite! I guess we're stuck with pillaging and plundering. No raping. The Hag help the poor sheep!"

CHAPTER 31

Cornelia's days were an endless torment of nakedness, and of being collared and walked on a leash. The only time Matres relinquished personal control of Cornelia's movements was when the young woman needed to squat for her toilet. Even then, day and night, two burly guards shadowed her. Their presence was a constant reminder of her cage.

The guards looked upon Cornelia with frustrated desire. Her first team of gaolers had taken her in the night and raped her to sate their lusts. That was their first mistake. Their second was to get drunk and brag about it. The men's skinless corpses, heaving with maggots, hung nailed to Lugudunon's gates. Their genitalia, slowly removed as Cornelia watched, were stuffed in their gaping maws before the flaying but while they yet lived. It was a lesson not lost on subsequent sentries, now forced to restrain carnal urges with lewd talk, whores, and masturbation.

Cornelia shivered. The humiliation of being Matres' pet bore down heavily on her mind. Much better to be a real slave than the gilded misery of her current life. Yet, of all the things that grated upon her spirit, the slowly changing colour of her hair weighed on her the most. Repeated applications of a paste of honey mixed with white wine, lemon juice, or olive oil had bleached her lustrous black tresses. Each day the sun was complicit in her transformation. Its rays lightened her hair while darkening her pale skin. Whispered gossip, although few cared whether she listened, pointed to her and uttered one word—Cathubodua.

***

The king of the Gaiscedach smiled. It was to be a rare sight this day. The object of his favour was Genovefa, now officially recognised as queen. Concolitanus looked with pride at the soft swell of his partner's belly. It was early days. Yet, Genovefa's obsession with keeping her body in perfect condition and not a hint of fat was proof enough to Concolitanus. He had already made offerings to the gods for the child to be a male—his successor and leader of the tribe. A scowl crossed his face. New life brought memories of his previous sons and daughter. He still blamed Matres for their deaths.

Concolitanus loved his mountains and the chaos of buildings made from wood, dirt and rock. He detested Lugudunon. "Bastard Greeks and Romans," he snarled as he gazed on nondescript buildings. To him, they were white-washed blocks built on terraces. The stepped incline served only to give the impression that the buildings perched on top of each other. Ordered streets gradually replaced meandering avenues. The king grunted. One advantage of this new order was that the path to Matres' Great Hall was broad and straight.

The outer wall of the hillfort was strong, high, and broad. It was edged with low, crenellated walls and was a formidable obstacle to an attacker. There was only one entrance on the eastern side. That was deceiving, as the entranceway was protected by two curved walls, each with their own gates. An attacking force having surmounted the first wall would find itself faced with an equally daunting task and at the mercy of Matres' slings. Concolitanus strongly suspected that there were tunnels under the settlement. He could not envisage Matres leaving herself without additional escape routes.

Accompanied by his queen and one hundred of his guard, Concolitanus cowered the hillfort's gate-keepers with a snarl and marched towards the Royal Hall and Matres' quarters. The long walk from his mountain fortress and tramp up the grassy incline to Lugudunon raised a film of sweat on his party's mostly unclad bodies. For Genovefa, she was totally naked, unless the snake tattoo that curled around her body was counted as a covering. Still, the Greek and Roman architectural influence waned the closer the party got to the Hall, as it was located in old Lugudunon.

A breathless messenger informed Matres of Concolitanus unexpected arrival in Lugudunon. She was angry at the apparent lack of civilities. Yet she was prepared as the Gaiscedach king entered her hall. Two hundred of her best warriors, alert and armed, lined the wooden walls of the room. That said, she was unprepared for the violence of Concolitanus' entrance as he almost took the entrance doors off their old iron hinges. The king did not look happy.

Concolitanus snorted, his posture was one of disdain for Matres' men. "Guards or king-slayers?" he roared. Accompanied by two of his men, he strode to the nearest of Matres' protectors, looked the man firmly in the eye and moved along the line. The inspection completed, the king moved back to the centre of the chamber. Matres watched. Her face, still as a statue, gave no clue to her thoughts. Concolitanus called the captain of his band to him and whispered in his ear. The man dipped his head, smiled and winked at another. Two spears were hurled with a swiftness and ferocity that did nothing to diminish their accuracy.

Pinned to the wall, two of Matres' men hung on iron spikes, their life-blood pooling at their feet. "King-slayers. You can tell by the strength of their gaze." Concolitanus laughed and sneered as Matres' remaining guards adopted a more aggressive stance. "Two hundred against my one hundred. Poor odds for you. Stand them down."

"By now, there's a thousand outside this Hall. You're a dead man, Concolitanus," snarled Matres.

Undaunted, the king gave a great belly laugh, "Even a thousand may not be enough. And, you will certainly die. A blast of a horn and I will have ten thousand outside your walls."

"And, those ten thousand will spill their guts on Lugudunon's walls," rasped Matres.

In the tense atmosphere of the unfolding theatre between Matres and Concolitanus, no-one observed Genovefa's serpentine glide across the wooden floorboards. She came to a halt within striking distance of Cornelia. A sharp yelp from Cornelia drew all eyes to the Roman. "What is this abomination?" the king shouted. "Do you think to replace Cathubodua with this creature?" Matres glared at her former partner. She was unnerved by the surprising movement of Genovefa, now returned to Concolitanus' side. A smug smile rested on Genovefa's painted lips. "Give the Roman whore up. She is to be killed and her ashes scattered to the wind. Otherwise, you'll bring the might of Rome and Brennus of the Senones against us."

"Never," spat Matres. "She is mine. Leave Lugudunon while you still can. Or your funeral pyre will warm my night."

A snapped order saw Concolitanus' party leave the Royal Hall. The cackling laughter of Matres rang in the king's ears as he retreated in the direction of the eastern gates. As the entrance came into view, Concolitanus gave an order to his second-in-command. "Kill the guards in the gatepost. Hold the gates until I return." The man dipped his head and smiled. The king and Genovefa marched away from the fort. Their army of ten thousand rested, hidden in the forested foothills of the Alpes.

"Did you accomplish your mission?"

Genovefa smiled, "Of course. Did you doubt that I could?"

Concolitanus laughed. "Matres will not be pleased."

News of Concolitanus' capture of the forward gates sent Matres into a rage. It was soon followed by the shouting of orders, liberally interspersed with threats. The single blare of a horn alerted her to the imminent arrival of the king's army. Meanwhile, Cornelia sat on a thick pelt on the right side of the throne. To her, and even though she was the catalyst for the upcoming battle, the whole episode seemed far from her fading grasp of reality. Cornelia reached a hand to her left shoulder and scratched what felt like an insect bite. Had she eyes in the back of her head, she would have noted two small circular punctures and the two slight scratches that trailed from them.

***

Lugudunon was situated at the confluence of two rivers, the Rodonos and the Souconna. Fortunately for Concolitanus, the hillfort was built on the western bank of the Souconna. Had it been built on the neck of land between the waters, then Matres would have had a formidable defensive position to add to her battlements. As it was, Concolitanus' army simply negotiated the slow-moving rivers. Matres watched from the eastern inner wall as her enemy marched upon her walls. Keeping out of spear and slingshot range, they quickly approached the east gateway.

Even with the loss of the outer entrance, Matres was confident in her ability to defend her ramparts. The courtyard between the outer and inner entranceway could accommodate fewer than five hundred warriors. Hence, the thousand warriors she placed on the eastern defences would always outnumber any enemy force. Lugudunon was an example of the strategic construction of defences. The only weakness was where the outer and inner convex walls joined and became one. It was here that the fiercest fighting would take place.

Matres placed her veterans at the two junctions. While the walls were broad, being about ten paces in breadth, and almost impregnable, only ten warriors could stand side-by-side across its width. She placed a cohort of one hundred of her best spearmen on each side. Standing in a block of ten rows, they would hold firm against any attacker. Any dead or severely injured would be pushed over the high walls, and it was left up to the gods to determine their fate.

From sunrise to sunset, the two sides railed and rallied. Matres' losses were minimal. Most of the blood splashed on the walls of Lugudunon belonged to Concolitanus' warriors. At dusk, the besiegers retreated to the warmth of their campfires and welcome food. Their tents were set up five hundred paces beyond the outer gate. At this distance, even a good slinger would be challenged to cause even a minor injury. Matres was anxious. This was not a tactic she had ever witnessed Concolitanus use before. His usual stratagems were either stealth and assassination, or all-out attack. As with his fellow Gaulish tribes, he rarely had the patience for a sustained siege.

Dawn brought a rumble of wheels, and then the sharp crack of battering rams thrust against stone walls. Matres cursed. Concolitanus grinned. The dismantled machines had been floated across the rivers during the night and assembled at sunrise. At the eastern wall, eight logs with sharpened and fire-hardened noses bashed the wall with little opposition. The rams were slung on chains and hung from a wooden frame. Each had a cover of wood and wet hides to protect from missiles, rocks, and fire. Several other rams were pushed into place further along the outer wall. Since the grassy mound that Lugudunon was built upon dropped sharply away from its walls, the remaining fortifications gave no ledge to support the massive siege machines.

A shrewd tactician, and now that he had bottled Matres up in her hillfort, Concolitanus had two immediate problems to solve. The first was how to keep his warriors from boredom and an inevitable drift away from the siege. The second was finding Matres' escape route. His solution to the first challenge was to send half of his force to rape, plunder, and burn the smaller settlements, mines, and farms that were scattered across the river valley. They were also to track down and engage Matres' warbands not trapped in Lugudunon at the start of the attack. Numbering in the thousands, these warriors, if properly commanded, were perhaps the most serious threat to Concolitanus' strategy. As to finding Matres' escape route, that was a matter of careful surveying of the ground around the fortress, time, and luck.

Matres leant over the crenellated wall and slapped the hard rock of her battlements with hands wrapped in leather strips. It was three sunsets since Concolitanus commenced his attack on Lugudunon. To the queen, it had become less of an attack. Actual combat was rare, and in most cases, her men were the victors. This smelt more of imprisoning her in a stone sarcophagus. She howled as she watched black smudges of soot stain clear blue skies. The bastard was dismantling her people's wealth, and likely dismembering her people as well. Matres prayed to the gods for vengeance and hoped her warriors beyond the hillfort had the sense to remain hidden, only attacking when the numbers were well in their favour. She would have need of her army to punish Concolitanus.

The queen's head pounded from the constant thumping of the rams. It was ironic that she had preferred stone to wooden defences. Rock was less flexible and more prone to crack than wood. Matres growled in frustration. Her face looked up sharply as a great cheer arose from the besiegers. Their labour had been rewarded with the appearance of several fissures in the wall. To Matres, it seemed like this gave them encouragement, and the incessant bashing of ram-heads against stone increased.

Several sunsets later, Matres looked at the ruins of her outer eastern wall and gateway. She heard the taunts of Concolitanus' men and the rumbling discontent of her warriors at the apparent impotence of their queen. When Concolitanus eventually departed, Matres would be forced to make examples of many to re-establish her authority. "Surely," she grumbled, "even Concolitanus must be bored with his plan."

Indeed, the king of the Gaiscedach was tired of his game. Rumours of other tribes raiding his borders angered him and needed to be answered. Yet one more piece needed to be moved on the fidchell board. A warrior, as tall, as broad, and as scarred as Concolitanus appeared at his side. The man was the king's shield-man and second-in-command. A fighter whose valour in battle rivalled the king. Hence, by Gaiscedach custom, he was a threat to the king's position. Only the fact that he was Concolitanus' friend from their youth and totally loyal had stayed the king's hand from disposing of him. Concolitanus looked at his friend and smiled as he dipped his head.

"It is done."

At the rumble and crash of stone, Matres dashed to Lugudunon's north-western wall. Or to be more precise, she ran to the edge of where the barrier should have been. At the foot of the hill, spread over the valley floor, lay the ruins of a large section of her defences. The faint smell of burnt timber tickled her nostrils, and she muttered, "Rot his balls." Raucous jeers from the besiegers as they retreated south across the Rodonos and Souconna, and eventually into the forests and their mountain strongholds, did little to improve the queen's humour. She had been outwitted, and by someone she considered of lower intelligence.

The realisation that Concolitanus never had any intention of conquering her bastion slithered into her mind. But why? Her humiliation, although painful, would pass and, in time, she would take her revenge. Matres felt a brisk northern breeze lift her hair and looked to the sky. Winter was not far off, and with it the violent wind known as the Máistir. She cursed. Was Concolitanus that cunning? Had she truly underestimated him? Was the weather to complete the destruction of Lugudunon? No! That could not be the full story. There had to be something else. A shiver of sudden comprehension travelled along her spine. The Roman bitch! A loud cry took flight from Matres' mouth.

"Cornelia!"

CHAPTER 32

404 B.C.—Cnocán-Mórrígan—Autumn

Tadhg kneeled on the slatted, wooden floor and puked. Unsteady, he tried to stand. Cramps seized his belly. Bent over double, he spewed again, watching the foul liquid seep through cracks in the floor to leave a splatter of undigested food. There was little left in his stomach, so when he tried to throw up for the third time, all he could manage was painful retching and muscle spasms. Bile and acid burned his throat and soured his mouth.

"No!" he howled.

Footsteps behind him signalled that his distress had been heard. Brocc was the first through the entrance. "Shite!" A trail of vomit and splashes of green-yellow bile led to Tadhg's feet. Beside him a wooden pail, its contents scattered, rocked slowly on its side. On Tadhg's bed of straw and pelts lay the body of Laoise. That the girl's head was angled unnaturally was due to it being severed from her body. Deep blue eyes stared at the entrance as if expecting her lover to enter. Long red hair formed a halo around her head. Its tips rested in a pool of slowly coagulating blood. A sword, presumably the one that took her head, rose up from between her breasts. The assassin's closing statement.

Brocc pushed his friends aside and knelt at the young woman's side. He placed his hand on her shoulder. "She's still warm." He looked at Tadhg, "How long have you been gone?" Stunned, Tadhg stared at Brocc, his mouth opening and closing without making a sound. Tight-lipped, Brocc turned to the small band, "This was bloody and happened very recently. Alert the watch. I want Cnocán-Mórrígan scoured for this woman-killer. Send runners to Conall, the Sidhe, and Crum Dubh."

Tadhg stared at Laoise for what seemed a long time. Soon his feelings numbed, and his mind took in the scene anew and with dispassionate objectivity. He took several steps towards her. Brocc made to stand between his friend and the corpse, but Tadhg shook his head, "I will mourn later. Laoise's spirit will not rest until her murderer is apprehended and executed."

The examination of Laoise had hardly commenced when Tadhg became mindful of another presence in the room. His awareness was prompted by the sharp pain on his cheek from a calloused, forceful hand, and a shriek of, "You cold-hearted, bastard. You set her up. And now she's gone." As his friends dragged a screaming Dufach from the roundhouse, Tadhg was left with the feeling that she was right.

"What do you notice about the body?" Tadhg's monotone question was directed at Brocc but was more an attempt to direct his own thoughts. Before Brocc could answer, Tadhg continued, "Cold, quick, and efficient. Killed by a sword thrust to her heart, then beheaded. The sword placed back into her chest as if sheathed." Tadhg gripped the hilt and tugged. "A strong man. The point is buried in the floor. A blade of no consequence. It will never be traced back to the murderer." Tadhg got off his knees and turned, "She did not suffer long. Not torture. Not passion. She bore a message for me."

He kneeled by Laoise's side once more. Tadhg lifted Laoise's hands, intending to lay them across her breasts. As he held them, he noted the dried blood and translucent slivers of skin that lodged under the nails. "She marked the bastard."

***

Lonán Ò Neill was not unsociable. Yet he preferred to live among other warriors rather than in society. Hence, and despite protestations from

Bláithín, he continued to reside in barrack accommodation. Today, his comfort level with humanity diminished to nothing. Spotted, as he returned to his quarters, by a baying crowd of loudmouths and miscreants fired up with beer and the urging of unseen agitators, he was judged guilty of Laoise's murder.

In some respects, the verdict of culpability was understandable. He was, indeed, covered in blood. Although, that was from an accident during a boar hunt. One of his companions had his femoral artery nicked by a tusk. Lonán was drenched in blood as he tried to prevent his friend from bleeding out. He failed, his comrade died, and hence, as he trudged back to the barracks, his mood was sombre. Lonán was in no frame of mind to tolerate the foibles of the mob and was very much in the mood to inflict pain.

New blood splattered Lonán's torso and scíath. Viscous droplets of crimson fell from the tip of the javelin grasped in his right hand. Previous attempts to overwhelm the Cróeb Ruad warrior had been met with pain and death. Never a man to be messed with, the warrior's resolve was simple. He would kill anyone who attacked him—male or female. Since he held the high ground on the raised walkway that ran along the hall's perimeter, his defensive position was excellent.

On the wooden steps leading to the entranceway, lay a cluster of bodies. Fools who had sought to tempt Fate. In the crowd, others lay dead or about to cross the veil. Lonán had identified them as leaders of the mob. Well within the range of a javelin throw, the thud of sharp iron ended their designs and severely wounded those directly behind. But the small supply of missiles stored near the barrack's entrance was quickly exhausted. He was down to a single spear and his sword. The mob was increasing in numbers although their leaders had slunk further back.

"Cróeb Ruad go Brách!" Lonán roared defiantly and contemptuously swatted away a fresh batch of stones, horse-shite and assorted rotting vegetables with his shield. The response of "Murderer!" from the crowd was predictable if puzzling to the broad-shouldered warrior.

He shouted, "Cróeb Ruad go Brách!" hoarsely, hoping for support from his Cróeb Ruad comrades. At the periphery of his vision, to his right and left, he saw men bludgeoning their way through the mob. He sighed in relief and ended one more assailant's life with a thrust to the throat. Another corpse was added to the mound of dead.

Muttering obscenities and threats that their courage would never allow them to act upon, the throng retreated as a hundred men formed a barrier across the front of the barracks. The clash of iron rims sounded as the shield wall locked into formation. The hedge of javelins, daunting for a well-prepared army, was frightening for a frenzied horde of civilians. Lonán sighed and breathed easier. It was then he noticed the third body of warriors carving a path through the middle of the mob.

Two bands of men, each one hundred strong, each armed to the teeth and each skilled in the use of their weapons, faced each other. They stood ten paces apart. There was little emotion on their faces. These were warriors. They took orders and fought. They killed. That was their job. Across the gap, friends and shield wall comrades looked into each other's eyes and knew no quarter would be given or expected. Brocc, Crum Dubh, and Tadhg strode into the space between the lines. "A right pig's arse of a situation," muttered Brocc, more than aware that a single wrong move could spark off a massacre. Worse, with over one thousand Cróeb Ruad warriors within the tribe, a spark in this tinder could destroy Clann Ui Flaithimh.

Crum assessed the situation quickly. The taint of sedition still hung in the air from the attack on Cnocán-Mórrígan. It was improbable that all the ringleaders had been caught and executed. This predicament gave the survivors a second bite at rebellion and had to be forestalled. He walked closer to the Cróeb Ruad shield wall. "Lonán, you are a commander in the army of Clann Ui Flaithimh. You know this cannot and will not be tolerated. Lay down your weapons. Come with us to the Great Hall." Any answer from Lonán was drowned out by calls for his death by the mob. Crum turned to face the crowd. "This matter will be addressed according to the Fénechas, and I am the arbiter of the Laws. Enough blood has been spilt. Disperse. Go back to your homes. No further action will be taken against you." Alas, the throng was past rational discourse. The rumble of threats continued. The crowd pressed forward.

The druid shook his head in frustration and looked with barely concealed anger at Tadhg. "*You* have a lot to learn about people. Go, fetch Conall *and* the Sidhe." Tadhg dipped his head in acknowledgement not only of the command but of the implication that the fire that had been lit was at his door. As he turned, Crum added ominously, "Tell Conall to bring more—many more men with him."

The sight of a grim-looking Conall, with his jaw set as if carved from granite and steel-blue eyes that seemed to pierce deep into each person, sent ripples of anxiety coursing through the rabble. In Conall's eyes, this was a coming together of the worst of the tribe. That the king of Clann Ui Flaithimh was accompanied by a sour-faced Fearghal with his longsword already unsheathed, and the Sidhe, whose usual presence struck fear and awe into anyone with an ounce of sense, only served to raise the level of unease of the crowd.

Conall shook his head as he gazed on Lonán and the shield wall that protected him. There was, he knew, no guilt to be laid at Lonán's feet. He cursed Cuán and the madness that had pulled together the tribe's malcontents and who, once again, were only too ready to cause trouble. He swore at their sheep-like followers. Anger at his own culpability knotted his belly. The king sighed heavily. How was he to deal with Lonán and a guard Conall would happily send out to slaughter his enemies? He stepped forward.

"Lonán, you know me. I need you to put down your weapons and come with me. Some things need to be resolved."

"That's not going to happen, my king." A blood enrobed Lonán came to the edge of the stairway. "These bastards," he pointed to the throng, "Have their blood up. I'll never make it through them alive.

They are too many. It would only take a thrown blade… even a well-placed slingshot, to end me." Conall scratched his head, all too aware that Lonán was right in his assertion. He called for the Sidhe, Crum, and Tadhg. After a few words and scurried actions, a table and seats were brought and set between the two rows of warriors. "In that case, Lonán, if you're agreeable to those present as your judges, then we'll conduct proceedings here." A bemused Lonán nodded his consent.

"First, the murder of Laoise…" A loud, rumbling chorus of "Murderer" gathered momentum through the crowd. "Quiet!" roared Conall. Soon, shouts of "Tyrant" were heard. Conall exhaled and called Brocc to him. In a voice loud enough to carry to the rear of the throng, he said, "Take charge of my caomhnóirí. Any citizen fomenting trouble is to be detained and held for trial and execution; any citizen wielding a weapon is to be executed instantly." A nervous hush descended on the mass, followed by the rustle of clothes as blades were secreted from view.

Conall's attention returned to Lonán. "Laoise scratched her assailant. Likely on the face or arms. There'll be fresh, deep lines of broken skin." The king looked at Lonán and groaned. The man was covered, from head-to-toe, in a shroud of blood. The warrior held out his arms and part of the casing of dried blood flaked from his body. Conall looked around and espied several barrels used to collect rainwater.

Sat in the shade, the water was very cold. Lonán gasped as several men hefted the casks and sluiced him down. To totally, although likely somewhat unnecessarily, clean the last vestiges of blood from his body, Lonán peeled off his wet pants and tossed them aside. "Not exactly a shrinking violet, is he?" muttered Fearghal to Mongfhionn. She just smiled and, like many other women in the mob, admired the sculpted, hard body presented to them. When Lonán was judged clean, Conall nodded to Tadhg.

Disconsolately, the young man trudged up the wooden steps to where Lonán stood. He felt a thousand pairs of eyes mock him as he inspected the warrior. In his heart, he knew that the examination would reveal no trace of Laoise's struggles on Lonán's torso and face. All that was visible were the lines of old battle scars. A hand touched his shoulder. He flinched, expecting it to be followed by a rock-hard fist. "You're a warrior like me. You're just doing your job," came a surprisingly soft voice. "I'm very sorry for your loss. She didn't deserve her end."

Tadhg dipped his head in appreciation. Together the two men thudded down the steps and walked to where Conall stood. A scream of, "No! He murdered Laoise," came from the spittle-flecked mouth of Dufach. She hurled herself forward pulling a blade from the sheath on her thigh. Sun glinted on the well-oiled dagger as it travelled towards Lonán's back. Brocc's actions were involuntary, honed by many battles and duels. As he stepped to protect Lonán, his scíath swung around catching Dufach on the chest. The sword in his hand moved in a shallow arc, parallel to the ground, and entered her side. Little resistance was met as the blade cut through skin and muscle. Dufach gasped and slumped against Brocc before sliding to her knees in the dirt.

"Why?" choked the anguished warrior who had dropped to his knees and held the woman.

"She was my daughter," came the reply.

"Lonán is innocent of the accusation."

"That may or may not be. I'll find out when I meet Laoise in Tír Tairngire." With a final burst of strength, she grasped Brocc's bloody hand. "Not your fault, son. Not your fault." Eyes closed, Dufach slumped forward, and the bean-sidhe collected another soul. Absolved of blame by Dufach, it would be a long time before Brocc forgave himself.

***

Many sunsets later, no-one had been caught. Justice for Laoise remained unserved. It was meán lae. Tadhg sat on a tree stump, lost in his own thoughts and unaware of the approach of the Sidhe. As her shadow fell across him, he looked up and stared into the face of his worst nightmare.

This was not the awesome, sometimes awful, beauty Mongfhionn customarily presented. It was the Hag, and her visage struck terror into Tadhg. His heart froze. His pulse seemed no more than a faint echo.

"Foolish *boy*," she snarled, "When you are *advised* by those wiser not to follow a course of action, take the counsel. I will not haunt your dreams. Rather, the eyes of an innocent will give you no peace."

Tadhg shivered. The Hag glanced upwards to the eagles circling above. "Fate and the Goddess still favour you." Tadhg exhaled a sigh of relief. "*But*, Conall has a geis to fulfil. I will tolerate no obstacle to his path. Fail him, and me, again, and whether you are favoured by the gods or not, I will pluck your beating heart from your chest and feed it to the ravens." With a swirl of her cloak, the Hag turned, and darkness descended on Tadhg.

Covered in the morning dew, Tadhg slowly awoke to a persistent prodding. "Do you think he's going to sleep all day?" Confused the young man looked up into the faces of Torcán, Brocc, and Deaglán. A sharp ache in his chest elicited a yelp. "I see you've been visited by our Lady Sidhe." There was a sympathetic tone to Torcán's observation. The pain in Tadhg's chest pulsed as if in concert with his heartbeat. He glanced down and saw the crimson, heart-shaped imprint on his chest.

"Oh shite!"

"The Lady does like to leave a reminder of her chastising," said Torcán, rubbing the red mark on his throat.

CHAPTER 33

404 B.C.—Late Autumn/Winter

The rivers in northern Aremorio flowed sluggishly southward, eventually joining with the Liga. They were vital to the region's trade in gold, wine, and slaves, and were a map for Mórrígan. The day drew to a close as the raiding party stood at the edge of a great loch. Bridle and halter fittings chinked as horses dipped heads and softly nickered. Frustrated by the smell of the water that was so close yet out of their reach, they pleaded for permission to drink.

Against the backdrop of an ochre sky, the golden sun drifted regally towards the horizon. It gave the lake the appearance of a fiery maw to the Otherworld. In the calm of dusk, only the slap of fish breaking through the glass-like surface of the waters and the cheerful evening birdsong disturbed the idyllic setting. That said, 'disturbed' was an inadequate description of the natural harmony on display.

From the cover of the lakeside forest, where leaves in autumn shades of orange and red had begun their short-lived dominance over the evergreens, Mórrígan and her chieftains scoured the vista and the river beyond. In the twilight, it was difficult to perceive the opposite bank. The hillfort of the Andecavi was a faint purple-grey shadow against the sky. A few torches flickered on its ramparts, but the fort was quiet. Sleep had overtaken the majority of its population, silencing the clamour and chaos of their daily routines. The few discernible people, likely the watch, were tiny, shimmering outlines.

The tributary's span was about a good slingshot, and at this point, it was shallow enough to cross without a problem. Mórrígan looked at Amodocus and Sarpedon. "Muffle the horse jewellery. We'll cross the tributary here and bypass the hillfort. A short canter along the bank of the Liga and we'll cross the border between the Andecavi and the Carnutes. We'll find a good campsite and rest until the sun rises." Both men dipped their heads in agreement.

As she gazed on the Liga, the queen of Clann Ui Flaithimh felt small and, unusually, a trifle nervous. Even the mighty Abha na Sionainne in Ériu or the Abhainn Dubh in northern Albu paled in comparison to it. "Perhaps we should have asked Pytheas for a few of his galleys," she muttered. So far, the journey south from Cnocán-Mórrígan had been free of serious incidents. There were always skirmishes by fools, driven by beer or bravado. Few had the strength to challenge Mórrígan's warband.

The memory of the shocking defeat by Conall was still uppermost in the minds of the tribes in Aremorio and the lands south to the Liga. Still, among the Celts, the propensity for in-fighting was never far from the surface. Tribes weakened by the battle faced raids from former allies, who sought to extend tribal borders. The queen was aware that Conall's cavalry under Íar and Nikandros had orders to raid deep into Veneti, Venelli, and Andecavi territories, capturing or destroying the fruit of the land. Conall wanted to sap the strength of the tribes through hunger and disease, leaving them unable to defend or endure a cold, wet winter. Gold, appropriated from the mines, would be added to Clann Ui Flaithimh's wealth. Without, the ability to trade food or buy goods, the economies of Aremorio's tribes would be devastated.

"We'll make camp here this evening. See to your horses. Keep the fires low. I don't want to alert anyone to our presence or burn the forest down." A ripple of laughs circulated among the band. It was followed by a cough from Crum Dubh. Mórrígan smiled and gave the druid a look that said she had not forgotten. "But first, we'll drop our sacrifices of thanks to the Goddess into the river and ask her blessing on the rest of our journey." The druid smiled and dipped his head in approval.

On the far side of the Liga, the flickering flames of torches and braziers outlined one of the strongholds of the Carnutes. Hands firmly gripping the rough bark of a lookout tower's guardrail, Acco of the Senones stared across the still waters. The chieftain was a guest of the Carnutes—an ambassador from Brennus. On Acco's arrival at the Carnutes' primary hillfort at Cenabum, Tasgiitios, ruler of the Carnutes and known as 'The Badger', remarked sarcastically that it was not often an envoy arrived with a bodyguard of a thousand warriors. Diplomatically, Acco simply bowed with appropriate deference, smiled, and requested permission to travel to the fort further downstream. Tasgiitios had little choice. The Senones under Brennus were not to be refused.

"Too late for fireflies or glow-worms. Could just be sióga," Acco murmured as he observed intermittent flickers of light in the forest. Did he imagine a faint scent of wood smoke and cooked fish? He breathed in deeper, but that only served to clog his nostrils with the smell of decay from rotting vegetation, and the piss and shite of the hillfort's residents and livestock. It also banished any idea of taking a refreshing morning swim in the river.

His orders from Brennus were explicit. Find the Clann Ui Flaithimh raiding party and assess its strength. Acco snorted. Translated, that meant engage the enemy and bring back its leader's head. He exhaled. By reputation, Mórrígan was not stupid. It would be surprising if she traversed the Liga this far downstream. There were too many settlements for her to raid on the far side. Why risk crossing a broad, if shallow, Liga? Probably she would also stay back from its marshy river plain. The soggy ground gave her riders no advantage. Acco shrugged. Battling the Dark Huntress was a contest that he relished. As for attacks on Carnutes settlements, that was not his concern. They were not of his tribe.

***

At twenty summers, Beacán was the youngest of the Ó Cathasaigh brothers. He smiled, dipped his head to his sister, and dismounted. With a movement smooth with practice, he unslung the bow from his back, released the bowstring, and carefully inserted the stave into its sheath. The young man considered himself only a passable archer. Nevertheless, he knew how to take care of his weapon. Unfastening his broad leather belt, he slipped the long scabbard and sword from it and fastened them to the mount's girth. They would be a hindrance for the task ahead. He retied the thick cord that kept his arse inside his green plaid pants around his waist. Then, after positioning a braided belt on his hips and over a moss-coloured shirt, he secured it with a fist-sized, wolfs-head buckle of gold and bronze. Beacán then slipped a silver-embossed baldric over his head, settling the soft inner pad on his left shoulder.

Next, he took up a short, iron sword. In length, it was little more than from the tip of his middle finger to his elbow and was based on the double-edged xiphos that Nikandros preferred. It was good for both slashing and stabbing. With a soft whisper, the sword was sheathed in the sheepskin lining of its scabbard and attached to the sash. Three throwing knives were placed into loops on the strap. A further two would be slipped into his soft leather boots.

Placement of the blades brought a smile to Beacán's face. To most, it was a toss-up as to whether Iasg or he was the better knife-thrower. In his head, he acknowledged she had the edge on him, but with more practice that could change. He scratched his chin and smirked. At the rate his nieces, Brighid and Danu, were progressing, they could quite possibly overtake both he and Iasg. With a final flourish, the warrior pushed two throwing axes into loops on his belt. The handles tapped gently against his arse as he settled all his weapons into place.

Amodocus laughed as he watched. "I think you may have some Thracian blood in you."

In contrast, Mórrígan's look was tinged with sadness. The Goddess' gift to Beacán was anonymity. Of average height, his body was slim yet muscular, and the long, flame-red hair of the Ó Cathasaighs smouldered rather than burned. He had a face that, while certainly not ugly, and which could be devastatingly charming when he smiled, was instantly forgettable. In a crowd, Beacán was unseen. He could cut the throats of a dozen persons and, even though drenched in blood, those around would swear the crime was committed by someone else. Also, with his strange loping gait he could cross ground quickly and almost invisibly. In short, the young man was the perfect scout—or assassin.

Further upstream, the Liga flowed in a gentle arc through a landscape entirely devoid of hills or mountains. The land's gentle undulations were mostly carpeted by a diversity of trees—ash and alder in the marshy areas close to the river, and oak, beech, and pine further away from the stream. Scattered farms and small settlements clustered around local forts. Most were built of rough wood. Stone was used if a quarry was close. By and large, each community was poorly defended. There was just too much ground to cover. No more than three-score of warriors and whatever men and boys laboured on the land usually manned the forts.

Ribbons of smoke smudged the sky behind Mórrígan. The cries of the terrorised constantly rang in her ears. The Goddess was merciful in that the dead made no sound. Amodocus sensed her thoughts and scowled at her once more. His men were displeased at the constraint with which she bound them—no raping of girls under fourteen summers. When first advised of the rule, the Thracian had thrown up his hands, exclaiming, "How on earth can my men tell how old they are? In the midst of battle, are we to politely ask their age and expect them to be truthful?" He further argued that he knew of girls younger than fourteen who had breasts as big as their mothers. Mórrígan's retort that she would be the arbiter of age and that any who broke her law would find their balls fed to the hounds brought a giggle from Gràinne, a smile to the druid's face, and a fiercer glare from Amodocus.

It was mid-afternoon as the Huntress looked at the minor hillfort, which sat on slightly raised earth at the apex of the river curve. It was more substantial than the previous ones, with a high, double-walled stockade and a ditch that ran around the perimeter. No doubt the trench held nasty surprises other than the inhabitants' sewage, and rotting meat and vegetables. Watchtowers were strategically placed to give maximum sightlines. The fort's main entrance was on the riverside. This made sense, as the presence of vast sandbanks, some made firm with a profusion of grasses and shrubbery, made the water eminently fordable at this point. The location was good for escape as well as reinforcement.

The queen nodded to her brother. Beacán smiled, knelt, and lifted a handful of ash from a cold fire. He rubbed the cinders over his decorated belts and weapons. Then he set off at a brisk lope in the direction of the hillfort. He was quickly out of sight. To her men, she said, "We'll camp in this glade tonight and await my brother's return. If his news is good, we'll attack from the west after the sun has reached its zenith."

***

Splashes at the river woke Mórrígan. She kicked a sleeping campfire, breaking its grey-black crust and tossed several logs onto it before striding in the direction of the sound. Beacán whirled around, throwing-axe in hand. His sister smiled and raised her hands, "Only friends here." She noticed the blood on his hands and arms, and the swirl of pinkish-red in the loch water. With concerned and experienced eyes, she quickly inspected her brother. An audible whisper of relief escaped her lips when she saw he was uninjured. "Trouble?"

"It's a trap. Sticks and stones!" Mórrígan looked questioningly at her brother. He chuckled, "Spears and slings."

"Carnutes?"

Beacán shook his head, "Senones—about a thousand of them. Veterans. In the forest on the eastern side of the ráth. The Carnutes in the fort are bait." He chuckled, "From the campfire conversations, about half of the Carnutes deserted once they realised their sacrificial role. So there's only about a score—thirty at the most—warriors inside the fort."

Strangely, both sides had the same tactic. Each wanted to fight on the firm, open ground between forest and fort. Except for the Cretans, Mórrígan's band were horse-fighters. Their horses were as much a weapon as the blades they carried. She preferred not to fight in the forest where limbs flung out from trees could knock a horseman from his mount. Or where fallen trees, moss-covered rocks, and brooks could result in torn tendons and broken fetlocks in the beast and broken necks in riders tossed from their perch.

As with most of the Gaulish tribes, Acco's warriors were spearmen first, swordsmen second, and tacticians last. After being fortified by beer and motivated by their chieftains, most rushed in a battle frenzy to throw themselves at the enemy. There was little finesse to their actions, being all slash and stab. There was also no great desire for prolonged battles. It was a strategy to win quickly or cut-and-run to fight another day. Like Mórrígan, Acco had little willingness for a struggle in the forest. Against the Huntress' cavalry, he preferred an area clear of obstacles where he could assemble a hedge of spears. The assumption, which was mostly correct, was that horses did not favour and would not charge a line of iron spikes.

Mórrígan hesitated to issue her next order, but she had little choice. She put her hand on Beacán's arm. "I'll send the hounds out when it's dark. Just their presence will make sleep fitful for the Senones." Beacán smiled in agreement. "Choose a handful of men and follow the dogs. Convey a message to the Senones that they will understand." The young man nodded and jogged off to select his companions.

The Huntress strode across the camp to where Sarpedon, Amodocus, and Gràinne sat. They carved pink-fleshed fillets from fish roasted over smoky fires, washing the throat-burning meat down with beer and wine. As usual, Amodocus was ogling Gràinne, while she charily, perhaps with too much emphasis, was avoiding his stare. With a shrug of resignation, Mórrígan joined the group. At least, while the Thracian's focus was on Gràinne, he was not bothering the queen.

Amodocus grinned and offered a fillet of the highly aromatic pink-fleshed fish. It proved irresistible. Mórrígan's stomach rumbled its demand to be satisfied, and she wolfed down the first piece. Slightly guilty of destroying the flesh so swiftly, Mórrígan restrained herself and savoured the next slice that was offered. She smiled. The cooked fish bore Sarpedon's imprint, and she was getting better at separating the various herbs he selected to enhance the food he prepared. With a sigh, she brought the light dinner conversation and Amodocus' drooling over Gràinne to a close. Looking at each of them, in turn, she said, "Sunrise. You know your roles. Stay with the plan."

***

"Bastards!" the rich, bass voice of a sleep-deprived Acco growled. He stood before two rows of battle-tested spearmen. As the sun rose, it cast a soft gold and pink hue over the eastern wall of the Carnutes hillfort. Its remarkable beauty was usurped by a nightmarish tableau of naked corpses. Headless cadavers, strung up by their wrists, swung from the upright posts of the hillfort's stockade. Braided leather ropes, damp with dew, creaked in synchronised harmony as the corpses gently rotated in the morning breeze.

Spiked on their own spears, skulls with sightless sockets—the eyes having been pecked clean by ravenous ravens—faced their comrades from a position midway between the opposing forces. In response, Acco's men and women averted their eyes, stretched muscles, stamped feet, and smacked spears on shields. The routine took their minds off the dead and a night haunted by growling wolfhounds and the odd opportunistic bite.

A slingshot's distance from the Senones, Mórrígan was barely able to distinguish one warrior from the next. They looked smaller than the wooden dolls carved by doting grand-das for their young kin. Alongside her, Beacán, Bricriu, and Amodocus leaned over the smooth velvet necks of their horses. Eyes strained to gain some useful insight. The druid, Crum Dubh, chose to remain with the group of disgruntled guards tasked with keeping an eye on the supply wagons and spare horses.

Mórrígan thanked the Goddess as the sun slipped behind streamers of pale grey cloud. Every advantage was welcome. They would be in their enemies faces before the full glory of the sun was seen again. She shouted, "Advance!" The mounts first stepped and then walked forward.

Acco tugged a scraggy blonde beard. Its poverty of fullness was a constant source of embarrassment to the tall, barrel-chested noble, and of merriment to his men who cruelly nicknamed him 'The Beard'. His men faced the oncoming riders. The Senones had little uniformity of armour. For many, their only protection was several layers of thick winter clothing. Calves and ankles were wrapped in long strips of woven wool or sheepskin if they were lucky. Both rows stood, spears stabbed into the dirt and shields slung on their backs. With slings ready, they were spaced to allow for swinging the potent but simple weapon. The hum of slings being readied brought a smile to Acco's face.

As Mórrígan's horse cantered past the speared skulls, the Huntress raised her hand. The warband encouraged their mounts to a gallop. Alongside them bounded the wolfhounds. Almost synchronous with the queen, Acco gave the order for the slings to be loosed. His men would only have a few volleys before the beasts and riders closed the gap. The queen's body ached with bruises and cuts from the slugs launched by the enemy's slingers. Several horses screamed and tossed riders from their backs. There were, however, no significant injuries. Slings were not very effective against a fast-moving target. Soon the barrage ceased as the Senones dropped their slings, gripped spears, and charged.

From the forest, Gràinne and Sarpedon watched. During the night, with wheels, tack, and hooves muffled, they had slowly felt their way to the position suggested by Mórrígan. Sarpedon knew there was a massive difference in distance between an arrow launched to kill its target and one meant to distract or injure. His job was to create chaos in the enemy's formation, and hence, his archers were little more than fifty paces distant from the charging spearmen. Thus, his bowmen were also dangerously close to Acco's men when, with arrows nocked, they emerged from the cover of the woods. As the edge of the Senones passed their position, the Cretans launched volleys of barbed shafts.

It was instinct, the ability to sense danger and act in self-preservation, that made Acco grab the warrior to his right and use him as a shield. Three arrows thumped into the unfortunate man's chest. Acco tossed him aside and looked along his line. Men cried out and stumbled as arrows thudded into poorly protected flesh. Others tripped over their comrades. The line trembled as men—and women—eyed with increasing anxiety the impact of unseen arrows launched from the edge of the forest.

A nod from Sarpedon brought a massive grin to Gràinne's visage. Screaming like a demented, half-naked—even Gràinne sought the comfort of plaid triubhas in the winter—bean-sidhe, Gràinne gripped a javelin. As they sprang from the cover of the forest edge, whips cracked above horse heads as charioteers cajoled their mounts to higher speeds. Given their head, the shaggy horses needed little encouragement. Nostrils flaring they snorted with joy, vying for position as they pulled the vehicles. Gràinne had changed the horses used from those favoured by Íar and Nikandros' riders to ones that had been bred from Eachdonn Breac's gift. She had a hunch that the smaller, longer-coated mounts would be better suited to the job. It looked as if she was right.

Gràinne, already hoarse yelling commands to her cohort, was relieved to finally reach the Senone line. The sigil-covered Cinn Péinteáilte warrior swept a long-sword from the sheath on her back. Holding the sword two-handed, she braced, balancing herself as the team of horses leapt in-tandem over several bodies and the cret bumped over the same. Dirt and mud splattered the Senones as the chariots wheeled and swerved among them. Warriors run at different paces. Thus, holes had appeared in the Senone lines. The chariots took advantage. Soon the whirling scythes on spoked chariot wheels and the swords wielded by the chariot-masters were covered in gore and shards of bone.

Faced by a resourceful enemy who wielded the disparate parts of her warband with ruthless efficiency, Acco watched his strategy falter. In succession, his force had been assailed by archers, chariots, and a horde of mounted warriors. His men were unnerved by the arrows and fast-moving vehicles. He watched as, on his right side, a band of screaming Thracians, their horses' heads and chests protected by chainmail, launched heavy iron bolts before switching to long-handled swords, axes, and maces. Men's skulls were reduced to a bloody pulp by the heavy-ended clubs. On the verge of panic, Acco's line trembled as he shouted commands to stay in formation and attack.

The Cretan archers now selected individual targets and the painted striapach's cruel chariots continued to rake his rear line, pouncing on any weakness and lagging clusters of warriors. Technically, his force, even with its losses, well-outnumbered their opponents. This did not, however, take into consideration the horses, which appeared to relish battle as much as their riders. Broad chests knocked men out of their path. Hooves trampled them into the dirt. Powerful jaws crushed bones. The sound of barking sent a shudder up his spine. He cursed. The wolfhounds had entered the affray.

A blood-curdling shriek drew his attention to his left flank. Acco cursed as he sighted the apparition known as the Dark Huntress. She was readily identified by the gold and silver embellished helmet. Trailing black feathers from its raven crest flared in the wind. Fortunately for Acco, Mórrígan's band, unlike the Thracians, had a lesser range of weapons and fought more traditionally, if only because no-one had yet devised a way for them to remain in motion and mounted while using their bows. The band of riders threw several volleys of javelins.

As the last javelin was loosed, Mórrígan's band slammed into the Senones. The whisper of blades unsheathed from scabbards and the creak of leather as axes were pulled from belts were drowned by the war cries of the Clann Ui Flaithimh. Momentum was with Mórrígan's men as they threw themselves at an already weakened Senone front line. The long spears of Acco's warriors gave little advantage when set against the slashing of long-handled cavalry weapons and the height of their fighting platform.

Although the sides were roughly equal, Acco knew that he fought an increasingly futile battle. Spear and shield worked in unison but seemed to do little other than provide fresh scars, but not mortal injuries. Assailed on his flanks, Acco saw his men flail as they coped with three fighting styles. The number of the dead was not worrying, but the steadily mounting toll of injured who had no sanctuary of retreat was ominous. Soon, both sides, man and beast, would suffer fatigue and the skirmish become a gore-soaked brawl. It would be at that stage, at the point of exhaustion, when mortal wounds would mount.

In desperation, Acco looked to the hillfort and cursed the ill-luck that placed the fort's entrance on the riverside. His men would have to slog through boggy land before reaching safety. A retreat across the river was unthinkable and would only serve to present his men's backs to the Clann Ui Flaithimh horsemen.

Acco bludgeoned a path closer to the Dark Huntress. Chips of wood flew from his shield as he considered the options before him. He could challenge the queen to a traditional duel, and she would be unable to refuse. Yet, as he watched Mórrígan swing twin, long-bladed daggers, slicing throats and opening up deep gashes on pale, pock-marked faces, Acco suspected that the odds of him winning were too finely balanced. In his calculation, he also knew of Mórrígan's gory reputation. Few survived an encounter with the queen. If she lost, would her men honour the result of a contest between them?

Those around Mórrígan and Acco sensed a confrontation between the leaders and moved back several paces. Acco stood, spear raised, before the queen's pale-gold horse. *It was a magnificent beast*, thought the Senone. As it snorted and stamped its feet, it was a mirror image of its master—gore-bespattered and defiant. The Huntress scowled. If this Senone chieftain wanted a duel, then she had no option but to concede to tradition. She also knew she could not remain mounted. That would be seen as ignoble. With a sigh, the Huntress swung her leg across her mount's shoulder and slid off the dillat and onto the dirt. Her blades remained firmly gripped in blood-stained hands.

It was Acco who gave the first hint of his intentions as he lowered his spear tip and took two steps backwards. The space allowed Mórrígan to move away from her horse. Skittish at the sudden change in tempo, the horse dipped its head, snorted and stamped the ground. Bricriu's hand on its reins calmed the beast. "We can fight, or we can talk. That choice is yours," called out Acco. In response, Mórrígan sheathed one blade and removed her helmet. Lank tresses of red hair fell onto her shoulders. The queen's usually lustrous hair smelt of travel dirt and sweat.

"What do we have to talk about, barbarian? You're plainly losing."

"You're too experienced, Mórrígan, Queen of Clann Ui Flaithimh, to believe that," Acco chuckled as he removed his helmet. It was a tall, conical bronze and iron helmet with little embellishment, noted Mórrígan. She observed her opponent as he scratched golden stubble. Acco preferred a head of very short hair. "Perhaps we could order our forces to stand down while we negotiate. It would at least let them gather their strength should our talks come to nothing."

"Your pragmatic demeanour is tinged, possibly tainted, with optimism."

Acco shook his head in mock disappointment. "Such cynicism." Mórrígan shrugged and dipped her head at Bricriu. A crisp, triple-noted phrase was repeated several times by a bronze hunting horn. It was accompanied by the deeper reverberations of a Senone warhorn. She pointed to a small clump of tree stumps several paces away. Acco nodded and walked towards the prospective seats. "Better this than sitting on our scíatha."

"What's your offer?"

"Simple. If you count the horses and those bloody chariots, our two forces are roughly equal. The warriors on both sides are all veterans. They will brawl in the mud until there is no strength left in their bodies."

He looked at Mórrígan and was pleased as her head bobbed in what he took as agreement. As he more closely examined her face, Acco was fascinated by the swirling berry-blue designs. He noted that her arms were also covered in similar sigils.

"The answer to your unspoken question is 'yes'. Much like those of the Cinn Péinteáilte, the tattoos cover all my body." Mórrígan pointed to Gràinne. "Much like her… only mine project a much more sinister tone."

Acco's Adam's apple moved up and down as he gulped. "My warriors and I are brother Celts. We have no interest in a long-drawn-out battle where both sides slash and batter each other to exhaustion." He pointed to Mórrígan's riders. "Neither is your warband configured for this type of skirmish. Your strength is in your horses."

"Brothers?" Mórrígan snorted, "Pray continue, *brother*."

"I propose we call a truce and both sides go their own way. I have achieved my goal of assessing your strength and tactics. You have given one of Brennus' best cohorts a bloody nose. Honour is satisfied for both of us. I see no sense in prolonging this engagement."

"Agreed," said Mórrígan and noted with some satisfaction the sigh of relief that slipped from Acco's lips. "Do you wish to share food with us? The sun is at its zenith."

Acco chuckled, "Thanks. But I think that might expect too much restraint from our men." Before he stood, the Senone added, "If you follow the Liga, you'll eventually come to Cenabum. It's impressively fortified and a major settlement of the Carnutes. Its importance, however, is as an economic and religious centre of the Gaulish nations. The druid who accompanies you will know well of the latter." Mórrígan flashed an irritated "we'll talk later" look at Crum Dubh, who had edged closer to the duo. Acco grinned, then looked more soberly at the Huntress, "My king, Brennus, considers it a duty to ensure Cenabum remains neutral and therefore, profitable. He will not tolerate anyone who disturbs its position in the region. Likely, your band will be endured in the hillfort and doubtless, welcomed by the merchants who will sell goods to anyone."

"And if we continue our education of the Carnutes to not be a nuisance to our clann?"

Acco scratched his head and spoke, "Kill, plunder, pillage as much as you wish. They are not my people. I have no responsibility for them. That is the duty of Tasgiitios." The Senone chuckled, "Your reception in Cenabum will, however, be frosty." The tall chieftain stood and stretched his arms and legs. Gathering his thoughts, in more ominous tone added, "Once beyond Cenabum, you will be in, or sufficiently close to, Senone lands. Brennus will not tolerate any armed force other than his own in his domain. I have a thousand men…"

"Not anymore," interrupted Mórrígan.

The Senone dipped his head in acknowledgement. "Brennus can field thirty thousand warriors. Even the famed An Fiagaí Dorcha of Clann Ui Flaithimh will not prevail against those numbers."

Mórrígan smiled and shook her head, "It is not my charge to conquer the Senones or their armies. That I will leave to my Rí Ruirech." She reached out a hand to Acco, and as they grasped forearms, she said, "We'll fight again."

"Yes. Yes, we will. The gods, I think, wish it."

As Acco walked away, Mórrígan called her brothers. "Gather the men and Gràinne, we should persuade the occupants of the hillfort to vacate their residence for a few nights while we rest. If they're reasonable, we'll not burn the fort down when we leave."

CHAPTER 34

404-403 B.C.—Cnocán-Mórrígan—Early Winter

The sun set as Torcán tramped back to the roundhouse. Even in the damp chill of the winter day, his body was covered in a film of sweat from training with Brocc and Deaglán. His usual musky odour was on the cusp of rancidity. As he sniffed the air, or more accurately under his arms, his nose crinkled. He needed to bathe but inwardly protested the idea. His nipples could punch holes in the thin ice that had started to enclose the ponds.

With a quick movement of his right hand, he pulled back the entrance's heavy covering. The hide kept the cold north winds from making the building inhospitable. A wave of welcome heat radiated from the roaring wood and peat fire at the centre of the home. The blaze gave needed warmth and relegated the yellow flames of the many rushlights to minor subjects. He smiled, delighting in his lover as she rose from the rough wooden seat. The homely tableau made Torcán glow unaided by the fire.

He considered the soft swell of Mòrag's belly and the bosom that cast a shadow on it. "Putting a bit of weight on?" The words had barely left Torcán's lips when the temperature of the room matched that of the exterior. He groaned at how his mouth had overruled his common-sense. He coughed, "What I meant..." It was too late. There was no recovery.

"Bastard!" shouted Mòrag. The friendly horn of beer in her hand became a missile, narrowly missing Torcán's head. Grabbing a heavy sheepskin-lined cloak, she stormed from the home.

Fear steadily built up in Torcán's mind, twisting his belly into knots. He had no idea how to remedy his foolish quip. Angst continued to sour his gullet at the thought of losing Mòrag. He paced the room, dredging the depths of his mind for inspiration. It soon dawned on him that the home was unusually quiet. Where were Barra and the hound? "The Hag," he mumbled, "I must be in deep shite." His anxiety notched up a few more levels. By the time Mòrag returned, his state was close to having gone ten rounds with Lonán Ò Neill.

"Sit down. We need to talk." Torcán's face fell at the awful words. He had really messed things up. In his mind and the absence of Barra, it all added up. Mòrag was going to end their relationship. He opened his mouth, but Mòrag's palm halted any words. In fact, the look on Torcán's face nearly broke the princess' heart. Her lover had never developed the ability to mask his emotions or his feelings. It was one of the reasons that she loved him and why she now felt so guilty.

"I have something important to say." Torcán groaned. Mòrag, caught between guilt and needing to speak, uncharacteristically burst into tears. In a trice Torcán was at her side, his arms around her shoulders. She cushioned her head against his chest, and the brash warrior felt tears soak the light covering of hair.

"Don't worry. It'll be alright. I'll just go. We can still be friends."

"Oh, shut up, you eejit. I'm carrying your child. Your leaving is not an option... never was." Torcán was speechless at the news. As his mind grappled with what he had been told, it seemed his hand performed the only sensible act and caressed Mòrag's belly. Soon he was on his knees covering her stomach with kisses. Mòrag ran her fingers through his hair and smiled. The unpolished and bluff warrior had learned a lot in their short time together.

"If you ever call me fat again, Torcán Ò Dubhghaill, I will cut your balls off." She sniffed the air, "And when was the last time you had a bath?"

***

It was mid-morning. In the broch at the centre of Cnocán-Mórrígan, the roaring fire threw out friendly warmth. Comforting aromas of roasted meats and bread baking on flat iron plates and hot stones added to the friendly aura. The demeanour of the chamber's occupants was in stark contrast. Across the table from Conall and his Chomhairle sat the five leaders of the local Gaulish tribes. All additional personal guards were barred from advancing beyond the ráth's frost-covered ramparts. Frustrated and taunted by the Clann Uí Flaithimh warriors who lined the stockade, they muttered curses, drew cloaks closer, and milled around. It was one more insult to be added to the long list of grievances that lined their weather-worn faces with helpless scowls.

For their part, the Chomhairle attempted to maintain an air of neutrality and stoicism. That said, their none-too-successful attempts at preventing the ends of their mouths lifting upwards into smirks did little to ameliorate the Gauls' humiliation. Yet, Conall's council were not all in-step. While most sat, the Sidhe stood, her staff of oak grasped firmly in porcelain fingers. Obsidian eyes alternately glared at the Gauls and Fearghal. The painted designs on her face seemed to glow and flow like liquid gold in the light of the fire. Mongfhionn's intimidating aura certainly increased the tribal leaders' anxiety, *which was good*, thought Conall. The impact on her partner was less visible. Only the set of Fearghal's jaw gave any indication as to his true feelings. Conall sighed, the clann's tempestuous couple were fighting again.

The Gauls came to Cnocán-Mórrígan to plead for relief. They needed a truce. Conall's incessant raids were impoverishing the kings and nobles. In the reckoning of injury, their people came a distant third. "You have my terms," said Conall in a firm but not overtly hostile voice. He had some sympathy for their plight and, in truth, his warriors and their partners and families wearied of the daily raids. None would consider refusing to carry out their orders, but most yearned to cuddle up with their loved ones, rut, and hibernate. The increasingly miserable weather—daily showers of cold rain and sleet and biting north winds—did little to lessen their yearning for a more cloistered winter.

"Cattle, grain, and gold," growled the putative leader of the group. He was the king of the Venelli. Once friends, under the late Dubnoreix, the Venelli had switched sides after a calamitous war with the Veneti. Both tribes had lost many fighters in that skirmish and even higher numbers in the battle for Cnocán-Mórrígan. The only consolation for the Venelli was that they had suffered less and were now stronger than the Veneti.

Conall nodded, "A tithe of your wealth to be delivered to me on the feasts of Samhain and Imbolg. Think of it as an incentive to encourage my people not to remain in Aremorio beyond the spring."

"Incentive, more like a bribe," grunted the Venelli king.

"Is that not the way of the Celts and Gauls?"

"Agreed," the king sighed, "To both the tax—and that we're all open to bribery."

***

It was unfortunate timing. Even as Conall sealed the armistice, a last scouting party set out on patrol before the onset of deep winter. They were on foot. With sharp ears, the sound of a bell struck or horn blasted on the ramparts could still be heard. Thus the group was reasonably close to Cnocán-Mórrígan. Most of the Venelli settlements and farms close to the community had already been razed to the ground. Expectations of trouble were low.

Swathed in multiple layers of pelts and tunics, Torcán still shivered. His metal helmet, with its woollen liner, was almost too cold to bear. He sensed something was amiss. While it was not surprising to come upon a handful of farm buildings, it was undoubtedly puzzling to see a trail of smoke curl upwards from what appeared to be the central roundhouse. There was none of the usual human activities or noises associated with a small-holding. That, however, could be explained by the farmer, his male kin, and slaves being in the woods. The women might be inside the roundhouse cooking or preparing and preserving victuals for the winter. However, the absence of any smells associated with such goings-on was curious. It added to Torcán's suspicion that all was not as it appeared.

Mòrag's thoughts travelled along the same path. She pointed to a large copse of pine and oak trees to the east. "That could hide a lot of warriors." Torcán nodded. He scanned the buildings once more. The tall barn to the left of the family home looked solid, defensible. The stockade and dry, stone walls around the croft lay scattered in the dirt. Obviously, the result of a previous raid. A closer look at the various structures showed black scorch marks and thatched roofs that, if they were to be weather-proof, would need substantial repair. Torcán pointed to the more substantial outbuilding. Mòrag nodded. The warband divided into two and with scíatha raised and weapons ready, the two lines of warriors strode watchfully across the field in the direction of the byre.

A sonorous war-horn heralded the attack. From two sides of the copse poured several large groups of warriors. In all, about five hundred charged Torcán and Mòrag's band. "In the name of the Hag, how did Íar's patrols miss this mob?" shouted Torcán. Caught in open ground, his hundred instinctively formed a shield-wall with fifty men in each row and faced their attackers.

There was no time for Mòrag's cohort to uncoil slings. Instead, her men divided and took up positions to protect her partner's flanks. Known as the Raven's Wings, it was a tactic that had rapidly gained acceptance within the armies of Clann Ui Flaithimh. They would shield the exposed ends of the wall while using their spears to drive the attackers onto the swords and javelins of the shield-wall. It seemed as if no time had passed between the first sighting of the enemy warbands and them being within spitting distance. Propelled by manic fervour and gaunt with hunger, they threw themselves at their enemy.

It was a moment of ill-fated misfortune that, just before the barbarians struck his part of the wall, Torcán glanced at Mòrag. His eyes met hers for no more than a brief moment before travelling down to the swell of her belly. The bull-necked warrior froze. He did not hear the scream of, "No!" from his lover.

A sharp tug on his shield tore Torcán from his momentary reverie, exposing his chest to the silver-grey blade of a war-axe. Helpless, in the slow motion of battle, Torcán watched the axe reach the apex of its arc before descending. A red-hot iron dragged slowly down his torso from chest to his lower abdomen. The pain was intense and thankfully brief before blackness took him.

"You bastard!"

The shriek was not what Torcán expected upon entry to Mag Mell. Nor did he think that the promised virgins awaiting him would all resemble a very angry Mòrag. He flinched as she raised her fists, thinking perhaps she was about to finish him off. The minor movement set his chest on fire and pushed daggers of pain deep into his head. He wanted to puke but knew that would definitely finish him off. He whimpered as an animal caught in a snare. The faint sound did, however, bring a look of contrition to Mòrag's face.

"You stupid man. What did you think you were doing?"

"Fear," he whispered hoarsely. The strong taste of iron in his mouth was unsettling. How badly was he hurt? Would he live? Was he missing any vital parts? Was he missing a particular part? Still in shock, with difficulty, he focused his gaze on Mòrag. Her countenance informed him that a single word was not going to suffice. Calling on any strength he might have, and with ragged breaths, he said, "I froze. Afraid for you… and our baby."

Mòrag exhaled. "I knew it. Your eyes told me." She loved Torcán more than life itself, and the thought of losing him gave her nightmares. Tears streamed down the warrior princess' cheeks. "You bloody stupid man. We're warriors. We're born to fight. It may be our only real talent. We'll most likely die a glorious and bloody death in battle, *but* you will die like a man, not a lovesick juvenile. You will cast fear aside and do what you normally do—kill our enemies without mercy."

"So, I'm not going to die?"

"You should be so lucky." Torcán sensed a tone of retribution in her voice. "The two men behind you reacted quickly, grabbed your mail-shirt at the neck and hauled you backwards. Otherwise, we'd be burying both halves of you." The princess paused, "The chainmail absorbed most of the axe blow, but the mail and undershirt are buried deep within the wound. Plus, congealed blood has bonded the mail to your body. We'll have to cut and peel the mail off you, then pick out each tiny piece of iron from the gash. And, that's before we clean the wound and sew you up."

"Mail cost me a fortune," gasped Torcán. Mòrag looked unsympathetically at the gold and silver bands that covered Torcán's muscled upper arm, and the heavy gold torc around his neck.

"Somehow, I don't think you're a pauper," she said. "Besides, I'm a princess. My credit is good."

"Knock me out."

"I considered that option, but it might do more damage to whatever brain you have left. Bite on this." Mòrag slipped a piece of wood wrapped in leather into Torcán's mouth and nodded to the others in the barn. It was not overlong before the sound of the stick breaking was heard. Morag winced as if sharing Torcán's pain. A single tear rolled down a dirt- and blood-smudged cheek as she watched her partner slip into blessed unconsciousness. She offered a prayer to the Goddess that it would not be her last memory of the warrior.

The gates of Clann Ui Flaithimh swung open as the party approached. Runners had been sent ahead with news of Torcán's injuries. The Sidhe, Fionnbharr, and several druids stood in the gateway. Torcán lay across three shields bound together and braced with poles cut from nearby trees. "Come back with your shield or on it." Conall looked with puzzlement at Nikandros as they watched the band tramp closer. The dark-haired, olive-skinned warrior smiled, "My mother told me that each time I left to fight."

"Her favourite son, were you?" Nikandros chuckled and turned to climb down the gatepost's ladder. He had an honorary Spartan to greet.

CHAPTER 35

403 B.C.—Cnocán-Mórrígan—Winter

It was winter. The weather was miserable. The people of Clann Ui Flaithimh, whenever they exited their accommodations, sloshed and tramped through pools of icy slush. Clothes quickly became soaked as rain, impregnated with hail, seemed to fall unceasingly from slate-grey skies. Many grumbled that, while the temperature might be a bit higher than in their native Ériu or Albu, the conditions were worse, especially when the north and northwest winds added their bite.

Amid the musky smells of stale sweat, piss, and rutting, another surfaced—decay. Clothes rotted. Boots and bróga disintegrated. Damp feet that never dried became foul-smelling and encrusted. Skin sloughed off, leaving feet raw and blistered. Men, women, and children expelled globs of phlegm, saliva, and snot. Eyes ran, and throats itched as seasonal coughs and sneezes increased. Few took the precaution to, or were courteous enough to, cover mouths and nostrils with a square of cloth. Even those that did promptly tossed the sodden article aside instead of burning it.

As in past winter seasons, the mass of the infected steadily increased. So too did the number of those who were taken by the mná-sidhe. Death and her servants culled the weak—the elderly, the very young, and the already sick. It was always sad, but was rationalised as making the clann stronger. The fittest survived to couple and produce a new tribal crop around Lugnasad. Yet this winter was different. There were more deaths, and not just of the weak. The healthy succumbed, not as rapidly as the sickly but nevertheless, they too died.

Speculation as to the source of the disaster focused on two culprits. The tribe was on a vital trade route to Albu. Therefore, merchants wishing to both sell and purchase goods were frequent visitors. Fionnbharr, the tribe's healer, recalled that some members of recent caravans did not appear to be in the best of health. Like Conall's friend, Pytheas, many came from the lands bordering the Great Sea. It did not take a seer to envision what potential maladies might arise from that region.

Yet, the more accepted malefactor was more visible and thus more acceptable: the uncommon number of rats and, in turn, the hundreds of fleas that each carried. Driven by predators from the forests surrounding Cnocán-Mórrígan and the small communities guarded by the tribal fortifications, thousands of rats invaded Clann Ui Flaithimh's lands. Around the settlement rose a crescendo of cursing, the smack of hands on flesh bitten by numerous fleas, and the slap of flat-bladed shovels crushing the skulls of vermin. Children wailed as they were nibbled while sleeping.

The clann's wolfhounds were set loose on the invaders. It was a forlorn effort. Even the crushing jaws of the hounds made little impact on the numerous long-tailed pests. Rescue came from another predator— feral cats. The progeny of pets stranded from Phoenician trading ships, the cats typically stayed in destructions in the woods, well away from humans, whom they quite rightly distrusted.

They, however, could not resist the feast placed before them. In smaller pounces, they moved onto the clann's domain. Soon they became the first line of defence and attack. More efficient killers than the dogs, the cats ripped through the besiegers. Yet, they were no friends to the people of Clann Ui Flaithimh and did not hesitate to use razor-sharp claws and teeth to reinforce their independence. Children wailed from the long scratches received, when they tried to pet the cuddly demons.

From the first wave of minor symptoms, it was not long before Fionnbharr began to see signs of headaches and fevers, and vomiting.

To his distress, this evolved rapidly to severe bruising, uncontrolled bleeding, and death. And so it was that Fionnbharr and Mongfhionn met with Conall to review and adopt a strategy to defeat an enemy that proved to be more dangerous than the tribes surrounding them.

"I have already lost one in twenty of my people to this curse. Am I helpless to prevent the deaths of more?"

The Sidhe was startled at the king's demeanour. Conall's voice lacked strength, and his breath was laboured. Trembling fingers constantly rubbed his temples. Ordinarily vibrant, observant eyes looked watery and red-rimmed. She started when the back of a hand dragged across his nose came away with faint streaks of blood. Momentarily, setting aside her concern for Conall, Mongfhionn stood.

"We persevere as we always have done. Burn the bodies. Crush and bury the bones. Use fire to clear the waste pits and ditches. Raise the homes of the afflicted to the ground and reduce them to ashes. The druids and healers will give succour to the ill and the healthy. With sacrifices, we will keep faith with the Goddess."

***

Conall knelt beside the stream and slipped his gift of gold and armour into its cold waters. He coughed briefly and spat on the ground. The phlegm was bloody. He felt tired and looked thinner. His strength was waning, and with difficulty, he raised his hands. "Too many things will go unaccomplished if your people perish, Goddess. Our enemies are many and will have no mercy on us. If your will is not to protect your people or your Hand, then I beseech you to keep safe my queen and children, that they might fulfil your will."

The eagle swept down, wings spread and talons open as if ready to strike. Conall felt the wind ruffle his hair as the great bird glided over him. From the breeze, he heard three words, "Fire and water." With little effort, the Goddess assumed her place with Fate in the skies above Conall. A piercing gold-flecked eye stared at Fate.

"Why? He is my chosen Hand."

Fate smiled. "Chosen he may be, but he is not immortal."

"Will he live?"

Fate screeched and wheeled away. He had sighted a sheep caught in a thicket of hawthorn. "Bastard!" Screamed the Goddess, then dived to beat him to the prey.

Several of Conall's guard, worried at his absence, found the king lying beside the stream. They laid him on several scíatha and carried him to the Sidhe. The only words spoken by the Rí Ruirech of Clann Ui Flaithimh were "Fire and water." Once uttered, the king's strength departed him, and he drifted into unconsciousness.

A worried Mongfhionn grasped Fearghal's arm so tight that the warrior winced. "The bean-sidhe has not called. There is still hope," said Fearghal, encircling his partner with strong arms. He trusted his words sounded more comforting than the despair he held in his heart.

***

Cúscraid stood alone on the western end of the fortifications. Cold, salty winds from the sea buffeted him, alternately trying to tear his cloak from his shoulders or shroud him in its sheepskin folds. The taciturn warrior stood resolute, unflinching as the elements battled to dislodge him from the wall. The scene perfectly summed up the warrior's life, except for the moment he stretched his arms upwards and roared, "Why?"

Earlier, head bowed, he stood with his friends at the funeral pyre of his beloved partner. She had been his sole companion since they were children. Never joined officially, Cúscraid prevailed on Crum to conduct a hand-fasting ceremony while she still held onto a spark of life. There was never a doubt that the Druid would refuse. Cúscraid remembered the smile on her lips as the words were spoken, the light cords that bound their hands together, and softness of her lips. Her scent, violet and wild strawberry, would forever command his nostrils.

With a great sigh, Cúscraid removed the urn from under his cloak. It seemed too small to contain all that she was. He hesitated, not wanting to carry out this final task. A sob escaped his lips. Tears streamed down weather-worn cheeks as he raised the vessel up and tipped out its contents.

Unseen and unknown, Fearghal and Mongfhionn stood well back from their friend. They kept watch over him—just in case. For a moment, the clouds parted, and it seemed in the moonlight that Cúscraid was at the centre of a vortex of shimmering silver. The Sidhe put her hand on Fearghal's arm. "We should go. His love watches over him as she has always done."

CHAPTER 36

403 B.C.—Cenabum—Winter

Like an over-scratched hive, the mound sat in a landscape that otherwise was flat as an oatcake. Mórrígan sat on a thick green dillat astride her mount and observed Cenabum for the first time. The weather was cold, but not unpleasantly so, and thankfully the incessant rain had ceased. The hillfort and settlement of Cenabum were shrouded in ribbons of bluish smoke from hundreds of fires. To those onlookers with a more poetic disposition, the fort appeared to have an ethereal quality. Perhaps the gods who protected it sought also to mark its spiritual role.

Cenabum was not, as many hillforts, built on elevated ground, a jutting headland, or an island surrounded by water. Generations of farmers, however, had deforested vast woods to produce the plain upon which Cenabum sat. In doing so, they gifted the citadel with exceptionally long sightlines. It was unsurprising that its defences included high wooden walls and multiple two-story round and square towers. A high-status and formidable fort, it stood at the point where the River Liga turned south and was proximal to the fluctuating borders of three major tribes—the Carnutes, the Senones, and the Biturges.

Given a choice, Mórrígan would have preferred to lead her band away from what she understood to be a heavily defended ráth. Yet there was no cover for her group to ghost past the settlement during the day. At night, the winter skies would be clear and the moon bright. There would be few shadows into which they could blend. Besides, her men were tired. They needed a rest from fighting and plundering Tasgiitios' lands. Hands and faces were ingrained with the soot and blood from many skirmishes. Her men smelt of smoke and horse sweat, piss, and shite. While not as fastidious as the Sidhe, the Huntress yearned for a bath. She had heard rumours of copper and bronze tubs filled with hot water for soaking. Surely, a fantasy, she thought.

Mórrígan pointed to the distant settlement, "We ride for Cenabum. Let's hope there's truth in Acco's assertion that the community, while being a Carnutes' ráth, is also neutral territory." She looked at her brothers, and Amodocus, Sarpedon, and Gràinne, "We kill no one… unless we have to." The Thracian grinned broadly. His infernal white teeth were even more striking with the added darkening of his skin.

Close-up, the hillfort was magnificent. It was approximately square with each side long enough to stand seven hundred warriors side-by-side. The walls, built as a series of timber boxes filled with earth and stone, were three spears high and ten to fifteen paces wide. A running fence of sharpened stakes topped the ramparts. An outer ditch and berm ran parallel to the palisade. At each corner was a two-story tower, approximately half of which jutted beyond the ramparts. The two on the west-facing wall were rectangular; the two on the east-facing were circular. Myriad shelters and workshops sprouted up along the battlements, using the rough wooden defences as an anchor wall. That, thought Mórrígan, could be a strength or a weakness. While it would be almost impossible to burn the fortifications down, the buildings could readily be fired.

"Now, there's a message," said Amodocus as he pointed to the substantial gates. On each gatepost were nailed six skulls. Pieces of skin still clung to the more recent additions. "Criminals, enemies, or poor artistic taste?" The gateway, which faced the east, was heavily fortified with a square tower on each side. The turrets were staggered to restrict vehicles—chariots and wagons—and people, and to provide defensive cross-fire if required. A wooden platform, which could be removed if the ráth was under attack, bridged the perimeter ditch.

"What's your business?" The thickly accented demand from the tower on the right side interrupted Mórrígan's inspection of the fort. Before she could answer, Crum Dubh had moved his horse forward.

"I am Crum Dubh, Leader of the Ériu, Albu, and Aremorio Councils of Druids. I have an audience with the Oracle, Rosmerta."

"You're full of surprises, Crum. I'll be interested in hearing your explanation for keeping this appointment from your queen... and king." The tone in Mórrígan's voice left no one in any doubt of her displeasure. As he looked on the queen's face, Crum shivered, for it seemed that the tattooed and painted sigils were much more noticeable. For the first time, he truly sensed the growing power emanating from Mórrígan. Its signature was not unlike that of the Sidhe.

"In good time, my Queen. I, however, may be your only passage into Cenabum. The settlement's neutrality will have been sorely tested by your ravaging of the Carnutes' lands. I doubt Tasgíitios has tender feelings towards you." A snarled response from Mórrígan was curtailed by another shout from the gate tower.

"The druid can enter. The rest can go to the Otherworld."

"That man is destined for a short life," murmured Mórrígan as, in an effortless movement, she unslung her bow. Crum shook his head. Indicating the group of riders with a flourish of a pale, blue-veined hand, he addressed the guard.

"These are my protectors. They will enter with me. You know the rules. A guest of Rosmerta cannot be refused. Do you wish to face *her* anger?"

A furious round of swearing and discussion was ended by the appearance of a burly warrior. With an air of authority that the previous guard lacked, he called out, "Druid, your 'protectors' are a murderous band of thieves led by the witch known as the Dark Huntress. The king has hitherto forbidden their entry to Cenabum. However, you place my king in an unenviable position. He has no wish to deny the Oracle." The man paused, largely for effect before continuing, "You may enter with a guard of no more than twenty. All will leave their weapons, apart from one dagger."

"At this time, I think this is the best we can do," said Crum.

Mórrígan nodded and then turned to her brothers, "Find the men shelter suitable for several sunsets rest. The nearby farms may have barns and outbuildings, as well as food, that can be bought. I'm sure the men can find suitable entertainment outside the fort." To Gràinne, Amodocus, and Sarpedon she said, "You will accompany me. Choose from the men to make up the rest of our party. Once inside, your first priority is to identify caches of weapons. Just in case."

As she walked her pale-yellow horse through the gateway, the stench and sound of civilisation burst unpleasantly upon Mórrígan's senses. A wave of claustrophobia swept over her. The cloying closeness of society pressed down on her. She had never witnessed so many packed into such a small space. Buildings were predominantly rectangular rather than circular. How could people live in homes no more substantial than an animal pen? She missed the chaos of diversity.

Before them stretched a broad avenue. Equally spaced, on either side, tall wooden posts displayed skulls, partially decayed corpses, armour, and banners—trophies from past battles? They were interspersed with life-size, carved stone statues of warriors, perhaps the heroes of those same battles. To either side of the avenue, arranged uniformly in streets on an east-west axis, were many rows of timber houses and workshops.

A cacophony of noise and odours ascended from the buildings. The clang of hammers striking anvils, grain ground on circular quern stones, and the rattle of looms weaving cloth. Young children with dirty faces and snot-encrusted noses ran barefooted, screaming in play. The poor and the orphaned scavenged for food or items of value to sell. Some stopped to squat or piss into the inner ditch that ran the length of the walls. The stench of sewage and decay rose up from the trenches. Mórrígan shook her head. If it was barely manageable in this cold season, what would the smell be like in the summer? Thankfully, there were also aromas of baked and roasted foods and the fragrance of wood fires.

At the end of the boulevard, but still at the centre of the settlement, was a fort-within-the-fort. "The Sanctuary," murmured Crum. His voice held a tone of reverence. The structure, built of timber and mudbrick, was segmented into two square structures, one resting within the other. The outer timber palisade was contained by a ditch and berm. A score of warriors stood guard on the raised bank. An elaborately carved gateway faced east and, as seemed to be the custom, was decorated with skulls.

Several large trees and shrubs provided natural cover, although their purpose, in part, was to hide a mound of crushed and burned bones, both human and animal. Crum pointed to an inner rectangle. It was much smaller but still had its own ditch, palisade and gateway, and guards. Beyond its entrance lay the sacrificial altar. Behind that, there appeared to be the living quarters.

"The Sidhe would be at home here," muttered Amodocus.

Mórrígan glared at the Thracian. Still, the thought had also occurred to her. Movement at the entrance to the inner sanctuary caught Mórrígan's eye. An old, she must have been at least three-score summers, female waddled, painfully towards them. In her youth, Mórrígan could envisage the small woman—she was a head less than the height of a javelin—as being quite pretty. Now, Rosmerta was severely disfigured. Deformed hip-joints gave her the odd gait. Her spine was unnaturally curved, making her head tip to the right and one half of her face looked frozen. Only steely eyes gave a hint of her power. She gripped a bronze-headed staff encrusted with gems. A substantial gold collar tipped with lion's paws rested heavily on a scrawny chest. Brooches, decorated with gold, amber and coral, held her outer cloak together.

She smiled at Crum and offered her cheek, "It has been a long time. Enter. We have things to discuss." Then her gaze fell on Mórrígan. Used to having people wilt under her stare, Rosmerta at first bridled and then chuckled as the queen's emerald eyes held her look without flinching. "An Fiagaí Dorcha. I have heard much about you. Not all good." A loud screech and the shadow of outstretched wings swept over the sanctuary. Somewhat chastised, Rosmerta continued, "You have the favour of the Goddess, but that can be a two-edged sword. Be wary. Your powers are growing. Likely, even now you still do not comprehend them." The elderly woman cackled, "Where is your brother?"

Mórrígan's answer did not please her. Irritated, she turned to Crum, "I expected the young man to accompany you. He cannot ignore his gift any longer. One day, he may take my place." Mórrígan scowled protectively at the manner to which her brother, Bricriu, had been referred. The Oracle ignored this, instead saying, "The king's palace is beyond this building. One of my acolytes will escort you to your accommodation. The kings request your presence at the evening feast."

"Kings?"

"Just so. One ascendant and one bruised."

***

Tasgiitios' palace was an imposing complex of four wooden buildings. A Great Hall sat at the centre with two small- and a medium-sized room conjoined on its left and right sides. The Hall functioned as a feasting chamber and where the king would meet his subjects and receive envoys. The larger of the remaining structures was the king's private quarters; the others were for guests. Smoke, sound, and the smells of roasting meat, mixed with sweat, puke, and beer, billowed out of the doors as Mórrígan, along with Gràinne, Amodocus, and Sarpedon, stepped from the half-light of dusk across the sill of the Hall's solid doorway. The doors slammed shut behind them, and heavy bars were slid into place to secure the room.

"It won't be easy to fight our way out of here," quipped Amodocus. Gràinne's hand instinctively reached over her shoulder for her longsword. She hissed, remembering it was secured elsewhere.

"There's a concealed doorway behind the throne chair." Sarpedon's sharp eyes had noticed the heavy tapestry hanging on the wall, move slightly under a draught. "It would be unusual for there not to be a concealed back entrance to the fort beyond that door. Kings are under the constant threat of assassination." Mórrígan acknowledged this with a smile and signalled for the group to move forward. The slatted wooden floor felt solid under their feet. The carpenter knew his job. Multiple fires in pits and hearths heated the room. Walls hung with pelts and richly coloured banners and tapestries, many with quite intricate designs, also added to the warmth.

That her group were still wearing heavy fur and sheepskin-lined winter cloaks substantially increased their personal temperatures. Beads of sweat formed on Mórrígan's brow as she walked forward. Surprisingly, there were few remarks from those seated around the tables that lined the chamber's longer sides. A few snarled and spat as she passed. Probably the chieftains of communities her warband had raided. Four sat at the high table—two kings and two shield-men. A great slab of oak, smooth and darkened with age, rested on wooden trestles. The whole assembly was placed on a raised plinth, giving those seated a commanding view of the Hall.

Mórrígan recognised Acco and dipped her head. It was acknowledged with a smile. To Acco's left, sat a red-haired man who exuded a confident arrogance. She assumed this was Brennus of the Senones. Curiously, while the others at the table, and indeed the room, had discarded their outerwear and sat in a riot of coloured woollen shirts and pants, Brennus retained a thick fur-lined cloak. On Brennus' left, Mórrígan deduced was the Carnutes king, Tasgiitios. His demeanour was distinctly unhappy. A scowl never departed his face all night.

"The famed Dark Huntress, Queen of Clann Ui Flaithimh. Scourge of the Carnutes." It was a rich, deep voice. Heavily accented, yet easy to understand. To Mórrígan, it seemed that Brennus derived an inordinate amount of pleasure at Tasgiitios' discomfort. It was with remarkable restraint, she thought, that the king of the Carnutes remained in his seat. Given the sour look on his face, he had plainly swallowed the bile that had risen up in his gorge. The shield-man next to Tasgiitios mirrored his master's aspect.

Silent and observant, Mórrígan stood, awaiting a sign from either king. Given the enmity between her and Tasgiitios, she was not clear why her presence had been requested. A natural instinct for survival heightened her senses. Was this to be an assassination? That seemed unlikely. Celts and Gauls had strict rules about guests, and even enemies, who shared food. "Come, remove your cloaks and sit. They'll serve you better when you leave. The food is good and the wine plentiful." Brennus' voice boomed across the Great Hall.

The queen nodded and unclasped the fist-sized bronze and gold brooch that held her fern-green mantle closed. She heard Gràinne's cloak fall to the floor, smiled and waited for the inevitable reaction. Apart from tactfully placed, oblique broad leather belts, both were naked. Although, that was a narrow interpretation. Both were clothed in swirling painted and tattooed sigils. The chamber erupted with loud shouts of, "Cinn Péinteáilte, witches, and whores!" More than a few simply leered at the women, rubbed their crotches and suggested a variety of positions for rutting.

"The entertainers have arrived." It was the first time that Tasgiitios spoke and, in truth, he would have been better to have kept his seat and his mouth closed. His dismissive tone grated on Mórrígan. Yet, his audience appreciated his words and resumed their lewder shouts. Apart from the methodical stroking of his beard, Brennus sat still and observed.

"This is Gràinne Ni Fearghal, a Queen of the Cinn Péinteáilte." Gràinne looked askance at the queen. It was highly unusual for her to be referred to by her Cinn Péinteáilte title. And she was not entirely comfortable with the memories it brought. Mórrígan continued, "If any of the brave men present wish to face her sword-to-sword, I am sure she will oblige." That brought a broad grin to Gràinne's face. The level of the noise in the Hall became more subdued. "I am Mórrígan, Queen of Clann Ui Flaithimh, named An Fiagaí Dorcha—The Dark Huntress, by the Goddess." She looked around the room. "My enemies tell that I am without mercy. Do not test me."

To Brennus and those in the Hall, it seemed as if a dark aura swathed Mórrígan. Dread began to intrude the minds of all present. "Enough!" barked Brennus whose mind had resisted the infiltration felt by others. "You have amply demonstrated that we underestimate you at our peril. Tasgiitios and I apologise for the lack of respect shown to a guest under our roof and protection. Come, sit and eat."

"I think not, Brennus. For, have we not accomplished what this encounter was really about? You should really pay more attention to the words, the warnings, of Rosmerta."

Brennus laughed, "Acco described you well, as did Rosmerta. You are welcome to stay, but you will also find a welcoming fire, food, and drink in your quarters. You are, after all, our guest."

Mórrígan bowed respectfully, "Until we meet again."

"Yes, and that is a prophecy that is sure to be fulfilled."

***

The farmer was too cooperative, the outbuildings and corral too perfect, and Mórrígan's brother's premonition too believable. Beacán slapped his brother, Bricriu, on the back, "Let's go talk to the owner." It was a substantial roundhouse. Much bigger than needed for a farmer, his wife and two young daughters. The home could comfortably house twenty or more. The brothers observed the family seated around an old table worn smooth with age. The woman looked anxiously at her daughters. They were twins and seemed no more than twelve summers old. By contrast, the farmer appeared quite nonchalant. Two leather pouches of gold thudded onto the table. They were quickly grabbed by the man.

"Where's the rest of your kin?" asked the older brother, Bricriu. The man seemed nonplussed at the question.

"What?"

"It's a big holding. Substantial buildings. Lots of land to till, plant, and harvest. There must be more than just the four of you. Where's everyone else?"

"At the fort. They're all at the fort." The man's eyes darted back and forward nervously as if searching for an escape route. He glared at the woman, but she gave him no succour. Instead, she bit her lip until it bled and held her girls closer.

"So, you're agreeable to the payment? The gold for all your food stores and feed for the horses. We'll take the livestock too." The man nodded vigorously.

Beacán nudged his brother and winked knowingly, making sure the man would notice. Then he looked lasciviously at the twins. "We'll take them too."

The mother screamed, "No!"

"Shut your mouth, woman." A lecherous smile drifted across the man's face. "That would be extra but sure, yes. Take them, too." Beacán nodded to the two men who had accompanied them. The girls were wrested from their mother and carried, kicking and screaming, outside. Sobs filled the air of the home as the mother rocked back and forward on the bench. The man placed his hands on the table and made to stand.

"If that's all."

The daggers that pierced and pinned his hands to the wooden slab elicited a high-pitched scream of pain. "That's the first honest sound that's come out of his mouth," said Beacán. "This is more my line of work than yours, brother." Bricriu sighed, took the woman by the arm and led her to the entrance. In the roundhouse, Beacán looked with contempt on the man, "You're either not the father, or you don't deserve to be the father."

Outside, the woman hugged her daughters and led them away from their home. She flinched at the sound of shrieking and pleading for mercy. In her heart, she knew there would be no pity. She did not care.

***

A hand clamped over Mórrígan's mouth. She struggled briefly and reached for her blades.

"It's a trap," whispered a voice.

It took Mórrígan a few moments to overcome the confusion of sleep and the surprise presence of Beacán at her cot. "What madness has infected you, brother? You should not have come here." Beacán quickly related the incident at the farm. In between begging for his life, the 'farmer' revealed that a large force of Senones was closing on the farm. An attack was imminent, likely just before dawn.

"Raise the others. What about the sentries?"

"There are no guards—anymore."

The fading light of rushlights forestalled a violent reaction to being suddenly awakened. Fortunately, having not remained at Brennus' feast, the remainder of the group were only slightly groggy as opposed to falling over drunk. "Perhaps we should leave Brennus a similar message," growled Amodocus as he took up his dagger, crossed the sill, and stepped over the bodies of those who had guarded them.

"I considered that," said Beacán, "But Brennus is no fool. His doorway is guarded by five warriors, three of which lie across the entrance. Killing the guards and then reaching him without a sound would be impossible." Beacán paused, "Besides, I don't think he's there." Mórrígan nudged her brother to continue. "By reputation, Brennus' snoring would shake the walls, and he has a frequent need to piss during the night. I heard no evidence of either." An impatient edge crept into his voice, "The alarm will soon be raised. We need to move quickly and silently to Cenabum's back gateway. Fifty paces beyond the entrance, horses and weapons are waiting."

In a few scattered copses, birds' plumage rustled in nests in anticipation of the dawn. Sharp shadows in the moonlight heralded Mórrígan's group as they ghosted into the farmholding's open yard. Hooves crunched on the frost-covered dirt. According to Beacán, there were three Senone encampments to the east, west, and south of the farm.

He did not think that there was a camp on the river side of the farm. This was perhaps in expectation that Mórrígan would not be foolish enough to take that route. The Huntress was impressed at the discipline of Brennus' men. There was no evidence of campfires to pinpoint their location.

That her riders were already mounted with horses' hooves covered in sheepskin and tack swathed in cloth to mute any noise, pleased Mórrígan. Gràinne found that her chariots had also been prepared for silent flight as well as having their scythes removed to avoid accidents. The spare mounts were loaded with as many supplies and weapons as they could carry. Several wagons were abandoned. More would be stolen if needed.

"You know your duties. Use the sandbanks to cross. We'll reunite upstream on the opposite side of the Liga."

The only retreat open to Mórrígan was to ride east along the river and to cross upstream. There was no alternative to an encounter with Brennus' eastern camp. Fortunately, the ground closest to the river was hard from winter frosts and was perfect for mounted warriors and chariots. The silver rays from the moon laid out the path before them. Hounds, horses, and chariots started off at a brisk canter, which soon increased to a full gallop. The charge would take the warband straight down the throats of the Senones.

Sleep-sealed eyes strained to open, and brains focused with reluctance. The Senone warriors, expecting to be the ones to surprise their enemy, were stunned to find a warband of over five hundred horses, war-dogs, and chariots rampage through the centre of the camp. From their advantage of height, axes, maces, and swords swung left and right at any target. Tents and shelters crashed to the ground. Some fell across slumbering fires and immediately sprang in a full blaze. Yet, the marauders were single-minded. There was no pause to consider making a stand or to cause further death and dismemberment. There would be no rescue of the inevitable, but hopefully few, who fell through misadventure or a sharp blade.

In another Senone camp, west of the farm, Brennus and Tasgiitios watched trails of smoke rise into the sky. With some justification, Brennus assumed that his men, eager to prove their superiority over the Carnutes and their comrades in the other camps, had attacked Mórrígan. As he approached the scene, his humour became dour and his expression dark. An early burst of sunshine mocked Brennus. The chaos and destruction of the Senone camp were evident. Already, the king began to compile a list of who to hold responsible for the debacle and how many would lose their heads.

As the sun climbed higher in the early morning sky, Brennus was interrupted from his thoughts by a cough from Tasgiitios. The king of the Carnutes pointed to movement across the river. The Liga was about five hundred paces wide at this point and details a challenge to discern. In the crisp air, sound flowed across the water with little distortion or drop in volume. The taunts, jeers, and cheers were quite clear and were accompanied by flashes of white arses.

"If she survives, she will learn to accept a victory and ride on." Brennus pointed to the large band rapidly closing on Mórrígan and took satisfaction at the disappointment on Tasgiitios' face. "She took the only possible escape route. I would have done the same. But I too have mounted warriors." It was a fierce and short encounter and witnessed only by the flocks of morning birds. The dissonant sounds of battle gave no clue as to whether there was a victor. Then there was silence.

Some time later, Tasgiitios directed Brennus' attention to a location further along the riverbank. Plumes of smoke curled up into the sky. "It would appear that the Dark Huntress survived and is not amused." Tasgiitios could barely restrain the smirk that fought to make an appearance on his face. "I wish you good luck in taming her."

Brennus spat. He knew there was no taming Mórrígan.

CHAPTER 37

403 B.C.—Winter

Beams of silvery moonlight followed the lone figure that walked barefoot along the broken walls of Lugudunon. Once mocked and cursed by men, women, and children, she had become the curse. Feral dogs growled and cowered as she passed. In the forests, the yellow eyes of wolves watched her path. Lynxes hissed at her presence. Bears stood on hind legs and roared their challenge. The apparition was still flesh, but only just, living in the twilight between life and death. Once slender, she, if she even merited the description, was now gaunt. Skin, once golden, was now the colour and texture of fermented milk and stretched over sharp bones. In the glimmer of the moon, her skull was visible through veined and transparent skin.

Men and women recoiled from her, avoiding her stare. Children who pointed were swiftly slapped and taken aside by frightened mothers. Their cries became music to her ears. Once scorned and derided, she now evoked visceral fear. The ills of Lugudunon, pestilence, hunger, and death, were laid at her feet. Matres looked upon her with wary eyes. The queen had resisted demands to kill her, to bury her deep in a mountain crevasse. Such a course of action was now beyond contemplation. She cursed Genovefa, whom she blamed for the poison that ravaged the Roman's body. Yet the queen was not guiltless and was fearful of what she helped create.

The poison spread like wildfire through Cornelia's body,

corrupting her blood and causing blemishes on the previously flawless skin. Weakened by constant bleaching, Cornelia's hair fell out in great clumps until she was bald. In a strange quirk of fate, her eyebrows retained the memory of her black, lustrous hair. The Roman had barely survived. Perhaps it would have been kinder for her to have passed away. The Gaiscedach queen shivered. She fervently wished that she could put the abomination out of its misery. Yet, when it came to Cornelia, Matres remained deeply conflicted and stayed her knife.

It was several cycles of the moon before the spectre that was Cornelia built enough strength to walk the ramparts of Lugudunon. As she passed the decaying remains of her former gaolers, twisting in the wind, thin lips drew back in a ghoulish grimace. She had no guards now. Several warriors had fallen on their swords rather than take up that duty. Cornelia looked up at the moon. Visions and dreams of another lifetime often disturbed her sleep although, in truth, she rarely slept. A solitary tear rolled down a pockmarked cheek. It always happened when a single word stumbled from her lips— "Gaius."

***

Genovefa lay back. A long, pink tongue flicked across full and slightly bruised lips. The salty taste of sweat pleased her. Her full breasts rose and fell, rapidly at first, but soon slowing to a sensual rhythm. Hard dusky pink nipples testified to her state of arousal, as did the dampness of her full-bushed triangle and the pulsating throb deep inside. Beside her lay Concolitanus. Swathed in sweat and leaking post-coital fluids, he impregnated the air with the musky fragrances of primal rutting. It was a perfume that Genovefa loved. She breathed deeply, as if trying to absorb every scintilla.

Concolitanus was a vigorous lover. Genovefa never ceased to be impressed by his level of recovery and the size and girth of his manhood. The latter was a weapon of dominance, wielded much like a spear in battle. It was thrust into her flesh, hard and fast. Its goal—to slay her resistance, to make her obedient, to brand and own her. As such, there

was no finesse about their rutting. Another woman would have shriv-
elled under such treatment, would have slowly died, if not physically,
then spiritually. Genovefa was no such woman. She enjoyed being taken
as an object to sate Concolitanus' passions. She climaxed fast, faster than
most men. But more than this, mentally Genovefa was much stronger
than her partner.

In the roundhouse, it was still warm enough not to need an over-lay-
er of thick pelts. A rustle of straw signalled that, as always, Concolitanus
had reached for the pitcher of cold spring water beside the cot. She listened to the gurgle of water flowing down his throat and the contented
sigh of thirst slaked. Genovefa smiled. It was a strangely comfortable
routine. It was predictable. It was fatal. Genovefa listened carefully to
the king's breathing. She turned, resting her head on her left hand and
watched his chest rise and fall. She traced a finger through pooled perspiration and along several prominent scars. There was no response
when she rubbed a nipple—usually an area of extreme sensitivity. She
smiled and lifted herself up.

Genovefa caressed his brow and watched the king's eyes open. "By
now you will have realised you cannot move." Fury and sadness filled
Concolitanus' fern-green eyes. "Brennus of the Senones sends his regards and his disappointment at your pathetic handling of Matres and
the Roman bitch." With a sigh, possibly of regret, Genovefa bent down
and kissed the tip of Concolitanus' manhood. "A memory of old times
to take with you." With a swift, fluid motion a knife was unsheathed and
drawn across the king's throat. As if to provide further assurance of his
demise, Genovefa stabbed the blade into Concolitanus' heart and twisted. Genovefa was, after all, an accomplished assassin.

The sole ruler of the Gaiscedach rose from the blood-soaked bed.
A basin of water rested on a nearby table. Slowly, she washed the gore
and sweat from her body. She shivered. The liquid was cold. She scowled
as she felt her belly. "Bastard," she muttered. There was, of course, no
child in her womb. The swell was fat. Had Concolitanus been more

observant, he would have noticed the increase of her food intake. The curse was for the exercise regime needed to regain her perfect figure.

It was dawn as Genovefa exited Concolitanus' quarters. She had a tribe to rule. Two guards dipped their heads as she walked past. The fine hairs on the back of her neck quivered. The warning was too late. As her hand dropped to her knife, spears punched into her, front and back. Brutally, the leaf-shaped heads were withdrawn. She kneeled in an ever-widening pool of blood. In her shock she heard a voice in her ear, "Brennus sends his regrets." A sword took her head.

***

Flowing down the mountains to the north of Lugudunon and along the valley of the Rodonos, the ancient wind, known as the Máistir, raged. The weakened defences of the fort and the rubble from the outer eastern gate which had not been cleared gave the cold wind an advantage it had long sought. Rocks of all dimensions from pebbles to boulders the size of men were lifted and hurled at the stronghold. Ice, formed from night-time frosts, filled and pushed apart cracks in the stone.

Like a conductor, the creature that was Cornelia held her audience in thrall. Only, this performer led her adherents not into euphoria but deep into the maw of the Otherworld. On the ramparts, she held up her arms to the storm clouds that flowed across the skies, blotting out the full moon. She revelled in the cold north-western breeze that had become a wind of wrath and rage. It swirled around her, whipping her thin shroud. To those who watched, she seemed to draw strength from the tempest.

It did no good for Matres to tell the people that the same wind had visited them for more generations than any could remember. That it would rage and then depart, its strength dissipated. That it would return again and again in the future. The tribe only felt the Máistir's fury and saw the apparition who commanded it. There were calls for Matres' removal. Guilt for nature's anger was laid at her feet, not the spectre's. Matres quenched all such rebellion, quickly and with no mercy. Whole families were strung up or staked on Lugudunon's walls.

***

Brennus' resourcefulness and the surprise attack at Cenabum drew reluctant admiration from Mórrígan, and a vow not to be snared in a like manner again. In total, she had lost one-fifth of her force, all veterans, in the vicious skirmish. Thirty had fallen in the encounter by the River Liga. A score more succumbed to their injuries on the journey to Lugudunon. It was many sunsets, many settlements raised to the ground, and many slaughtered until the Huntress forgave her lack of omniscience.

They arrived before the storm peaked. Its ferocity astounded the Gaels, but not the Thracians and Cretans, who had experienced its like before. Fortune was with the warband, as by chance they came upon the entrance to a labyrinth of caves. A curtain of rain and the cascading waters from the mountain sealed the mouth of the cave. Deep pools of water filled the hollows carved by generations of rainfall. They made the entrance hazardous to negotiate. It was a gift from the Goddess that Mórrígan gratefully accepted. Now, with awe, they watched nature's unrelenting assault on Lugudunon.

Many sunsets later, the storm abated. There was a sense of satisfaction in the air as if, this season, the Máistir was well-pleased with its trail of destruction. In the fading light of dusk, Mórrígan stared at the lone figure that walked the shattered walls of the hillfort. Something about the creature sent a shiver up the queen's spine and made the fine hairs on her neck stand on end. Instinct told her that this was Cornelia. Her mind prayed it was not.

Full and pale yellow, the moon looked huge as it sat on the horizon before rising to take its place as queen of the nocturnal skies. The night was clear and calm if a touch chilly. As the orb rose higher, its light cast deep shadows across the land and the hillfort of Lugudunon. From gloom-to-gloom Mórrígan, her brothers, and a small group of escorts crept closer to the fort. It was sparsely guarded, especially where Cornelia walked. The western section of the wall was not high, being about the height of three men. Large fissures in the stone provided an abundance of hand- and footholds. It was a much less daunting climb than that of the cliffs of Ráth na Lairig Éadain in Ériu.

Mórrígan's soft boots crunched on the grit and pebbles scattered over the ramparts by the Máistir. She crouched low, waiting as her eyes adjusted to the half-light. Her bow was unslung and a black shaft with red and white fletching already nocked. The scrape of feet on gravel told her that the rest of her band had scaled the wall and taken up positions around her. The Huntress pointed. Two remained with her, the rest had other tasks to accomplish.

The queen was almost taken by surprise by the appearance of Cornelia. The Roman's footfall was as silent as the night, adding to her disquieting air. For a moment, Mórrígan inspected Cornelia. She was filled with a sense of outrage and sorrow for what the Roman had become. This was not the young beauty with lustrous, raven-black hair and blemish-free, golden skin described by Gaius. She felt deep grief for Gaius and his partner. She feared for an already unstable Gaius' mind should he cast eyes on his beloved Cornelia. Behind her, Mórrígan heard breaths quickly withdrawn, and curses uttered. The words 'bean-sidhe' escaped lips thinned with sorrow and horror.

As Mórrígan stood, the apparition started. She was unaccustomed to anyone else braving the walls when she passed by. "Cornelia," whispered Mórrígan, "Come with me, Cornelia. Gaius waits for you. We have healers to restore your health. Our Goddess is merciful."

Memories flooded the mind of the piteous creature. A silver-gold tear rolled down her face. Reminiscences that should have brought happiness and tears of joy now stabbed Cornelia with a viciousness that took the breath from her. She could not deal with thoughts of hope, of rescue, of love. Unseen were the chains that bound Cornelia to the hillfort. Yet they held her stronger than iron. For a brief moment, she became the Roman princess. Her shoulders and back straightened and her head was held high. "No," was all she uttered before turning around and disappearing like a ghost.

Despairing at her failure to convince Cornelia to escape her cage, Mórrígan turned her attention to more practical matters. Conall, the armies, and the people of Clann Ui Flaithimh were unlikely to arrive in the Rodonos Valley before early summer. Her warband's job was to assess and map the terrain, but more so to spread fear among the inhabitants of the vale and encourage their exodus. With grim resolution, An Fiagaí Dorcha—the Dark Huntress, called her captains to her.

As the dawn sun enveloped the white walls of Lugudunon in golden pastels, a shriek arose to shatter nature's dawn chorus. Matres shouted, "Cut them down!" Before her, the blood of the night's watch seeped from slashed throats and stained the white stone square in front of her quarters. Mórrígan smiled. The first message had been received.

CHAPTER 38

403 B.C.—Exodus to Lugudunon—Late Spring

Eye-watering odours of fire and smoke filled the night sky. The people of Clann Ui Flaithimh raised their gaze to witness the raging inferno that was Cnocán-Mórrígan. While the dirt ramparts still stretched from coast to coast, anything that could burn or be torn down was destroyed. The majestic broch at the centre of the hillfort was a pile of rubble. All homes and halls were slowly transformed into ash and lumps of charred stone. In time, the forests and wildwoods would take back their domain. A collective sigh arose from the sprawling camp of the tribe. Once more, they were itinerant. Many hoped and prayed to the Goddess that this would be their last journey.

The winter's travails had weakened the people and the army of Clann Ui Flaithimh. A full tithe of the tribe, over one thousand souls, had journeyed beyond the veil. It was hoped that few had entered the Otherworld. Of the remainder, many were in poor condition. Some would not survive the journey.

Much to the disappointment of the local tribes, the trek to Lugudunon had commenced closer to Bealtaine. The pace was agonisingly slow. Venelli and Veneti scouts watched impatiently from higher grounds as the long millipede plodded along the banks of the tributaries that flowed into the Liga. Still, they were powerless to facilitate a faster march. The Gaulish tribes of Aremorio had also suffered disease and death.

Led by the famed shield wall and, even though the clann walked in ragged rows of ten across, the beast that was Clann Ui Flaithimh stretched back until the rear-guard was an indistinct blur on the horizon. The pace was unavoidably slow. Hundreds of wagons pulled by mules and oxen trundled along, carrying the wealth, possessions, and supplies of the tribe. The horsemen, under a watchful Íar and an uncharacteristically distracted Nikandros, regularly patrolled the length of the caravan. Carmag's forest warriors, supported by Brandubh's Ravens, flowed into the woods on both sides of the river. Hunters made frequent sorties into the woodland in search of fresh meat. Fishers had an easier task. So plentiful were the shoals of fish that some said that it was possible to walk across the river on their silver backs. Only the odd irate bear challenged the strangers who competed for its food source.

Conall gasped and rolled as the covered wagon lurched without warning. The vehicle had solid wooden wheels and even the layers of thick pelts could not soften the impact of every rut and rock. The king of Clann Ui Flaithimh had not fully recovered from the pestilence that had struck him down. Conall's path to health, as with many of the clann, proved to be slow and frustrating. Kingly privilege had assigned him a cart for travel. His faithful horse Toirneach trotted beside the wagon, as did his wolfhounds. A grunt and hiss of pain from his companion made Conall chuckle.

"There's two of us. Stay on your own side. No royal dispensations in this wagon." The rasping voice of Torcán was a surprising comfort to Conall. He had overruled the Sidhe and Fionnbharr's wish that he travel alone and, on the whole, remained happy with his decision. Still, when the warrior let loose with one of his signature farts, which was quite often, Conall wished he was very far away. Nevertheless, these were the days when kings were part of their clann, and not set apart.

It was in-character for Torcán to put on a bold face and joke with his friends. Yet, all knew that his grip on life had been tenuous. The bean-sidhe had hovered close to his door. His nearly mortal wound meant that he too had some ways to go before he fought in battle again. Mòrag had been inconsolable at the thought of losing him. Even her sceptical brother, Brandubh, was won over and accepted that his sister and Torcán were an ideal, if an unconventional, couple. He had freely given his consent when death stood close to their door, and Mòrag and Torcán had signalled their wish to be hand-fast partners.

The hide flap of the wagon's cover was pulled aside. Barra Mac Connell, now three summers old, bounced into the box with a laugh and shouts of "Da!" He was followed by a now obviously pregnant Mòrag, who hesitated briefly before climbing into the cart. She smiled weakly at both men and mouthed, "Awkward." Both Conall—by blood—and Torcán—by hand-fasting—could rightly claim the title of "Da." The two men looked at each other and to Mòrag's relief roared with laughter. The red-haired Barra, for he favoured his mother, had more than enough hugs and kisses for two fathers.

It was just after dawn, and the occupants of the wagon rested, having enjoyed their first meal of the new day. There was, thought Torcán, a definite advantage to having the king as a companion in his recuperation. The food was definitely superior, the service excellent, and there was no responsibility for cleaning up. Fresh bedding and clothes were delivered regularly. There were daily visits by the Sidhe and Fionnbharr to ensure that their ailments were treated. The bluff warrior let out a long sight of contentment. Yes, he could become accustomed to this lifestyle.

Torcán's appreciation of the good life was abruptly terminated when the cover of the wagon was unceremoniously pulled off the wooden frame. Sunlight flooded in, as did the omnipresent spring mizzle. It was with outrage that the burly warrior spluttered, to the as yet unseen pranksters, "The king will have your heads for this." For his part, Conall gauged that, being at the centre of the large camp, it was most unlikely he was in any danger. Therefore, he was merely curious about what was happening while being amused at his companion's reaction. A shadow fell across the gate of the wagon as it was dropped. The massive frame of Urard almost succeeded in blotting out the sun. The smile on the warrior's face sent a shiver up Conall's spine. Urard did not smile unless he was in Iasg's presence.

With a curt nod to signal his words applied equally to Torcán, Urard said, "Time to get fit, my king. Fearghal, Fionnbharr, and Mongfhionn have decided that, since you have shown excellent signs of recovery, it is time to accelerate your reintegration into the army." The edges of Urard's lips crinkled upwards, "I have been put in charge of this *therapy*."

Torcán groaned, "We're dead men, my king. At least he hasn't brought that bloody great axe with him. We can overpower him and make our escape to friendlier arms." Conall looked incredulously at his companion and was about to comment when another voice, full of faux mockery, was added to the conversation.

"In your dreams, warrior. While Urard is responsible for the king's new therapy, I volunteered to help with yours."

"Bollocks!" croaked Torcán as Urard was joined by Lonán Ó Neill. The tall warrior plainly enjoyed Torcán's dismay as he sported a grin as wide as his face.

As he stumbled from the cart, Conall stretched out a hand to steady himself. His legs had all the strength of cheese curds. A wave of nausea was followed by the rapid departure of blood from his brain. Beads of sweat formed on his forehead. To Conall, it was uncertain whether he would throw up or faint. Moments later, he was assisted to rest on a tree stump. From the sour odour and damp patch on his shirt, Conall concluded he had achieved both.

Meanwhile, Torcán found himself equally unsteady on his feet and staring at the ground. Having the constitution of a wild boar, the warrior had bulled his way through the wave of queasiness while managing to maintain his senses. "Straighten up arsehole," came an unsympathetic rejoinder from Lonán. Torcán's brain feverishly attempted to accomplish what on the surface should have been a simple task. His body, or more precisely his chest and abdomen, stubbornly refused. Lonán at first tried to help the younger man straighten up, but the screams of agony made him stop.

"Let's take a look at you."

A firm grasp on Torcán's shirt was followed by the sound of the garment being torn down the middle. "The Hag's arse!" exclaimed Lonán, "Why are you alive?" Shock, dismay, and admiration coloured his voice. A garish, purple-red scar traced a ragged line from the top of Torcán's chest to below his belt. In a more understanding tone, Lonán added, "You'll likely not believe me, but you're lucky at our timing." Torcán's look told him this was not uppermost in his mind. "Each day, that scar is tightening up. As it heals, it pulls on all the flesh around it— inside and out. Three or four more cycles of the moon and that scar would have settled, and you would be walking stooped like an old man for the rest of your life."

"Iasg's got a good salve for scars. Her people needed it," said Urard. "Stinks like horse shite and fish guts, but it does the job." Torcán groaned. He wondered if he could convince Mòrag to administer the balm. Probably not, he mused. She would likely tell him to pitch his tent elsewhere. It was not comforting to hear Lonán mutter to Urard, "Let's hope his insides aren't totally screwed."

The army and people took as their guide a narrow hunting path that ran alongside the tributary. By the time the rear-guard passed, the track resembled a broad road pounded into place by thousands of feet. Clann Ui Flaithimh's members, from the lowest slave to its nobles, had little to smile about, save that they were still alive. Yet the sound of blades striking scíatha raised hope that their beloved Rí Ruirech had finally escaped the grasp of the bean-sidhe. In the skies above, the Goddess screeched approval. Her Hand had passed Fate's trial.

It was slow and painful at first, but after just one cycle of the moon, under Urard and Lonán, Conall and Torcán showed a vast improvement. Several cycles later, and within sight of the Liga and the land of the Canutes, while neither man had regained their previous weight, wasted muscles had been strengthened. Each now had a taut body with little fat. Torcán still gasped at the sharp spikes of pain in his chest, but could stand upright. Held in Fearghal's arms, Mongfhionn smiled as she watched Conall battle against Urard. It was, she thought, quite remarkable that such were the strong ties between king and clann that as Conall became stronger, so did the people.

"Did you expect anything else?" It was as if Fearghal was able to read her mind.

The Sidhe smiled, "No."

* * *

While travelling south-east through Aremorio, the tribe faced few challenges from the region's tribes. All had armies significantly diminished after the battle with Conall and the subsequent raids of attrition. They too had suffered the ravages of the pestilence that swept through Clann Ui Flaithimh. If anything, they were much less prepared to resist and lessen its impact. Without a full complement of workers, along the fertile river plain, hundreds of small, family-based farms and communities had fallen into disrepair. Fences and walls were broken, and fields lay fallow and overgrown.

At the head of his men, Gaius Aurelius Atella marched alongside Aquila and the Greek surgeon, Alkaios. The men's bronze shields were slung across their backs, and long sarissas rested on square shoulders. Recently polished breastplates and greaves glinted in the sun. Now that he was on a journey that would lead to his beloved, Cornelia, the Roman's humour was much improved and his mind clearer. This was a great relief to Aquila, who had feared for his leader and friend's sanity. Even the fact that the Romans formed the rear-guard did not appear to have a negative impact on Gaius' disposition. Aquila reflected that this might change when drier and warmer weather caused a stoor to rise from thousands of boots.

Gaius thanked his gods that his men had not suffered as severely as the people of Clann Ui Flaithimh. The number of fully battle-ready men stood at six hundred, including the teams for operating the ballistae. A frown hovered over his brow. The thought of the missile-throwers brought the fate of the traitor Crispus Galerius Donatus to Gaius. He shrugged. The gods had taken that judgement out of his hands.

Crispus had been imprisoned until such times that Conall and Gaius would decide his fate. Shackled and chained, his presence was overlooked during the upheavals that faced Cnocán-Mórrígan. Crispus had first languished and then succumbed to the pestilence that raged through the community. He died ignored and without any to say a kind word over his pyre.

***

Of stocky build, and with a matting of coarse, dark hair that covered a well-muscled body replete with battle scars, Tasgiitios, king of the Canutes, cut an imposing figure but would never be considered a handsome man. The areas of his face not covered by a thick, dark beard, or concealed by straight, shoulder-length hair, were deeply pock-marked. Taunted in his childhood and youth for his countenance, life had endowed Tasgiitios with a passion for fighting and an absence of mercy. His beard was parted by a thin white line—another gift from skirmishes.

Sat astride a broad-backed grey, Tasgiitios snarled, "Bastards," as he watched the long caravan, like the river Liga, carve its way through his territory. The king still smarted from what he considered to be the recent insult from Brennus of the Senones. His precarious strategic position with the Senones to his east and the Biturges to the south did nothing to ameliorate his mood. The Carnutes did not need a third enemy to confront. Thankfully, the striapach queen of Clann Ui Flaithimh was long gone from his territory, but the scars of abandoned farms, widows, and orphans remained.

That said, honour demanded that he take some sort of action against the barbarians from Ériu and Albu. During the last cycle of the moon, three warbands, each comprising several hundred warriors, had been sent against what were considered the weak flanks of the Clann

Ui Flaithimh. The people and the wagons. Before they died, his men had discovered two unsettling facts. First, that the ordinary people were armed with spear and shield and were quite capable of defending the long convoy. Second, the tribe's horsemen were veteran fighters who despatched justice with long-handled blades. A few hundred spearmen on foot were no match for a thousand horsemen.

Tasgiitios hacked up a glob of phlegm and saliva and spat over the head of his horse. This time his ire was aimed at the grasping merchants and traders. Those from his major population centres around the hill-forts of Tourones and Cenabum insisted that they should be allowed to trade with his enemy. "The opportunity was too great to ignore or take advantage of," they said. "Think of the taxes," they argued. Many of his Council argued on behalf of the merchants. The king spat once more. "Bribes," he snarled.

Furthermore, his spies had informed him that a string of farms, along the river plain, had been left untouched by Mórrígan's raiders. The owners had come to an understanding with Mórrígan that they would be given a favourable price for their produce and livestock. That the alterna-tive was death and destruction as suffered by their neighbours, made the decision clear-cut. Along the Liga, an unusual number of flat-bottomed galleys, most originating from ports in the Great Sea, were also laden with goods to trade. The implicit threat from these longstanding Greek, Roman, and Phoenician traders, and probably instigated by that bastard, Pytheas, was that the Liga was not the only route they could take in the future.

"Gold!" he shouted, "A curse on us all."

***

Fearghal cantered alongside Conall and pointed, "A reception party?" Conall nodded. He had observed the Canutes form up across the north-ern side of the river plain. They halted about one thousand paces ahead, between the marshy land and the edge of the forest. "I count about a thousand men. I assume the one on the horse with the impressive winged helmet is their leader." Conall patted the velvet shoulder of Toir-neach and again nodded. "Are we in a talkative mood?" Conall chuck-led. His battle commander had expressed on many occasions concerns about what he perceived as his king's interpretation of the process of negotiation and diplomacy.

"Ask Mongfhionn, the Lady Bláithín, Cúscraid, Deaglán, Íar, and Nikandros to join us. Also, ask Deaglán to round up my caomhnóirí. I think that should impress them." Catching sight of Mòrag, who al-ways seemed to be nearby when a fight was imminent, Conall muttered, "She and Torcán are well-suited." But Conall was not about to put a heavily pregnant Raven princess at risk. He called her over, "Mòrag." The princess' emerald eyes lit up in expectation, only for her hopes to be dashed. "Send riders to your brother and to Carmag. Ask them to move up parallel with the Carnutes force but to remain hidden. They'll know what to do if negotiations don't go as we hope." The ends of Mòrag's lips dropped in disappointment, but then a glimmer of a smirk appeared. It did not go unnoticed by Conall. "*You*, personally, will *not* go to or with either Brandubh or Carmag. That is my command." The stream of swear words that flowed from Mòrag's lips as she turned on her heels and stormed off, brought a cheer from those around.

Tasgiitios' somewhat bruised and fragile ego suffered what he per-ceived as another slight. As he watched the leaders trot forward, they were accompanied by only several hundred warriors. He wondered whether they were insulting him by implying that his men could be de-feated by this much smaller force. Although, he did admit that the lead-ers, men, and beasts looked striking and much better turned out than his warriors. A quick flourish of his hand signalled for his shield-bearer and ten burly warriors to step forward. With a sigh, Tasgiitios directed his mount to walk in the direction of his enemy.

The kings' parties met mid-way and, for a short time, stood about ten paces apart as they took the measure of each other. After a sufficient pause, Conall walked Toirneach forward to within a spear's length of

Tasgiitios. Slowly he reached up and removed his helmet. Released from confinement, tresses of auburn hair fell on his shoulders. A quick cough cleared his throat. In a loud, firm but not unpleasant voice, he said, "I am Conall Mac Gabhann, Rí Ruirech of Clann Ui Flaithimh and also known as the Hand of the Goddess. What are your terms for peaceable passage through your domain?"

To Conall, the scowl on Tasgiitios' face was discouraging. The harsh tone of his voice, as he called out his response, was of further concern. Conall had little idea as to what Tasgiitios was saying, and he suspected therefore that the king had not much comprehension of his words. With a hand raised, palm towards the king of the Carnutes, Conall smiled, turned his horse around and walked back to his leaders. "Tasgiitios' language is vaguely familiar but is so heavily accented that I can barely understand one word in ten. I'm open to suggestions?" Conall looked at each of his leaders, in turn, only to be presented with blank looks. It was with a note of consternation that he added, "We don't have a lot of time here before events turn nasty and very bloody."

"You need to travel more. Broaden your horizons. Meet new peoples—preferably ones that you do not slaughter," snapped Mongfhionn. Fearghal looked at his partner in astonishment, then caught the glint in eyes that were so deeply coloured that they appeared black.

"Bloody Aes Sidhe warped sense of humour. Can you help or not?"

The Sidhe took up the reins of her horse and walked to stand next to Conall. Both horses had coats as dark as midnight. Indeed, their only distinguishing marks were that Mongfhionn's mount had white socks and a white blaze shaped like lightning. "Shall we go restart the conversation?" From Tasgiitios demeanour and posture, it was clear that he was a traditional thinker and had no room for women in leadership positions. His scowl deepened and he made to turn away.

With a voice that could crack ice, Mongfhionn thundered, "I am Mongfhionn, Lady Sidhe of the Aes Sidhe, Counsellor to Conall Mac Gabhann, Defender of the people of Clann Ui Flaithimh. Insult me and turn your back on me once more, and I will remove you, your men, and your people from the earth." As if to add emphasis, a peel of thunder rolled across the sky. With a quick flick of her wrist, the Sidhe slipped off her cloak and hood to rest on her horse's back. Golden hair with highlights of flame red flared into a corona about her head. The swirling designs on exposed flesh seemed to have a life of their own. An oaken staff, blackened with age, pointed at Tasgiitios.

The reaction of Tasgiitios' men was confused. Many muttered the global language of, "Shite!" Others fell to one knee. For Tasgiitios, the scales had tipped against him. For all his flaws, the king was a man who was faithful to the gods. He dismounted and with as much dignity as he could martial, strode to stand before the Sidhe. With a bow, he spoke, "I apologise my Lady. I was not aware of your presence."

"Accepted. I will act as an interpreter for as long as necessary between you and Conall. I will take no side, save I think either is being unreasonable."

Conall had neither fear of battle nor doubt in his army's ability to triumph. Yet the many seasons since his exile from Ériu had tempered his youthful brashness. Thus, it was not in Conall's mind to humiliate the king of the Carnutes. He was also mindful that many of the clann still suffered from physical and spiritual scars caused by the winter plague. He swung his leg across Toirneach's back, slipped off his sword belt and axe and, accompanied by Mongfhionn, approached Tasgiitios with his arms spread in what he hoped was a conciliatory gesture.

The omens were not propitious as Tasgiitios launched into a long tirade about the rape, plunder, and pillaging of his lands by Mórrígan's riders. Yet Conall sensed that the litany of complaints was in large part for Tasgiitios' warriors. After all, it was a normal part of Celtic life to raid their neighbours' domains. Fighting was deeply ingrained in the culture. It was why the Celts and Gauls made invaluable mercenaries. Eventually, Tasgiitios monologue drew to a close with a final exclamation of, "Leave my lands or face my spears!"

"Time for my king to argue our case," said Fearghal. There was more than a hint of mock sarcasm in his rich voice.

Conall looked Tasgiitios in the eye and held the leader of the Carnutes' gaze. "The Dark Huntress had fewer than three hundred warriors in her band. I have *many* more. Deny us journeying privileges. Punish those who choose to sell goods to us, and you will discover the extent of my retribution. I will level your hillforts and devastate your lands. For generations to come, your people will dig in the dirt for roots to feed themselves. They will seek shelter in the forests, for they will have no roundhouses. Your neighbours will carry them off as slaves. *Your* name will be remembered in shame."

Behind him, Fearghal groaned, "So much for diplomacy," and loosened the loop from his long-sword. The metallic clang of shields behind him told Fearghal, the two hundred warriors of Conall's caomhnóirí were ready to fight.

"*But,*" continued Conall, "If we can come to an accommodation, then the Carnutes and its people will not fear war from Clann Ui Flaithimh. A fair price will be paid for goods. The king's coffers will grow from taxes." Conall paused and smiled, "And when we leave the lands of the Carnutes, our enemy will be the Senones. While we traverse Brennus' land, he will be more occupied with our presence than your borders. I bring you peace. If only for a time."

Tasgiitios was more convinced with Conall's promise of vengeance than the supposed benefits of accommodation. Something in the barbarian's eyes made the Canutes' king uneasy. It seemed that the warrior king was too comfortable with a policy of revenge. In his mind, Tasgiitios was already reconciled to having to suffer the intrusion of Clann Ui Flaithimh for a season. Yet doubts remained as to whether Conall would live up to his promise to simply cross Canutes' territory. "I agree to your terms but with one condition." The sigh of impatience from the Ériu leaders did not dissuade Tasgiitios. "You will leave a noble as my guest for as long as you are in my lands. He will be returned when you reach Cenabum or leave my lands."

"No!" exclaimed Conall. "I will not ask one of my Chomhairle to be a hostage."

"Not a prisoner. Nor a hostage. A guest. He will be treated as befits his status and will be under my protection. We are Celts. You well know our laws concerning all who eat under our roof." Conall looked with suspicion at Tasgiitios, and his mind remained set to decline the offer. He would not willingly sacrifice any of the clann, preferring to take his chances in battle. The decision was removed from him.

"I will go with the king of the Canutes." It was Bláithín who spoke. To Tasgiitios she said, "I am Bláithín Ni Néill, a noble-woman of the Clann Uí Néill, Banríon Clochar, and a member of Clann Ui Flaithimh's Chomhairle.

"That's settled. We have a treaty," said Tasgiitios.

"No," came the response, "Not quite." All held their breath. "The lady will be accompanied by my queen's brother, Brocc Ó Cathasaigh, and a hundred chosen warriors. It would disrespect the lady's honour and position to allow her to travel without an adequate guard."

For the first time, Tasgiitios laughed, "Agreed. Do you play fidchell? If not, you should take it up. I'd not like to wager against you." The Carnutes king took a step closer and offered his hand, which was accepted by Conall. Tasgiitios looked at the sky, then at the galleys that bobbed on the slow-moving waters of the Liga. "I doubt your people will travel much further this day." With a nod towards the ships, he added, "A feast is in order. The least you can do is to provide the food and drink."

Conall laughed, "Agreed." Then he raised his arm. From the woods emerged Carmag and Brandubh's warriors. Tasgiitios and his men flinched in anticipation of treachery. Conall shook his head, "I would never insult the king of the Carnutes by opposing him with just two hundred men. Although that would be a good fight. Two thousand gives me much better odds." Tasgiitios dipped his head, his honour and ego had been somewhat restored. And he pondered whether he could convince the Rí Ruirech to support his raids on the Biturges.

"Now that's diplomacy," whispered Mongfhionn in her partner's ear.

"A brave decision by the Lady Bláithín, and an intriguing choice of the guard to accompany her," murmured Fearghal.

"Conall is quite observant. Bláithín and Brocc have been dancing around each other since the death of Cuán. Some time away from the tribe will help them to decide if they want a future together."

CHAPTER 39

403 B.C.—Cenabum—Early Summer

Bláithín missed her children. Yet, as she leaned against the parapet and watched Brocc work through his exercise routine, she had a deep sense of contentment and ample measure of lust. Shoulder-length, red hair, its unruly locks braided by herself, swung wildly as Brocc ducked and weaved to avoid the painful slap of the heavily-weighted training sword. Her lover's naked upper body glistened with sweat from his exertions. She smiled broadly as Brocc taunted his mentor and second-in-command, and laughed aloud at the stream of oaths when a blow from the grizzled veteran overcame Brocc's guard.

These were days of happiness without the burden of duty. The Ériu noble basked in the anonymity of the vast settlement that was Cenabum. Although guests of Tasgiitios, and treated with all the respect reserved for her position, she and Brocc could effortlessly disappear in the crowds that thronged the fort. With the intimacy afforded, their feelings for each other had grown stronger. Only faint traces of guilt from the misfortunes associated with her late partner, Cuán, remained. Mostly, these concerned how her young boys would view Brocc living with them permanently. Would they accept him as their father?

Like a butterfly, a frown lit on her lips and just as quickly fluttered away. Several sunsets past, a rider brought news that Conall and the people of Clann Ui Flaithimh drew nearer. In two evenings, they would be encamped around Cenabum. Then, she and Brocc would have no choice but to address the burning questions that both continued to avoid. Did they have a future together and was it within Clann Ui Flaithimh? A shout from Brocc brought an end to her thoughts.

"Come, my lady, pick up a sword and try your luck." It was no idle challenge. The Cróeb Ruad tattoo on Bláithín's right arm testified to her prowess in battle.

Bláithín laughed, "You say that when I'm dressed like this." She indicated her loose, long-sleeved, ankle-length, gold and red dress. It was a gift from Tasgiitios, who informed her that it was a Chinese style. The king said it was a material called silk that was traded to him for local goods. Bláithín had no idea what was meant by 'Chinese' or 'silk' but loved the feel of the garment against her skin. It was so light, she could imagine it not being there.

Brocc grinned. "Mòrag and Gràinne's preference is to fight with large amounts of flesh exposed. Even Mórrígan has gone into battle naked. Perhaps, you might consider their example?"

"Are you suggesting that you don't see me naked often enough?" Retorted Bláithín with a huge grin on her face. "As for comparing me to Mòrag, you flatter me if you consider my breasts to be in that league." Brocc roared with laughter. It was a happy, infectious laugh and another reason why she loved him. "Time you bathed that sweat from your body. We are invited to eat with Tasgiitios. Besides, there's no chance of you lying in our cot with that odour."

Brocc bowed exaggeratingly low, "As you wish, my lady." Then added, as if sensing her troubled thoughts, "It's time for us to talk."

"It is," sighed Bláithín.

***

It was well after meán lae and a pleasant summer's day when the people and armies of Clann Ui Flaithimh finally reached Cenabum. The remaining hours of sunshine were used to set up a sprawling camp around the settlement. A thankful tribe tossed gifts of gold and armour into the Liga. A tribute to the Goddess for keeping them safe. They also gave thanks to Conall. He had informed the civic leaders, flatha, and army captains and commanders that they would rest at Cenabum for a half-cycle of the moon. It would be a welcome rest.

Following this, they would turn south to cross the mountains that stretched from the Liga to the valley of the Rodonos. According to Tasgiitios, the area to be traversed was one of great natural beauty—rivers, forests, lakes, and hills. Although mountainous, the peaks were much less treacherous or lofty than the Alpes. At this season, their foremost enemies would be the weather—sun and storms—flies, and a variety of small, nomadic tribes.

The Carnutes of the settlement and fort mostly chose not to interact with Clann Ui Flaithimh. Those who, by chance, had cause to meet viewed Conall's tribe with suspicion. As always, the exceptions were the children, who grasped any opportunity to make new play-friends, thieves in the hope of easy victims, and all who had goods or services to sell—merchants, traders, artisans, and tradesmen. The latter group saw the tribe's arrival as a blessing from the gods. Galleys from the Great Sea lined the river bank and rocked on the gentle swell of the water. Everything from basic necessities to luxuries of wine, jewellery, and cloth, to whores was available—for a price.

Conall was delighted to be reunited with Bláithín and Brocc and relieved they had been treated well. His intuition suspected that they were now more reserved in the company of king and Chomhairle than during their enforced exile from the clann. Conall chuckled. He was not much older than the couple, and here he was, playing matchmaker, and apparently poorly. The couple were distinctly pink- if not red-faced when hailed by Bláithín's brother-in-law, Lonán. With a voice that could be heard at the far end of Cenabum, he greeted them.

Bláithín bit her lip and gripped Brocc's hand tightly, for Lonán was accompanied by her sons. Ultán was eleven summers old, and Fionn was twelve. The look of joy on her face when the boys flung themselves at her with cries of, "Ma!" was surpassed by her tears when both extricated themselves from her arms. They stood back, looked at each other and then at Brocc. With a nod and a shout, they launched themselves at Brocc. Lonán turned and winked at Conall, "Wise beyond their years those two. We should make a discreet retreat." Conall nodded.

The following sunset as he ate with Mongfhionn, Fearghal, Cúscraid, Íar, and Gaius, Conall tried to dampen Cúscraid's enthusiastic assertion, brought on by a strong local beer, that in his opinion Clann Ui Flaithimh's army could without much difficulty besiege and take Cenabum. Conall was pleased his commander of defence had regained some semblance of his old nature. That said, Conall firmly emphasised that they needed more allies and friends, not enemies.

Conall's reasoning with Cúscraid was distracted by a shout of, "I hope there's more beer and food left. I'm starvin'!" A dust-covered Bricriu gave the reins of his horse to a young boy as he walked towards the campfire. "Well?" he asked, with arms outstretched, "Is no one happy to see me? I've ridden a long way to get here, and my arse is sore." It was not long before the young man was the subject of heavy slaps on the back, manly embraces and recommendations of accommodating females who would happily tend his bruised cheeks.

"An unexpected pleasure, Bricriu," said Conall and then added, "I hope you bring good news."

"Mostly," he replied. Conall quickly picked up on the worried look Bricriu glanced at Gaius. "My sister thought it would be useful for one of us to make the journey back to Cenabum. Among other things, I will be your guide to Lugudunon."

"Is there something else?" asked Conall.

Bricriu hesitated, "Well, Mórrígan was a bit mysterious. She said I should make a point of meeting an Oracle called Rosmerta."

***

The king of the Carnutes had overcome his misgivings and was overjoyed that the economy of Cenabum profited greatly from the new arrivals. His treasury would be much healthier. He was also delighted and mightily relieved that Conall's intention to move on was not a bluff. A potential fight with Clann Ui Flaithimh had given the king many restless nights. Even if the Carnutes prevailed, the Senones and Biturges would happily tear his weakened kingdom apart.

Celts rarely need an excuse for a feast and céili. Hence, it was unsurprising to receive the invitation from Tasgiitios. Conall's offer of a harpist and a seanachaí was appreciated. More so, when the audience discovered the impressive talents of Craiftine and Tadhg. As the pair played and sang, both were taken aback by the volume of small discs tossed them. Coins were a rarity for the Gaels, but when assured that they were gold, Craiftine remarked to Tadhg that they should convince Fionnbharr to take up the bodhrán. "We'd make a killing here!"

It was during a lull in the feasting that Tasgiitios remarked, "You have strange allies, Conall, Rí Ruirech of Clann Ui Flaithimh." The Carnutes' king addressed Gaius directly. "That you, Gaius Aurelius Atella, are still alive is surprising and speaks well of you as a warrior." A tint of unease coloured the king's words. "Your enemy, Marcus Fabius Ambustus, is well known to us. He is powerful... and very wealthy. There's a king's ransom in gold for the delivery of your head... the head of a traitor. Even here in Cenabum, your presence will have been noted, and word will almost certainly be on its way to Marcus."

"I am no traitor," snarled Gaius.

"I care not whether you are or are not. I would, however, prefer that your stay in Cenabum is brief. As part of Conall's retinue, you are my guest. Yet, it pains me to admit, that even I cannot guarantee your safety."

"Cornelia?"

Tasgiitios exhaled sharply. It was evident that he did not want to answer. "She was kidnapped by slavers working for Matres. Marcus was furious. This news would not be well-received by the Senate in Rome or Cornelia's father. Thus, Marcus paid for her execution. Orders were given that she was to disappear without a trace. The Gaiscedach from the

Alpes south of the Rodonos were given the contract. Brennus and the Senones were tasked with ensuring no one lived to tell any tales. From what I hear, Brennus kept his part of the deal."

"Not fully, though, if you know of the contract… and its outcome," Conall interjected.

"We're Gauls and Celts. Ply us with strong wine and beer or bribe us with enough gold and our lips loosen."

"Cornelia?" The single word from Gaius brought Tasgiitios' attention back to the Roman.

"She lives, and is at Lugudunon. Purportedly, she remains a prisoner of Matres." The relief in Gaius' face was manifest, his eyes brightened, and his frame appeared to straighten up. As a gesture of thanks, he dipped his head to Tasgiitios before rising from the table and walking away. With hope now a fire kindled in his breast, he had many things to consider. Aquila nodded to Conall and Tasgiitios and followed his leader to the hall's entrance.

When they reached the doorway, Conall raised an eyebrow, "Your choice of words was curious—purportedly?"

"I sense, and alien as it may seem to me, that you are a friend to this Roman," began Tasgiitios, "If you are, dampen his expectations. Rumour and gossip have it that the question of whether Cornelia is a prisoner of Matres or vice versa has yet to be answered. This may be foolish superstition, but there is talk of a spectre that holds all in its thrall and walks the walls of Lugudunon. Your queen will have confirmation—or not—of the tale. I pray that I am wrong." Tasgiitios looked several seats along the table to Bricriu. "I also suspect that the brother of Mórrígan knows much more than he will say in public."

***

It was an odd group that approached the inner sanctum of Cenabum and a peculiar couple that received them. In a break with a period of pleasant weather with clear blue skies and warm sunshine, the firmament was now a deep, vibrant grey. It made all colours appear more intense. The distant rumbling thunder and flashes of lightning on the horizon added an ominous backdrop to the meeting. Mongfhionn, cloak unhooded and oak staff in hand, stepped forward. The glare she threw at Crum Dubh would have reduced an average man to a quivering mass. Thus, it was a compliment to the druid that it only appeared to cause his jaw to drop and his vocal cords to do little more than elicit a hoarse croak. The Sidhe's dark stare fell next on Rosmerta.

"I thought you would be dead by now, old woman."

"Wishful thinking on your part, Mongfhionn," retorted Rosmerta.

Conall nudged Fearghal with his elbow, "There is some history here. I'm not sure whether they're friends or implacable enemies."

Fearghal shrugged, "I'm not convinced either makes that distinction."

Suddenly the subject of both women's glares, the two men shut up. There was a prolonged silence between the women that seemed uncomfortable to only those not involved in the unheard conversation. Fearghal risked the wrath of the pair and murmured, "Perhaps, they can read each other's thoughts and have no need for words?" Conall grunted. He was unwilling to go as far as speaking. Fearghal raised an eyebrow, "Coward."

"You and I have many issues that have never been resolved. Possibly, they never will. I no longer lose sleep over them. It is not that I care not. It is simply an acknowledgement that other challenges have priority. I have two requests..." Rosmerta paused and stared at Bricriu, "*He cannot be allowed to ignore his gift. If he does, it will kill him... and not just him. It disturbs me that you have allowed him the freedom to kick against his gift.*" Mongfhionn chewed on her lip at the Oracle's admonishment. That said, in this area, she knew that Rosmerta was in the right.

"Your second request, old woman?"

There was a definite glint of glee, and possibly of retribution, in Rosmerta's eyes. "A request? No. I *will* join Clann Ui Flaithimh. My time at Cenabum is done. Crum and I have agreed on who will stand in the Sanctuary in my place. When a new Oracle is elected, he or she will return to Cenabum." Once more, Rosmerta looked at Bricriu and point-ed, "*He* will be my apprentice."

Silence descended for what seemed like many cycles of the moon. Both women stood unyieldingly. "Agreed," snapped Mongfhionn and with a swirl of her cloak, strode away from the group. Rosmerta smiled and nodded to Crum. Together they walked back to the Sanctuary.

"Do I get a choice or even a merit an opinion in this?" asked Bricriu.

"Apparently not," said Conall rubbing the stubble on his chin thoughtfully. "But then, I'm Rí Ruirech, and I was not consulted either."

CHAPTER 40

403 B.C.— Lugudunon—Late Summer

The feast of Lugnasad was not far off when Clann Ui Flaithimh's people and armies emerged from the mountains of the Carnutes and spilt onto the vast river plain of the Rodonos. They were about a sunset's walk from their final destination. Hope and optimism were tempered, as all knew there were battles to be fought and blood to be spilt before they could claim the land as theirs. The tribe's encampment sprawled untidily across the landscape. On Conall's orders, the camp was quickly ringed with sharpened stakes and thorn bushes. Trees were felled for lumber and firewood but also for defence as they were dropped, branches outward, along the perimeter. The people's militia, organised by fine, patrolled with spears, slings, and shields, ready to repel attacks by man or animal.

On the new sunrise, and to rousing cheers of, "No retreat, no surrender!" and "Conall Abu!" the might of Clann Ui Flaithimh, accompanied by Mongfhionn and Crum's score of druids, set its face to and marched towards Lugudunon. Carmag Mac an t-Sionnaich's forest people and Brandubh Mac Artair's Ravens, resplendent in their nakedness, formed the flanks. A fuming Mòrag, having just given birth to a baby girl, Ròs, was commanded by her brother, her partner, Torcán, and the king to remain with the citizenry. To be sure that she stayed as ordered, she was accompanied by one hundred warriors who had express orders to restrain the princess, if necessary.

At the centre of the army marched three thousand five hundred shield-wall warriors—male and female—in three columns. Each ceannairí céad and his sergeant ensured their platoon kept pace and formation and that their weapons and armour were in prime condition. Ranging ahead of the foot soldiers were Gràinne's chariots, and Íar's riders. Much to Íar's chagrin, the cavalry now included a small contingent of female fighters. Even worse for Íar, his unassuming wet nurse, Aoibheann, was one of the first to volunteer and was proven to be well-qualified as a warrior and accomplished rider.

To the rear of Conall's divisions, led by Aquila, tramped six centuria of Romans with sarissas resting on their shoulders and round, bronze shields gripped in their left hands. Bronze helmets, cuirasses, and greaves reflected the orange tones of the morning sun. Ballistae and their teams followed in the wake of the centuria. Gaius rode his grey at the front with Conall and his commanders. Finally, rearmost was the army's quartermaster, Sárán Mac Craobhach. His heavy wagons, piled high but orderly, were pulled by teams of mules and oxen. Peals of laughter and delight came from several carts. They contained the young boys and girls who would thump the bodhráns and play bone and wood flutes as the army stormed into battle. They also carried the black, red, and gold banners of king and tribe.

It was not unexpected to find Conall at the head of the army. Relishing the comfort of a thick gold dillat fringed with red tassels, the king sat upon Toirneach, grey-blue eyes constantly scanned the landscape around him. Like most of the army, he wore only plaid pants. His were red and black, tied at the waist, and finished with soft leather boots tied around his calves with thongs. At this stage, the weather was too warm for full battle armour. That would be donned before the fight began.

Around Conall were his battle commanders, ceannairí na míle, and the Sidhe. At his side rode Mongfhionn, Fearghal, Cúscraid, and Gaius. Behind him Brocc, Craiftine, Deaglán, Fionnbharr, Torcán, and Tadhg who, with varying success, attempted to control their mounts. All were much more comfortable walking rather than riding. With no challenges to impede their progress, they would make camp at dusk, once the hill-fort was in sight.

***

The blackness of the night sky was broken only by a pale, yellow moon and the shimmering blue-white light of countless stars. To the west of Lugudunon, the usual dark shadows that shrouded the landscape were under attack. Matres cursed as she lost count of the multitude of camp-fires sparking into life. The blazes were in two swathes. One ribbon was distant and faint, she surmised it was the encampment of the people of Clann Ui Flaithimh. The closer band was her true foe, Conall's army. She grimaced as she recalled her daughter, Cathubodua, and how this single-minded bastard's long trek for vengeance had started. She cursed Mórrígan for the arrow that gave her a permanent limp.

Dawn broke to a chorus of birds and the groans of men. As it climbed above the horizon, the sun gained strength. Shafts of light painted Lugudunon's whitewashed buildings with a wash of gold and orange. Matres watched the army of Clann Uí Flaithimh assemble. She spat over the thigh-high crenellated wall that edged the battlements. It was a measure of her contempt. Cerulean eyes squinted, trying to assess the number and quality of the enemy. She was likely outnumbered. That caused her little concern. Her faith in the rock of the hillfort remained absolute. Although not fully restored from Concolitanus' assault or the ravages of the Máistir and winter rains, the ramparts were strong. If Concolitanus and his witch could not dislodge Matres from her strong-hold, neither would this barbarian rabble.

Only the artisans of war—the blacksmiths, spear-, and scíath-mak-ers—lingered in Lugudunon. Upon news of the invader's arrival, the ci-vilian population fled to the safety of the Alpes with their families and as much as they could carry. Matres had no doubt that she would prevail over Conall's army. Then, she sneered, the slaughter and massacre of the people of Clann Ui Flaithimh would commence. She would extinguish all trace of their existence.

Lugudunon's ramparts were lined with Matres' veterans. To the queen, they were loyal, hard-bitten, and battle-tested warriors. To others, they were thieves, thugs, and murderers. They would give no quarter and die rather than fail their queen. Calloused, bare feet drew strength from the rock beneath them. By and large, the buildings in Lugudunon ran east-west in five broad avenues. From these paths was spun a spider's web of narrow streets. Each of the boulevards was barricaded in several places by wagons, household furniture, rocks, and any useable debris. In each building, Gaiscedach assassins waited. At the centre, all of the faces of Matre's Great Hall were guarded by high banks of dirt and stone.

The enemy would not attack before meán lae. It made no sense to fight with the sun in their eyes and, as she grudgingly admitted, Conall and his commanders were no fools. She was uncertain what had caused her to look to the north. A flicker of movement in the corner of her eye drew Matres' attention from an assessment of her assets. On a face that had not been favoured with a smile in a long time, frown lines deepened. Matres clenched her teeth and watched, stone-faced, as Mórrígan's band wheeled in a wide curve that deliberately took them past the stronghold's walls.

***

A growing cloud of dust alerted Conall to Mórrígan's imminent arrival. Horses were quickly brought, and soon he trotted out to meet his partner together with his closest leaders and advisers. Behind, the army grabbed weapons and shields and trotted in their wake.

"I have missed you." Mórrígan smiled at Conall's words. They were simple and not extravagant, but their warmth was undeniable. Conall grinned broadly at the dirt-encrusted Mórrígan as she came to a halt several paces from him. Toirneach snorted his own welcome at the queen's golden mount and strained to move forward. In a whimsy of the Goddess, a fleeting zephyr flung the smell of Mórrígan and her party at

Conall's group. All diplomatically smiled. Well, almost everyone. Torcán, true to form, opened his mouth before his brain could overrule.

"You smell as bad as a bean-sidhe's arse."

Coming from Torcán, who was not known for his fondness for bathing, this was indeed an insult. Still, the young man under Mórag's tutelage was becoming more socially aware. That all around was silent, although a few, including the Sidhe, had fists in their mouths to prevent unseemly laughs and titters, brought a, "My apologies, my Queen."

Fortunately, Torcán was rescued by Brighid, Danu, and Aodán, who with shouts of, "Ma!" brought their ponies alongside their mother. Sadly, the levity and joy of the long-awaited reconciliation of Clann Uí Flaithimh's royal family was curtailed. Mórrígan walked her horse to stand beside Gaius' grey. The Roman's eyes were filled with a hope that was beyond her to fulfil. "She is alive, Gaius." Joy flickered in his eyes but was quickly supplanted by a look of puzzlement. He peered beyond Mórrígan, hoping to catch sight of his beloved, Cornelia. The Huntress stretched out a hand, resting it on Gaius' forearm. "She would not come." A protest formed on the Roman's lips but was cut short. "We will talk at length—very soon. But my first duties are to family and tribe."

* * *

True to her word, and accompanied by Conall, Mórrígan met with Gaius at sunset. There was no balm, no remedy for the dismay that consumed Gaius as he listened to the Queen's tale. Tears in Mórrígan's eyes and her stricken look told the Roman that, if anything, she spared him far worse details. Still, in the absence of hope and Cornelia, Gaius' tenuous hold on rational thought threatened to shatter. Reason fled from his eyes. He stood, howled curses at the gods, and then, reeling from the fire, became lost in the darkness.

Cold water splashed over Gaius' face. He spluttered, his face red with misinformed outrage. The Roman pulled at the thongs that bound him firmly to the wooden seat. Blood on his hands and nails cracked and torn to the quick perplexed him. Across a hastily constructed table were Conall and Mórrígan. Their faces were troubled. On their right sat Fearghal and the Sidhe; on the left were Crum Dubh and Rosmerta. Arranged in a rough semi-circle behind the bench stood the remaining members of the Chomhairle, the ceannairí na míle, and Aquila.

"I told you that no Roman is to be trusted," Mongfhionn pointed at Gaius and glared at Conall, "When they look at us all they see are barbarians and slaves-to-be. They measure us by the gold that we will fetch on the slave blocks. He has caused the deaths of our men. Cast him out. Better still give him to me. I will sacrifice him to the Goddess."

"There are mitigating circumstances."

A sense of shock and bewilderment rippled around the gathering. The Sidhe's eyes narrowed in disbelief. For, it was Mórrígan who spoke, and she was well-known for her hostility towards all things Roman. Without flinching, she held Mongfhionn's stare and asked, "If Fearghal likewise sought to avenge you. Would you demand his death? *You* have not seen the pitiful creature that Matres of the Gaiscedach made of Cornelia. I have."

A cough brought attention to Gaius. "May I ask that my bonds are cut? I doubt that I am a threat to anyone present. I have no memory beyond my talk with Conall and Mórrígan at sunset. Will someone please tell me what I am accused of?"

"You got roaring drunk, strapped on your armour—although how is a mystery to me—grabbed weapons, and tried to assault the walls of Lugudunon." There was a hint of admiration in Fearghal's voice.

"I'm not clear how this action, although foolish, has brought me to be judged."

"A score of men—yours and ours—followed you to the walls of the fort. I presume they simply wanted to bring you back, not join in your attack," spat the Sidhe. "Nine corpses now lie at the foot of Lugudunon's walls." Gaius bowed his head and sat in grim silence. There was little he could say. If he were in Conall's place, probably he would already have given the orders for him to be stripped, scourged, and beheaded.

Conall nodded to Crum. The sallow-faced druid stood. He coughed once to clear his throat. "I, together with counsel from those present, am here to administer the Law, to judge and pronounce sentence—if needed. The Fénechas are for the Celts. Yet, justice and fairness state that I treat you as one of the clann." The druid paused at the vigorous shaking of the Sidhe's head before continuing, "The men who followed you and died, did so of their own free will. It is my ruling that their deaths cannot be laid at your feet." Ignoring a further snarl from Mongfhionn, Crum added, "Yet, they would not have died had you not attempted your understandable but foolish mission. As laid down by the Law, you will pay agreed reparations to the families of the dead and to those whose injuries will cause hardship."

Gaius stood and bowed to Crum and then to Conall. "Your judgement is reasonable. Much fairer than I could expect. I will abide by the conditions." The Roman drew himself up to what he hoped was some semblance of a commander of Rome. "I would ask that, in the battle that is to come, my men and I are given a chance to show our appreciation of the kindness shown to us."

Conall, Rí Ruirech of Clann Ui Flaithimh, looked first to Fearghal, his battle commander, and then to Gaius. A smile played on his lips, "Well, about that…"

CHAPTER 41

403 B.C.— Siege of Lugudunon—Late Summer

"Are they mad?" Without comprehension, Matres watched as six hundred Romans marched, one hundred abreast, towards the walls of Lugudunon. They strode without their long sarissas. Neither Gaius nor Conall expected Matres to fight on open ground. Instead, each man carried several swords and as many daggers and throwing axes that their belts and baldrics could hold. Behind them trundled wagons loaded with ballistae and long scaling ladders. The Gaiscedach queen turned to her second-in-command, "Hold this wall or die."

"They look impressive, Conall," said Mórrígan. Both sat on their horses, watching the Roman advance.

"They always do."

"We aren't just going to watch them die?" It was Fearghal who spoke. The hissed "Yes" from Mongfhionn, astride her black mount, left no one in doubt as to her view.

Conall looked to Fearghal's right, "Cúscraid informs me that the walls cannot be breached by any weapon we have. We have no rams and no machines that can hurl great rocks at such barriers. We could dig tunnels under the walls or build dirt banks to match the height of the ramparts, but that would take a long time. Celts have no patience for such a strategy."

Cúscraid nodded his agreement. "Can we not draw them out?"

"Would *you* abandon such strong walls? I doubt it. Rock and spears are a compelling advantage."

"Only one way in then," grunted Fearghal.

"The walls are in bad repair. Lots of grips and footholds. We scaled the heights of Ráth na Lairig Éadain in full battle armour and weapons. These ramparts are not nearly as high."

"True, but the defenders of that ráth were not expecting us, *and* we had a diversion. And it wasn't this bloody hot!"

"As I recall, you complained that it was raining then."

Fearghal grinned at the riposte. "The Goddess has guided us to Lugudunon and provided Gaius and his men. I am hoping that the mere presence of Roman warriors will unsettle Matres, make her hesitate. The cavalry and chariots have already departed for the eastern gate. The slings and arrows of Brandubh, Mórrígan, and Sarpedon will keep Matres' warriors occupied on the southern and northern walls while we climb the western. I have left it up to Gaius as to how he deploys the ballistae."

Fearghal dipped his head and then shouted, "Send Brocc, Carmag, Lonán, Torcán, and Urard to me. I need brawlers to lead our assault." Conall looked at Fearghal. A boyish smirk played on his lips. Fearghal exhaled, "As for you, your caomhnóirí will not want you at the front of the attack, but they will forever blame me if they miss this fight. Besides, I doubt if even the Lady Sidhe would be able to stop you from being at my side." A low growl from Mongfhionn confirmed Fearghal's assessment.

* * *

Shouting orders to her men and watching the steady approach of the Romans, Matres limped up and down the western wall. She cursed as she observed two groups of wagons break right and left. Her ire deepened as she watched the ballistae assembled. Even her slings could not match the range of a bolt from one of those machines.

A slight movement on her left drew Matres attention to the ethereal figure of Cornelia. Hands placed on the roughly hewn stones that edged the battlements, Cornelia peered at the advancing soldiers. The lines glinted as sunshine reflected off polished bronze shields, cuirasses, and greaves. Red cloaks flapped. Crimson plumes on helmets flared in the slight breeze. The look on her face was one of concentration and frustration. It was as if she was wrestling to bring some long-hidden memory to the fore.

"Come to watch your lover die on my walls?" spat Matres.

Adrenalin coursed through Matres' veins, and she paced the walkway. The impending clash dulled the Gaiscedach queen's dread of the spectre. She drew pleasure as a frown formed on Cornelia's brow. About to claim victory before the battle started, Matres opened her lips to speak, but stopped. A loud cry from the skies forced her gaze upward. A brace of eagles circled Lugudunon. Above them was a dark cloud of ravens. "Means nothing," she muttered, "Only flesh and blood can kill." Ululating shrieks from the midst of Conall's army echoed off the mountains bordering the valley. "Witches!" she exclaimed and shivered.

The queen turned to hobble away but was halted as Cornelia's skeletal arm rose, and a bony finger pointed. In a voice that held little of humanity, Cornelia spoke. "My spirit clings to this shell by the thinnest of threads. *I* have no fear of death." Long submerged, but now remembered, strains of Roman nobility coursed through Cornelia's veins. With patrician contempt, she presaged, "*You*, the gods have turned their back on. Your death is assured, and you will suffer… very painfully."

Cornelia's diaphanous white garment lifted in the breeze. Like a ribbon, it fluttered over the parapet. It should have been impossible to discern the material against the rampart's stone. Yet the movement caught Gaius' eye as he scanned the wall for signs of weakness. The distance between them was too great for recognition. Still, in that instant when their eyes met, both knew. And, at that same moment, Cornelia panicked. She was not the young woman Gaius remembered. She was skeletal. Her mind was twisted, and her body diseased and broken. She looked around for an escape.

It came at the edge of Matres' blade. There was little pain when the dagger was drawn across Cornelia's throat. The spectre was beyond physical hurt. As she slumped against Matres, she kissed the queen with bloody lips and rasped, "My kiss seals your fate." Helpless to intervene, Gaius watched the corpse of Cornelia lifted up and nailed to a stake on the walls of Lugudunon. The growing crimson stain on the white robe left little doubt that her spirit was free and walking the Elysian Plain.

With a wracking sob, Gaius fell to his knees and pounded the dirt. His eyes and heart saw only the raven-haired, blue-eyed beauty who had kissed him goodbye in Rome. Moments later, resolute and grim-faced, he stood, and deliberately adjusted his armour and swung his shield onto his back. He turned to face his men. "Aquila, take command of the ballistae. Soak the ramparts in blood." Gaius paused, raised his sword and pointed to Lugudunon, "Kill them all. No quarter." With a roar and to the sound of the crack of ballistae, the legion of Gaius Aurelius Atella marched forward.

***

"Shite! Was he not supposed to wait for us?" asked Fearghal, "There goes the battle plan."

Conall laughed and slapped Fearghal on his back. "We're Celts. Tears and tragedy flow in our blood." He sighed in resignation, "Think of the epic tale Tadhg will recount over and over to our sons and daughters."

Fearghal dismounted, and Conall slipped from Toirneach. The horse looked disappointed. "Not this time, my friend." Both men stripped off their heavy armour. Speed would be of more value. Behind, Conall heard a collective thud as thousands mimicked their king and battle commander. Clad only in light plaid pants, the army waited, their torsos glistening with sweat in the rising heat. Baldrics, waist and shoulder belts, bandoliers, and boots bristled with blades.

The king looked around at the assembled army. He felt their anticipation. Relished their readiness. Settling his raven-crested helmet on his head, he tightened the leather chin-straps. Finally, he slipped the battle-axe from its loop. With a shout of, "Bog ar aghaidh. Ionsaí!" Conall raised his weapon and charged forward. In reply, the host of Clann Ui Flaithimh shouted, "Conall Abu! No retreat, no surrender!" and as one followed their king. The sun-dried and wind-swept river plain trembled as the Celts charged.

* * *

It was no surprise that Gaius was the first to scramble over the crenellated wall. Scaling ladders generally allowed two options: the besieger could hold a shield, or a weapon, but not both. The free hand was used to grip the rungs of the ladder. Some also clamped a dagger between their teeth. However, Gaius considered this to give the climber too many options to ponder at a moment when the enemy was likely bearing down quite fast. Gaius chose to climb with his shield gripped in one hand. To the veteran, this afforded some protection from rocks, debris, and the occasional body as it flailed on its way down.

Faced with two Gaiscedach spears, out of habit, Gaius immediately swung his shield in a wide arc roughly parallel to the stone walkway. The usual outcome was the attacker taking a step back. This afforded the time to pull sword from sheath. This day the gods smiled on Gaius. One of the attackers was a head smaller than the Roman. The edge of the shield crushed his throat. As his comrade fell to his knees clutching his ruined neck, the second spearman lunged. The spear point gouged a track along the right side of the cuirass. Caught off-balance, Gaius' shield slammed into his assailant's chest and face. Now, close enough to smell his opponent's sour breath, Gaius' short sword plunged into his belly. A kick from the Roman released his sword and sent the man toppling over the rampart.

Footfalls behind and to his sides told Gaius that he was no longer alone on the narrow parapet. "Form around Cornelia. Protect her body," he shouted. The stake that she hung on was approximately at the midpoint of the western wall. "Cowards, murderers, without honour," he railed at the Gaiscedach as he heard more of his men join him. On the walkway, the better order and discipline of the Romans soon told as they forced a broad section clear. Cornelia's corpse at the centre of their attack was a grim reminder of their commander's and her suffering. Blood flowed like a crimson river on the ramparts.

Standing back from the main skirmish, and balancing on two upright stones, the Gaiscedach queen surveyed her bloodied defences. Rocks and boiling oil, water, and embers had taken a horrendous toll on the Romans. The odour of cooked flesh mingled with shite and piss loosened from failing bowels. Bodies lay broken at the foot of the hill of Lugudunon. The constant moaning of the injured rose up to blight the ears of those on the battlements. Matres grudgingly admitted that Gaius' men fought with determination, neither expecting nor giving mercy. Her western wall was littered with the bodies of the Gaiscedach. Indeed, such was the ferocity of the fight that some were locked in a rictus of death with Roman hands around their throats. More lay at the foot of the inner walls, kicked aside by Roman boots.

Matres reckoned that over five hundred of her warriors had died at the hands of the Romans. Many more were injured. This for the loss of two hundred of Gaius' men. Now the Romans had a firm foothold on the wall. A blast of horns from outside the defences made the Gaiscedach queen swear. Distracted by the ferocity of the Roman assault and the cursed ballistae whose bolts continued to harvest reinforcements, Matres' attention now turned to a much bigger threat. Hundreds of grappling hooks clanged, scraped, and gouged stone to find purchase. Ladders thunked as they slammed against her defences. In between the ragged breaths from the exertions of the ascent, the taunts, threats, and curses of Clann Ui Flaithimh became ominously clear. A cry of alarm from Lugudunon's eastern gateway told her that it too was besieged.

Hoarse with shouting commands, Matres spat to clear her throat. She became aware of a dark cloud overhead. At first, she dismissed it as the cloud of ravens that seemed to follow Conall's army. Then the shrieking and cursing began. Joining the ballistae bombardment of the western wall, a storm of stones and arrows plunged from the sky, falling on the southern and northern defences. It was followed by a second and third volley. Matres swore, but like her men, ducked and raised her shield to avoid serious injury.

Fearghal panted as his muscles groaned with each lunge upwards to find a foothold and the next knot on the rope. The weight of the shield and javelins slung on his back seemed to have quadrupled in the short climb. "Thank the Goddess," he muttered, as the summit of the wall came within sight. "I hope Gaius has done his job and Mórrígan remembers that she's only supposed to attack the walls we're not climbing," grunted the granite-muscled battle commander to no-one in particular.

Conall laughed, "I told you to use the ladders."

On the grassy incline at the foot of the southern walls, Mórrígan called Sarpedon to her. "Two more volleys. Then we climb and take charge of the walls. Tell your men to pick your targets. This day we take no prisoners, no slaves." The Cretan dipped his head. On the northern wall, Brandubh gave similar orders to the five hundred with him; the remainder he had put under Mórrígan's command. He looked at Carmag, "It is time to climb." With a roar of sheer joy, the wild-haired warrior ran to the wall and began his ascent.

Conall and Fearghal tumbled over the low crenellated wall. Rising from a crouching halt and, in a motion made a habit by many battles, shields were unslung and javelins grasped. The throwing spears were immediately loosed on a group of Gaiscedach who, having sufficiently recovered from Mórrígan's barrage, approached Gaius' front lines, red-faced and angry. There was little attempt at accuracy, and only the good fortune of the Goddess directed any of the missiles to find flesh and bone. They did, however, stall a putative Gaiscedach advance. More quickly clambered over the crest in Conall's footsteps.

On one side of Conall and Fearghal, Lonán, Brocc, Bláithín, Cúscraid, and Deaglán grunted in unison as they surmounted the wall and tumbled onto the blood-splattered walkway. Cúscraid was bemused.

He usually found himself defending a position. On Conall's other flank were Torcán, Urard, Iasg, and the three Ó Cuileannáin brothers. The walls of Lugudunon were between five and ten paces in breadth, with the west and east walls being the widest. Thus, six or seven warriors could span it. Fearghal grinned at Conall and trotted over to join Lonán's group; Conall took charge of Torcán's. Both units hefted their remaining javelins, locked scíatha, and strode to relieve Gaius' men. They intended to clear a wider section of the wall and secure a foothold for the mass of the warriors in their wake.

Of Conall's party, it was no surprise that Urard was the first to confront the enemy. Powerful legs propelled him forward and the axe, Breith, flashed in the sun as it arced downward seeking its first victim. The surprise was that Iasg beat her partner to first blood. One of her knives neatly and precisely entered the eye of Urard's chosen quarry. The warrior howled in pain, but this was cut short as Urard's axe cleaved his head. Gore splattered Urard, making him look even more fearsome. The tall, burly fighter looked at Iasg, shook his head, and growled, "Mine." Iasg wiped a blood splatter from her cheek, grinned, and threw another blade. This time the recipient, with blood spurting from a deep wound to his forehead, stumbled to his knees. Iasg indicated the fallen Gaiscedach and mouthed, "Mine."

Training and exercise hone skills and increase endurance, but nothing can mimic the ferocity and turmoil of battle conditions. Bláithín ignored Brocc's exhortations that she remain with Sárán and the supply wagons. Now, side-by-side with him and Lonán, the Ulaid noblewoman grimaced as her short-handled axe carved through flesh and bone. Arms ached as she swung the axe and defended with the small shield. Ears rang from many blade strikes on her helmet. Her spine was likely bruised an angry purple from the scíath pressed hard against her back. Long gouges in her breastplate made her thankful for the skills of her armourer. Yet, in the middle of this, Bláithín was quite annoyed about a minor indiscretion. In the midst of the skirmish, she had pissed herself. That was a habit she would have to break.

Amodocus, Íar, and Gràinne cursed at the eastern gate's obdurate resistance to their attempts to knock, pull, or hack it down. "The Hag's arse, the battle will be over, and we'll still be outside," complained Gràinne. The young Cinn Péinteáilte's blood boiled that her longsword remained unbloodied. She looked at the square stone guard towers on either side of the gate and then at Íar. "Can yer men pitch javelins into the tower?" Íar looked as if he had been insulted at such a slur on his riders skills but nodded. Then Gràinne turned to Amodocus and with a grin issued her challenge. "I'll take the left tower. Do ye think ye can handle the right one?"

Gràinne's chariot pulled up adjacent to the guard tower. Facing the wall, the Cinn Péinteáilte warrior deftly stepped onto the cret's rail and quickly found purchase on the rough stones. With a scream of defiance, Gràinne started to climb. "Shite!" cursed Íar and ordered his men to toss javelins into the towers. Amodocus watched as, lizard-like, the young woman scaled the rampart. Still exasperated, Íar stared at the Thracian. "Are you going to watch Gràinne's arse or take the other tower?" Amodocus sighed and cantered to the wall.

Nikandros felt marginalised. Although a member of the quartet of leaders assigned to capture the eastern gateway, the others appeared to act in harmony without the benefit of his input. He wondered if what he sensed as a chilling of relations with the other members of the Chomhairle and ceannairí na míle was all in his imagination. The only exception was Mórrígan, who remained friendly. As the gateway was thrown open, the Spartan gripped his long doru and cantered forward. He needed to remember who and what he was, and take heed of the stiffening hairs on the back of his neck.

***

Matres surveyed the battle. Due to the narrowness of the rampart, the clash on the west wall soon became a bloody stalemate with neither side making headway. The injured were pulled back and quickly replaced.

She watched the blood-dripping axe of a massive warrior destroy three shields as if they were made of kindling. Without another glance, the queen knew the men were lost. Kicked from the rampart by friend and foe, they joined the growing heap of corpses that lay at the foot of the defences. Deep blue eyes narrowed. The men's kin and comrades would have noted the shoddy workmanship of the scíatha. No doubt there would be less one armourer after the battle.

A bellowed battle cry from the northern wall drew Matres' attention. Her gaze fell on a brawny, near-naked red-haired warrior who tumbled over the rough wall. Immediately, he swung a heavy-headed club, smashing skulls to a pulp. On the narrow parapet, those who followed lagged to avoid the reach of his swing. The queen shrugged. Lugudunon's north wall was lightly manned and quickly overrun as more tattooed Cinn Péinteáilte warriors joined the hirsute warrior.

Cries from the southern wall drew curses from Matres. She watched as men spun around, falling to their deaths. That said, the black-shafted arrows protruding from their backs more than likely suggested that they were already journeying to Mag Mell. A snarl escaped Matres as she spotted the Dark Huntress and her Cretan mercenaries. With uncanny accuracy, the queen of Clann Ui Flaithimh sent arrow upon arrow into Matres' warriors. At Mórrígan's side, the Cretan leader and his men seemed to have an incredible rate of fire. And they were no less accurate.

It had never been Matres intention to fight the primary battle for Lugudunon from the hillfort's ramparts. Less than a quarter of her force manned the battlements. The remainder were secreted in the numerous homes, workshops, and other buildings of the fort. Still, she had hoped that strength of stone would have told and sufficiently weakened Conall's army to give her an advantage for the real fight. Matres cursed Cornelia once more. It was conceivable that Marcus and Concolitanus were right. Had she executed Cornelia, then Gaius would not have had cause to storm Lugudunon's walls. Perhaps Conall and his tribe would have chosen another territory to conquer.

The queen spat and looked to the horizon. Sunset was not far off. She signalled a nearby warrior. Gaiscedach horns sounded out. Those who could, turned from the skirmish and dashed for the stone stairways and into the next battleground—the streets of Lugudunon.

***

Conall leant against what had been a white stone wall. It was now a garish pink, splattered with blood and gore. The abrupt exit of Matres' forces took him by surprise. Blade slashes, javelins, and arrows claimed a further proportion of the retreating Gaiscedach, but not enough to make a discernible difference. Clann Ui Flaithimh's warriors and their Roman allies held the walls of Lugudunon, but that was of doubtful utility.

"Well?" The question was posed to the commanders and captains who stood before him.

It was Cúscraid who provided the assessment. "The light is departing fast with the onset of dusk, but as far as I can tell from reports around the walls, they've disappeared." Conall raised an eyebrow. "Oh, they're inside the defences. Íar has the eastern gates well-guarded. No-one will get past the horses and chariots." Cúscraid gestured in the direction of Lugudunon's centre. "About one thousand guard Lugudunon's Great Hall. I presume Matres is within the building. The rest? The rats have gone to ground. Their nests are hidden in the many buildings. The main streets are blocked off. I suspect we'll face hidden snares and other traps."

"The buildings are all stone?"

Cúscraid nodded unhappily, "A few have wood and thatch roofs, but the majority are all stone. Burning them out is not an option."

"Advice?" In his heart, Conall knew what the answer would be and who should be in command of the next tactic.

"A night of blood and nightmares."

The words were spoken with no great pleasure. Unlike in the past, Mórrígan took little delight in the darker side of her character. "The wolfhound pack will be set loose as soon as it is dark. Beacán will command my men. He and Amodocus will divide their men into small teams. Like ghosts, they will strike and retreat. Sarpedon's men will take up positions within sight of the Great Hall. Like gnats, their arrows will bite Matres' guard throughout the night. Any building that can be set alight will be. The Gaiscedach will not know sleep from sunset to sunrise."

"And you?"

Mórrígan sighed and replied with no great pleasure in her voice, "The Lady Sidhe, Gràinne, and I will provide the nightmares." A cold shiver ran up Conall's spine.

***

Blood flowed, and the mná-sidhe wailed during the dark hours. Beacán, his torso streaked in gore, let another warrior drop at his feet. Her throat bore a deep slash from a dagger forever stained with the blood of many nameless victims. This one he held longer than most. He heard her sigh as life departed and felt the warmth of her body wane. What it would have been like to embrace her and lie in her arms, he wondered? Absent-mindedly he passed his hand across his dry lips. The metallic taste of her blood jerked him from his musing. A chuckle. It was pitch black in the home. She could be as ugly as the Hag.

The night was filled with the unrelenting song of the mná-sidhe as souls—both Clann Ui Flaithimh and Gaiscedach—were harvested. On the walls three solitary figures, arms stretched to the stars, glowed as moonlight flowed through the swirling designs that covered their bodies. As they chanted, a miasma of horror radiated from them and into the minds of the Gaiscedach. Of the trio, it was most difficult for Gràinne. She had never sung the Tuireadh—the death chant of her tribe—and yet without prompting, it seemed to be on her lips. It promoted emotions she did not like. She felt tainted.

Night retreated with the rising sun, and so did Beacán and Amodocus', bands. The night became one of legend. Yet, over the campfires of many Celt and Gaul tribes, it was in hushed tones that warriors debated who were the better assassins—Clann Uí Flaithimh or Gaiscedach. The three women, exhausted and covered in sweat from the night's exertions, departed Lugudunon, each retreating to find a sanctuary in the woods and a river where they could cleanse away the horror that still lingered in their minds.

As the sun climbed to its zenith, so did the stench of Lugudunon. The hillfort became a stone-walled cauldron, simmering with a sickening brew of decaying corpses and ruptured guts. Mórrígan and Sarpedon's archers patrolled the battlements, looking for targets of opportunity. The persistent stream of warriors weaving between blood-stained buildings, frantically searching for escape routes, provided ample fodder for their bows. Sarpedon shrugged as he watched as another arrow thudded into its victim. The man spun around under the impact. He leant against the whitewashed wall and, as he slowly slid to his final rest, fresh blood smeared the brick.

For those who made it past the archers and skirmishing parties to the gateway, there was to be no escape. Their fate was to be chased and cut down by merciless riders. Still, the archers and mounted warriors had a less onerous task than the bulk of the army. Divided into five parties, the foot warriors of Clann Uí Flaithimh walked slowly along avenues that ran east-west and finally converged on the large square where Matres' Great Hall stood.

The pace was excruciatingly slow and perilous. Barriers had to be dismantled, and the side streets searched. Ambushes were frequent. From a sudden stab in the back from a spear as an entrance was passed, to warbands of fifty or more men suddenly appearing in front and behind. In the closeness of the fort, there was little room to swing axes and longer swords. This was mostly a brawl with shields, daggers, fists, and whatever body part could inflict the most damage.

Torcán signalled his hundred to rest. He looked down at his chainmail gloves—a present from Craiftine. Strings of skin and small white shards of bone spattered the metal surface. In the narrow alleyways, he had long since laid his shield aside and fought with short-sword and knife as well as fists and, of course, his head. Now at an intersection between an avenue and a major street, he paused to look to his left. Lonán stood bent over, hands pressed down on his knees.

The Cróeb Ruad warrior's sweat and blood-covered chest heaved as he tried to suck in air. "Bastard heat," he mouthed at Torcán, wiping his brow of the beads of perspiration. He prayed to the Goddess for a cold drink, and then for the safety of the young boys and girls who followed and risked their lives to bring skins of water to the warriors. Several damp patches in the dirt told a tale of those whose lives ended with a spear thrust or cut throat. A loud bellow from the furthest avenue on his left brought a smile that cracked the dried blood on his face.

Carmag started the day cursing and continued in the same vein. "You'd have thought he would be happy to be in a fight at last," muttered Lonán. His men chuckled. It was a speck of relief on a gloom-laden day. The burly warrior chieftain from Northern Albu was not, however, complaining about the brawl. It was that in the streets there was little room to swing his beloved hammer. His men, fearing for their own wellbeing—several had narrowly avoided being maimed—appealed to Carmag to fight in the broader avenue. The next challenge was to prevent the red-haired hulk from moving so far ahead that he risked being cut off from the main body of his men.

In the central, and broadest avenue of Lugudunon, a similar problem faced Urard. Iasg had lost count of the number of times she had had to dive aside to avoid the arc of Breith's blade. It was noticeable that Conall, Cúscraid, and Fearghal gave the warrior a very wide berth. Still, Urard's mastery of the axe had cut a gory swathe through the ranks of the Gaiscedach. Iasg found herself limited to the two hand-axes she carried. Her considerable inventory of throwing knives had gradually been depleted, mainly due to her victims stumbling away, or their bodies refusing to give up the small weapons.

"I think we're here," said Fearghal, his voice made thick with battle

347

dust and debris. A step took Clann Ui Flaithimh's battle commander into the main square of Lugudunon. Before the tall building at the centre of the yard stood a defiant Matres, queen of the Gaiscedach, and what remained of her army. With scíatha raised and spears held steady, they stood as bold as their queen. "Likely, mostly veterans protect her," said Fearghal, "This will not be easy."

Conall took a skin of water from the dirty-faced, young girl who appeared at his side. She was no older than his daughters. His thirst slaked, he handed the pouch to Fearghal and then turned to face the child. "This is no place for you." His tone was severe—the brutality of battle overwhelming compassion. The girl's face fell at the rebuke and her green eyes clouded with tears. A cough from Fearghal made Conall look at his friend, "What?" he snapped. The look in Fearghal's hazel eyes was all that was needed for the father in Conall rise to the surface.

The intemperate nature of Conall's retort shamed him. The king dropped to one knee and faced the child. With a finger, he gently wiped away the tear that had commenced its journey down her cheek. "My daughters would hold me to account for my graceless thanks." Reaching up to his neck, Conall took off a thick gold torc and placed it around the girl's neck. "A small gift from a very grateful king. Tell your ma and da to come visit me after the battle. Bring your brothers and sisters too." The smile on the youngster's face for a brief moment made Conall forget about the fight. It was fleeting. The king stood, "Go, and may the Goddess keep you safe." As she scampered away, he turned to face his enemy.

"Glory, honour, and a tale for Tadhg to recount, or a slaughter to be whispered in the shadows?" Conall pitched the question to his commanders as they studied the ranks of the Gaiscedach. Arrayed ten rows deep, with each row having two hundred warriors, the formation bristled with spears held by those who undoubtedly were expert in their use.

"We're fortunate that Íar is not among us." Conall's brow furrowed at Fearghal's comment. The bluff warrior continued, "Íar, after all, is the most honourable of us."

"I have a hand-fast partner and a baby that I have not seen. Finish it. We've left enough of our comrades and blood in the dirt of this place." There was an audible gasp of surprise among the members of the small group. It was not at the sentiment, but at its deliverer. For it was Torcán, the brawler, the wild boar by reputation and by name who spoke. He looked at the astonishment on the faces of his friends.

"What? A man can change."

"Send for Mórrígan and Sarpedon's archers. Tell Sárán to bring all the javelins he has forward." Conall paused and then with a trace of sadness and inevitability he looked to Gaius and Aquila, "Have the ballistae teams brought to the front." The age of war machines had arrived for Clann Ui Flaithimh. The air of resignation among the group was broken by a chuckle from Torcán. He pointed to the Gaiscedach.

"Besides, we'll have our glorious and bloody fight. If you don't think that those bastards will charge when the first arrow leaves the bow, then you're an eejit."

Torcán was right.

***

In this battle, her defeat became inevitable. Trapped in a stone cage, it was too late when Matres came to the realisation that the Gaiscedach's real strength was outside—in the fields, the forests, the mountains, and the night. Now, the army lay broken and bleeding on the white stones of Lugudunon. It would take many seasons for the rains to wash away the dark red stains. Perhaps they never would. The irony that the blemishes would be an eternal reminder to Conall not to make the same mistake failed to amuse Matres.

Her veterans of war, terror, and assassination had been fought to a standstill on their own ground. Conall's men fought toe-to-toe with her warriors and, with ruthless efficiency, ground her men like meat. The Cinn Péinteáilte and Ravens of Northern Albu, their bodies painted crimson, howled like wolves as they swung their great clubs and used wickedly sharp spears. The cursed Dark Huntress and her archers swept her captains aside. Bolts from the cursed Roman ballistae carved grisly paths among the Gaiscedach ranks. Matres lost a third of her men, crippled or dead, in the first barrage. As Torcán had predicted, the rest broke ranks and charged the Clann Ui Flaithimh. At least when both sides closed the storm of iron ceased.

Outside the gates, in their thirst for blood and vengeance, the mounted warriors of Clann Ui Flaithimh gave no quarter. There were no Gaiscedach injured. None were taken in chains to be sold as slaves. To all the neighbouring tribes, the message was clear. Perfidy brought a death sentence. Now Conall's forces closed in on all sides of her palace.

Concolitanus' discovery and destruction of her tunnels on the western side of Lugudunon had constrained but not eliminated Matres' escape options. The queen of the Gaiscedach was both wily and pragmatic. That she could sacrifice her daughter and sons for whom she had genuine feelings—although love was too strong a word—in a failed attack on Conall and his family, was a measure of the low value she placed on the warriors who guarded her. As she saw it, her fortress was overrun, and therefore the only hope for the remnant of her people scattered in the hills was her survival.

Selecting a score of her most trusted men—any more would be suspicious—Matres made her way to a room that few entered. Those that did never spoke or saw again. A circular trapdoor was located at the centre of the chamber. Matres nodded. It took four to lift the heavy, wooden access flap. Its heavy iron hinges stubbornly resisted, but soon screamed and yielded. A stale smell rose from the blackness. The queen pointed to the hole and, using iron rungs set into the stone, half of her men proceeded to climb down. Matres followed, and then the rest of her guard.

A stench of ancient shite and piss assaulted the group's nostrils as they broke the surface crust and tramped through a thick sludge. Matres smiled. It was fortunate that the previous occupiers of Lugudunon had built the sewage tunnel. The brick-faced shaft ran east to the River

Souconna. There was a precipitous drop at its end, but the river was deep enough to break any fall. The Souconna would also perform a secondary function of washing the sewage from them. From there, they would travel east to the gentle foothills, and then the snow-covered slopes of the Alpes.

✴✴✴

The end, as was the beginning, was bloody. On his chestnut-bay, Íar removed his helmet as he surveyed Lugudunon. He turned to Aoibheann and shook his head. She sensed his torment. "Were they honourable people who deserved an end celebrated for all-time by the stories of the seanachaí?"

With a sad shrug of his broad shoulders, Íar whispered, "No."

✴✴✴

"She escaped." Tadhg's report was short and unwelcome. Gaius banged his fists on the table. Conall raised an eyebrow for more details. "We found a tunnel entrance in one of her chambers. It leads to the river. She's likely heading for the Gaiscedach strongholds in the Alpes."

"Bitseach!"

Conall dipped his head in agreement with Mórrígan's interjection. The Huntress made to speak again, but a palm before her face stopped her. "Before you say anything, you are right. I should have sent you after Matres in Albu." He paused, "That woman has more lives than a feral cat."

✴✴✴

Farther to the east, as she began to climb the mountain, Matres turned, cleared her throat and spat. Only one thought—one word—filled her mind—revenge. The bitter taste of defeat soured her belly. She swore vengeance on Conall, his queen, and his children; on Gaius; on Concolitanus and his witch—Matres was unaware that this pair had already met their fate—and on Marcus Fabius Ambustus and his sons. With another spit, she turned and limped away.

351

CHAPTER 42

403 B.C.—Lugudunon—Late Summer

A thin blanket of warm rain shrouded the forests to the north of Lugudunon. While welcome, Conall knew that it would take more than a light drizzle to cleanse the streets of the blood spilt. Exhausted from the battle and indifferent to the weather, men and women rested where they collapsed. Only the Sidhe seemed to take pleasure in the change in conditions. Rain, clouds, and thunder all refreshed her spirit and her powers.

Hands on the wet rampart stone, Conall peered into the distance. He derived no comfort from the beauty of the valley and the distant mountains. The back of his neck itched. He rubbed it until it burned pink. *This*, thought Fearghal, *was not a good sign*. A mournful wail of war-horns broke the pastoral harmony. "Shite!" growled Conall as the voices of thousands of Gaulish warriors joined the horns. The horde erupted from the forest edge and tramped at a fast pace towards the hillfort.

"Eejits," muttered Fearghal, "They'll be dog-tired by the time they reach us."

"Might not matter," remarked Cúscraid, "I make their numbers between fifteen and twenty thousand." He faced Conall, "From the banners, it seems that Brennus is paying us a visit."

Conall shrugged weary shoulders, looking with a wry smile at the eagles soaring high above. They were joined by a conspiracy of ravens who answered the war-horns with their own cries of *kraa kraa*. Taking a deep breath, Conall roared, "Archers, ballistae, and slings to the northern walls." He looked at Brandubh, Mórrígan, and Sarpedon, "I need every sling and arrow to fire once the enemy is within range." Then he looked at Gaius, "Place the ballistae to best effect. Your men, along with Bláithín and Brocc's céadta, will form a last line of defence."

"Fearghal, rouse the ceannairí céad and ceannairí na míle. Form the shield wall with full battle armour twenty paces from the north wall." Conall paused and looked around. He smiled when he spotted the familiar orange plaid of Sárán Mac Craobhach. "You will ensure the fighters have a supply of javelins. Arrange the wagons behind the shield wall. Assign people to feed weapons to the warriors."

"Carmag, this is a fight you will enjoy. Form up on the right flank of the shield wall. Your Cinn Péinteáilte will attack the enemy's flank on my command." Carmag smiled, hefted his heavy club, and shouted orders to his men. Without hesitation, they streamed out of the gates of Lugudunon. To Íar, Nikandros, and Gràinne, Conall said, "Take a wide path to the east. Harass Senones' flanks and rear. Drive the Gauls onto our swords."

"And us?" The question came from behind Conall.

"Us?"

With a flourish of her milk-white hand, Mongfhionn indicated the presence of Rosmerta and Crum. "You are aware of my talents. The old lady, much as I would prefer to ignore, does have a unique set of gifts. Like me, she is not to be underestimated. As for Crum and his score of druids, their prayers and swords will strengthen the walls." Crum nodded. Rosmerta gave the Sidhe a sour look.

"As you wish. After all, who am I to question the spiritual leaders of Clann Ui Flaithimh." All three snorted derisively.

***

The envoy, although that was a large name for a small boy of no more than twelve summers, galloped into the camp of Clann Ui Flaithimh. As he slowed his horse to a walk, hazel eyes with gold and amber flecks searched feverishly for someone in authority. He had no idea what the civic leader of the tribe looked like. Born out of experience, he had spent most of his short life avoiding the clann's elders. They were more likely to cuff his ears and tell him to "Clear off!" than hold a conversation. The steady clack of wood-on-wood drew his attention, and he trotted in the direction of the source.

Mòrag, to allay her boredom and being the only professional warrior left in the encampment, had taken it upon herself to organise training sessions for the militia. A few, mainly fools apparently unaware of her reputation, mocked her. In their eyes, she was an entitled princess, and they doubted that a young woman could teach them anything. For her part, Mòrag chose to use these eejits as dummies for target practice. The few healers left in the camp were later to admonish Mòrag for the sudden jump in broken bones and cracked ribs.

Today, however, Mòrag had a much more pleasant duty. She watched over Barra and his friends, as they tried to emulate their older role models. Sat on an oak stump, Mòrag called out instructions as she nursed Ròs, the recent addition to her family. The baby girl sucked happily, and with some force, on her mother's nipple. Mòrag chuckled. It was good that Ròs had no teeth.

And so, the young messenger came upon this scene. Open-mouthed, and with the honesty of the young, he looked down—for he was still astride the chestnut bay loaned to him—and stared at Mòrag's breasts. It was not that the sight of an infant suckling at exposed nipples was a rare sight in the clann. In fact, it was quite common-place. Yet, rarely had the young man seen such a well-shaped and ample-sized pair. The stirring in his groin reminded him painfully of his adolescence, As the horse's shadow fell across Mòrag, she glanced up and quickly understood the situation. She smiled. The boy's lechery was honest, if not innocent.

"You may watch for as long as you wish, *But*, if I see your hand slide under your pants, I will pull you from that horse, take your pants down and beat your arse until it looks like an under-cooked steak." Suddenly, the envoy remembered his mission, leapt down from the mount and knelt before Mòrag. Once his thoughts were organised the boy related his message from Conall and the urgent need for the militia to take the field in support of the army. "That you were entrusted with so serious a message, speaks well of you. *But*, learn your priorities. You will have a short life if easily distracted by a pair of tits." The severe look from Mòrag was punishment enough, and the young man's eyes kept to the dirt as the warrior princess strode away to assemble the militia.

***

Brennus, having discarded his mount, marched towards the hillfort. Much to the consternation of the men who formed his personal guard, his long stride ensured that he was well to the fore of his army. Given the time of the year, his dress—light woven pants and calf-boots, and armour, hardened leather breastplate and a helmet which he carried under his left arm—was minimal. Brennus' right hand rested on the smooth metal pommel of his sword. The weapon was sheathed in a wood and leather scabbard and hung from a leather baldric. The king of the Senones was a tall man. Yet the blade's length was such that the sheath scrapped the dirt. With cutting edges honed sharp and a rounded tip, this was a sword for slashing. An oblong wooden scíath and several spears were slung on his back.

Close enough to assess the assembly of Conall, Brennus raised his hand, and the Senones slowed their pace. To many Gaulish leaders, the backdrop of Lugudunon's walls was ill-omened. The white fortifications looked as if they were bleeding. Before them stood several ranks of locked shields, all red with a black painted raven. Above the scíatha, two apparitions in dark cloaks prowled the walls. Their arms were raised high and nightmarish ululating shrieks scythed through the air. Soon they were joined by the monotone chanting of Crum's druids. On the horizon, Brennus could see grey clouds gathering, Feint traces of the sharp, fresh smell that accompanies thunder and lightning tickled his nostrils.

Unease rippled through the Senone horde.

Acco looked at Brennus, "Send the full force against them."

Brennus had never lost a major battle, and Acco knew it was his leader's intention to test Conall with five thousand men, albeit veterans. According to the king, a quick and bloody victory would send Conall's invaders packing and sound a clear message to the neighbouring Gaulish tribes not to challenge him. Additionally, but likely of more weight than other considerations, Brennus wanted Mórrígan's head to decorate his doorpost. The Dark Huntress' campaign of destruction and terror across his lands had resulted in Brennus losing face among his people.

"If we lose the veterans, the rest will falter."

Acco made one last appeal to reason. As he surveyed the defences of Lugudunon, a shiver travelled up his spine. What strength lined the parapets? Where were the damned horses and chariots? By his reckoning, the warriors on the field were evenly matched in numbers. That Conall's men chose to fight outside of the hillfort's protection did not bode well. He licked dry lips.

"Are you with me?" asked Brennus.

"Stupid bloody question." Acco's cheeks flushed at the implied insult. "Of course, I am. Next to you, there is no better warrior in the Senones."

Brennus chuckled. "Sound the war-horns."

***

"I don't think they're taking us seriously," opined Fearghal as he watched a third of the Senone force detach from the main body and stride towards the walls of Lugudunon. Conall laughed. It was a brief respite from his anxiety. His men were exhausted. Scabby wounds, soon to be re-opened, pulled at inflamed pink skin. No doubt, they would fight bravely for king, tribe, and family, but for how long? Brennus had chosen his time well. Conall's hope lay in his missiles.

About to call out to Mórrígan, the whoosh of disturbed wind informed Conall there was no need. His queen conducted her orchestra with an innate sense of timing. First, Brandubh's one thousand slings launched a storm of metal and stone. Soon they were joined by the squeal of tightened skeins, the grunts of men, and the thud and crack of wood as arm-sized bolts with vicious iron heads were hurled into the midst of the Senones. Mórrígan and Sarpedon's bows, having the shortest range, were the last to add their barbs to the symphony.

"My hairy arse!" exclaimed Fearghal in awe of the bombardment.

It was a sentiment that echoed among the ranks of the Senones. Battlefield philosophers wondered if this was the future of war—to be sent to Mag Mell by an unseen enemy. Brennus' advance faltered, exploding in a mist of iron and blood. There was little need for accuracy with the slings. All that was required was volume and height. Rocks and metal slugs rained down on the approaching horde. Deadly leaf-shaped bolts carved tracks deep into the Senone horde, cleaving heads and limbs effortlessly. Those tipped with long iron spikes punched holes in flesh with more ease than a knife in freshly-made butter. Exiting their prey in a gush of gore and bone, they travelled on to the next victim. In contrast, archers added finesse to the mix. The last to enter the barrage, they shifted tactics from quantity to precision as Brennus' men drew closer.

Brennus grimaced as he felt his army shudder under the bombardment. He pushed from his mind the vision of the dead and injured from the lethal response to his assault. The attack slowed, but still pressed forward. There was no choice. Men and women raised shields and crouch-walked to make themselves smaller. The charge became a laboured tramp to survive until they could engage the sciátha of Conall. Brennus bellowed encouragement to those around him. In this, he was alone. Acco's blood was splashed over his chest and face. The second-in-command fell to a bolt that left his head attached to his neck by slivers of skin and gristle.

Suddenly, apart from arrows that appeared to be picking off his chieftains, the barrage ceased. Brennus wondered why. He straightened up and saw red and black sciátha, arrayed in four rows of five hundred warriors, move forward. At fifty paces, the shield wall launched the first volley of javelins. The king of the Senones scowled when a javelin head sliced a well-muscled forearm. By the time Brennus' warriors closed the gap to a score of paces, two more volleys had been thrown. A clash of shield rims signalled that the ranks of the Conall's human wall had closed.

A wave of Senones crashed against Conall's sciatha with all the fury of a violent sea. Like a cliff of granite, anchored by the rear three rows, the shield-wall held. Harsh words were first into battle. An aerosol of spit was carried on breaths fortified by rotten teeth, diseased gums, and garlic. The front row retained one javelin, and it was now thrust through the gap created by the waists of the oblong shields. The rear rows stabbed over the shoulders of their comrades. Before long, most of the spears were lost, trapped by flesh unwilling to give up the cause of its demise. Swords were drawn, and the sciatha moved forward, one agonisingly slow, bloody pace at a time. Legs, throats, faces were slashed. Conall's mounting injured were pulled to the rear and replaced. Brennus' attackers had no such luxury, and were trampled underfoot by their comrades.

A horn from the walls of Lugudunon sounded. To Brennus' left a loud cheer arose and, with weapons raised high, Carmag's forest people entered the affray. Clubs pounded the left flank of the Senones. It was a distraction that Brennus could have done without. The savage glee with which they fought startled him. The Senone king knew that the weaknesses of Conall's shield wall were its right side and rear, where no shields afforded protection. Hence, warbands had been dispatched to outflank Conall's formation. They lay in the dirt, slaughtered by Cretan arrows. Senone war-horns reverberated across the battlefield, directing the attack, attempting to shift the balance of the fight to the right. Carmag's entrance frustrated that strategy.

In the slop of battle, the count of the dead and injured mounted. Clann Ui Flaithimh showed no sign of surrender or retreat. The Senones had no answer to the relentless slashing swords of the shield wall. At a signal from Brennus, the war-horns sounded again. His warriors disengaged, retreating, although not in a panic. They came to a halt just beyond the range of the missiles of their enemy. Conall's men leaned heavily on their shields. Their ragged breathing was the only sound disturbing the lull. Teams of healers and their helpers scurried from Lugudunon to bring the badly injured within the hillfort.

"Bastard's up to something." Conall nodded.

"Like me, Brennus knows we're at a standoff. And, like me, he's likely calculating the costs and prospects of his options."

Fearghal pointed to the mass of the Senones, and snorted, "We have options? Enlighten me. He could throw his whole army at us. We're well outnumbered."

"I don't reckon that Brennus is that rash. He'll know that we can always retreat to behind the walls of Lugudunon and bombard him with rocks, bolts, and arrows. He'll not want that. Too much damage to his army, and for a territory that is far from his kingdom." Conall shrugged, "Besides, Celts and Gauls have no patience for sieges. Fight, feast, and rut. That's our way."

Fearghal pointed a bloody finger at an advancing figure, "We have movement."

A change of tactics was needed, and Brennus was a formidable strategist. He also figured he could beat Conall in a straight fight—man-to-man. The tall Senone king strode away from his army. Naked from the waist up, Brennus cradled a heavy, broad-bladed sword in his arms. His sole defence was his iron and bronze helmet with its curling horns. He came to a halt mid-way between the two armies. His intent was obvious.

"Shite!" groaned Fearghal. Conall just smiled, tightened the straps on his helmet and settled his shield on his arm. Fearghal slipped the battle axe from its loop on the king's back and handed it to Conall. Barely had Conall taken a few steps when he was faced by Urard. The big man held the axe Breith in his hands.

"Any advice?" asked Conall.

"Let me fight him."

Conall smiled and shook his head, "This is between kings." Urard dipped his head and stood aside.

Brennus steadily advanced on Conall, gripping the longsword in both hands. Several paces from each other, the Senone king raised his weapon above his head and charged. The impact of the blade on Conall's shield numbed his arm and brought him down on one knee. He was thankful for the sturdy construction of the scíath as more strikes quickly followed.

A wild swing of Conall's axe drew a curse from Brennus, making him take a step backwards. The blade had sliced through the king's boots. Fortunately, the edge was still keen and neatly opened a thin gash on Brennus' ankle. It was a painful cut, but not debilitating. It did, however, give Conall the opportunity to attack. Scíath and axe worked in unison as the king of Clann Ui Flaithimh battered and slashed his opponent. The flourish ended with a clash of metal as Brennus head-butted Conall and pushed him away. Both circled each other, probing defences and looking for weaknesses to exploit.

Conall's fleeting glance at the fresh wound on Brennus' right arm curled the ends of the Senone king's mouth upwards. The gesture was unseen, masked by the king's bushy beard and whiskers. Brennus moved his sword to counter an attack on his right. It was a feint, and Conall's axe sliced open the muscles on Brennus' upper left arm. The Senone growled and swung his weapon around in frustration as Conall pirouetted away. Clann Ui Flaithimh's Rí Ruirech intended to get behind his opponent and bury the axe in his back. Not the most gentlemanly act, but needs must.

However, and as with many battles, fortune is fickle. Brennus' unplanned sword stroke coincided with the point in Conall's dance when his back was most exposed. The weapon's tip tracked down Conall's spine, causing the young king to grunt in pain. Now, in this, Conall had every reason to be thankful to the Goddess. Brennus' sword was meant for slashing, and hence only its long edges were honed. The tip was rounded—never intended for stabbing. Plus, unlike Brennus, Conall was wearing chainmail. The king of Clann Ui Flaithimh received a very painful strike along his spine but, although he would be in pain for several sunsets, it was not a mortal wound.

To Conall, it seemed that the cheers from both armies at each strike, feint, and block, were getting closer. Indeed, the forces of the Senones and Clann Ui Flaithimh had edged closer to the combatants. Although not close enough to start the fighting again. In the tradition of the Celts, wagers on the duel were soon rippling through the armies. There was little advantage to either king. All acknowledged that both were skilled fighters. Loud approval sounded out, especially when one of them attempted a particularly dirty move.

Nevertheless, as the armies watched, all could see that their champions were tiring. Blood streamed from numerous cuts on arms and legs and in Brennus' case on his torso. Most were shallow, but some were deep enough to need stitching. Tiredness and blood loss slowed the movement of each fighter and dulled their minds. The Senone king was the stronger of the duellists, but even his vaunted potency had its limits. Conall was lighter and faster, and under Urard and Fearghal's tuition was a skilled warrior with axe and sword. But his chainmail was heavy. His stamina flagged, and his arm and leg muscles burned. Desperation resided in both men's eyes. Both wanted to win. Neither wanted to lose through a mistake.

With a snarl of frustration, Brennus flung his helmet at his opponent. Conall ducked and took several paces backwards. Brennus watched suspiciously as Conall removed his helmet, and tossed it aside along with his scíath and axe. Conall's chainmail followed next. Both men stood with naked torsos and bare fists. Brennus laughed aloud. Only arrogance led the Clann Ui Flaithimh king to a contest of brute strength. The

Senone king threw his sword aside. Both men advanced.

"This is not a good idea," Lonán Ó Neill said to Torcán. The two renowned brawlers of Clann Ui Flaithimh were in agreement. Beside them, Fearghal shook his head, rubbed his stubbled chin, and, as if looking for inspiration, glanced to the ramparts where Mongfhionn watched. The Sidhe was equally concerned about the strategy of her champion. In the sky, the Goddess stretched long wings to their fullest and wheeled in a wide circle. No cry came from her. She too was perturbed at her Hand's action.

There was a slap of flesh-on-flesh as the men met. Fists flew, thudding into chins, bellies, and ribs. Brennus fought with renewed strength. *It was*, the king thought, *hubris for Conall to believe he could best me in a battle of brute force. Pride was his weakness and would be his downfall.* His chance to end it came when Conall fell, almost too readily, into his vice-like embrace. The sound of bones popping brought joy to Brennus as he held his opponent in a great bear-hug. As Brennus' hands clasped behind Conall's back and the hold tightened, Conall gasped for breath. The host of Clann Ui Flaithimh held their breath as they watched their king slump in Brennus' grip.

The creeping lassitude of battle combined with a sense of impending victory. Brennus relaxed his grip. The viper held to his bosom struck. A sharp pain in his side made him gasp and loosen his hold on Conall. The brawny king looked down at the Clann Ui Flaithimh king. Before, when defeat seemed imminent, the blue eyes appeared unfocused. Now, they gleamed. The short-bladed dagger held in Conall's right hand was a fingertip's depth into Brennus' flesh.

"I can plunge the blade in to its hilt, or we can talk."

"You devious bastard! Where did you hide that? In your arse?" snarled Brennus, angry at being outwitted.

***

The mood was sombre in the ravaged camp of the Senones. While the armies of Brennus either watched or fought, the riders and chariots of Clann Ui Flaithimh had destroyed the encampment. Smoke curled up from the ruins of tents and supply wagons. Those left to guard the site, along with armourers and blacksmiths, were headless corpses. The whores who followed Brennus' army scattered into the hills and forests. They would bide their time. Their trade did not depend on tribe or clann. Only on who was willing to pay for their services.

Hands held high, the messenger walked the strawberry roan into the camp of the Senones. The smell of smoke lingered in the morning air. While the horse appeared to be undaunted by the circumstances, the rider was nervous—and unarmed. On reflection, he thought that being armed would not be a significant deterrent should a group of Senones choose to take his head. A crowd of warriors, their tempers worsened by a sleepless night and with looks on their faces that did not indicate a friendly disposition, surrounded the envoy. It quickly became impossible to move in any direction.

"I am Tadhg Ó Cuileannáin, ceannairí na míle and ambassador of Conall Mac Gabhann, Rí Ruirech of Clann Ui Flaithimh. I wish an audience with Brennus, King of the Senones." The prolonged silence that followed his words was disconcerting. Perhaps, they did not understand his words or brogue. "Shite," he mumbled. That was all he needed. Maybe, if he spoke louder, they would understand. On the other hand, possibly they would be insulted and skewer him on one of the many charred tent poles scattered across the site. Tadhg sucked in his chest and filled his lungs as he prepared to shout his request.

Thankfully, Tadhg was saved when the crowd parted, and Brennus strode forward. He walked up to Conall's envoy, but paid him no attention. Instead, Brennus stroked the velvet head of the roan. The horse nickered in approval. *Traitor*, thought Tadhg. "Dismount. I'll talk to no-one who looks down on me." Tadhg bowed, swung a leg across the mount's shoulder, and dropped to the ground. At a signal from Brennus, one of his men approached and led the beast away. Tadhg raised an eyebrow. Brennus laughed, "A fine horse. It was a gift. Wasn't it?"

***

The pavilion was erected mid-way between Lugudunon and the camp of the Senones. It was a rickety construction of wooden poles and tapestries scavenged from Matres' quarters. In all probability, it would collapse in a brisk wind. Fortunately, there was not a breath of air. The early morning mists had been burned off by the rising sun. Brennus threw aside the entrance flap and stepped inside. He rolled his eyes as the poles wavered like rushes at the riverside. It was unexpectedly light in the shelter. A section of the roof had been pinned back to allow for natural light. It was a welcome sight, given that he had anticipated a gloomy interior to mirror a rancorous conversation.

Seated at a solid wooden table were Conall, Mórrígan, Mongfhionn, Rosmerta, Crum, and Fearghal. Brennus grunted and sat down opposite the group. The five warriors who accompanied him remained standing. It was a clear statement that only Brennus spoke for the Senones. He growled at Mórrígan, who bared her teeth and smiled quite sweetly at the king. In truth, Brennus respected the ruthless efficiency of the queen of Clann Ui Flaithimh. "Is this a meeting between kings or witches?" he rasped, placing large, calloused hands on the table. He winced as the edges of the deep gashes on his arms pulled against the neat row of catgut stitches. The Senone king's gaze hovered over the Sidhe and the Oracle.

"The mother and her whelp."

This brought disconcerted looks from Conall and Fearghal and followed by stern *"We'll talk about this later"* stares from both men. Brennus was amused at the irritation his words provoked. "A word of advice. Heed it or not. Trust this pair at your peril." Brennus then peered at the druid, "And this one's rise to priestly prominence may warp the partiality of his counsel." To give him his due, Crum Dubh appeared to be genuinely affronted at Brennus' slur.

"Keep to your task, Brennus," Rosmerta spoke quietly, but there was no doubting the menace in her voice.

Brennus looked at Conall and, with a grin that actually made his face look attractive, pronounced, "A tithe of all Clann Ui Flaithimh's possessions is my price for you to remain in these lands."

Conall found it difficult not to admire the shaggy-haired, arrogant king who sat before him. "Javelins, bolts, and stones have caused you great injury and death. My shields staunched the flow of your warriors. Many of your chieftains lie with black shafts in their chests. As for my riders, they have not begun to cause real mischief. You have already paid too great a price for land, which is Gaiscedach territory—a tribe for which you care nothing, and far from your home. We have claimed this valley and the Rodonos waterway with our blood. We will hold it by battle."

"Your army is well-outnumbered, and you too have suffered many injuries and deaths. Your army is much smaller than mine, and your losses have a bigger impact on your strength. Numbers always count. Cede the tithe. We'll shake hands, feast, get drunk, and part with respect."

"Your point is well made," said Conall. A fleeting change in Brennus' demeanour spoke of relief. The king wanted to avoid another battle, even against this smaller force. Brennus looked warily at the young king. Conall's countenance did not suggest surrender. In fact, there was a somewhat smug look on his face. It was the same look when he held a dagger to Brennus' side. Alarmed, Brennus looked around, wondering if he had walked into a trap. His hand hovered over his sword's pommel. Conall's head shook in mock disappointment.

"We're not the Gaiscedach. We don't murder our guests."

"You were about to say something."

"Our numbers are not far apart, and we hold the hillfort of Lugudunon."

"Not far apart? By my reckoning, you have less than three thousand fighting men. The rest are exhausted, injured, or dead. You are outnumbered five-to-one." Brennus paused. He was perturbed. Conall did not appear concerned by his calamitous situation. What had he missed? "Be reasonable, Conall. I have ten summers on you. Believe me, you can't win every battle. Sometimes you have to swallow pride and compromise."

"Walk with me to the walls of Lugudunon?" Surprised at the request, but confident that Conall meant him no harm, Brennus pushed away from the table. He winced again at the sharp pains that stabbed his arm and side. "Our Greek healer, Alkaios, has great salves that will reduce the pain and help the healing of those wounds." The Senone king nodded his thanks.

"A sow's arse!" Brennus gazed around Lugudunon. Bodies, limbs, and streamers of guts were strewn around the fort. Maggots feasted on, and clouds of flies hovered over decaying corpses. Ravens pecked at succulent eyes. Long veins of dark red blemished the pristine white walls. "If you don't get this under control, I'll not need to fight. I'll just wait outside the walls until disease takes you."

"True, but that is not what I wished to show you," Conall pointed to the west, "Tell me what you see."

"Bastard!" Brennus eyes had fallen on Mòrag and the clann's militia.

"They should be here before meán lae. Five thousand fresh spears should even up the battle—maybe even tilt it in my favour."

"You play a mean game of fidchell," said Brennus, waving a group of fat, blue-black flies away from his face. "Let's get out of this shite-hole. We need to agree on how both of us save face."

***

Several sunsets later, Conall watched the Senones march to the foothills of the Aedui and disappear into the dense forests. There was little doubt that the Senones and Clan Uí Flaithimh would fight again. It was in their blood, and Brennus was a king with lofty ambitions of ruling Gaul. Still, on this day, with the return of his wounded and a supply of food, beer, and salves for the journey, the two kings grasped hands, embraced, and parted as friends. An assurance had been given that Conall would not sever the valued trade routes of the Liga and Rodonos unless Brennus resumed hostilities. For his part, Brennus agreed to allow unhindered access to Cenabum and to the Senones' fort at Sens for merchants from Clann Ui Flaithimh. Time would tell how long the agreements would last.

There was a sigh of relief from Conall as Brennus departed. The militia numbered less than two thousand five hundred—not the five thousand he boasted of to Brennus. Earlier, Cúscraid had informed him that the price paid by Clann Ui Flaithimh's army was over one thousand injured and five hundred dead. It would take many seasons to regain full strength. The disposition of the neighbouring Gallic tribes towards the invader was uncertain, but likely his new borders would be tested before the winter.

To the west, and to the accompaniment of singing, bodhráns, and horns, the people of Clann Ui Flaithimh flowed into the Rodonos valley and its foothills. It would be a prosperous land. "Home," Conall breathed into the air, giving Mórrígan a hug that tested her ribs. Then the pungent smell of decay swamped his nostrils. Work had begun on clearing Lugudunon of the dead. The funeral fires burned long into the night, but the season's high temperatures only accelerated the corruption of the bodies, exacerbating the risk of disease. Powder-blue skies, clear of clouds, gave no hint or promise of rain, although the rumble of distant thunder gave Conall hope that storms would come to his rescue and cleanse the hillfort.

"Over there," said Conall, pointing to the spar of land bounded on two sides by the Rodonos and the Souconna. "That is where we will build our citadel of wood and rock." He gestured at the buildings within Lugudunon. "Too small, too regular."

Mórrígan snorted, "You're just an uncivilised barbarian." Then she indicated several biremes with their square black sails pulling up to a wooden jetty. A small, deeply-tanned man with gleaming black hair jumped from the leading vessel. Spying Conall and Mórrígan on the parapet, he smiled broadly and waved. "Well, that didn't take long. I think we will see much more of Pytheas now that Massalia is closer."

Conall laughed. "He will always be welcome. However, now that we control the Rodonos, perhaps I should rethink his offer of partnership. Let's go meet our guest."

***

A brace of eagles soared high above Lugudunon. "I presume you're satisfied with your Hand and An Fiagaí Dorcha." The smaller, although not by much, of the eagles spoke. There was a note of dry wit in his shriek. That is if an eagle's cry can be assigned such qualities.

"He has done well. The Sidhe guides him well. The likelihood of a tyrant's path to the Otherworld recedes with each day. As for the Huntress, her powers grow much faster than anyone, even Mongfhionn, realises." Bright golden eyes briefly held a dark shadow. "It is a good thing. Rosmerta's influence on the Sidhe is unpredictable. Mórrígan may be an excellent foil."

"The Oracle's an old woman, and mortal. Tantalised by the gift of foresight, she renounced the gifts of the Aes Sidhe many years ago. Her days may not be long."

"Is that a hint?"

Fate laughed. It was an odd strangled sound from the great bird's throat. His attention was suddenly diverted at the sight of a lamb struggling in a thicket of thorns, and he swept downwards. "You tease like a striapach," screeched the Goddess. Several beats of her mighty wings propelled her towards the target. She could almost taste the creature's warm flesh.

EPILOGUE

402 B.C.—Rome—Winter

Marius Furius Camillus looked to the three barbarians before him. They were mounted on the best horses that Marius had set eyes on for a long time. The Roman's eyes reflected his envy. One huge warrior carried a massive battle-axe on his back. The second, a tall, willowy warrior with restless eyes constantly scanned the surroundings. The third, of average height, bore the burden of authority on broad shoulders. One hundred mounted warriors, all veterans by the hard looks on their faces, were arrayed in a single rank behind the three.

It was against the advice of the captain of his personal guard that Marius met with the barbarians in the snow-covered clearing, north of Rome. One hundred faced one hundred. Restless hands brushed against well-used weapons. All were loosed from their safety loops. Still, there was unspoken discipline in the pine encircled glade.

The silence was broken as the leader of the barbarians dismounted, handed his reins to the slender, sandy-haired warrior, and removed an ornate, black-plumed helmet. The helmet was taken by the giant. The burly warrior grunted a few words in a dialect with which Marius was unfamiliar. The leader smiled, unsheathed his sword, and pulled his axe from its belt loop. They disappeared into a massive paw.

Across grass brittle with ice, the barbarian leader's fleece-lined boots crunched. Five paces from the Roman he stopped and bowed in respect. Marius pulled his heavy purple cloak closer and with firm steps walked to stand several paces from the barbarian. The barbarian smiled at the Roman's patrician reserve. He was impressed when the Roman dipped his head.

"You are Conall, king of Clann Ui Flaithimh?" Marius' voice had no warmth in its tone.

Conall nodded, "I regret that I bring no good news for you."

The king of Clann Ui Flaithimh turned his head and with a raised hand signalled. A large wagon trundled through the line of horses. Some snorted and dipped heads as if in respect. Plumes of steam curled upwards, forming an arch of white ribbons. The wagon came to a halt alongside Conall. After securing the reins of the horse team, the driver stood and leapt onto the snow-covered ground.

"Perhaps your men could take the wagon." Pale-faced, Marius nodded and signalled to his guard. Two men approached and jumped up onto the wagon's seat. "Go gently with it," said Conall. "It holds a precious cargo." With a quick flick of the reins, the vehicle started to move. As it passed alongside Marius, he held up a hand. The cart's wheels slipped on the icy ground before shuddering to a halt. Two men dropped the back. In the wagon rested a man-length cedar-wood box.

With a deep breath, Marius watched as the men levered the top of the box. The squeal of iron nails grated on ears already sore with the deep cold. Their task complete, the soldiers wiped red-rimmed eyes and held out a hand to aid the father of Cornelia as he climbed into the wagon-box. Cries of anguish echoed around the clearing as his eyes fell on the body of his only daughter. He fell sobbing to his knees.

Cornelia rested on a bed of ice. She was covered in a white, muslin shroud. Ice-blue eyes had opened during the journey. Through the slit in the covering, they stared accusingly at her father. The eyes told Marius all he needed to know about his daughter's suffering. He berated himself. This was an ending he could and should have prevented. Unsteady and grim-faced, he rose and, still standing on the frost-covered wagon floor, turned to face Conall.

"You have my thanks for returning my daughter."

"My advice, from one father to another," said Conall, his faced etched with sadness. Marius looked at him expectantly. "Do not remove the shroud. She would not want it." A moan of grief escaped from Marius' thin, red lips. It was followed by a snarl of imminent revenge.

"Who?"

"Matres of the Gaiscedach. She evaded us." Conall bowed once more and turned to walk back to his men.

"Gaius?"

"Rome cast him out. I gave him a home. He is a good man. Betrayed by enemies and those he held as friends." Marius flinched at the rebuke. "The loss is yours—and Rome's." Marius nodded.

"Will we meet in battle, barbarian?"

"Unless Rome deals with Marcus Fabius Ambustus and his sons, then yes, Roman, we will."

***

The white muslin and silk hangings in the Temple of Vesta billowed and flapped in the bitterly cold winds that chased one another around the tall columns. Watched over by the statue of Minerva, only the Eternal Flame provided any semblance of warmth. It was mid-day. The six Vestals having attended the fire, now filed out through the Sacred Grove. They had other duties to attend.

They were passed by a tall figure enrobed in a heavy cloak of silver wolf-pelts. The figure limped and used a spear to compensate for the weakness on its left side. Thick boots tread unevenly and warily, making little noise in the snow. The shape's voluminous outline made it difficult to determine whether the person was male or female. It took a circuitous route to the eastern temple entrance.

Inside the circular temple, the figure peered around the dimly lit edifice. "Marcus," she hissed like the viper she was. There was no answer. She spat, "You know that it is perilous for me to be here. Reveal yourself."

"It is indeed unsafe for you, and will become even more so." The voice of Marius Furius Camillus was calm, but Matres sensed the rage beneath the surface and shivered.

"Stand back, old man, or I'll send you to meet your daughter."

There was a brittle laugh. "So foolish to imagine I would fear that?"

A short sword appeared in Matres' right hand. The spear now snuggled firmly under her left armpit swept a low arc in front of her. Marius snapped his fingers, and a cordon of his heavily-armed guard appeared from the shadows of the temple. All held shields. All carried spears. For a moment, Matres panicked. Then, acknowledging that she was already dead, she launched herself with a scream at Marius.

She wondered at the cruel smile that appeared on his lips. That he did not move or flinch was disturbing. It was then she heard the scuffle of nets dropping. Lead weights clanged against her helmet. She screamed, "No!" as the netting bore her to the marble floor.

In her ear, she heard Marius whisper, "No. You will not leave this life so quickly or easily. That would disappoint The Persian. He is looking forward to working on you. As for me, I am looking forward to many days and nights of your screams." In the chilly air of the temple a single bead of sweat formed on Matres' temple. She had little chance to ponder her fate as a spear butt smacked into her forehead, and the blackness took her.

A black pit of hopelessness took Matres and never slackened its grip. She screamed at first in rage and then begged for pity as she watched an increasing number of body parts displayed on the blood-stained table before her. The Persian informed her that in time, her full body would be dismembered and laid on the table. Stumps of ears, fingers, and toes throbbed. They smelt of charred flesh and corruption. Rats feasted on the long slices of meat filleted from her torso and limbs. Over the odours of shite and piss, she could smell the putrescence of her body's decay. The torturer left her with her sense of smell and hearing. One eye he took on the fourth day.

"She's gone." It was a week since the Persian started his work on Matres.

"Pity. I thought she would last longer."

"The trauma and shock were too much for her mind. The guilt of her daughter's death weighed heavily on her spirit. Her body might have lasted longer with a stronger mind and more to live for. I can offer a discount if you're disappointed."

"That will not be necessary." A heavy, maroon purse of gold clinked as it slid across the black, marble table. "As a final service, throw the carcass in the cesspits. Let the vermin have her."

The Persian bowed, "As you wish."

As he turned to leave, the second pouch of gold thudded on the table. Eyebrow raised, he looked to Marius for an explanation.

"I have one more service you can perform for me." The Persian smiled and dipped his head.

***

No longer in his prime, Marcus' skin hung on his bones like a flesh-coloured shroud. "It is fortunate," he muttered, "that wealth and power cover my imperfections." He leered at the two young women who attended him in his bath. Both were no more than sixteen years of age. One was tall and slender with small breasts and a skinny ass. The other was voluptuous. Youth held her breasts in its firm embrace. The sway of her hips and ass as she walked was enough even to cause a stirring in his old groin. He smiled. They were not slaves, although he had many of those to use. They were the daughters of men who wanted to curry favour with him.

He signalled to the slender one. She had full lips and a long, swan-like neck. The disgust in her eyes told Marcus that she knew what was expected. Her revulsion only added to his enjoyment. He opened his legs and watched as she kneeled between them. She had barely commenced her ministration when the door to the chamber swung open.

Outraged, Marcus screamed at the interruption. He pushed the girl aside and stood up, his semi-erection visible to his sons and the servants and guards who followed them into the room. "You had better have a good reason for this," he snarled, grabbing a cloak and snatching a bronze goblet of wine from a slave.

His eldest son, Quintus, strode forward. "A messenger brought this." In his hand, he held a cedarwood gift-box. Marcus seized the box from Quintus and slid open the lid. In shock he slipped to the floor, his mouth flapped, and long bony fingers trembled. Sitting on a bed of green velvet were two hands. One was the right hand of his youngest son, Caeso. The ring on the middle finger confirmed the identity. The other was that of Matres.

"Where is the messenger?" shrieked Marcus.

"Gone. He left the box and disappeared."

Marcus mourned for several weeks. The rest of Caeso's body never was recovered. No demand for gold was received. No message, verbal or written, of responsibility was delivered. And yet all of Rome knew who had been held to account for the death of Cornelia.

The End

TECHNICAL NOTES

The technical section is not meant to be an exhaustive detailing of archaeology, culture or technology. That is taken care of by the references listed as Suggested Reading in this and the preceding books in the series. Rather it is a sampling of phenomena—large and small—that tickled my curiosity.

***

Siege weapons (ballistae) are introduced in Conall IV. With author's licence, I have likely presented this type of weapon 10 to 20 years before history would 'officially' concur. It is generally reckoned that the catapult made its appearance in 399 B.C. in Sicily and under the then-leadership of Dionysios I. However, it is also unreasonable to suggest that ballistae suddenly appeared. Instead, the weapon's development is likely to have taken place over decades and in several countries.

Ballistae launched a large projectile at a distant target. Early versions projected heavy darts or spherical stone projectiles of various sizes for siege warfare. Two levers with torsion springs were used instead of a prod (the bow part of a modern crossbow), the springs consisted of several loops of twisted skeins. It was possible to launch lighter projectiles with higher velocities over a longer distance. All components that were not made of wood were transported in the baggage train. The weapon would be assembled using local wood parts.

The smaller ballistae, such as those that Gaius transported, delivered lighter munitions (thus producing less energy on impact) it is a widely held opinion that they were used more as an anti-personnel role, or to destroy lighter structures. Rainy weather, humid air, or even the morning dew could negatively affect the performance of the springs.

**

Little is written about the Iron Age settlements of Tours (Tourones), Orléans (Cenabum) or Lyons (Lugudunon). In Gallic times Tours was important as a crossing point of the Loire.

The territory of the Carnutes had the reputation among Roman observers of being the political and religious centre of the Gaulish nations. The description of Cenabum (Orléans) is based on the archaeology of Mont Lassois (Vix) circa 480 B.C. and Gournay-Sur-Aronde circa 260 B.C. The latter was particularly apt since it had an impressive sanctuary and Cenabum was reputed to be both a religious and economic centre. The city had strong fortifications, and also controlled a bridge over the Loire of considerable financial and strategic importance.

I continue to be amazed at the ingenuity of Iron Age engineers. Mont Lassois was a large planned settlement with a central north-south axis and several phases of buildings. It had extensive fortifications with walls up to 26ft. thick. At its centre was a complex of two to three buildings, one of which was about 115x70x40ft, i.e., the dimensions of a modern church or small palace. It was a high-status settlement featuring massive fortifications, a citadel, a lower town, rare and imported materials, and numerous rich burial mounds.

The description of Rosmerta's Sanctuary of Cenabum is based on one discovered at Gournay-Sur-Aronde and which appeared to have been a permanent ritual site. It had two square structures, one inside the other, and was constructed of timber and mudbrick. The entire area 45-60ft per side. The central square is the temple with an altar and surrounded by a square ditch and palisade with a large timber gate.

The outer building was enclosed by a massive timber palisade and ditch on either side. Its single entrance—a large timber gate facing east— was a monumental gateway with skulls nailed to the gate. There were many signs of animal sacrifice and the triumphant display of the remains of enemies killed in battle or sacrificed to the gods. Tall wooden posts with collections of weapon trophies and beheaded corpses lined the street to the sanctuary. It is estimated that on the grounds were the crushed and burned bones of around 1000 enemies!

Lugudunon was originally located in Fourvière, France, which is a district of modern-day Lyon. It was situated on a hill immediately west of the old part of the town, rising abruptly from the river Saône and then gently sloping down to the north-west. It could be said that Lyon is the result of urban sprawl across the confluence of the Saône and the Rhône. The settlement eventually was renamed Lugdunum in 43 B.C. following its capture by Rome.

***

The character of the Oracle, Rosmerta, is based on a princess or seer who lived in Mont Lassois and died aged about 35 to 40. She was quite small at 5'3", had hip-joint issues, and her head tipped to the right, giving her a waddling gait. Buried with her were: a bronze-headed staff, a heavy gold collar with two bulbous ends shaped as lion paws, Baltic amber beads, pins, ankle bronze rings, eight fibulae (brooches) decorated with gold, amber and coral, and ceramic, bronze and silver vessels. Interestingly the lady must have been fond of her wine, since huge (1,500 bottles capacity) bronze vessels of Greek designs, and used for mixing/storing wine were interred with her. Fragments of Chinese silk were also found in the grave.

***

The Máistir is, of course, *Le Mistral*—a violent, cold, north or northwest wind that accelerates when it passes through the valleys of the Rhône and the Durance Rivers to the coast of the Mediterranean around the Camargue region. It affects the northeast of the plain of Languedoc and Provence to the east of Toulon, where it is felt as a strong west wind. It has a significant influence on agriculture and the climate along the Mediterranean coast of France, and often causes sudden storms in the Mediterranean between Corsica and the Balearic Islands.

The wind usually blows in winter or spring, though it occurs in all seasons, and produces sustained winds often exceeding 41 mph, sometimes reaching 115 mph. Many of the trees in its path are forever bent in the direction of the prevailing wind. By reputation, the wind was capable of lifting large rocks.

***

I found the language of the Gauls to be a mystery. Unlike their fellow Celts from Ireland, Scotland and Wales who, against the odds, managed to preserve their language—Gaelic, in the face of the Roman invaders, the Gaulish nations of mainland Europe succumbed. Most place and personal names that are considered Gallic in fact comprise only a few components or syllables—if that. The rest have been 'Romanized', and likely by Julius Caesar. Thus, in the novel, I have consulted listings of the names of Gaulish kings and gods and selected those that appeared 'less Roman.' Place names have been taken back to as ancient a language format as I could research.

Of interest to this Celt/Gael, while Latin is considered a dead language and spoken by none, Gaelic continues to survive and in some areas of Ireland and Scotland thrives. Perhaps, after all, the final victory was to the Celts and not Caesar!

***

Somewhat related to language is swearing, and in this, I have accepted defeat. Even Melissa Mohr's highly recommended and very readable, *Holy Sh*t: A Brief History of Swearing*, only goes back as far as Ancient Rome. Most of the terms considered as taboo and swear words, such as penis and vagina, are today mostly medical terms. Hence, they both lose their impact and are clunky in a novel such as this. That said, the one rule of swearing appears to be that it has to involve bodily functions/excretions and a reference to a deity.

***

The paradox of the Celts is their acknowledged fierceness in battle and their love of design, art, and culture. Many of the more ornate pieces of armour (helmets and shields) and jewellery described in the novel are based on actual items uncovered in excavations. And yes, Cingetorix king's winged headpiece was remarkable by having a life-size metal bird perched on its crest. The wings also flapped. By the same token, Blaithin's helmet is based on a real piece of armour.

***

Finally, a quick word on the 'elephant in the room.' Were, the Celts cannibals? The evidence would certainly appear to suggest that a proportion of the Celtic nation practised cannibalism. Ritual sacrifice is well documented. Certainly, several tribes went into battle with the skulls of recently deceased enemies hanging from their belts. As described earlier, the gateways to hillforts were often decorated by having skulls nailed to the door posts.

SUGGESTED READING

T. Douglas Price, *Europe Before Rome: A Site-by-Site Tour of the Stone, Bronze and Iron Ages*, Oxford University Press, 2013

R. Ewart Oakeshott, *The Archaeology of Weapons: Arms and Armour from Prehistory to the Age of Chivalry*, Dover Publications, Inc., 1996

Mags McCartney, *Warfare and Violence in the Iron Age of Southern France*, BAR International Series 2403, 2012

Marilynne E. Raybould & Patrick Sims-Williams, *Introduction and Supplement to the Corpus of Latin Inscriptions of the Roman Empire Containing Personal Names*, CMCS, Aberystwyth, 2009

Melissa Mohr, *Holy Sh*t: A Brief History of Swearing*, Oxford University Press, 2013

Patrick Sims-Williams, *Ancient Celtic Place-Names in Europe and Asia Minor*, Blackwell Publishing, 2006

Tracey Rihill, *The Catapult: A History*, Westholme Publishing, 2013

DRAMATIS PERSONNÆ

CLANN UI FLAITHIMH

Conall Mac Gabhann

Eirnín Mac Gabhann (brother of Conall)

Mórrígan Ni Cathasaigh (joined with Conall Mac Gabhann)

Brion Ó Cathasaigh (brother of Mórrígan, king of Na Mèadaidh)

Brocc Ó Cathasaigh (brother of Mórrígan and Brion)

Bricriu Ó Cathasaigh (brother of Mórrígan and Brion)

Beacán Ó Cathasaigh (brother of Mórrígan and Brion)

Barra Mac Conall (son of Conall and Mòrag Ni Artair)

Brighid Ni Conall (daughter of Conall and Mórrígan, twin of Danu)

Danu Ni Conall (daughter of Conall and Mórrígan, twin of Brighid)

Aodán Mac Conall (son of Conall and Mórrígan)

Fearghal Ruad (Battle Commander of Clann Ui Flaithimh)

Mongfhionn (the Sidhe)

Neamhain Ni Fearghal (daughter of Fearghal and Mongfhionn)

Craiftine Ó Cuileannáin (famed harpist)

Fionnbharr Ó Cuileannáin (a healer)

Tadhg Ó Cuileannáin (famed storyteller)

Cuán Ó Néill (Ériu noble)

Bláithín Ni Néill (Wife of Cuán)

Lonán Ó Néill (Brother of Cuán)

Cúscraid Mac Conchobar (Master of Defences)

Deaglán Ó Néill (Ceannairí na míle)

Íar Mac Dedad (son of Deda mac Sin, King of Curraghatoor)

Sorchae Ni Íar (adopted daughter of Íar)

Aoibheann Ni Finnseach (wet nurse of Sorchae)

Nikandros (the Spartan and former assassin)

Sárán Mac Craobhach (Quartermaster)

Torcán Ó Dubhghaill

Mòrag Ni Artair (sister of Brandubh)

Ròs Ni Torcán (daughter of Torcán and Morag)

Urard (Protector of the Twins)

Iasg (partner of Urard)

CLANN UI FLAITHIMH/CINN PÉINTEÁILTE

Brandubh Mac Artair (son of Artair)

Carmag Mac an t-Sionnaich (Ceannairí na míle)

Crum Dubh (The druid)

Gràinne Ni Fearghal (adopted daughter of Fearghal Ruad)

Brianag Ni Brion (daughter of Brion Ó Cathasaigh and Gràinne)

THE GREEKS

Alkaios (Greek Surgeon)

Pytheas (Merchant and sailor)

THE ROMANS

Gaius Aurelius Atella (centurion in Marcus' army)

Marcus Fabius Ambustus (Pontifex of Rome)

Quintus Fabius Ambustus (son of Marcus)

Numerius Fabius Ambustus (son of Marcus)

Caeso Fabius Ambustus (son of Marcus)

Marius Furius Camillus (General of Rome)

Cornelia Furius Camillus (daughter of Marcus and wife of Gaius)

Aquila (second-in-command of Gaius' legion)

Crispus Galerius Donatus (centurion of Marcus, ballistae commander)

THE GAULS

Ambigatos (King of the Aedui)

Brennus (King of the Senones)

Acco (shield-man of Brennus)

Brennus the Ignored (a distant relative of Brennus)

Cingetorix (King of the Veneti)

Albiorix (Gaul champion)

Concolitanus (King of the Gaiscedach)

Genovefa (Queen of the Gaiscedach)

Matres (a queen of the Gaiscedach)

Cathubodua (daughter of Matres)

Dubnoreix (King of the Venelli)

Brigindos (daughter of Dubnoreix)

Divico (shield-man of Dubnoreix)

Dufach (leader of Venelli whores)

Laoise (daughter of Dufach)

Tasgiitios (King of the Carnutes)

THE THRACIANS

Amodocus (leader of Thracian mercenaries)

THE CRETANS

Sarpedon (leader of Cretan mercenaries)

OTHERS

Aveta (a slaver)

Rosmerta (The Oracle)

LOCATIONS MENTIONED

Albu (Britain)
Alkebulan (Africa)
Andion (Jersey, Channel Islands)
Aremorio (Northwest France)
Ériu (Ireland)
Gaul (France)
Germania (Germany)
Bibracte (Autun near Burgundy, Aedui major settlement)
Cenabum (Orléans, major settlement of the Carnutes)
Lugudunon (Lyon, France, hillfort of Matres)
Mai Dún (Maiden Castle, England)
Massalia (Marseille, France)
Rinn-Campáil (Danebury, England)
Sens (Sens, major settlement of the Senones)
Tourones (Tours, major settlement of the Carnutes)
Aedes Vesta (The Temple of Vesta, Rome, Italy)
Albanus Lacus (Lago Albano, Italy)
Alpes (The Alps)
Cebenna (The Cévennes mountains)
Choir-Gaur (Stonehenge, England)
Donaris (The Danube River)
Great Sea (The Mediterranean)
Liga (The Loire River, France)
Máistir (Mistral wind)
Muir nIocht (English Channel)

Rénos (Rhine River)
Rodonos (The Rhône River, France)
Souconna (The Saône River, France)

ABOUT THE AUTHOR

Born in Belfast, Northern Ireland, David H. Millar is the founder, owner, and author-in-residence of Houston-based 'A Wee Publishing Company'—a business that promotes Celtic literature, authors, and art.

Millar moved to Nova Scotia, Canada, in the late 1990s. After ten years shovelling snow, he decided to relocate to warmer climates and has now settled in Houston, Texas. Quite a contrast!

An avid reader, armchair sportsman, and Liverpool Football Club fan, Millar lives with his family and Bailey, a Manx cat of questionable disposition known to his friends as "the small angry one!"

Conall IV: A Brace of Eagles is the fourth novel in the Conall series. All are available in print and eBook formats from all major online and retail channels and distributors. If any of the books are not on the shelf of your local bookstore, then ask them to order a copy for you.

LET'S CHAT

I would love to hear from any readers of the Conall series. Comments and feedback will be greatly appreciated. You can find me at any of the following:

BLOG

http://aweepublishingco.com/david-h-millar.html

FACEBOOK

https://www.facebook.com/aweepublishingco/

GOODREADS AUTHOR PAGE

https://www.goodreads.com/DavidHMillar

INSTAGRAM

Author.DavidHMillar

TWITTER

@DavidHMillar